The Penguin Book of
Christmas Stories

The Penguin Book of Christmas Stories

*From Hans Christian Andersen
to Angela Carter*

Edited by
JESSICA HARRISON

PENGUIN CLASSICS
an imprint of
PENGUIN BOOKS

PENGUIN CLASSICS

UK | USA | Canada | Ireland | Australia
India | New Zealand | South Africa

Penguin Books is part of the Penguin Random House group of companies
whose addresses can be found at global.penguinrandomhouse.com.

This collection first published in Penguin Classics 2019
This edition published 2021

001

Cover design and illustration by: Coralie Bickford-Smith

The acknowledgements on pp.270–72 constitute an extension of this copyright page
The moral right of the editor has been asserted

Printed and bound in Great Britain by Clays Ltd, Elcograf S.p.A.

The authorized representative in the EEA is Penguin Random House Ireland,
Morrison Chambers, 32 Nassau Street, Dublin D02 YH68

A CIP catalogue record for this book is available from the British Library

ISBN: 978–0–241–45565–4

www.greenpenguin.co.uk

Contents

Contents

Contents

HANS CHRISTIAN ANDERSEN

The Fir Tree

Translated by Tiina Nunnally

Out in the forest stood such a charming fir tree. It was in a good spot where it could get sunshine and there was plenty of air. All around grew scores of bigger companions, both firs and pines, but the little fir tree was so eager to grow up that it didn't think about the warm sun or the fresh air. It didn't pay any attention to the farm children who walked past, chattering, whenever they were out gathering strawberries or raspberries. Often they would come by with a whole pitcher full or they would have strawberries threaded on a piece of straw. Then they would sit down near the little tree and say, 'Oh, how charming and little it is!' That's not at all what the tree wanted to hear.

The following year it was a full length taller, and the year after that yet another. On a fir tree you can always tell how many years it has been growing by how many layers of branches it has.

'Oh, if only I were a big tree like the others,' sighed the little tree. 'Then I could spread out my branches all around and from the top I could gaze out on the wide world. The birds would build nests in my branches, and when the wind blew, I could nod so grandly, like all the others.'

The tree took no pleasure in the sunshine, in the birds, or in the crimson clouds that sailed overhead both morning and evening.

When it was winter, and the snow lay all around, glittering white, a hare often came bounding along and sprang right over the little tree. Oh, how annoying that was! But two winters passed and by the third the tree was so tall that the hare had to go around it. 'Oh, to grow and grow, to get bigger and older. That is the only lovely thing in this world,' thought the tree.

In the autumn the woodcutters would always appear to chop down some of the biggest trees. It happened every year, and the young fir tree, which was now quite grown-up, would start trembling because the tall, magnificent trees would topple to the ground with a groan and a crash. Their branches would be cut off, and they looked so naked, tall and slender. They were almost beyond recognition. But then they were loaded onto wagons, and horses carried them away, out of the forest.

Where were they going? What was in store for them?

In the spring, when the swallow and stork appeared, the tree asked them: 'Do you know where they were taken? Have you seen them?'

The swallows didn't know anything, but the stork looked thoughtful, nodded his head, and said, 'Oh, yes, I think so. I met many new ships as I flew here from Egypt. On the ships were magnificent mast trees, and I'd venture to say they were yours. They smelled of fir. I bring you many greetings. How they swaggered and swayed!'

'Oh, if only I too were big enough to fly across the sea! What is the sea like, anyway? How does it look?'

'Well, it's much too complicated to describe,' said the stork and flew off.

'Enjoy your youth!' said the rays of sunlight. 'Enjoy your fresh growth and the young life inside you!'

The wind kissed the tree, and the dew shed tears over it, but the fir tree did not understand.

When Christmastime came, quite young trees were felled, trees that were often not even as tall or as old as the fir tree, which could never find any peace but was always eager to be off. These young trees, and they were the most beautiful of all, always kept their branches. They were loaded onto wagons, and horses carried them away, out of the forest.

'Where are they going?' asked the fir tree. 'They're no bigger than I am. There was even one that was much smaller. Why do they keep all their branches? Where are they being taken?'

'We know! We know!' chirped the sparrows. 'In town we've looked in the windows. We know where they're being taken. Oh, they end up in the greatest splendor and glory you could ever imagine. We've looked in the windows and seen them being planted in the middle of the warm parlor and decorated with the loveliest things: gilded apples, gingerbread, toys, and hundreds of candles!'

'And then?' asked the fir tree, all its branches aquiver. 'And then? What happens next?'

'Well, that's all we saw. But nothing could match it.'

'Maybe I was meant to take this glorious path,' rejoiced the fir tree. 'That's even better than going across the sea. What an agony of longing! If only it were Christmas. Now I'm as tall and broad as the others that were carried off last year. Oh, if only I were on that wagon right now. If only I were in the warm parlor with all that splendor and glory! And then . . . ? Well, then something even better is bound to happen, something even more wonderful, or why would they decorate me like that? Something even grander, even more glorious is bound to happen. But what? Oh, how I'm suffering! Oh, how I yearn! I just don't know what's come over me.'

'Take pleasure in us!' said the air and the sunlight. 'Take pleasure in your fresh youth out in the open!'

But the fir tree felt no pleasure at all. It grew and grew. Both winter and summer it was green; dark green it stood there. Everyone who saw it said, 'That's a lovely tree!' And at Christmas, it was the very first to be cut down. The ax bit deep into its marrow, and the tree fell to the ground with a sigh. It felt a pain, a weakness, it couldn't even think about happiness. It was sad to part with its home, with the spot where it had sprouted up, for the tree realized that it would never see its dear old companions again: the small shrubs and flowers all around, maybe not even the birds. Leaving was certainly not pleasant.

The tree didn't recover until it was unloaded in a courtyard with all the other trees and it heard a man say, 'That one is magnificent. That's the one we want.'

Then two servants in fine livery came and carried the fir tree into an enormous, beautiful room. Portraits hung on all the walls, and next to the large woodstove stood big Chinese vases with lions on the lids. There were rocking chairs, silk-covered sofas, big tables covered with picture books, and toys worth a hundred times a hundred *rigsdaler* – at least that's what the children said. And the fir tree was set in a large wooden tub filled with sand, but no one could tell that it was a wooden tub because green fabric was wrapped all around it, and the tub stood on top of a big, colorful carpet. Oh, how the tree trembled! What was going to happen next? Then the servants and the maids proceeded to decorate the tree. On one branch they hung little woven baskets cut of colored paper; each basket was filled with sweets. Gilded apples and walnuts hung on the tree as if they had grown there, and more than a hundred little candles, red and blue and white, were fastened to the branches. Dolls that looked as lifelike as human beings swayed in the boughs. The tree had never seen anything like it before. And at the very top they put a big star made from shiny gold paper. It was magnificent, quite incomparably magnificent.

'Tonight,' they all said, 'tonight the tree will shine!'

'Oh,' thought the tree. 'If only it were evening. If only they'd light the candles soon. And what will happen after that? Will trees come from the forest to look at me? Will the sparrows fly past the window? Will I take root and stand here, decorated like this, all winter and summer long?'

Oh yes, the tree thought it knew all about it. But it had a terrible bark-ache from sheer yearning, and bark-aches are just as bad for trees as headaches are for the rest of us.

Finally the candles were lit. What splendor, what magnificence! Every branch of the tree trembled so much that one of the candles set fire to a bough. How it stung!

'God help us!' shrieked the maids, and hastily put out the fire.

Now the tree didn't even dare tremble. Oh, how awful! It was so afraid of losing any of its finery. It was quite bedazzled by all the splendor. And then the double doors flew open, and a crowd of children rushed in, as if they were about to topple the whole tree. The grown-ups followed more sedately. The children stood in utter silence, but only for a moment. Then they began shouting again so their voices echoed through the room. They danced around the tree, and one present after the other was plucked from the branches.

'What are they doing?' thought the tree. 'What's going to happen?' And the candles burned all the way down to the boughs, and as they burned down, they were put out, and then the children were allowed to plunder the tree. Oh, how they rushed at it, making all the branches groan. If the tree hadn't been tied to the ceiling by its top and the gold star, it would have toppled right over.

The children danced around with their splendid toys. No one paid any attention to the tree except for the old nursemaid, who walked around it, peering in among the branches. But she was only checking to see that not a fig or apple had been overlooked.

'A story! A story!' shouted the children, pulling a stout little man over to the tree, and he sat down right underneath. 'Because we're out in the forest,' he told them, 'and it may do the tree some good to listen along! But I'm only going to tell you one story. Do you want to hear the one about Ickety-Ackety or the one about Clumpa-Dumpa, who fell down the stairs but still ended up on the throne and won the hand of the princess?'

'Ickety-Ackety!' cried some of the children. 'Clumpa-Dumpa!' cried the others. They shouted and shrieked, and only the fir tree stood in silence and thought, 'Won't I get to take part? Won't I get to do anything?' It had been part of the celebration, after all; it had done what it was supposed to do.

And then the man told the story of Clumpa-Dumpa, who fell down the stairs but still ended up on the throne and won the hand of the princess. And the children clapped their hands and shouted, 'Tell us more, tell us more!' They wanted to hear the one about 'Ickety-Ackety' too, but he would only tell them the story about Clumpa-Dumpa. The fir tree stood quite still and pensive. The birds in the forest had never mentioned anything like this. 'Clumpa-Dumpa fell down the stairs, and yet won the hand of the princess. Well, well, so that's the way the things are out in the world,' thought the fir tree, believing that it was all true because such a nice man had told the story. 'Well, well! Who knows, maybe I too will fall down the stairs and win the princess.' And the fir tree looked forward to the next day when it would be adorned with candles and toys, gold and fruit.

'Tomorrow I won't tremble,' it thought. 'I will fully enjoy all my glory. Tomorrow I'll hear the story about Clumpa-Dumpa again, and maybe the one about Ickety-Ackety too.' And the tree stood still and pensive all night long.

In the morning a servant and a maid came into the room.

'Now the finery is going to start again!' thought the tree. But they dragged it out of the parlor and up the stairs to the attic. And there, in a dark corner where no daylight shone, they left it. 'What does this mean?' thought the tree. 'I wonder what I'm supposed to do here? I wonder what I'm going to hear now?' It leaned against the wall and stood there thinking and thinking. And it had plenty of time for that, because day after day and night after night went by. No one came up to the attic, and when someone finally did, it was only to put some large boxes in the corner. The tree stood quite hidden; you would almost think it had been completely forgotten.

'Now it's winter outside,' thought the tree. 'The ground is hard and covered with snow. The people wouldn't be able to plant me. No doubt that's why I'm standing here, safe indoors until springtime. What a good plan! How kind the people are! If only it wasn't so dark in here and so terribly lonely. There's not even a little hare. It was so nice out there in the forest when the snow lay on the ground and the hare came running past. Yes, even when it leaped right over me, although I didn't like it much at the time. But up here it's terribly lonely.'

'Squeak, squeak!' said a little mouse at that very moment and came scurrying. And then another little mouse appeared. They sniffed at the fir tree and scurried in and out of its branches.

'It's awfully cold,' said the little mice. 'But otherwise it's quite blissful to be here. Don't you agree, you old fir tree?'

'I'm not old at all!' said the fir tree. 'There are plenty of trees that are much older than I am!'

'Where did you come from?' asked the mice. 'And what do you know?' They were awfully curious. 'Tell us about the loveliest place on earth! Have you ever been there? Have you been in the pantry where cheeses are lined up on the shelves and hams hang from the ceiling? Where you can dance on tallow candles? Where you go in skinny but come out fat?'

'I don't know that place,' said the tree. 'But I do know the forest, where the sun shines and the birds sing.' And then the tree told them all about its youth, and the little mice had never heard anything like that before. They listened closely and said, 'Oh, you've seen so much! How happy you've been!'

'Me?' said the fir tree, thinking about everything it had just described. 'Why yes, I suppose those were quite delightful days, after all.' But then the tree told them about Christmas Eve, when it was decorated with cakes and candles.

'Oh!' said the little mice. 'How happy you've been, you old fir tree!'

'I'm not old at all!' said the tree. 'It was only this winter that I came here from the forest. I'm in the prime of my life, I've just stopped growing.'

'How wonderfully you describe things!' said the little mice, and the following night they brought along four other little mice who wanted to hear what the tree had to tell. And the more the tree told them, the more clearly it remembered everything and thought, 'Those actually were quite enjoyable days. But they can come again, they can come again! Clumpa-Dumpa fell down the stairs, yet he won the hand of the princess. Maybe I too can win a princess.' And then the fir tree thought about a charming little birch tree that grew out in the forest. For the fir tree, the birch was a real and lovely princess.

'Who's Clumpa-Dumpa?' asked the little mice. And then the fir tree told them the whole story; it could remember every single word. And the little mice were ready to run all the way to the top of the tree out of sheer glee. The next night many more mice came, and on Sunday there were even two rats. But they said the story wasn't amusing, and that made the little mice sad, because then they thought less of the story themselves.

'Is that the only story you know?' asked the rats.

'The only one,' replied the tree. 'I heard it on the happiest evening of my life, but back then I didn't realize how happy I was!'

'It's an exceptionally tedious story. Don't you know any about bacon and tallow candles? Any pantry stories?'

'No,' said the tree.

'Well, thanks for nothing!' replied the rats, and they went back home.

Eventually the little mice disappeared too, and then the tree sighed, 'It was so nice having those nimble little mice sitting around me and listening to what I told them. Now that too is over. But I'm going to remember to enjoy myself when they finally take me out of here.'

But when would that happen?

Well, one day in the early morning, servants came up to the attic and started rummaging around. The boxes were moved aside, and the tree was pulled out. Now, it's true that they threw it to the floor rather hard, but then a man dragged it at once toward the stairs, where daylight was shining.

'Now life will begin again!' thought the tree. It could feel the fresh air, the first rays of sun. And then it was out in the courtyard. Everything happened so fast that the tree forgot all about taking a look at itself. There was so much to see all around. The courtyard was next to a garden, and everything was in bloom. The roses hung so fresh and fragrant over the little fence, the linden trees were blossoming, and the swallows flew about, saying, 'Kirra-virra-vit, my husband has arrived!' But it wasn't the fir tree they meant.

'Now I'm going to live!' rejoiced the tree, spreading its branches wide. But alas, its boughs were all withered and yellow. In the corner among the weeds and nettles was where the tree came to rest. The star made from gold paper was still on its top, shimmering in the bright sunshine.

In the courtyard several of the lively children were playing who had danced around the tree at Christmastime, taking such delight in it. One of the youngest children came over and tore off the golden star.

'Look what's still sitting on the horrid old Christmas tree!' he said, stomping on the branches so they groaned under his boots.

And the tree looked at all that floral splendor and freshness in the garden. Then it looked at itself and wished that it had stayed in the dark corner of the attic. The tree thought about its fresh youth in the forest, about the joyous Christmas Eve, and about the little mice who had listened so happily to the story about Clumpa-Dumpa.

'It's over, it's over!' said the poor tree. 'If only I had enjoyed it while I could. It's over, it's over!'

And the hired man came over and chopped the tree into little pieces; it made a whole stack. How lovely the tree flared up under the big copper cauldron. And it sighed so deeply; each sigh was like the sound of a little shot. That's why the children who were playing came running over and sat down in front of the fire, staring into the flames and shouting, 'Bang, snap!' But with each sharp crack, which was a deep sigh, the tree thought about a summer day in the forest, or about a winter night out there, when the stars were shining. It thought about Christmas Eve and about Clumpa-Dumpa, the only story it had ever heard and knew how to tell. And before long the tree had burned up.

The boys played in the courtyard, and on his chest the youngest one had the gold star that the tree had worn on its happiest evening. Now it was over, and the tree was gone, along with the story. It was over, over, and that's what happens to every story!

PETER CHRISTEN ASBJØRNSON AND JØRGEN MOE

The Cat on the Dovrefjell

Translated by George Webbe Dasent and D. L. Ashliman

Once upon a time there was a man up in Finnmark who had caught a large white bear, which he was going to take to the King of Denmark. It so happened that he came to the Dovrefjell on Christmas Eve. He went to a cottage where a man lived whose name was Halvor, and he asked the man for lodging for himself and his white bear.

'God bless us!' said the man, 'but we can't give anyone lodging just now, for every Christmas Eve the house is so full of trolls that we are forced to move out, and we'll have no shelter over our own heads, to say nothing of providing for anyone else.'

'Oh?' said the man, 'If that's all, you can very well let me use your house. My bear can sleep under the stove here, and I can sleep in the storeroom.'

Well, he begged so hard, that at last he got permission to stay there. The people of the house moved out, but before they went, everything was made ready for the trolls. The table was set with cream porridge and fish and sausages and everything else that was good, just as for any other grand feast.

When everything was ready, in came the trolls. Some were large, and some were small. Some had long tails, and some had no tails at all. And some had long, long noses. They ate and drank and tasted everything.

Then one of the troll youngsters saw the white bear lying under the stove, so he took a piece of sausage, stuck it onto a fork, and went and poked it against the white bear's nose, burning it. Then he shrieked, 'Kitty, do you want some sausage?'

The white bear rose up and growled, and then chased the whole pack of them out, both large and small.

A year later Halvor was out in the woods at midday of Christmas Eve, gathering wood for the holidays, for he expected the trolls again. As he was chopping, he heard a voice shouting from the woods, 'Halvor! Halvor!'

'Yes?' said Halvor.

'Do you still have that big cat?'

'Yes,' said Halvor. 'She's lying at home under the stove, and what's more, she now has seven kittens, far bigger and fiercer than she is herself.'

'Then, we'll never come to your place again,' shouted the troll in the woods, and since that time the trolls have never eaten their Yule porridge with Halvor on the Dovrefjell.

A Christmas Party and a Wedding

Translated by Ronald Meyer

The other day I saw a wedding . . . but no! I'd better tell you about the Christmas party. The wedding was nice; I liked it very much, but the other event was better. I don't know how it was that I recalled that Christmas party as I watched the wedding. This is what happened. Exactly five years ago, on New Year's Eve, I was invited to a children's party. The person who invited me was a certain well-known businessman with connections, a circle of acquaintance and intrigues, so that one might think that the children's party was a pretext for the parents to get together and talk about some interesting matters in an innocent, casual and extemporaneous way. I was an outsider; I didn't have any business matters whatsoever, and therefore I spent the evening rather left to my own devices. There was another gentleman as well who seemed to be neither kith nor kin, but who, like me, had chanced upon this bit of family happiness . . . He was the first to catch my eye. He was a tall, thin man, quite serious, and quite decently dressed. But it was obvious that he was in no mood for celebrations and family happiness: he would walk over to some corner, immediately stop smiling and knit his bushy black brows. Apart from the host, he didn't know a single soul at the party. It was obvious that he was terribly bored, but that he was valiantly playing the part of the thoroughly entertained and happy man to the very end. I learned afterwards that this was a certain gentleman from the provinces who had some sort of crucial, puzzling business in the capital, who had brought a letter of recommendation to our host, and whom our host was patronizing by no means *con amore* and who had been invited to the children's party as a courtesy. They didn't play cards with him, they didn't offer him cigars, no one struck up a conversation with him, recognizing from afar, perhaps, the bird by its feathers and, therefore, my gentleman was forced to stroke his side whiskers all evening just so he had something to do with his hands. The side whiskers indeed were quite handsome. But he stroked them so very zealously that looking at him, one might very well think that first just the side whiskers had been brought into the world, and then later the gentleman was attached to them in order to stroke them.

Apart from this figure, who was taking part in the family happiness of our host (who had five chubby boys), I liked one other gentleman. But he was a completely different sort of character. This was a personage. His name was Yulian Mastakovich. Just one glance was enough to see that he was an honoured guest and that he was on the same terms with the host as the host was with the gentleman stroking his side whiskers. The host and hostess showered him with compliments, waited on him, made sure he had something to drink, pampered him, brought their guests to him to be introduced, but didn't take him to be introduced to anybody. I noticed that our host's eyes began to sparkle with tears when Yulian Mastakovich observed in regard to the evening that rarely did he spend his time in such a delightful fashion. I became somewhat terrified in the presence of such a personage and therefore, after admiring the children for a bit, I left for the small drawing room, which was completely empty, and sat down in the hostess's flowery arbour that took up almost half of the whole room.

The children were all unbelievably sweet and flatly refused to behave like *grown-ups*, despite the exhortations of their governesses and doting mothers. They stripped bare the entire Christmas tree in a flash, down to the last candy, and had already managed to break half of the toys before they found out which one was meant for whom. Particularly winsome was one boy, with dark eyes and curly hair, who kept wanting to shoot me with his wooden gun. But his sister attracted more attention than anyone, a girl about eleven years old, charming as a little cherub, quiet, thoughtful, pale, with big, pensive, prominent eyes. The children had somehow hurt her feelings, and so she had come into the same drawing room where I was sitting and busied herself in the corner – with her doll. The guests were respectfully pointing out a certain rich tax-farmer, her father, and somebody remarked in a whisper that 300,000 roubles had already been set aside for her dowry. I turned around to cast a glance at those who were intrigued by this circumstance, and my glance fell on Yulian Mastakovich, who, with his hands clasped behind his back and his head inclined a bit to one side, seemed to be listening with special attention to the idle chatter of these gentlemen. Afterwards I could not but marvel at the wisdom of our hosts in distributing the children's presents. The little girl who already possessed a dowry of 300,000 roubles received the most expensive doll. Then came the presents which decreased in value in accordance with the decrease in rank of the parents of these happy children. Finally, the last child, a boy of about ten years old, a skinny, little, freckled redhead, received only a little book of stories that expounded on the grandeur of nature, the tears of emotion, and so forth, without pictures and even without a single vignette. He was the son of a poor widow, the governess of our hosts' children, a boy who was extremely cowed and frightened. He was dressed in a jacket made out of some cheap nankeen. After receiving his book, he hovered for a long time near the other toys; he wanted terribly to play with the other children, but he didn't dare; it was clear that he sensed and understood his position. I like to observe children very much. Their first manifestation of independence is extremely interesting. I noticed that the little red-haired boy was so tempted by the other children's expensive toys, in particular the theatre in which he very definitely wanted to play a part, that he made up his mind to wheedle his way in. He smiled and started to play with the other children, he gave away his apple to a pudgy little boy who already had a lot of presents tied up in his handkerchief, and he had even undertaken giving a ride on his back to another boy, just so he wouldn't be chased away from the theatre. But a minute later some troublemaker thrashed him good. The child didn't dare cry. Then the governess, his mother, appeared and ordered him not to bother the other children who were playing. The child went into the same drawing room as the girl. She welcomed him and the two of them quite diligently set about dressing the expensive doll.

I had already been sitting for half an hour in the ivy arbour and had almost dozed off listening to the faint murmur of the red-haired boy and the beauty with a dowry of 300,000 as they busied themselves with the doll, when suddenly Yulian Mastakovich entered the room. He had taken advantage of a deplorable episode of the children quarrelling to leave the room quietly. I noticed that a minute earlier he had been talking quite ardently with the papa of the future wealthy bride, with whom he had just become acquainted, about the advantages of one line of work over another. Now he was standing lost in contemplation and seemed to be counting something on his fingers.

'Three hundred . . . three hundred,' he whispered. 'Eleven . . . twelve . . . thirteen and so forth. Sixteen – five years. Let's say four per cent interest – 12 times 5 equals 60, and on that 60 . . . well, let's say, for five years in all – four hundred. Yes! That's it . . . But he won't settle for four per cent, the swindler! He might get eight or even ten per cent. Well, let's say five hundred, five hundred thousand, at the very least, that's for certain; well, and what's left over can go towards the glad rags for the trousseau, hmm . . .'

His contemplation concluded, he blew his nose and was about to leave the room, when he suddenly glanced at the little girl and came to a stop. He didn't see me behind the pots of greenery. He seemed to be extremely agitated. Either his calculations were having their effect on him, or something else, but he rubbed his hands and couldn't stand still. This agitation increased to *nec plus ultra*, when he came to a stop and cast another, decisive glance at the future bride. He was on the verge of moving forward, but had a look around first. Then, on tiptoe, as though he were feeling guilty, he started to approach the child. He walked up with a little smile, bent down and kissed her on the head. Not expecting an assault, she cried out in fear.

'And what are you doing here, dear child?' he asked in a whisper, looking around and patting her on the cheek.

'We're playing . . .'

'What, with him?' Yulian Mastakovich looked askance at the boy.

'And you, my dear boy, should go into the ballroom,' he said to him.

The boy kept silent and looked at him with his eyes wide-open. Yulian Mastakovich again took a look around and again bent down towards the girl.

'And what is that you have, a dolly, dear child?' he asked.

'A dolly,' the girl answered, knitting her brow and quailing a bit.

'A dolly . . . And do you know, dear child, what your dolly is made of?'

'No, I don't . . .' the girl answered in a whisper, looking down at the ground.

'Why, it's made out of rags, my darling. My dear boy, you should go to the ballroom and be with your playmates,' Yulian Mastakovich said, after casting a stern look at the child. The girl and boy knitted their brows and grabbed hold of each other. They didn't want to be separated.

'And do you know why they gave you this dolly?' Yulian Mastakovich asked, lowering his voice more and more.

'No, I don't.'

'Because you were a sweet and well-behaved child all week long.'

Then Yulian Mastakovich, unable to contain his agitation, took a look around and, lowering his voice more and more, asked finally in an inaudible voice that faltered with agitation and impatience:

'And will you love me, my dear girl, when I come to visit your parents?'

Having said this Yulian Mastakovich wanted to kiss the sweet girl one more time, but the red-haired boy, seeing that she was on the verge of tears, clasped her by the hands and started to whimper in complete sympathy with her. Yulian Mastakovich became angry in earnest.

'Get out, get out of here, get out!' he said to the little boy. 'Go to the ballroom! Run along to your playmates!'

'No, don't! You get out of here,' the girl said, 'leave him alone, leave him alone!' she said, almost bursting into tears.

Someone made a noise at the door, Yulian Mastakovich took fright and immediately raised his majestic body. But the red-haired boy was even more frightened than Yulian Mastakovich; he abandoned the girl and quietly, hugging the wall, passed from the drawing room into the dining room. So as not to arouse suspicion, Yulian Mastakovich went to the dining room as well. He was as red as a crayfish, and after taking a look at himself in the mirror, he apparently became ashamed of himself. Perhaps he had become annoyed at his impetuousness and his impatience. Perhaps he was so struck by the calculation he'd made on his fingers, so tempted and inspired that, despite all his respectability and importance, he had decided to act like a little boy and take his object by storm, despite the fact that this object could not become a real object for at least another five years. I followed the estimable gentleman into the dining room and witnessed a strange sight. Yulian Mastakovich, all red with vexation and fury, was threatening the red-haired boy, who kept moving further and further away – he didn't know where to run to in his fear.

'Get out, what are you doing here, get out, you ne'er-do-well, get out! You're filching fruit here, are you? Filching fruit, are you? Get out, you ne'er-do-well, get out, you sniveller, get out, run along to your playmates.'

The frightened boy, having resolved on a desperate measure, tried crawling under the table. Then his persecutor, exasperated to the utmost, took out his long cambric handkerchief and started to flick it under the table at the child, who had become as quiet as quiet can be. It should be noted that Yulian Mastakovich was a bit on the heavy side. This was a man who was somewhat portly, ruddy, thickset, with a paunch, with fat thighs, in a word, as they say, a hearty fellow, as round as a little nut. He broke out into a sweat, was panting and became terribly flushed. In the end, he became almost frenzied, so great was his feeling of indignation and, perhaps (who knows?), jealousy. I doubled over with laughter. Yulian Mastakovich turned around and, all his importance notwithstanding, became thoroughly flustered. At this moment the host entered through the door opposite. The little boy crawled out from under the table and brushed off his knees and elbows. Yulian Mastakovich hurried to raise to his nose the handkerchief that he was holding by one end.

The host looked at the three of us in some bewilderment; but, as a person who knows life and looks upon it with some seriousness, he immediately made use of the fact that he had caught his guest alone.

'That's the boy, sir,' he said, after pointing out the redhead, 'about whom I had the honour to request . . .'

'What was that?' Yulian Mastakovich answered, still not fully recovered.

'The son of my children's governess,' the host continued in a tone befitting a request, 'a poor woman, a widow, the wife of an honest official; and therefore . . . Yulian Mastakovich, if it were possible . . .'

'Oh no, no,' Yulian Mastakovich hurriedly cried out, 'no, forgive me, Filipp Alexeyevich, that's quite impossible, sir. I've made enquiries: there aren't any vacancies, and if there were, there would already be ten candidates a great deal more entitled to it than he . . . What a pity, what a pity . . .'

'A pity, sir,' the host repeated, 'the boy is modest, quiet . . .'

'A big mischief-maker, from what I've seen,' Yulian Mastakovich answered, hysterically curling his lip, 'off with you, boy, why are you standing there, run along to your playmates!' he said, addressing the child.

Here, it seems, he couldn't restrain himself and he shot a glance at me with one eye. I also could not restrain myself and began to laugh right in his face. Yulian Mastakovich turned around at once and asked the host rather distinctly so that I should hear it, who that strange young man was. They started to converse in whispers and left the room. I then saw how Yulian Mastakovich shook his head warily as he listened to the host.

Having laughed my fill, I returned to the ballroom. There the great man, surrounded by the fathers and mothers of families, by the hostess and host, was heatedly explaining something to a lady to whom he had just been introduced. The lady was holding by the hand the little girl with whom, ten minutes ago, Yulian Mastakovich had had the scene in the drawing room. Now he was singing the praises of and going into raptures over the beauty, talents, grace and good manners of the dear little child. He was conspicuously playing up to the mother. The mother was listening to him practically with tears of rapture. The father's lips had a smile on them. The host rejoiced in the outpouring of universal joy. Even all the guests sympathized, even the children's games were stopped so as not to interfere with the conversation. The very air was suffused with reverence. I then heard how the mother of the interesting little girl, touched to the bottom of her heart, requested in the most elegant language that Yulian Mastakovich do her the particular honour of favouring their home with his precious acquaintance; I heard the genuine rapture with which Yulian Mastakovich accepted the invitation and later how the guests as they were breaking up to go their separate ways, as dictated by decorum, sang the heart-swelling praises of the tax-farmer, the tax-farmer's wife, the little girl and Yulian Mastakovich in particular.

'Is that gentleman married?' I asked, almost aloud, to one of my acquaintances who was standing closest to Yulian Mastakovich.

Yulian Mastakovich threw me a searching and spiteful glance.

'No!' answered my acquaintance, who was distressed to the very depths of his being by the blunder that I had intentionally committed . . .

Not long ago I was walking past —skaya Church; I was struck by the crowd and the throng of carriages. All around there was talk of a wedding.

The day was overcast, it had started to drizzle; I fought my way through the crowd into the church and saw the groom. He was a small, roundish, portly little man with a paunch, decked out to the hilt. He was running around, bustling about and giving orders. At last, word spread that the bride had arrived. I elbowed my way through the crowd and saw the marvellous beauty for whom the first spring had scarcely begun. But the beauty was pale and sad. She looked about absentmindedly; it even seemed that her eyes were red with recent tears. The classical severity of every feature of her face imparted a certain gravity and solemnity to her beauty. But through this severity and gravity, through this sadness still shined the first childish look of innocence; one sensed something utterly naive, unformed, youthful, which seemed to be silently begging for mercy.

People were saying that she had just turned sixteen. After taking a careful look at the groom, I suddenly recognized him as Yulian Mastakovich, whom I had not seen in exactly five years. I took another look at her . . . My God! I started to elbow my way out of the church as quickly as I could. In the crowd they were saying that the bride was rich, that the bride had a dowry of 500,000 . . . plus so much for glad rags for her trousseau.

'All the same, a fine bit of calculation!' I thought to myself, as I elbowed my way to the street . . .

PAUL ARÈNE

St Anthony and His Pig

Translated by J. M. Lancaster

St Anthony pushed open the door and saw in his cabin half a dozen little children who had come up from the village, in spite of the storm, to bring him some honey and nuts, dainties which the good hermit allowed himself to enjoy once a year, on Christmas Day, on account of his great age.

'Sit around the fire, friends, and throw on two or three pine knots to make a blaze. That's right. Now make room for Barrabas; poor, faithful Barrabas, who is so cold that his tail is all out of curl.'

The children coughed and wiped their noses, and Barrabas – for that is the real name of St Anthony's pig – Barrabas grunted, with his feet comfortably buried in the warm ashes.

The saint threw back his hood, shook the snow from his shoulders, passed his hand over his long gray beard, all hung with little icicles, and having seated himself, began:

'So you want me to tell you about my temptation?'

'Yes, good St Anthony; yes, kind St Anthony.'

'My temptation? But you know as much as I do about my temptation. It has been drawn and painted a thousand times, and you can see on my wall – God forgive me this piece of vanity – all the *prints*, old and new, dedicated to my glory and that of Barrabas; from Épinal's sketch which costs a sou including the song, to the admirable masterpieces of Teniers, Breughel, and Callot.

'I am sure your mothers must have taken you to the marionnette theater at Luxembourg, to see my poor hermitage, just as it is here, with the chapel, the cabin, the bell hanging in the crotch of a tree, and myself at prayer, while Proserpine offers me a cup, and a host of little devils dancing at the end of a string are tormenting and terrifying poor Barrabas.

'After a while, when you have learned to read, you will see behind the glass doors of your father's bookcase these words:

'*The Temptation of St Anthony*, by Gustave Flaubert, in letters of gold on the back of a handsome book.

'This M. Flaubert is a clever fellow, though he does not write for little children like you, and what he says about me is all very true. The artists, of whom I spoke to you just now, have not omitted any of the devils which have tormented me at different times; in fact, they have added a few.

'That is the reason, my children, that I am afraid I should weary you if I should tell you again things that you already know so well.'

'Oh, St Anthony! Oh, good St Anthony!'

'Let me tell you something else –'

'No, no; the temptation, the temptation!'

'Well, well,' said St Anthony, 'I see that I shall not escape the temptation this year; but as you have been unusually good, I will tell you about one which no artist has ever painted, and which M. Flaubert knows nothing about. Nevertheless it was a terrible temptation – was it not, Barrabas? – and kept me a long time on the slope at whose foot the fires of hell are glowing.

'It was at midnight, just such a night as this, that the thing occurred.'

At this beginning, Barrabas, evidently interested, raised himself on his two front feet to listen, the children shivered and drew closer together, and here is the Christmas story which the good saint told them:

'Well, my friends, I must tell you that after a thousand successive temptations, the devils, all at once, stopped tormenting me. My nights were once more peaceful. No more monsters with horns and tails, carrying me through the air on their bat's wings; no more devil's imps with he-goat's beards and monkey faces; no more infernal musicians trying to frighten Barrabas, with their stomachs made of a double bass, and great noses which sounded like an unearthly clarion; no more Queen Proserpines in robes of gold and precious stones, graceful and majestic.

'And I said to myself, "All's well, Anthony; the devils are discouraged." Barrabas and I were as happy as we could be, on our rock.

'Barrabas followed me about everywhere, delighting me with his childish gaiety. As for me, I did what all good hermits do. I prayed, I rang my bell at the proper times, and between my prayers and offices, I drew water from the spring for the vegetables in my garden.

'This lasted six months or more; six delightful months of solitude.

'I slept in perfect security, but unhappily the Evil One was still awake.

'One day, near Christmastime, I was about to sun myself in my doorway, when a man presented himself. He wore hobnailed shoes and a square-cut velvet coat, and carried on his back a pedlar's pack.

'He called out:

'"Spits, spits, spits! Buy some spits!" with a slight Auvergnese accent.

'"Do you want a spit, good hermit?"

'"Go your way, my good man. I live on cold water and roots and have no use for your spits."

'"All right, all right. I am only trying to sell my wares.

'"However," added he, with a fiendish glance at Barrabas, who, more sagacious than I, was grunting furiously in a corner, "however, that fellow there looks so fat and sleek, that I thought – God forgive me! that you might be keeping him for your Christmas Eve supper."

'The fact was that Barrabas, the rascal, had grown very fat, now that the devils no longer troubled his digestion.

'I suddenly became aware of this fact, but was far enough from any thought of feasting upon my only friend, so when I saw the pedlar go down the path, spit in hand, I could not help laughing at the idea. Little by little, however, like the growth of a noxious weed, the infernal idea – for it was evidently a devil from hell disguised as a pedlar, who had tried to sell me the spit – this infernal idea of eating Barrabas took root in my mind. I saw spits; I dreamed of spits. In vain I increased my mortifications and penances. Penances and mortifications availed nothing, and fasting – fasting only seemed to sharpen my appetite.

'I avoided looking at Barrabas. I no longer dared take him with me on my expeditions, and when, at my return, he ran to rub the rough bristles on his back against my bare feet, I turned away my eyes right quickly and had not the heart to caress him.

'But I am afraid, children, that this does not interest you much and perhaps you would prefer –'

'No, good St Anthony!'

'Go on, kind St Anthony!'

'Well, then I will go on, however painful it may be to me to recall those terrible memories. What temptations! What trials! The devil often makes use of the most innocent things to lead a man astray.

'Near my hermitage there was a little wood (I think there are still a few trees there) where some good people had given me permission to take Barrabas to eat acorns.

'It was our favourite walk at sunset, when the oak leaves smell so good.

'I read, while Barrabas gorged himself with acorns, and often while he rooted about in the damp leaves, he turned up rough-looking black balls, which smelled very nice indeed, and these he ate greedily.'

'Perhaps they were truffles, good St Anthony.'

'Yes, my little friend, truffles; a cryptogamous plant which I had scorned till that time, but whose odour struck me all at once as very delicious and appetizing.

'So that from that moment every time that Barrabas dug up a truffle, I made him drop it by hitting him a sharp blow on the snout with a stick, and then – wretched hypocrite that I was – threw him a chestnut or two so that he might not become discouraged.'

'Oh, St Anthony!'

'In that way I collected several pounds.'

'And you were going to cook Barrabas's feet with truffles?'

'Well, I had not altogether decided to do so, but I acknowledge I was thinking about it.

'Beside my door,' continued the hermit, 'a seed brought by the wind had sprouted and grown up between the rock and the wall. Its long leaves of a grayish green smelled very nice, and in the spring the bees came to steal honey from its little purple flowers. I loved this modest plant, which seemed to grow for me alone. I watered it. I cared for it. I put a little earth about its roots.

'But, alas, one morning as I broke off a little sprig and smelled it, I had a sudden and tempting vision of quarters of pork roasting on a spit, deluging with their golden gravy, bits of an herb thrust into the meat and shrivelling and curling in the heat of the fire. My plant, my modest little plant, was the sage so dear to cooks, and its savoury odour thenceforth called to mind only images of spareribs and roast pig. Ashamed of myself, I pulled up my sage, and gave all the truffles at once to Barrabas, who had a grand feast on them.

'But I was not to get off so cheaply. The sage pulled up, the truffles thrown away, my temptation still continued.

'They became more frequent, more irresistible as Christmastime approached.

'Put yourselves in my place: with a robust stomach, for years poorly nourished with roots and cold water, what I saw pass at the foot of my rock, on the high road which leads to the city, was well fitted to ruin a holier man than I. What a procession, my friends! The country people – good Christians as they were – were preparing for the Christmas Eve feast a week beforehand, and from morn till night nothing went by but eatables. Carts full of deer and wild boars, nets full of lobsters, hampers full of fish and oysters; cocks and hens hanging by their feet under the wagons; fat sheep going to the slaughterhouse; ducks and pheasants; a flock of squawking geese; turkeys shaking their crimson wattles; not to mention the good country women carrying baskets full of fruit ripened on straw, bunches of grapes, and white winter melons; eggs and milk for custards and creams; honey in the comb and in jars; cheeses and dried figs.

'And, greatest temptation of all, the despairing cries of some poor pig, tied by the leg and dragged squealing along.

'At last Christmas came. The Midnight Mass over at the hermitage, and everybody gone, I locked the chapel and shut myself up quickly in my hut. It was cold: as cold as it is today. The north wind blew and the fields and roads were covered with snow. I heard laughing and singing outside. It was some of my parishioners who were going to eat their Christmas Eve feast in the neighbourhood. I looked through the hole in my shutter. Here and there over the white plain the bright fires shone out from the farmhouse windows, and down below the illuminated city sent up a glow to heaven, like the reflection from a great furnace. Then I called to mind the Christmas Eve feasts of my gormandizing youth. My grandfather presiding at the table, and christening with new wine the great backlog. I saw the smoking dishes, the white tablecloth, the firelight dancing on the pewter pots and platters on the dresser; and at the thought of myself alone with Barrabas, when all the world was feasting, sitting before a miserable fire, with a jug of water and a wretched root, a sudden sadness seized me. I cried, "What a Christmas feast," and burst into tears.

'The tempter was only waiting for this moment.

'For the last few minutes the silence of the night had been broken by the sound of invisible wings. Then came a shout of laughter, and a series of discreet little knocks on door and shutter.

'"The devils! Hide, hide, Barrabas!" cried I, and Barrabas, who had good reason to hate all sorts of devilish tricks, took refuge behind the kneading trough.

'The slates on my roof rattled as if it were hailing. The infernal gang was once more let loose about my head.

'But now we come to the strangest thing. Instead of the terrific noises and discords by which my enemies generally announced their coming – cries of foul night-birds, bleating of he-goats, rattling of bones, and clanking of iron chains – this time they were low sounds; at first quite vague, like those which the chilly traveller hears from out an inn whose doors are closed, and which, growing more and more distant, resolve themselves into a marvellous music of turning of spits, stirring of saucepans, clinking of glasses, emptying of bottles, rattling of forks and plates, and sizzling of frying pans.

'All at once the music ceased. The walls of my cabin trembled, the shutter blew open, the door slammed back, and the wind, rushing in, put out my lamp.

'I expected to smell brimstone and sulphur. But, no! Not at all! This time the infernal wind was laden with pleasant odours of burned sugar and cinnamon. My cabin smelled very sweet.

'Just then I heard a squeal from Barrabas. They had found out his hiding place.

'"Come, come," said I, "the old jokes are beginning again. They are going to tie fireworks on his tail once more." These devils have not much invention. And forgetting myself, I prayed Heaven to grant my companion strength to bear the trial. But as he cried louder and louder, I ventured to open my eyes, and my lamp being suddenly relighted, I saw the unfortunate martyr held fast by his tail and his ears, and struggling for dear life, surrounded by white devils.'

'White devils! Good St Anthony!'

'Yes, my friends, white devils. The very whitest of the white, I assure you, disguised as they were as scullions and potboys, in short jackets and caps. They brandished larding needles and pranced about with dripping-pans.

'However, in the middle of the room they had placed a long board on two trestles, and on this they stretched Barrabas. Near the board was a big knife, a pail, a little broom and a sponge. Barrabas squealed, and I knew that they were about to cut his throat.

'What a soul-destroying thing is gluttony! While the blood was running and Barrabas was still squealing, my soul was greatly disquietened. But Barrabas once silent – "Bah," said I to myself, "since he is dead" – and with guilty coolness and even with a certain interest, I looked at Barrabas in the hands of the assassins. The innocent Barrabas, the dear companion of my solitude, cruelly torn to pieces and marvellously transformed into a multitude of savoury things.

'I saw him cut open, cleaned and scraped, hung by the feet along a ladder, washed as white as a lily, and smelling very good already in the steam of the boiling water; then cut, chopped, salted, made into sausages, pâté meat, all with diabolical rapidity; so that in a twinkling my hearthstone was covered with a bed of live coals (the devils are never at a loss for anything). I was surrounded by steaming kettles, gridirons and spits, where, amid perfumes as fragrant as ambergris, in gravies and sauces ruddy as gold, bubbled, sizzled, fried, boiled – and that, I confess, to my great joy and satisfaction – the remains of him who was my friend, now transformed into pork.

'All of a sudden everything changes. What a spectacle! A palace instead of a cabin; no more cooking and no more live coals. The broken walls were hung with tapestry; the floor of beaten earth was covered with a carpet.

'Only the slates of the roof kept their places, but these were transformed into a wonderful vine trellis, and through their openings were seen the blue sky and the stars. I had already admired one like it at the house of a rich man in the city, where I had preached repentance for sin. And through these openings ascended and descended a host of little scullions carrying dishes, catching on by the brittle vine twigs, sliding down the branches and covering a table beside me with meats done to a turn.

'There was everything on that table. Ah! My friends, my mouth waters at the thought – Stop, what was I going to say? No; at the very thought of it, my heart is full of remorse. Four hams, two big and two little; four truffled feet; only one head, but stuffed so full of pistachio nuts; steaks;

galantines blushing through their mantle of quivering amber jelly; dainty forcemeat balls; twisted sausages; puddings black as hell.

'Then the roasts; the hashes; the sauces; and I, with staring eyes and dilated nostrils, wondered that so many savoury things could be contained under the bristles of a humble animal, and my heart ached at the thought of poor Barrabas.'

'But did you eat any of him?'

'Almost. I almost ate some, my friends. I had already stuck my fork into the crackling skin of a black blood-pudding, offered me by a very polite little devil. The fork was in; the devil smiled.

'"Get thee behind me, get thee behind me!" cried I. I had just recognized the smile of the diabolical little pedlar, the cause of all my temptations, who two months before had tried to sell me a spit. "Get thee behind me, Satan!"

'The vision fled: it was daybreak and my fire had just gone out. Barrabas, well and happy, shook himself and rang the little bell about his neck, and instead of a host of white devils, snowflakes as big as your fist whirled in the door and window, which the storm had burst open.'

'And what next?' said the children, eager for more of the beautiful story.

'Next, my dear friends, with a heart full of penitence, I shared my meal of roots with Barrabas, and since then no more devils have ever come to disturb our Christmas Eve feast.'

ANTON CHEKHOV

Boys

Translated by Constance Garnett

'Volodya's come!' someone shouted in the yard.

'Master Volodya's here!' bawled Natalya the cook, running into the dining-room. 'Oh, my goodness!'

The whole Korolyov family, who had been expecting their Volodya from hour to hour, rushed to the windows. At the front door stood a wide sledge, with three white horses in a cloud of steam. The sledge was empty, for Volodya was already in the hall, untying his hood with red and chilly fingers. His school overcoat, his cap, his snowboots, and the hair on his temples were all white with frost, and his whole figure from head to foot diffused such a pleasant, fresh smell of the snow that the very sight of him made one want to shiver and say 'brrr!'

His mother and aunt ran to kiss and hug him. Natalya plumped down at his feet and began pulling off his snowboots, his sisters shrieked with delight, the doors creaked and banged, and Volodya's father, in his waistcoat and shirt-sleeves, ran out into the hall with scissors in his hand, and cried out in alarm:

'We were expecting you all yesterday? Did you come all right? Had a good journey? Mercy on us! you might let him say "how do you do" to his father! I am his father after all!'

'Bow-wow!' barked the huge black dog, Milord, in a deep bass, tapping with his tail on the walls and furniture.

For two minutes there was nothing but a general hubbub of joy. After the first outburst of delight was over the Korolyovs noticed that there was, besides their Volodya, another small person in the hall, wrapped up in scarves and shawls and white with frost. He was standing perfectly still in a corner, in the shadow of a big fox-lined overcoat.

'Volodya darling, who is it?' asked his mother, in a whisper.

'Oh!' cried Volodya. 'This is – let me introduce my friend Lentilov, a schoolfellow in the second class . . . I have brought him to stay with us.'

'Delighted to hear it! You are very welcome,' the father said cordially. 'Excuse me, I've been at work without my coat . . . Please come in! Natalya, help Mr Lentilov off with his things. Mercy on us, do turn that dog out! He is unendurable!'

A few minutes later, Volodya and his friend Lentilov, somewhat dazed by their noisy welcome, and still red from the outside cold, were sitting down to tea. The winter sun, making its way through the snow and the frozen tracery on the window-panes, gleamed on the samovar, and plunged its pure rays in the tea-basin. The room was warm, and the boys felt as though the warmth and the frost were struggling together with a tingling sensation in their bodies.

'Well, Christmas will soon be here,' the father said in a pleasant sing-song voice, rolling a cigarette of dark reddish tobacco. 'It doesn't seem long since the summer, when Mamma was crying at your going . . . and here you are back again . . . Time flies, my boy. Before you have time to cry out, old age is upon you. Mr Lentilov, take some more, please help yourself! We don't stand on ceremony!'

Volodya's three sisters, Katya, Sonya, and Masha (the eldest was eleven), sat at the table and never took their eyes off the newcomer.

Lentilov was of the same height and age as Volodya, but not as round-faced and fair-skinned. He was thin, dark, and freckled; his hair stood up like a brush, his eyes were small, and his lips were thick. He was, in fact, distinctly ugly, and if he had not been wearing the school uniform, he might have been taken for the son of a cook. He seemed morose, did not speak, and never once smiled. The little girls, staring at him, imme-diately came to the conclusion that he must be a very clever and learned person. He seemed to be thinking about something all the time, and was so absorbed in his own thoughts, that, whenever he was spoken to, he started, threw his head back, and asked to have the question repeated.

The little girls noticed that Volodya, who had always been so merry and talkative, also said very little, did not smile at all, and hardly seemed to be glad to be home. All the time they were at tea he only once addressed his sisters, and then he said something so strange. He pointed to the samovar and said:

'In California they don't drink tea, but gin.'

He, too, seemed absorbed in his own thoughts, and, to judge by the looks that passed between him and his friend Lentilov, their thoughts were the same.

After tea, they all went into the nursery. The girls and their father took up the work that had been interrupted by the arrival of the boys. They were making flowers and frills for the Christmas tree out of paper of different colours. It was an attractive and noisy occupation. Every fresh flower was greeted by the little girls with shrieks of delight, even of awe, as though the flower had dropped straight from heaven; their father was in ecstasies too, and every now and then he threw the scissors on the floor, in vexation at their bluntness. Their mother kept running into the nursery with an anxious face, asking:

'Who has taken my scissors? Ivan Nikolaitch, have you taken my scissors again?'

'Mercy on us! I'm not even allowed a pair of scissors!' their father would respond in a lachrymose voice, and, flinging himself back in his chair, he would pretend to be a deeply injured man; but a minute later, he would be in ecstasies again.

On his former holidays Volodya, too, had taken part in the preparations for the Christmas tree, or had been running in the yard to look at the snow mountain that the watchman and the shepherd were building. But this time Volodya and Lentilov took no notice whatever of the coloured paper, and did not once go into the stable. They sat in the window and began whispering to one another; then they opened an atlas and looked carefully at a map.

'First to Perm . . .' Lentilov said, in an undertone, 'from there to Tiumen, then Tomsk . . . then . . . then . . . Kamchatka. There the Samoyedes take one over Behring's Straits in boats . . . And then we are in America . . . There are lots of furry animals there . . .'

'And California?' asked Volodya.

'California is lower down . . . We've only to get to America and California is not far off . . . And one can get a living by hunting and plunder.'

All day long Lentilov avoided the little girls, and seemed to look at them with suspicion. In the evening he happened to be left alone with them for five minutes or so. It was awkward to be silent. He cleared his throat morosely, rubbed his left hand against his right, looked sullenly at Katya and asked:

'Have you read Mayne Reid?'

'No, I haven't . . . I say, can you skate?'

Absorbed in his own reflections, Lentilov made no reply to this question; he simply puffed out his cheeks, and gave a long sigh as though he were very hot. He looked up at Katya once more and said:

'When a herd of bisons stampedes across the prairie the earth trembles, and the frightened mustangs kick and neigh.'

He smiled impressively and added:

'And the Indians attack the trains, too. But worst of all are the mosquitoes and the termites.'

'Why, what's that?'

'They're something like ants, but with wings. They bite fearfully. Do you know who I am?'

'Mr Lentilov.'

'No, I am Montehomo, the Hawk's Claw, Chief of the Ever Victorious.'

Masha, the youngest, looked at him, then into the darkness out of the window and said, wondering:

'And we had lentils for supper yesterday.'

Lentilov's incomprehensible utterances, and the way he was always whispering with Volodya, and the way Volodya seemed now to be always thinking about something instead of playing . . . all this was strange and mysterious. And the two elder girls, Katya and Sonya, began to keep a sharp look-out on the boys. At night, when the boys had gone to bed, the girls crept to their bedroom door, and listened to what they were saying. Ah, what they discovered! The boys were planning to run away to America to dig for gold: they had everything ready for the journey, a pistol, two knives, biscuits, a burning glass to serve instead of matches, a compass, and four roubles in cash. They learned that the boys would have to walk some thousands of miles, and would have to fight tigers and savages on the road: then they would get gold and ivory, slay their enemies, become

pirates, drink gin, and finally marry beautiful maidens, and make a
plantation.

The boys interrupted each other in their excitement. Throughout the
conversation, Lentilov called himself 'Montehomo, the Hawk's Claw',
and Volodya was 'my pale-face brother'!

'Mind you don't tell Mamma,' said Katya, as they went back to bed.
'Volodya will bring us gold and ivory from America, but if you tell Mamma
he won't be allowed to go.'

The day before Christmas Eve, Lentilov spent the whole day poring
over the map of Asia and making notes, while Volodya, with a languid
and swollen face that looked as though it had been stung by a bee, walked
about the rooms and ate nothing. And once he stood still before the holy
image in the nursery, crossed himself, and said:

'Lord, forgive me a sinner; Lord, have pity on my poor unhappy Mamma!'

In the evening he burst out crying. On saying good-night he gave his
father a long hug, and then hugged his mother and sisters. Katya and
Sonya knew what was the matter, but little Masha was puzzled, completely puzzled. Every time she looked at Lentilov she grew thoughtful
and said with a sigh:

'When Lent comes, nurse says we shall have to eat peas and lentils.'

Early in the morning of Christmas Eve, Katya and Sonya slipped
quietly out of bed, and went to find out how the boys meant to run away
to America. They crept to their door.

'Then you don't mean to go?' Lentilov was saying angrily. 'Speak out:
aren't you going?'

'Oh dear,' Volodya wept softly. 'How can I go? I feel so unhappy about
Mamma.'

'My pale-face brother, I pray you, let us set off. You declared you were
going, you egged me on, and now the time comes, you funk it!'

'I . . . I . . . I'm not funking it, but I . . . I . . . I'm sorry for Mamma.'

'Say once and for all, are you going or are you not?'

'I am going, only . . . wait a little . . . I want to be at home a little.'

'In that case I will go by myself,' Lentilov declared. 'I can get on without you. And you wanted to hunt tigers and fight! Since that's how it is,
give me back my cartridges!'

At this Volodya cried so bitterly that his sisters could not help crying too. Silence followed.

'So you are not coming?' Lentilov began again.

'I ... I ... I am coming!'

'Well, put on your things, then.'

And Lentilov tried to cheer Volodya up by singing the praises of America, growling like a tiger, pretending to be a steamer, scolding him, and promising to give him all the ivory and lions' and tigers' skins.

And this thin, dark boy, with his freckles and his bristling shock of hair, impressed the little girls as an extraordinary remarkable person. He was a hero, a determined character, who knew no fear, and he growled so ferociously, that, standing at the door, they really might imagine there was a tiger or lion inside. When the little girls went back to their room and dressed, Katya's eyes were full of tears, and she said:

'Oh, I feel so frightened!'

Everything was as usual till two o'clock, when they sat down to dinner. Then it appeared that the boys were not in the house. They sent to the servants' quarters, to the stables, to the bailiff's cottage. They were not to be found. They sent into the village – they were not there.

At tea, too, the boys were still absent, and by supper-time Volodya's mother was dreadfully uneasy, and even shed tears.

Late in the evening they sent again to the village, they searched everywhere, and walked along the river bank with lanterns. Heavens! what a fuss there was!

Next day the police officer came, and a paper of some sort was written out in the dining-room. Their mother cried ...

All of a sudden a sledge stopped at the door, with three white horses in a cloud of steam.

'Volodya's come,' someone shouted in the yard.

'Master Volodya's here!' bawled Natalya, running into the dining-room. And Milord barked his deep bass 'bow-wow'.

It seemed that the boys had been stopped in the Arcade, where they had gone from shop to shop asking where they could get gunpowder.

Volodya burst into sobs as soon as he came into the hall, and flung himself on his mother's neck. The little girls, trembling, wondered with terror what would happen next. They saw their father take Volodya and Lentilov into his study, and there he talked to them a long while.

'Is this a proper thing to do?' their father said to them. 'I only pray they won't hear of it at school, you would both be expelled. You ought to be ashamed, Mr Lentilov, really. It's not at all the thing to do! You began it, and I hope you will be punished by your parents. How could you? Where did you spend the night?'

'At the station,' Lentilov answered proudly.

Then Volodya went to bed, and had a compress, steeped in vinegar, on his forehead.

A telegram was sent off, and next day a lady, Lentilov's mother, made her appearance and bore off her son.

Lentilov looked morose and haughty to the end, and he did not utter a single word at taking leave of the little girls. But he took Katya's book and wrote in it as a souvenir: 'Montehomo, the Hawk's Claw, Chief of the Ever Victorious.'

JOAQUIM MARIA MACHADO DE ASSIS
Midnight Mass

Translated by Margaret Jull Costa and Robin Patterson

I've never quite understood a conversation I had with a lady many years ago, when I was seventeen and she was thirty. It was Christmas Eve. Having arranged to attend midnight mass with a neighbour, I had agreed that I would stay awake and call for him just before midnight.

The house where I was staying belonged to the notary Meneses, whose first wife had been one of my cousins. His second wife, Conceição, and her mother had both welcomed me warmly when, months before, I arrived in Rio de Janeiro from Mangaratiba to study for my university entrance exams. I led a very quiet life in that two-storey house on Rua do Senado, with my books, a few friends, and the occasional outing. It was a small household, consisting of the notary, his wife, his mother-in-law and two slavewomen. They kept to the old routines, retiring to bed at ten and with everyone sound asleep by half past. Now, I had never been to the theatre, and more than once, on hearing Meneses announce that he was going, I would ask him to take me with him. On such occasions, his mother-in-law would pull a disapproving face, and the slavewomen would titter; he, however, would not even reply, but would get dressed, leave the house, and not return until the following morning. Only later on did I realize that the theatre was a euphemism in action. Meneses was having an affair with a lady who was separated from her husband and, once a week, he slept elsewhere. At first, Conceição had found the existence of this mistress deeply wounding, but, in the end, she had resigned herself and grown accustomed to the situation, deciding that there was nothing untoward about it at all.

Good, kind Conceição! People called her 'a saint', and she did full justice to that title, given how easily she put up with her husband's neglect.

Hers was a very moderate nature, with no extremes, no tearful tantrums and no great outbursts of hilarity. In this respect, she would have been fine as a Muslim woman and would have been quite happy in a harem, as long as appearances were maintained. May God forgive me if I'm misjudging her, but everything about her was contained and passive. Even her face was average, neither pretty nor ugly. She was what people call 'a nice person'. She never spoke ill of anyone and was very forgiving. She wouldn't have known how to hate anyone nor, perhaps, how to love them.

On that particular Christmas Eve, the notary went off to the theatre. It was around 1861 or 1862. I should have been in Mangaratiba on holiday, but I had stayed until Christmas because I wanted to see what midnight mass was like in the big city. The family retired to bed at the usual time, and I waited in the front room, dressed and ready. From there I could go out into the hallway and leave the house without disturbing anyone. There were three keys to the front door: the notary had one, I would take the second, and the third would remain in the house.

'But Senhor Nogueira, what will you do to fill the time?' Conceição's mother asked.

'I'll read, Dona Inácia.'

I had with me a novel, *The Three Musketeers*, in an old translation published, I think, by the *Jornal do Comércio*. I sat down at the table in the middle of the room, and by the light of an oil lamp, while the rest of the house was sleeping, I once again climbed onto D'Artagnan's scrawny horse and set off on an adventure. I was soon completely intoxicated by Dumas. The minutes flew past, as they so rarely do when one is waiting; I heard the clock strike eleven, but barely took any notice as if it were of no importance. However, the sound of someone stirring in the house roused me from my reading: footsteps in the passageway between the parlour and the dining room. I looked up and, soon afterwards, saw Conceição appear in the doorway.

'Still here?' she asked.

'Yes, it's not yet midnight.'

'Such patience!'

Conceição came into the room, her bedroom slippers flip-flapping. She was wearing a white dressing gown, loosely tied at the waist. She was quite thin and this somehow lent her a romantic air, rather in keeping with my adventure story. I closed the book, and she went and sat on the chair next to mine, near the couch. When I asked if I had unwittingly woken her by making a noise, she immediately said:

'No, not at all. I simply woke up.'

I looked at her and rather doubted the truth of this. Her eyes were not those of someone who had been asleep, but of someone who had not yet slept at all. However, I quickly dismissed this observation – which might have borne fruit in someone else's mind – never dreaming that I might be the reason she hadn't gone to sleep and that she was lying so as not to worry or annoy me. She was, as I said, a kind person, very kind.

'It must be nearly time though,' I said.

'How do you have the patience to stay awake while your neighbour sleeps? And to wait here all alone too. Aren't you afraid of ghosts? I bet I startled you just now.'

'I was a little surprised when I heard footsteps, but then you appeared immediately afterwards.'

'What were you reading? Don't tell me, I know: it's *The Three Musketeers*.'

'Exactly. It's such a good book.'

'Do you like novels?'

'I do.'

'Have you read *The Dark-haired Girl*?'

'By Macedo? Yes, I have it at home in Mangaratiba.'

'I love novels, but I don't have much time to read any more. What novels have you read?'

I began listing a few titles. Conceição listened, leaning her head against the chairback, looking at me fixedly through half-closed eyelids. Now and then, she would run her tongue over her lips to moisten them. When I finished speaking, she said nothing, and we sat in silence for a few seconds. Then, still gazing at me with her large, intelligent eyes, she sat up straight, interlaced her fingers and rested her chin on them, her elbows on the arms of the chair.

'Perhaps she's bored,' I thought. Then, out loud, I said:

'Dona Conceição, I think it must be nearly time, and I . . .'

'No, no, it's still early. I just looked at the clock and it's only half past eleven. You still have time. If you ever do miss a night's sleep, can you get through the next day without sleeping at all?'

'I have in the past.'

'I can't. If I miss a night's sleep, I'm no use for anything the next day and have to have a nap, even if it's only for half an hour. But then I'm getting old.'

'What do you mean "old", Dona Conceição?'

I spoke these words with such passion that it made her smile. She usually moved very slowly and serenely, but now she sprang to her feet, walked over to the other side of the room and paced up and down between the window giving on to the street and the door of her husband's study. Her modestly rumpled appearance made a singular impression on me. Although she was quite slender, there was something about that swaying gait, as if she were weighed down by her own body; I had never really noticed this until then. She paused occasionally to examine the hem of a curtain or to adjust the position of some object on the sideboard; finally, she stopped in front of me, with the table between us. Her ideas appeared to be caught in a very narrow circle; she again remarked on her astonishment at my ability to stay awake; I repeated what she already knew, that I had never attended midnight mass in Rio and did not want to miss it.

'It's just the same as mass in the countryside, well, all masses are alike really.'

'I'm sure you're right, but here it's bound to be more lavish and there'll be more people too. After all, Holy Week is much prettier in Rio than it is in the countryside. Not to mention the feasts of St John or St Anthony . . .'

She gradually leaned forward, resting her elbows on the marble table top, her face cupped in her outspread hands. Her unbuttoned sleeves fell back to reveal her forearms, which were very pale and plumper than one might have expected. This was not exactly a novelty, although it wasn't a common sight either; at that moment, however, it made a great impression on me. Her veins were so blue that, despite the dim light, I could count every one. Her presence was even better at keeping me awake than my book. I continued to compare religious festivals in the countryside and in the city, and to give my views on whatever happened to pop into my head. I kept changing the subject for no reason, talking about one thing, then going back to something I'd mentioned earlier, and laughing in the hope that this would make her smile too, thus affording me a glimpse of her perfect, gleaming white teeth. Her eyes were very dark, almost black; her long, slender, slightly curved nose gave her face an interrogative air. When I raised my voice a little, she told me off:

'Ssh! You might wake Mama!'

Much to my delight, though, she didn't move from where she was, our faces very close. It really wasn't necessary to speak loudly in order to be heard; we were both whispering, I even more softly than her, because I was doing most of the talking. At times, she would look serious – very serious – even frowning slightly. She eventually grew tired and changed position and place. She walked round to my side of the table and sat down on the couch. I turned and could just see the toes of her slippers, but only for the time it took her to sit down, because her dressing gown was long enough to cover them. I remember that the slippers were black. She said very softly:

'Mama's room is quite some way away, but she sleeps so very lightly, and if she were to wake up now, it would take her ages to get back to sleep.'

'I'm the same.'

'What?' she asked, leaning forward to hear better.

I went and sat on the chair beside the couch and repeated what I'd said. She laughed at the coincidence of there being three light sleepers in the same house.

'Because I'm just like Mama sometimes: if I do wake in the night, I find it hard to go back to sleep, I toss and turn, get up, light a candle, pace up and down, get into bed again, but it's no use.'

'Is that what happened tonight?'

'No, not at all,' she said.

I couldn't understand why she denied this, and perhaps she couldn't either. She picked up the two ends of her dressing-gown belt and kept flicking them against her knees, or, rather, against her right knee, because she had crossed her legs. Then she told some story about dreams, and assured me that she had only ever had one nightmare, when she was a child. She asked if I ever had nightmares. The conversation continued in this same slow, leisurely way, and I gave not a thought to the time or to mass. Whenever I finished some anecdote or explanation, she would come up with another question or another subject, and I would again start talking. Now and then she would hush me:

'Ssh! Speak more softly!'

There were pauses too. Twice I thought she had dropped asleep, but her eyes, which had closed for an instant, immediately opened again with no sign of tiredness or fatigue, as if she had merely closed them in order to see more clearly. On one such occasion, I think she became aware of my rapt gaze, and she closed her eyes again, whether quickly or slowly I can't recall. Other memories of that night appear to me as truncated or confused. I contradict myself, stumble. One memory does still remain fresh, though; at one point, she, who I had only thought of as 'nice-looking' before, looked really pretty, positively lovely. She was standing up, arms folded; out of politeness, I made as if to stand up too, but she stopped me, placing one hand on my shoulder and obliging me to sit down again. I thought she was about to say something, but, instead, she shivered, as if she suddenly felt cold, then turned and sat in the chair where I had been sitting when she entered the room. From there, she glanced up at the mirror above the couch and commented on the two engravings on the wall.

'They're getting old, those pictures. I've already asked Chiquinho to buy some new ones.'

Chiquinho was her husband. The pictures exemplified the man's main interest. One was a representation of Cleopatra, and I can't remember the other one, but both were of women. They were perhaps rather vulgar, but, at the time, I didn't think them particularly ugly.

'They're pretty,' I said.

'Yes, but they're rather faded now. And frankly I would prefer two images of saints. These are more suited to a boy's bedroom or a barber's shop.'

'A barber's shop? But you've never been in one, have you?'

'No, but I imagine that, while they're waiting, the customers talk about girls and love affairs and, naturally, the owner brightens up the place with a few pretty pictures. The ones over there just don't seem appropriate in a family home. At least, that's what I think, but then I often have strange thoughts. Anyway, I don't like them. On my prayer-stool I have a really beautiful statuette of Our Lady of the Conception, my patron saint, but you can't hang a sculpture on the wall, much as I would like to.'

The word 'prayer-room' reminded me of mass, and it occurred to me that it might be getting late and I was just about to mention this. I did, I think, get as far as opening my mouth, but immediately closed it again to listen to what she was saying, so gently, touchingly, softly, that my soul grew indolent and I forgot all about mass and church. She was talking about her devotions as a child and as a young girl. She then moved on to stories about dances, about outings she'd made, memories of Paquetá, all woven almost seamlessly together. When she grew tired of the past, she spoke about the present, about her household duties and the burdens of family life, which, before she married, she had been told were many, but which were not, in fact, burdensome at all. She didn't mention that she was twenty-seven when she married, but I knew that already.

She was no longer pacing up and down as she had to begin with, but stayed almost frozen in the same pose. She no longer kept her large eyes fixed on me, but glanced around at the walls.

'This room needs repapering,' she said after a while, as if talking to herself.

I agreed, simply in order to say something and to try to shake off that strange, magnetic sleep or whatever it was trammelling my tongue and my senses. I both wanted and didn't want to end that conversation; I made an effort to take my eyes off her, and I did so out of a sense of respect, but then, fearing that she might think I was bored, when I wasn't at all, I quickly brought my gaze back to her. The conversation was gradually dying. Out in the street, utter silence reigned.

We sat without speaking for some time, I don't know for how long. The only sound came from the study, the faint noise of a mouse gnawing away at something, and this did at last rouse me from my somnolent state; I tried to speak, but couldn't. Conceição appeared to be daydreaming. Then, suddenly, I heard someone banging on the window outside, and a voice shouting:

'Midnight mass! Midnight mass!'

'Ah, there's your friend,' she said, getting up. 'How funny! You were the one who was supposed to wake him up, but there he is waking you. Off you go. It must be time.'

'Is it midnight already?' I asked.

'It must be.'

'Midnight mass!' came the voice again, accompanied by more banging on the window.

'Quick, off you go. Don't keep him waiting. It was my fault. Goodnight. See you tomorrow.'

And with the same swaying gait, Conceição slipped silently back down the corridor. I went out into the street, where my neighbour was waiting. We set off to the church. More than once during mass, the figure of Conceição interposed itself between me and the priest, but let's put that down to my seventeen years. The following morning, over breakfast, I described the mass and the congregation, but Conceição showed not a flicker of interest. During the day, she was her usual natural, benign self and made no mention of our conversation the previous night. At New Year, I went home to Mangaratiba. By the time I returned to Rio in March, the notary had died of apoplexy. Conceição was living in Engenho Novo, but I neither visited her nor met her again. I later heard that she had married her late husband's articled clerk.

SAKI

Reginald's Christmas Revel

They say (said Reginald) that there's nothing sadder than victory except defeat. If you've ever stayed with dull people during what is alleged to be the festive season, you can probably revise that saying. I shall never forget putting in a Christmas at the Babwolds'. Mrs Babwold is some relation of my father's – a sort of to-be-left-till-called-for cousin – and that was considered sufficient reason for my having to accept her invitation at about the sixth time of asking; though why the sins of the father should be visited by the children – you won't find any notepaper in that drawer; that's where I keep old menus and first-night programmes.

Mrs Babwold wears a rather solemn personality, and has never been known to smile, even when saying disagreeable things to her friends or making out the Stores list. She takes her pleasures sadly. A state elephant at a Durbar gives one a very similar impression. Her husband gardens in all weathers. When a man goes out in the pouring rain to brush caterpillars off rose trees, I generally imagine his life indoors leaves something to be desired; anyway, it must be very unsettling for the caterpillars.

Of course there were other people there. There was a Major Somebody who had shot things in Lapland, or somewhere of that sort; I forget what they were, but it wasn't for want of reminding. We had them cold with every meal almost, and he was continually giving us details of what they measured from tip to tip, as though he thought we were going to make them warm under-things for the winter. I used to listen to him with a rapt attention that I thought rather suited me, and then one day I quite modestly gave the dimensions of an okapi I had shot in the Lincolnshire fens. The Major turned a beautiful Tyrian scarlet (I remember thinking at the time that I should like my bathroom hung in that colour), and I think that at that moment he almost found it in his heart to dislike me. Mrs Babwold put on a first-aid-to-the-injured expression, and asked him why he didn't publish a book of his sporting reminiscences; it would be *so* interesting. She didn't remember till afterwards that he had given her two fat volumes on the subject, with his portrait and autograph as a frontispiece and an appendix on the habits of the Arctic mussel.

It was in the evening that we cast aside the cares and distractions of the day and really lived. Cards were thought to be too frivolous and empty a way of passing the time, so most of them played what they called a book game. You went out into the hall – to get an inspiration, I suppose – then you came in again with a muffler tied round your neck and looked silly, and the others were supposed to guess that you were *Wee MacGreegor*. I held out against the inanity as long as I decently could, but at last, in a lapse of good-nature, I consented to masquerade as a book, only I warned them that it would take some time to carry out. They waited for the best part of forty minutes while I went and played wineglass skittles with the page-boy in the pantry; you play it with a champagne cork, you know, and the one who knocks down the most glasses without breaking them wins. I won, with four unbroken out of seven; I think William suffered from over-anxiousness. They were rather mad in the drawing-room at my not having come back, and they weren't a bit pacified when I told them afterwards that I was *At the end of the passage*.

'I never did like Kipling,' was Mrs Babwold's comment, when the situation dawned upon her. 'I couldn't see anything clever in *Earthworms out of Tuscany* – or is that by Darwin?'

Of course these games are very educational, but, personally, I prefer bridge.

On Christmas evening we were supposed to be specially festive in the Old English fashion. The hall was horribly draughty, but it seemed to be the proper place to revel in, and it was decorated with Japanese fans and Chinese lanterns, which gave it a very Old English effect. A young lady with a confidential voice favoured us with a long recitation about a little girl who died or did something equally hackneyed, and then the Major gave us a graphic account of a struggle he had with a wounded bear. I privately wished that the bears would win sometimes on these occasions; at least they wouldn't go vapouring about it afterwards. Before we had time to recover our spirits, we were indulged with some thought-reading by a young man whom one knew instinctively had a good mother and an indifferent tailor – the sort of young man who talks unflaggingly through the thickest soup, and smooths his hair dubiously as though he thought it might hit back. The thought-reading was rather a success; he announced that the hostess was thinking about poetry, and she admitted that her mind was dwelling on one of Austin's odes. Which was near enough. I fancy she had been really wondering whether a scrag-end of mutton and some cold plum-pudding would do for the kitchen dinner next day. As a crowning dissipation, they all sat down to play progressive halma, with milk-chocolate for prizes. I've been carefully brought up, and I don't like to play games of skill for milk-chocolate, so I invented a headache and retired from the scene. I had been preceded a few minutes earlier by Miss Langshan-Smith, a rather formidable lady, who always got up at some uncomfortable hour in the morning, and gave you the impression that she had been in communication with most of the European Governments before breakfast. There was a paper pinned on her door with a signed request that she might be called particularly early on the morrow. Such an opportunity does not come twice in a lifetime. I covered up everything except the signature with another notice, to the effect that before these words should meet the eye she would have ended a misspent life, was sorry for the trouble she was giving, and would like a military funeral. A few minutes later I violently exploded an air-filled paper bag on the landing, and gave a stage moan that could have been heard in the cellars. Then I pursued my original intention and went to bed. The noise those people made in forcing open the good lady's door was positively indecorous; she resisted gallantly, but I believe they searched her for bullets for about a quarter of an hour, as if she had been a historic battlefield.

I hate travelling on Boxing Day, but one must occasionally do things that one dislikes.

The Legend of the Christmas Rose

Translated by Velma Swanston Howard

Robber Mother, who lived in Robbers' Cave up in Göinge forest, went down to the village one day on a begging tour. Robber Father, who was an outlawed man, did not dare to leave the forest, but had to content himself with lying in wait for the wayfarers who ventured within its borders. But at that time travellers were not very plentiful in Southern Skåne. If it so happened that the man had had a few weeks of ill luck with his hunt, his wife would take to the road. She took with her five youngsters, and each youngster wore a ragged leathern suit and birch-bark shoes and bore a sack on his back as long as himself. When Robber Mother stepped inside the door of a cabin, no one dared refuse to give her whatever she demanded; for she was not above coming back the following night and setting fire to the house if she had not been well received. Robber Mother and her brood were worse than a pack of wolves, and many a man felt like running a spear through them; but it was never done, because they all knew that the man stayed up in the forest, and he would have known how to wreak vengeance if anything had happened to the children or the old woman.

Now that Robber Mother went from house to house and begged, she came one day to Övid, which at that time was a cloister. She rang the bell of the cloister gate and asked for food. The watchman let down a small wicket in the gate and handed her six round bread cakes – one for herself and one for each of the five children.

While the mother was standing quietly at the gate, her youngsters were running about. And now one of them came and pulled at her skirt, as a signal that he had discovered something which she ought to come and see, and Robber Mother followed him promptly.

The entire cloister was surrounded by a high and strong wall, but the youngster had managed to find a little back gate which stood ajar. When Robber Mother got there, she pushed the gate open and walked inside without asking leave, as it was her custom to do.

Övid Cloister was managed at that time by Abbot Hans, who knew all about herbs. Just within the cloister wall he had planted a little herb garden, and it was into this that the old woman had forced her way.

At first glance Robber Mother was so astonished that she paused at the gate. It was high summertide, and Abbot Hans' garden was so full of flowers that the eyes were fairly dazzled by the blues, reds, and yellows, as one looked into it. But presently an indulgent smile spread over her features, and she started to walk up a narrow path that lay between many flower-beds.

In the garden a lay brother walked about, pulling up weeds. It was he who had left the door in the wall open, that he might throw the weeds and tares on the rubbish heap outside.

When he saw Robber Mother coming in, with all five youngsters in tow, he ran toward her at once and ordered them away. But the beggar woman walked right on as before. She cast her eyes up and down, looking now at the stiff white lilies which spread near the ground, then on the ivy climbing high upon the cloister wall, and took no notice whatever of the lay brother.

He thought she had not understood him, and wanted to take her by the arm and turn her toward the gate. But when the robber woman saw his purpose, she gave him a look that sent him reeling backward. She had been walking with back bent under her beggar's pack, but now she straightened herself to her full height. 'I am Robber Mother from Göinge forest; so touch me if you dare!' And it was obvious that she was as certain she would be left in peace as if she had announced that she was the Queen of Denmark.

And yet the lay brother dared to oppose her, although now, when he knew who she was, he spoke reasonably to her. 'You must know, Robber Mother, that this is a monks' cloister, and no woman in the land is allowed within these walls. If you do not go away, the monks will be angry with me because I forgot to close the gate, and perhaps they will drive me away from the cloister and the herb garden.'

But such prayers were wasted on Robber Mother. She walked straight ahead among the little flower-beds and looked at the hyssop with its magenta blossoms, and at the honeysuckles, which were full of deep orange-coloured flower clusters.

Then the lay brother knew of no other remedy than to run into the cloister and call for help.

He returned with two stalwart monks, and Robber Mother saw that now it meant business! With feet firmly planted she stood in the path and began shrieking in strident tones all the awful vengeance she would wreak on the cloister if she couldn't remain in the herb garden as long as she wished. But the monks did not see why they need fear her and thought only of driving her out. Then Robber Mother let out a perfect volley of shrieks, and, throwing herself upon the monks, clawed and bit at them; so did all the youngsters. The men soon learned that she could overpower them, and all they could do was to go back into the cloister for reinforcements.

As they ran through the passage-way which led to the cloister, they met Abbot Hans, who came rushing out to learn what all this noise was about.

Then they had to confess that Robber Mother from Göinge forest had come into the cloister and that they were unable to drive her out and must call for assistance.

But Abbot Hans upbraided them for using force and forbade their calling for help. He sent both monks back to their work, and although he was an old and fragile man, he took with him only the lay brother.

When Abbot Hans came out in the garden, Robber Mother was still wandering among the flower-beds. He regarded her with astonishment. He was certain that Robber Mother had never before seen a herb garden; yet she sauntered leisurely between all the small patches, each of which had been planted with its own species of rare flower, and looked at them as if they were old acquaintances. At some she smiled, at others she shook her head.

Abbot Hans loved his herb garden as much as it was possible for him to love anything earthly and perishable. Wild and terrible as the old woman looked, he couldn't help liking that she had fought with three monks for the privilege of viewing the garden in peace. He came up to her and asked in a mild tone if the garden pleased her.

Robber Mother turned defiantly toward Abbot Hans, for she expected only to be trapped and overpowered. But when she noticed his white hair and bent form, she answered peaceably, 'First, when I saw this, I thought I had never seen a prettier garden; but now I see that it can't be compared with one I know of.'

Abbot Hans had certainly expected a different answer. When he heard that Robber Mother had seen a garden more beautiful than his, a faint flush spread over his withered cheek. The lay brother, who was standing close by, immediately began to censure the old woman. 'This is Abbot Hans,' said he, 'who with much care and diligence has gathered the flowers from far and near for his herb garden. We all know that there is not a more beautiful garden to be found in all Skåne, and it is not befitting that you, who live in the wild forest all the year around, should find fault with his work.'

'I don't wish to make myself the judge of either him or you,' said Robber Mother. 'I'm only saying that if you could see the garden of which I am thinking you would uproot all the flowers planted here and cast them away like weeds.'

But the Abbot's assistant was hardly less proud of the flowers than the Abbot himself, and after hearing her remarks he laughed derisively. 'I can understand that you only talk like this to tease us. It must be a pretty garden that you have made for yourself amongst the pines in Göinge forest! I'd be willing to wager my soul's salvation that you have never before been within the walls of a herb garden.'

Robber Mother grew crimson with rage to think that her word was doubted, and she cried out: 'It may be true that until today I had never been within the walls of a herb garden; but you monks, who are holy men, certainly must know that on every Christmas Eve the great Göinge forest is transformed into a beautiful garden, to commemorate the hour of our Lord's birth. We who live in the forest have seen this happen every year. And in that garden I have seen flowers so lovely that I dared not lift my hand to pluck them.'

The lay brother wanted to continue the argument, but Abbot Hans gave him a sign to be silent. For, ever since his childhood, Abbot Hans had heard it said that on every Christmas Eve the forest was dressed in holiday glory. He had often longed to see it, but he had never had the good fortune. Eagerly he begged and implored Robber Mother that he might come up to the Robbers' Cave on Christmas Eve. If she would only send one of her children to show him the way, he could ride up there alone, and he would never betray them – on the contrary, he would reward them, in so far as it lay in his power.

Robber Mother said no at first, for she was thinking of Robber Father and of the peril which might befall him should she permit Abbot Hans to ride up to their cave. At the same time the desire to prove to the monk that the garden which she knew was more beautiful than his got the better of her, and she gave in.

'But more than one follower you cannot take with you,' said she, 'and you are not to waylay us or trap us, as sure as you are a holy man.'

This Abbot Hans promised, and then Robber Mother went her way. Abbot Hans commanded the lay brother not to reveal to a soul that which had been agreed upon. He feared that the monks, should they learn of his purpose, would not allow a man of his years to go up to the Robbers' Cave.

Nor did he himself intend to reveal his project to a human being. And then it happened that Archbishop Absalon from Lund came to Övid and remained through the night. When Abbot Hans was showing him the herb garden, he got to thinking of Robber Mother's visit, and the lay brother, who was at work in the garden, heard Abbot Hans telling the Bishop about Robber Father, who these many years had lived as an outlaw in the forest, and asking him for a letter of ransom for the man, that he might lead an honest life among respectable folk. 'As things are now,' said Abbot Hans, 'his children are growing up into worse malefactors than himself, and you will soon have a whole gang of robbers to deal with up there in the forest.'

But the Archbishop replied that he did not care to let the robber loose among honest folk in the villages. It would be best for all that he remain in the forest.

Then Abbot Hans grew zealous and told the Bishop all about Göinge forest, which, every year at Yuletide, clothed itself in summer bloom around the Robbers' Cave. 'If these bandits are not so bad but that God's glories can be made manifest to them, surely we cannot be too wicked to experience the same blessing.'

The Archbishop knew how to answer Abbot Hans. 'This much I will promise you, Abbot Hans,' he said, smiling, 'that any day you send me a blossom from the garden in Göinge forest, I will give you letters of ransom for all the outlaws you may choose to plead for.'

The lay brother apprehended that Bishop Absalon believed as little in this story of Robber Mother's as he himself; but Abbot Hans perceived nothing of the sort, but thanked Absalon for his good promise and said that he would surely send him the flower.

Abbot Hans had his way. And the following Christmas Eve he did not sit at home with his monks in Övid Cloister, but was on his way to Göinge forest. One of Robber Mother's wild youngsters ran ahead of him, and close behind him was the lay brother who had talked with Robber Mother in the herb garden.

Abbot Hans had been longing to make this journey, and he was very happy now that it had come to pass. But it was a different matter with the lay brother who accompanied him. Abbot Hans was very dear to him, and he would not willingly have allowed another to attend him and watch over him; but he didn't believe that he should see any Christmas Eve garden. He thought the whole thing a snare which Robber Mother had, with great cunning, laid for Abbot Hans, that he might fall into her husband's clutches.

While Abbot Hans was riding toward the forest, he saw that everywhere they were preparing to celebrate Christmas. In every peasant settlement fires were lighted in the bath-house to warm it for the afternoon bathing. Great hunks of meat and bread were being carried from the larders into the cabins, and from the barns came the men with big sheaves of straw to be strewn over the floors.

As he rode by the little country churches, he observed that each person, with his sexton, was busily engaged in decorating his church; and when he came to the road which leads to Bösjo Cloister, he observed that all the poor of the parish were coming with armfuls of bread and long candles, which they had received at the cloister gate.

When Abbot Hans saw all these Christmas preparations, his haste increased. He was thinking of the festivities that awaited him, which were greater than any the others would be privileged to enjoy.

But the lay brother whined and fretted when he saw how they were preparing to celebrate Christmas in every humble cottage. He grew more and more anxious, and begged and implored Abbot Hans to turn back and not to throw himself deliberately into the robber's hands.

Abbot Hans went straight ahead, paying no heed to his lamentations. He left the plain behind him and came up into desolate and wild forest regions. Here the road was bad, almost like a stony and burr-strewn path, with neither bridge nor plank to help them over brooklet and rivulet. The farther they rode, the colder it grew, and after a while they came upon snow-covered ground.

It turned out to be a long and hazardous ride through the forest. They climbed steep and slippery side paths, crawled over swamp and marsh, and pushed through windfall and bramble. Just as daylight was waning, the robber boy guided them across a forest meadow, skirted by tall, naked leaf trees and green fir trees. At the back of the meadow loomed a mountain wall, and in this wall they saw a door of thick boards. Now Abbot Hans understood that they had arrived, and dismounted. The child opened the heavy door for him, and he looked into a poor mountain grotto, with bare stone walls. Robber Mother was seated before a log fire that burned in the middle of the floor. Alongside the walls were beds of virgin pine and moss, and on one of these beds lay Robber Father asleep.

'Come in, you out there!' shouted Robber Mother without rising, 'and fetch the horses in with you, so they won't be destroyed by the night cold.'

Abbot Hans walked boldly into the cave, and the lay brother followed. Here were wretchedness and poverty! and nothing was done to celebrate Christmas. Robber Mother had neither brewed nor baked; she had neither washed nor scoured. The youngsters were lying on the floor around a kettle, eating; but no better food was provided for them than a watery gruel.

Robber Mother spoke in a tone as haughty and dictatorial as any well-to-do peasant woman. 'Sit down by the fire and warm yourself, Abbot Hans,' said she; 'and if you have food with you, eat, for the food which we in the forest prepare you wouldn't care to taste. And if you are tired after the long journey, you can lie down on one of these beds to sleep. You needn't be afraid of oversleeping, for I'm sitting here by the fire keeping watch. I shall awaken you in time to see that which you have come up here to see.'

Abbot Hans obeyed Robber Mother and brought forth his food sack; but he was so fatigued after the journey he was hardly able to eat, and as soon as he could stretch himself on the bed, he fell asleep.

The lay brother was also assigned a bed to rest upon, but he didn't dare sleep, as he thought he had better keep his eye on Robber Father to prevent his getting up and capturing Abbot Hans. But gradually fatigue got the better of him, too, and he dropped into a doze.

When he woke up, he saw that Abbot Hans had left his bed and was sitting by the fire talking with Robber Mother. The outlawed robber sat also by the fire. He was a tall, raw-boned man with a dull, sluggish appearance. His back was turned to Abbot Hans, as though he would have it appear that he was not listening to the conversation.

Abbot Hans was telling Robber Mother all about the Christmas preparations he had seen on the journey, reminding her of Christmas feasts and games which she must have known in her youth, when she lived at peace with mankind. 'I'm sorry for your children, who can never run on the village street in holiday dress or tumble in the Christmas straw,' said he.

At first Robber Mother answered in short, gruff sentences, but by degrees she became more subdued and listened more intently. Suddenly Robber Father turned toward Abbot Hans and shook his clenched fist in his face. 'You miserable monk! did you come here to coax from me my wife and children? Don't you know that I am an outlaw and may not leave the forest?'

Abbot Hans looked him fearlessly in the eyes. 'It is my purpose to get a letter of ransom for you from Archbishop Absalon,' said he. He had hardly finished speaking when the robber and his wife burst out laughing. They knew well enough the kind of mercy a forest robber could expect from Bishop Absalon!

'Oh, if I get a letter of ransom from Absalon,' said Robber Father, 'then I'll promise you that never again will I steal so much as a goose.'

The lay brother was annoyed with the robber folk for daring to laugh at Abbot Hans, but on his own account he was well pleased. He had seldom seen the Abbot sitting more peaceful and meek with his monks at Övid than he now sat with this wild robber folk.

Suddenly Robber Mother rose. 'You sit here and talk, Abbot Hans,' she said, 'so that we are forgetting to look at the forest. Now I can hear, even in this cave, how the Christmas bells are ringing.'

The words were barely uttered when they all sprang up and rushed out. But in the forest it was still dark night and bleak winter. The only thing they marked was a distant clang borne on a light south wind.

'How can this bell ringing ever awaken the dead forest?' thought Abbot Hans. For now, as he stood out in the winter darkness, he thought it far more impossible that a summer garden could spring up here than it had seemed to him before.

When the bells had been ringing a few moments, a sudden illumination penetrated the forest; the next moment it was dark again, and then the light came back. It pushed its way forward between the stark trees, like a shimmering mist. This much it effected: The darkness merged into a faint daybreak. Then Abbot Hans saw that the snow had vanished from the ground, as if someone had removed a carpet, and the earth began to take on a green covering. Then the ferns shot up their fronds, rolled like a bishop's staff. The heather that grew on the stony hills and the bog-myrtle rooted in the ground moss dressed themselves quickly in new bloom. The moss-tufts thickened and raised themselves, and the spring blossoms shot upward their swelling buds, which already had a touch of colour.

Abbot Hans' heart beat fast as he marked the first signs of the forest's awakening. 'Old man that I am, shall I behold such a miracle?' thought he, and the tears wanted to spring to his eyes. Again it grew so hazy that he feared the darkness would once more cover the earth; but almost immediately there came a new wave of light. It brought with it the splash of rivulet and the rush of cataract. Then the leaves of the trees burst into bloom, as if a swarm of green butterflies came flying and clustered on the branches. It was not only trees and plants that awoke, but crossbeaks hopped from branch to branch, and the woodpeckers hammered on the limbs until the splinters fairly flew around them. A flock of starlings from up country lighted in a fir top to rest. They were paradise starlings. The tips of each tiny feather shone in brilliant reds, and, as the birds moved, they glittered like so many jewels.

Again, all was dark for an instant, but soon there came a new light wave. A fresh, warm south wind blew and scattered over the forest meadow all the little seeds that had been brought here from southern lands by birds and ships and winds, and which could not thrive elsewhere because of this country's cruel cold. These took root and sprang up the instant they touched the ground.

When the next warm wind came along, the blueberries and lignon ripened. Cranes and wild geese shrieked in the air, the bullfinches built nests, and the baby squirrels began playing on the branches of the trees.

Everything came so fast now that Abbot Hans could not stop to reflect on how immeasurably great was the miracle that was taking place. He had time only to use his eyes and ears. The next light wave that came rushing in brought with it the scent of newly ploughed acres, and far off in the distance the milkmaids were heard coaxing the cows – and the tinkle of the sheep's bells. Pine and spruce trees were so thickly clothed with red cones that they shone like crimson mantles. The juniper berries changed colour every second, and forest flowers covered the ground till it was all red, blue and yellow.

Abbot Hans bent down to the earth and broke off a wild strawberry blossom, and, as he straightened up, the berry ripened in his hand.

The mother fox came out of her lair with a big litter of black-legged young. She went up to Robber Mother and scratched at her skirt, and Robber Mother bent down to her and praised her young. The horned owl, who had just begun his night chase, was astonished at the light and went back to his ravine to perch for the night. The male cuckoo crowed, and his mate stole up to the nests of the little birds with her egg in her mouth.

Robber Mother's youngsters let out perfect shrieks of delight. They stuffed themselves with wild strawberries that hung on the bushes, large as pine cones. One of them played with a litter of young hares; another ran a race with some young crows, which had hopped from their nest before they were really ready; a third caught up an adder from the ground and wound it around his neck and arm.

Robber Father was standing out on a marsh eating raspberries. When he glanced up, a big black bear stood beside him. Robber Father broke off an osier twig and struck the bear on the nose. 'Keep to your own ground, you!' he said; 'this is my turf.' Then the huge bear turned around and lumbered off in another direction.

New waves of warmth and light kept coming, and now they brought with them seeds from the star-flower. Golden pollen from rye fields fairly flew in the air. Then came butterflies, so big that they looked like flying lilies. The bee-hive in a hollow oak was already so full of honey that it dripped down on the trunk of the tree. Then all the flowers whose seeds had been brought from foreign lands began to blossom. The loveliest roses climbed up the mountain wall in a race with the blackberry vines, and from the forest meadow sprang flowers as large as human faces.

Abbot Hans thought of the flower he was to pluck for Bishop Absalon; but each new flower that appeared was more beautiful than the others, and he wanted to choose the most beautiful of all.

Wave upon wave kept coming until the air was so filled with light that it glittered. All the life and beauty and joy of summer smiled on Abbot Hans. He felt that earth could bring no greater happiness than that which welled up about him, and he said to himself, 'I do not know what new beauties the next wave that comes can bring with it.'

But the light kept streaming in, and now it seemed to Abbot Hans that it carried with it something from an infinite distance. He felt a celestial atmosphere enfolding him, and tremblingly he began to anticipate, now that earth's joys had come, the glories of heaven were approaching.

Then Abbot Hans marked how all grew still; the birds hushed their songs, the flowers ceased growing, and the young foxes played no more. The glory now nearing was such that the heart wanted to stop beating; the eyes wept without one's knowing it; the soul longed to soar away into the Eternal. From far in the distance faint harp tones were heard, and celestial song, like a soft murmur, reached him.

Abbot Hans clasped his hands and dropped to his knees. His face was radiant with bliss. Never had he dreamed that even in this life it should be granted him to taste the joys of heaven, and to hear angels sing Christmas carols!

But beside Abbot Hans stood the lay brother who had accompanied him. In his mind there were dark thoughts. 'This cannot be a true miracle,' he thought, 'since it is revealed to malefactors. This does not come from God, but has its origin in witchcraft and is sent hither by Satan. It is the Evil One's power that is tempting us and compelling us to see that which has no real existence.'

From afar were heard the sound of angel harps and the tones of a

56

Miserere. But the lay brother thought it was the evil spirits of hell coming closer. 'They would enchant and seduce us,' sighed he, 'and we shall be sold into perdition.'

The angel throng was so near now that Abbot Hans saw their bright forms through the forest branches. The lay brother saw them, too; but behind all this wondrous beauty he saw only some dread evil. For him it was the devil who performed these wonders on the anniversary of our Saviour's birth. It was done simply for the purpose of more effectually deluding poor human beings.

All the while the birds had been circling around the head of Abbot Hans, and they let him take them in his hands. But all the animals were afraid of the lay brother; no bird perched on his shoulder, no snake played at his feet. Then there came a little forest dove. When she marked that the angels were nearing, she plucked up courage and flew down on the lay brother's shoulder and laid her head against his cheek.

Then it appeared to him as if sorcery were come right upon him, to tempt and corrupt him. He struck with his hand at the forest dove and cried in such a loud voice that it rang throughout the forest, 'Go thou back to hell, whence thou art come!'

Just then the angels were so near that Abbot Hans felt the feathery touch of their great wings, and he bowed down to earth in reverent greeting.

But when the lay brother's words sounded, their song was hushed and the holy guests turned in flight. At the same time the light and the mild warmth vanished in unspeakable terror for the darkness and cold in a human heart. Darkness sank over the earth, like a coverlet; frost came, all the growths shrivelled up; the animals and birds hastened away; the rushing of streams was hushed; the leaves dropped from the trees, rustling like rain.

Abbot Hans felt how his heart, which had but lately swelled with bliss, was now contracting with insufferable agony. 'I can never outlive this,' thought he, 'that the angels from heaven had been so close to me and were driven away; that they wanted to sing Christmas carols for me and were driven to flight.'

Then he remembered the flower he had promised Bishop Absalon, and at the last moment he fumbled among the leaves and moss to try and find a blossom. But he sensed how the ground under his fingers froze and how the white snow came gliding over the ground. Then his heart caused him even greater anguish. He could not rise, but fell prostrate on the ground and lay there.

When the robber folk and the lay brother had groped their way back to the cave, they missed Abbot Hans. They took brands with them and went out to search for him. They found him dead upon the coverlet of snow.

Then the lay brother began weeping and lamenting, for he understood that it was he who had killed Abbot Hans because he had dashed from him the cup of happiness which he had been thirsting to drain to its last drop.

When Abbot Hans had been carried down to Övid, those who took charge of the dead saw that he held his right hand locked tight around something which he must have grasped the moment of death. When they finally got his hand open, they found that the thing which he had held in such an iron grip was a pair of white root bulbs, which he had torn from among the moss and leaves.

When the lay brother who had accompanied Abbot Hans saw the bulbs, he took them and planted them in Abbot Hans' herb garden.

He guarded them the whole year to see if any flower would spring from them. But in vain he waited through the spring, the summer and the autumn. Finally, when winter had set in and all the leaves and the flowers were dead, he ceased caring for them.

But when Christmas Eve came again, he was so strongly reminded of Abbot Hans that he wandered out into the garden to think of him. And look! as he came to the spot where he had planted the bare root bulbs, he saw that from them had sprung flourishing green stalks, which bore beautiful flowers with silver white leaves.

He called out all the monks at Övid, and when they saw that this plant bloomed on Christmas Eve, when all the other growths were as if dead, they understood that this flower had in truth been plucked by Abbot Hans from the Christmas garden in Göinge forest. Then the lay brother asked the monks if he might take a few blossoms to Bishop Absalon.

And when he appeared before Bishop Absalon, he gave him the flowers and said: 'Abbot Hans sends you these. They are the flowers he promised to pick for you from the garden in Göinge forest.'

When Bishop Absalon beheld the flowers, which had sprung from the earth in darkest winter, and heard the words, he turned as pale as if he had met a ghost. He sat in silence a moment; thereupon he said, 'Abbot Hans has faithfully kept his word and I shall also keep mine.' And he ordered that a letter of ransom be drawn up for the wild robber who was outlawed and had been forced to live in the forest ever since his youth.

He handed the letter to the lay brother, who departed at once for the Robbers' Cave. When he stepped in there on Christmas Day, the robber came toward him with axe uplifted. 'I'd like to hack you monks into bits, as many as you are!' said he. 'It must be your fault that Göinge forest did not last night dress itself in Christmas bloom.'

'The fault is mine alone,' said the lay brother, 'and I will gladly die for it; but first I must deliver a message from Abbot Hans.' And he drew forth the Bishop's letter and told the man that he was free. 'Hereafter you and your children shall play in the Christmas straw and celebrate your Christmas among people, just as Abbot Hans wished to have it,' said he.

Then Robber Father stood there pale and speechless, but Robber Mother said in his name, 'Abbot Hans has indeed kept his word, and Robber Father will keep his.'

When the robber and his wife left the cave, the lay brother moved in and lived all alone in the forest, in constant meditation and prayer that his hard-heartedness might be forgiven him.

But Göinge forest never again celebrated the hour of our Saviour's birth; and of all its glory, there lives today only the plant which Abbot Hans had plucked. It has been named CHRISTMAS ROSE. And each year at Christmastide she sends forth from the earth her green stalks and white blossoms, as if she never could forget that she had once grown in the great Christmas garden at Göinge forest.

O. HENRY

A Chaparral Christmas Gift

The original cause of the trouble was about twenty years in growing. At the end of that time it was worth it.

Had you lived anywhere within fifty miles of Sundown Ranch you would have heard of it. It possessed a quantity of jet-black hair, a pair of extremely frank, deep-brown eyes and a laugh that rippled across the prairie like the sound of a hidden brook. The name of it was Rosita McMullen; and she was the daughter of old man McMullen of the Sundown Sheep Ranch.

There came riding on red roan steeds – or, to be more explicit, on a paint and a flea-bitten sorrel – two wooers. One was Madison Lane, and the other was the Frio Kid. But at that time they did not call him the Frio Kid, for he had not earned the honours of special nomenclature. His name was simply Johnny McRoy.

It must not be supposed that these two were the sum of the agreeable Rosita's admirers. The broncos of a dozen others champed their bits at the long hitching rack of the Sundown Ranch. Many were the sheeps'-eyes that were cast in those savannas that did not belong to the flocks of Dan McMullen. But of all the cavaliers, Madison Lane and Johnny McRoy galloped far ahead, wherefore they are to be chronicled.

Madison Lane, a young cattleman from the Nueces country, won the race. He and Rosita were married one Christmas Day. Armed, hilarious, vociferous, magnanimous, the cowmen and the sheepmen, laying aside their hereditary hatred, joined forces to celebrate the occasion.

Sundown Ranch was sonorous with the cracking of jokes and sixshooters, the shine of buckles and bright eyes, the outspoken congratulations of the herders of kine.

But while the wedding feast was at its liveliest there descended upon it Johnny McRoy, bitten by jealousy, like one possessed.

'I'll give you a Christmas present,' he yelled, shrilly, at the door, with his .45 in his hand. Even then he had some reputation as an offhand shot.

His first bullet cut a neat underbit in Madison Lane's right ear. The barrel of his gun moved an inch. The next shot would have been the bride's had not Carson, a sheepman, possessed a mind with triggers somewhat well oiled and in repair. The guns of the wedding party had been hung, in their belts, upon nails in the wall when they sat at table, as a concession to good taste. But Carson, with great promptness, hurled his plate of roast venison and frijoles at McRoy, spoiling his aim. The second bullet, then, only shattered the white petals of a Spanish dagger flower suspended two feet above Rosita's head.

The guests spurned their chairs and jumped for their weapons. It was considered an improper act to shoot the bride and groom at a wedding. In about six seconds there were twenty or so bullets due to be whizzing in the direction of Mr McRoy.

'I'll shoot better next time,' yelled Johnny; 'and there'll be a next time.' He backed rapidly out the door.

Carson, the sheepman, spurred on to attempt further exploits by the success of his plate-throwing, was first to reach the door. McRoy's bullet from the darkness laid him low.

The cattlemen then swept out upon him, calling for vengeance, for, while the slaughter of a sheepman has not always lacked condonement, it was a decided misdemeanour in this instance. Carson was innocent; he was no accomplice at the matrimonial proceedings; nor had any one heard him quote the line 'Christmas comes but once a year' to the guests.

But the sortie failed in its vengeance. McRoy was on his horse and away, shouting back curses and threats as he galloped into the concealing chaparral.

That night was the birthnight of the Frio Kid. He became the 'bad man' of that portion of the State. The rejection of his suit by Miss McMullen turned him to a dangerous man. When officers went after him for the shooting of Carson, he killed two of them, and entered upon the life of an outlaw. He became a marvellous shot with either hand. He would turn up in towns and settlements, raise a quarrel at the slightest opportunity, pick off his man and laugh at the officers of the law. He was so cool, so deadly, so rapid, so inhumanly blood-thirsty that none but faint attempts were ever made to capture him. When he was at last shot and killed by a little one-armed Mexican who was nearly dead himself from fright, the Frio Kid had the deaths of eighteen men on his head. About half of these were killed in fair duds depending upon the quickness of the draw. The other half were men whom he assassinated from absolute wantonness and cruelty.

Many tales are told along the border of his impudent courage and daring. But he was not one of the breed of desperadoes who have seasons of generosity and even of softness. They say he never had mercy on the object of his anger. Yet at this and every Christmastide it is well to give each one credit, if it can be done, for whatever speck of good he may have possessed. If the Frio Kid ever did a kindly act or felt a throb of generosity in his heart it was once at such a time and season, and this is the way it happened.

One who has been crossed in love should never breathe the odour from the blossoms of the ratama tree. It stirs the memory to a dangerous degree.

One December in the Frio country there was a ratama tree in full bloom, for the winter had been as warm as springtime. That way rode the Frio Kid and his satellite and co-murderer, Mexican Frank. The Kid reined in his mustang, and sat in his saddle, thoughtful and grim, with dangerously narrowing eyes. The rich, sweet scent touched him somewhere beneath his ice and iron.

'I don't know what I've been thinking about, Mex,' he remarked in his usual mild drawl, 'to have forgot all about a Christmas present I got to give. I'm going to ride over tomorrow night and shoot Madison Lane in his own house. He got my girl – Rosita would have had me if he hadn't cut into the game. I wonder why I happened to overlook it up to now?'

'Ah, shucks, Kid,' said Mexican, 'don't talk foolishness. You know you can't get within a mile of Mad Lane's house tomorrow night. I see old man Allen day before yesterday, and he says Mad is going to have Christmas doings at his house. You remember how you shot up the festivities when Mad was married, and about the threats you made? Don't you suppose Mad Lane'll kind of keep his eye open for a certain Mr Kid? You plumb make me tired, Kid, with such remarks.'

'I'm going,' repeated the Frio Kid, without heat, 'to go to Madison

Lane's Christmas doings, and kill him. I ought to have done it a long time ago. Why, Mex, just two weeks ago I dreamed me and Rosita was married instead of her and him: and we was living in a house, and I could see her smiling at me, and – oh! h—l, Mex, he got her: and I'll get him – yes, sir, on Christmas Eve he got her, and then's when I'll get him.'

'There's other ways of committing suicide,' advised the Mexican. 'Why don't you go and surrender to the sheriff?'

'I'll get him,' said the Kid.

Christmas Eve fell as balmy as April. Perhaps there was a hint of far-away frostiness in the air, but it tingled like seltzer, perfumed faintly with late prairie blossoms and the mesquite grass.

When night came the five or six rooms of the ranch-house were brightly lit. In one room was a Christmas tree, for the Lanes had a boy of three, and a dozen or more guests were expected from the nearer ranches.

At nightfall Madison Lane called aside Jim Belcher and three other cowboys employed on his ranch.

'Now, boys,' said Lane, 'keep your eyes open. Walk around the house and watch the road well. All of you know the "Frio Kid", as they call him now, and if you see him, open fire on him without asking any questions. I'm not afraid of his coming around, but Rosita is. She's been afraid he'd come in on us every Christmas since we were married.'

The guests had arrived in buckboards and on horseback, and were making themselves comfortable inside.

The evening went along pleasantly. The guests enjoyed and praised Rosita's excellent supper, and afterward the men scattered in groups about the rooms or on the broad 'gallery', smoking and chatting.

The Christmas tree, of course, delighted the youngsters, and above all were they pleased when Santa Claus himself in magnificent white beard and furs appeared and began to distribute the toys.

'It's my papa,' announced Billy Sampson, aged six. 'I've seen him wear 'em before.'

Berkly, a sheepman, an old friend of Lane, stopped Rosita as she was passing by him on the gallery, where he was sitting smoking.

'Well, Mrs Lane,' said he, 'I suppose by this Christmas you've gotten over being afraid of that fellow McRoy, haven't you? Madison and I have talked about it, you know.'

'Very nearly,' said Rosita, smiling, 'but I am still nervous sometimes. I shall never forget that awful time when he came so near to killing us.'

'He's the most cold-hearted villain in the world,' said Berkly. 'The citizens all along the border ought to turn out and hunt him down like a wolf.'

'He has committed awful crimes,' said Rosita, 'but – I – don't – know. I think there is a spot of good somewhere in everybody. He was not always bad – that I know.'

Rosita turned into the hallway between the rooms. Santa Claus, in muffling whiskers and furs, was just coming through.

'I heard what you said through the window, Mrs Lane,' he said. 'I was just going down in my pocket for a Christmas present for your husband. But I've left one for you, instead. It's in the room to your right.'

'Oh, thank you, kind Santa Claus,' said Rosita, brightly.

Rosita went into the room, while Santa Claus stepped into the cooler air of the yard.

She found no one in the room but Madison.

'Where is my present that Santa said he left for me in here?' she asked.

'Haven't seen anything in the way of a present,' said her husband, laughing, 'unless he could have meant me.'

The next day Gabriel Radd, the foreman of the XO Ranch, dropped into the post-office at Loma Alta.

'Well, the Frio Kid's got his dose of lead at last,' he remarked to the postmaster.

'That so? How'd it happen?'

'One of old Sanchez's Mexican sheep herders did it! – think of it! the Frio Kid killed by a sheep herder! The Greaser saw him riding along past his camp about twelve o'clock last night, and was so skeered that he up with a Winchester and let him have it. Funniest part of it was that the Kid was dressed all up with white Angora-skin whiskers and a regular Santy Claus rig-out from head to foot. Think of the Frio Kid playing Santy!'

IRÈNE NÉMIROVSKY

Noël

Translated by Sandra Smith

As the title of the film and list of actors scroll down the screen, we first see appear, initially as a background, then as detailed photographs, all the most conventional and unsophisticated images that accompany the idea of the Christmas holidays.

First, heavy, blinding snow that falls slowly from above. Then it turns to rain, forming a light wintery mist over the streets of Paris.

Garlands of holly and mistletoe turn to dead leaves and are carried away by the flowing water.

A large log disintegrating into sparks cuts to the image of radiators.

A panorama of snow, an idyllic scene, turns into a small street in Montmartre, and the songs of children gradually become nasal, unpleasant.

Everywhere, shop signs are shining brightly. Christmas Eve. Dinner parties, etc. The songs become clearer; we recognize words like:

> *Childhood*
> *Innocence . . .*
> *Dawn of the world . . .*
> *Dawn of love*
> *The most wonderful days . . .*

Accompanied by the shrill music of an organ grinder.

The music stops, the vague images disappear and the movie begins.

In a large, dark drawing room, two men are carrying a Christmas tree, still undecorated; its branches drag along the floor. They wipe the sweat from their brows. A valet enters holding a coin.

'Here's your tip.'

The men frown: 'That's it? Well, really now . . .'

The servant shrugs his shoulders. 'Our boss is a real cheapskate . . .'

The men leave, grumbling. On the white walls in front of the door to the pantry, a hand is writing: *The stairs are high, and the tips are low . . .* while a man whistles contemptuously as he goes down the steps. The servant looks at the tree, indifferently gives it a kick to prop it up and leaves the room.

In the hall, two well-dressed children, followed by a nanny, run out of their room.

'Is that the Christmas tree? Is it pretty?' they ask, excited.

'Very pretty, Mademoiselle Christiane, the Christ Child has just brought it,' says the valet, forcing, with difficulty, his sour face into an affectionate grimace.

'Christiane, Jeannot, come along,' the nanny says, sharply. 'What are you doing?'

We catch a glimpse of the large, bare tree in the dark drawing room. Outside the window, the winter rain is falling, mixed with snow, lit up by a streetlight. Then rumbling from the street. Images of Paris on Christmas Eve. Stacks of pine trees tied together on the quayside. Brightly lit signs on the department stores, the shopfronts of *Potin, Potel* and *Chabot* weighed down with turkeys and oysters. Pyramids of bottles of champagne, *Chez Nicolas*. The rush of cars and buses; shops selling candy, florists, feverish salesgirls rushing about.

'Two kilos of candied chestnuts . . . a basket of orchids,' etc.

The hustle and bustle of conversations, a record spinning around. Then the street. Dazed little children dragged along by their exhausted parents, some affectionate and happy, others irritable, weary. A serious-looking father with a goatee, holding a skinny little rascal by the ear says with indignation:

'I buy him a car that costs nearly twenty francs. And now little Sir wants a garage to put it in . . . Greed and ingratitude are two terrible vices, my boy . . . And at your age . . .' His voice trails off amid the noise of the crowd.

Other children leap with curiosity around the wrapped packages their parents have under their arms. We hear their joyful chirping:

'Mama, what is Santa Claus going to bring me? Tell me!'

'Santa Claus isn't real, you know,' one little girl says to another, 'it's like the stork; it's really Papa . . .'

Lovers hold each other tight and kiss as they walk by.

Then we see, always very quickly, very rapidly, department store shelves full of toys, Christmas trees, decorated, sparkling, swaying, going round and round. The noise finally dies down. The salespeople hurry, pulling down the iron shutters over the storefronts. The rumbling of Paris grows fainter, distant, ends in silence. In a children's bedroom in front of a small low table, Christiane and Jeannot are colouring Christmas trees. They are humming: 'Three angels came tonight to bring me such wonderful things . . . ,' a tune that has gradually been adapted from Chevalier's words, spoken through a record player in the next room. There, Marie-Laure and Claudine, their two older sisters, aged twenty-two and twenty, are getting dressed to go to a ball. Their dresses and fine lingerie are laid out on the bed, amid the chaos of a young woman's bedroom. Marie-Laure is putting on makeup in front of the mirror. Claudine, still wearing her peignoir, is standing at the window, watching the rain, thinking.

'Claudine!' calls Marie-Laure, 'Claudine! Hey! I'm talking to you! Why are you making that face?'

Claudine shudders. 'What?'

'You've had your head in the clouds for some time now . . . Trouble with your love life? Your Ramon? . . . Really, don't make such a fuss . . . Men – they come, they go . . . No importance whatsoever . . . Are you ever going to get dressed? It's nearly nine o'clock . . .'

We see the children again, half asleep in their chairs. The young women slip on their dress shoes, help each other put on their pearls.

The nanny knocks at a door; we hear shrill voices. Monsieur and Madame are getting dressed, and arguing. He is bald, short and ugly. He is in a bad mood and grumbles:

'You slave away just to make ungrateful people rich . . . that's my fate . . . What a stupid custom to go out to celebrate Christmas Eve, poisoning yourself and eating disgusting things at a restaurant instead of staying peacefully at home!'

Madame: she is wearing makeup, worried about her clothes, old and fat.

'If you'd listened to me, we would have gone to the Midi!'

Monsieur breaks a nail putting on one of his cuff-links and impatiently stamps his foot on the floor.

Madame: 'Oh, no, please, go and let off steam somewhere else . . . It's not my fault that it's Christmas, really!'

Monsieur: 'It's the same with this Christmas tree, and the children's tea party . . . It's going to cost a fortune . . . The children don't need all that to enjoy themselves . . . We're giving them a taste for unbridled luxury!'

Madame (bitterly): 'It's not because I enjoy it, you know, but we have to return invitations to people who have invited us, it's only polite . . . And besides, if you'd rather people know you're about to go bankrupt!'

Monsieur (horrified): 'Shh, shh . . .'

They finally hear the nanny discreetly knocking at the door.

'Who's there? Come in . . .'

The nanny: 'It's nine o'clock. The children are falling asleep.'

'Well, then put them to bed.'

'But . . . they want to hang their stockings in front of the fireplace . . . They've been waiting since seven o'clock.'

Madame: 'Oh, my God, yes. I'd forgotten, bring them in.'

Christiane and Jeannot enter, in their pyjamas, holding their stockings.

The children kiss their parents, put their stockings over the fireplace and kneel down.

'Dear Jesus, please bring me a real donkey, a train set with tracks and a little brother 'cause there's too many girls in this house.'

Meanwhile, his father, who is having a bit of trouble putting on his boots because of his fat stomach, interrupts him:

'All right, all right, that's enough, dear Jesus is not very rich this year, my boy.'

Madame, who had been moved at first, has lost interest. 'Yes, tighter,' she says to her maid who is lacing up her corset, 'tighter, it's fine.'

'But Madame, there's no way.'

'Yes, there is.'

Then, annoyed, looking at herself in the mirror: 'My God, this dress makes me look so fat.'

The frame fades. Far-off music plays: 'Three angels came tonight . . .'

A fireplace full of toys – miniature trumpets and toy dolls – appears in the darkness; they transform into real trumpets and live dolls in a nightclub.

Dancing, jazz, drunkards, dust, etc.

Meanwhile, Marie-Laure and Claudine and their parents are in the car, their father and mother in the back, the two young women wearing bright dresses, ball gowns decorated with ermine, sit in the front. Monsieur and Madame continue to argue.

Monsieur: 'What a way to behave . . . Young women these days don't even deign to invite their parents to the parties they give! . . . Very nice, very appropriate, you have to admit.'

Marie-Laure (annoyed): 'But, Papa, I told you that Nadine's mother and aunt will be there; I should think that's enough!'

Monsieur (without listening to her): 'Really, this habit of letting young women come home by themselves, at God knows at what time, accompanied by such scoundrels!'

Madame: 'Well, then you can go and pick them up yourself!'

Marie-Laure: 'Actually, Édouard Saulnier, from the Saulnier Sugar Factory family is going to bring us home.'

Father (attentive): 'Oh?'

Marie-Laure (mockingly): 'Well, well – that seems to reassure you.'

Father: 'He's obviously a suitable young man.'

Marie-Laure: 'And rich!'

Father: 'You know what I think about that, my dears . . . For a marriage to be truly happy, like your parents' marriage for example, you must be united, understand each other, get along well, be in love, in short . . . like the perfect union we have been giving you as an example since you were children. Now, considering that business is going from bad to worse, if you both were to marry well . . .'

Madame: 'My God, you really can't wait to get rid of them . . . they're still children . . .'

Father (baulking): 'Are you afraid of becoming a grandmother, eh, is that it?'

The car stops.

Madame, forcing herself to sound strict as the chauffeur opens the car door: 'I forbid you to come home later than two o'clock. Do you hear me, girls?'

'Yes, Mama.'

In the entrance hall, Marie-Laure pokes her sister: 'Listen, pull yourself together, you look upset.'

Claudine (anxious): 'Really?'

Marie-Laure: 'But what . . . what's wrong?'

Claudine (annoyed): 'Nothing, my God, nothing . . . I was tired but I'm all right now, I'm all right . . .'

Her final words are lost in the general commotion. Laughter, music. A debutante ball. Only very young men and women, everyone very merry. In a little room off to one side, two serene old women – they look like sheep in profile – the lady of the house and her sister, are knitting. Music in the distance. One of the old lady sighs:

'Ah, how happy the young are . . . It's a pleasure to listen to them! Do you remember, Louise?' (She sighs.)

Claudine goes into the ballroom, anxiously looking for someone among the dancers; she replies to the young people who say hello as they pass by with a smile, a nod. At the same time, a hand slips around her waist. 'Shall we dance?' the voice says. She turns quickly around, recognizes Ramon, a handsome, elegant young man.

They dance.

We see the old women again. A laugh that is a little too forced and shrill jazz music have made them start. One of them whispers, worried: 'Perhaps . . . we should go and see . . .'

'The youngsters don't like it when we are obviously watching them, and besides, what can we do? It's us, the adults, with our suspicions who put evil thoughts in their minds.'

The other lady (hesitant): All the same, my dear, we're meant to be chaperoning them.'

We see the ballroom where about twenty couples are holding each other tightly and dancing a sensual tango in the semidarkness.

Nadine, the young lady of the house, wearing very modern clothes, notices her mother and her aunt coming over to them, and tells everyone in a playful whisper: 'Yikes! The cops are here!'

Everyone immediately starts behaving impeccably. The lights are switched on. The jazz band plays a lovely waltz.

The two old women are touched: 'They're so charming.'

The camera pans and reveals little dark corners here and there around the brightly lit ballroom. In one of them, a couple is kissing, in another, all we see is the bottom of a young woman's dress. She is sitting down and her fashionable full skirt is pulled up to her knee, revealing her beautiful legs. As the two old women get closer, the dress is slowly lowered, and we hear a very serene voice, very 'virginal', reply: 'Oh, yes, Madame, thank you so much; we're having such a lovely time . . .'

On the banister of the staircase, two young men are standing very close to a young woman. The old woman comes closer, raises her lorgnette and sweetly asks: 'What game is this you're playing, children? My eyes are so bad, I can't tell.'

'Just an innocent little game, Madame.'

'Oh, really? I didn't know you still played those kinds of games, like I did when I was young . . . Keep going, my dears.'

Meanwhile, Claudine and Ramon are dancing.

'You look especially lovely tonight, Claudine.'

'Oh, Ramon, I've been trying to see you for a week.'

'Oh, I've had a lot on my mind . . . problems,' he says, with a barely noticeable hint of coldness in his voice.

'I needed to speak to you about something important.'

'Oh?' he replies, with a slight gesture of suspicion.

When the two old women appear, they look at Claudine affectionately.

'Look at that little Claudine . . . she's just charming . . . What I especially like about her is how virtuous she looks . . . she looks so "virginal", don't you think? I was like that when I was young.'

'She and Ramon make a handsome couple. Is she going to marry him?'

'Oh, I don't think so. Nadine told me he already has a fiancée back home, in Buenos Aires. She found out by chance.'

Meanwhile, two young people disappear into a little adjoining room. You can hear music in the distance.

Claudine (secretly): 'I'm going to have a baby, Ramon.'

She is standing, looking very fragile and childlike in her white dress. Ramon makes an irritated gesture and says, faltering: 'Good heavens . . . that's a nuisance.'

Claudine, with a hint of a smile: 'Yes . . . rather.'

In the ballroom, they are giving out streamers and confetti. The dancers form a long chain that stretches from one end of the room to the other and under a door decorated with mistletoe. We see a front view of couples kissing: the good girls who laugh and offer their cheeks, the little sly ones who make sure that the kiss on the cheek ends up near their lips, and, finally, the spinster, going to seed, dressed like a child, who offers her mouth to her doleful cavalier and who, peeved, gets a peck on the forehead. Then Marie-Laure appears with a young man, Édouard Saulnier; he is short, ugly, with a kind, timid appearance. He wants to kiss her.

She pushes him away: 'Oh, no, dear boy!'

Him, annoyed: 'So everyone except me?'

'*You* will have to marry me first . . .'

'Charming . . . And why?'

She sighs. He looks at her with some admiration.

'You have many faults, Marie-Laure, but no one could really accuse you of hiding your feelings.'

She shrugs her shoulders: 'You want to kiss me. *I* don't want you to. It's give-and-take. I'll say it again: marry me. Until then, no kissing.'

Édouard, hissing: 'Little bitch . . .'

'What did you say?'

'Nothing.'

Under the mistletoe, she offers her hand for him to kiss, and little by little, manages to let her arm drift under the young man's nose several times. She laughs, sounding provocative and cunning:

'Still, I think you would prefer Claudine, wouldn't you? Too bad she only has eyes for Ramon, eh? But I'm a nice girl; I know very well that I'm just a consolation prize to you, but I'm not angry about it.'

Claudine and Ramon again. He is holding her hand.

'Listen, my little one . . . we must be reasonable . . . What can you do? It's life . . . that is keeping us apart . . . You know very well that if I could marry you, I would, and with joy . . . with the greatest happiness . . . But my father is uncompromising. I'm leaving . . . (She makes a sudden movement.) I'm leaving tomorrow morning, my poor darling, I'm going back home and getting married there . . . I'm so sorry, I swear, so very sorry . . . Oh, we shouldn't have let ourselves get carried away.'

She makes a weary gesture: 'Oh . . .'

'It's true . . . it's true, I blame myself more than you think . . .'

She pulls her hand from his.

'Claudine . . .'

'Leave me alone . . .'

She goes back inside the ballroom. He throws away his cigarette and says with sincere pity: 'Poor girl . . . Good Lord, this is annoying . . . What a problem . . . (He thinks for a moment.) If it's true, of course . . .'

Back to the ball. Then to two young women in a corner. One of them tries to stop her stocking from running with a damp finger. 'Damn! A pair of stockings ruined! . . . And Georges still hasn't asked me to marry him . . . What a business it is to be a young woman!'

Ramon, surrounded by a group of young people: 'Well, my dear friends, I have to say my farewells tonight . . . Yes, I'm leaving tomorrow morning . . .'

'Really?' says a stocky young lad with a grin on his face, 'I thought you weren't leaving until next week.'

Ramon elbows him in the ribs so he stops talking.

We hear: 'Well, good-bye, good-bye, then.'

Now the young women have all come closer and are watching – their eyes bright with curiosity and maliciousness – as Claudine and Ramon are going to say good-bye to each other. Meanwhile, other couples are dancing.

Ramon, embarrassed: 'Good-bye, Claudine . . .'

Claudine looks at him. He lowers his eyes. The young women snigger. She offers him her hand, making a great effort to remain calm.

'Good-bye Ramon . . . Bon voyage.'

The couples start dancing again, turning round and round. Claudine stands apart, alone. Édouard Saulnier appears behind her.

'What's the matter? You were so cheerful before . . . What's wrong?'

'Nothing, Édouard, it's nothing. Thank you,' she whispers, holding back her tears.

Then pan to the cabaret where her parents have been celebrating. At first, we hear the church bells calling the religious to Midnight Mass, but they are drowned out by the sound of jazz. There are so many people in the nightclub that all we can see are a mass of couples crushed in under a cloud of confetti and streamers that are flying around. We see the points of two paper hats. The hats are taken off, revealing the pitiful face of Claudine's father and another older gentleman.

'Oh, it's horrible, horrible; who would have thought that the Chantace stocks would drop by twenty-five percent in two months?'

'*I would*, but you didn't listen to me,' says the other man, bitterly.

'But you have some of their stock too!'

'Of course, and that's *your* fault, I was taken in by your blind confidence.'

'We tell ourselves that they can't go any lower . . . which is a mistake . . . We have to get it in our heads that stocks can always go down.'

Streamers landing on his nose make him fall silent. The black musicians twist and turn like contortionists. Meanwhile, Claudine's mother is dancing with an Argentinian, shorter than her, whom she holds tightly, lovingly, in her arms.

'Do you love me?'

Him: A cascade of incomprehensible Castillian *r*'s.

Her (nearly fainting): 'Oh, when you look at me like that, I tremble all over.'

The faithful come out of Midnight Mass. The partygoers leave the restaurant. A drunken man holds his toy dolls close to his heart. When people bump into him, he complains.

'Oh, my little dolls, let me keep my little dolls, you mean people.'

A very small bellboy, as tiny as can be, leads him to his car with maternal care.

'Yes, Monsieur, no one will touch your little dolls, this way, Monsieur . . .'

Once again we see the ballroom where Marie-Laure and her friends are dancing. The young Nadine is cajoling her mother: 'Mama, go up to bed, this is ridiculous, you'll feel awful tomorrow.'

'Well, Nadine, will you all be good?'

Nadine opens her eyes in wide innocence: 'What do you mean, Mama?'

'I mean . . . you won't make too much noise?'

'Oh, no, Mama, I promise.'

Semidarkness. Songs playing quietly on the record player. Divans, plush armchairs, flirting, kissing.

Nadine: 'Mama made a point of telling us not to make too much noise.'

Laughter.

A young man quietly sings a blues song.

Claudine to Édouard: 'You're a kind friend . . . but it's my fault. I've been stupid. I should have behaved like everyone else here, flirt, rather than fall in love. I didn't know and I only got what I deserve.'

'But . . . Claudine . . .'

Claudine (sharply): 'Oh, don't go imagining anything out of the ordinary happened. No, I admit that I . . . I was very fond of Ramon, and that it hurts that he's leaving . . . so . . .'

Nadine, wearing a top hat, dances, twisting and turning.

Claudine (angrily):

'If I have a daughter, I can tell you she won't be raised like her, or like me!'

Édouard, smiling: 'Well, you have plenty of time to think about that.'

Marie-Laure calls out: Édouard, where on earth are you?' Then quietly, angrily, to Claudine: 'Listen, what you're doing is disgusting! We promised each other: I wouldn't go near your Ramon and you wouldn't go near Édouard! Besides, I'm the eldest . . .'

Claudine (quietly): 'Leave me alone, Marie-Laure.'

'You, dear sister, have done something stupid.'

Nighttime. We see the brightly lit sign a department store: Santa Claus is going down a chimney with lots of presents. We can see the windows lit up, the shadows of people dancing. Jeannot and Christiane's room, them in bed. They wake up with a start when the heavy courtyard door noisily opens.

Jeannot: 'Perhaps it's Santa Claus . . .'

Christiane: 'You're so stupid, he comes down the chimney, that's the grown-ups coming home.'

Downstairs, Marie-Laure and Claudine come into the entrance hall, on tiptoe.

Marie-Laure: 'Damn! It's after five o'clock. We're going to get told off . . .'

75

Claudine: 'We have to be quiet.'

Marie-Laure knocks over a piece of furniture, making a terrible noise. They switch on the lights.

'Well, well, our parents aren't home yet,' says Marie-Laure, 'we shouldn't have been so worried.'

We see the servants who are celebrating on the sixth floor.

Then, in the car, their parents, who disappear under a mass of streamers and confetti.

Marie-Laure and Claudine get undressed.

'You know, I think this is it, this time. I told Édouard to come over tomorrow. He asked if Papa would be home.'

Claudine: 'Do you love him?'

Marie-Laure (shrugging her shoulders): 'He's rolling in it . . .'

Claudine (pensively): 'He seems like a good man. You're lucky.'

She starts brushing her hair. Marie-Laure is humming; her sister says, sharply: 'Oh, do be quiet!'

'Mademoiselle is nervous. Oh, of course, that was your Ramon's favourite tango.'

'Yes, it was.'

'Goodness, you really are old-fashioned! We flirt, we part, that's life . . . True love only comes when you're married, and I don't mean with your husband, naturally.'

Claudine drops down onto the bed, sobbing: 'Oh, Marie-Laure, if only you knew! There's nothing more I can do, except kill myself, do you understand?'

Marie-Laure (suddenly very harshly): 'What do you mean?'

'I'm going to have Ramon's baby . . . Ramon . . . who knows and who is going away . . . (a gesture of despair) I loved him, I thought he would marry me, of course, yes, I thought I knew everything, that I was very smart, but I was actually just as stupid as everyone else.'

Marie-Laure (furious): 'What are you going to do?'

'Do you think I know?'

The image fades. We see the parents coming home, in a bad mood.

'What disgusting champagne . . . and who was that little Argentinian who kept dancing with you?'

'A charming young man.'

We see Marie-Laure who is finishing saying something to Claudine; all we can hear is: 'Now listen to me, I'm giving you good advice!' and Claudine who says over and over again: 'No, no, I don't want to . . .'

Fade to the children's bedroom. The first dawn of winter. Christiane, leaning on one elbow, watching, enraptured, the snow that has fallen onto the windowsill during the night. A bird is pecking at something. A perfect Christmas card image. A taxi full of drunkards passes by on the street. In front of the doors to the nightclubs, people are sweeping up piles of streamers, confetti and crushed toy dolls.

Then the first church bells rings. We see families going to Mass. Well-dressed children, wearing white gloves, holding their little prayer books. A light snow is falling. Through the windows of several different houses, we see children in their parents' rooms, on large beds, with new toys. We hear the children shouting and laughing.

Christiane and Jeannot solemnly walk into their parents' bedroom. We see the fireplace full of toys, hear the little ones saying 'oh' in amazement, then, the bed, where their parents – puffed up, snoring, wrinkled – their balding father, and their mother wearing a chin strap, are sleeping. Jeannot is busy playing with his toys, but Christiane looks at her parents, lowers her head and seems upset and unhappy. A sleepy, moaning voice comes from under the covers: 'Take them out, dear Nannie, can't you see I have a headache?'

The servants set the table for the guests who have been invited to the Christmas party. We see the tall tree decorated with toys.

In her bedroom, their mother, who has recovered somewhat, is now talking to Marie-Laure and Claudine. She gives each of them a little pendant. Claudine, very upset, murmurs as she kisses her: 'Mama . . .'

'Yes?'

'I need to talk to you.'

The mother (annoyed): 'Well, talk fast . . .'

'It's just that . . . it's too difficult . . . this way . . . Mama . . .'

'Well then, we'll do it another time, my child. You can see I'm in a hurry.'

Marie-Laure sniggers as she leaves the room, prodding her sister with her elbow.

'You see? You're still fooling yourself, come on . . . Can you picture

Mama raising your kid, and Papa telling you: "Miserable girl; you've disgraced me, but I forgive you!" Well, can you? All *I'm* asking you, and I think I do have a say in all this, is that there be no scandal!'

'What has it got to do with you?'

'Well, that's a good one. What about my marriage?'

The scene fades. Paris, Christmas morning. The shops are closed. In the street, the last pine trees have been taken away; people are sweeping up the needles left on the sidewalk. Trash in Les Halles food market. Then we see how Claudine's parents spend this family holiday. Her father is with his mistress. An insignificant little actress who greets him rather coldly. He says (sounding pitiful): 'I brought you your little Christmas present, my sweetie . . .'

He gives her a pendant exactly like the one given to his daughters. She grumbles: 'Yeah, I see you didn't knock yourself out.'

She's stretched out on the bed in her pyjamas. She hangs the pendant from her toe, swings it there for a moment, then kicks it onto the rug. He goes over to her, whispers: 'My Louloute . . .'

She sighs and lets him kiss her.

A barrel organ grinds away in the courtyard:

> *Childhood, innocence*
> *Dawn of life . . .*

Then Christane and Jeannot appear on a path in the Bois de Boulogne. The voice of the invisible nanny nags them, scolding: 'Christiane, stand up straight . . . Jeannot, don't get your gloves dirty, stop jumping,' etc.

The songs continues:

> *Love is for the young*
> *In the springtime, the birds all agree . . .*

Fade to the bachelor pad of the little Argentinian. In the bathroom, Madame is pulling in her bosom with a tight, invisible band made of pink rubber.

Then the voice of the little Argentinian: 'I have so many difficulties . . . My father who owns an enormous farm wrote to me saying that this year, he can't send me my allowance because the bulls won't mate with the cows . . .'

(Superimposed: bulls turn away in disgust when the cows, mooing sadly, pass by.)

The music plays again. Madame sighs: 'Oh, it's so romantic.'

Finally, in a poor neighbourhood, one of those terrible areas where every window has a sign that says DENTIST'S OFFICE in gold letters, we see Claudine walking quickly; she looks weary and desperate. The morning snow has turned into water and mud. A woman offers her a branch of mistletoe.

'It brings happiness, Mademoiselle!'

After Claudine has given her some money and walked away, the woman watches her go and sighs: 'Some people are lucky,' then begins shouting in the gathering fog: 'Mistletoe for happiness! Come and get it! Plenty for everyone!'

Her voice merges with the animated sound of the children gathered around the Christmas tree as it is being lit up. They are playing, singing, dancing. We hear only their voices, their laughter as the doors open very slowly, a fairy tale, mysterious atmosphere, to reveal the magnificent pine tree with hundreds of little lit candles.

In the little adjoining room sit Édouard and Marie-Laure.

Édouard: 'Where is Claudine?'

'She went out.'

'She seemed so sad yesterday.'

'She's been depressed since her Ramon left. It serves her right; she shouldn't have thrown herself at him.'

Claudine is wandering in the street, anxiously looking for an address. Finally, she goes through a door, whispers a name to the concierge who replies with a snigger and a shrug of her shoulders.

'Fifth floor, door on the left.'

Claudine climbs the stairs; we see the look of despair on her face. The staircase is horrible, narrow, dark, with a very small gaslight on the landing, lighting up a shiny sign: MIDWIFE.

Claudine has stopped on the landing. We see only her shadow. At that moment, a young woman comes down holding a baby in her arms. He's a tiny little thing, ugly; he's asleep. As the mother passes by Claudine, she covers, with infinite care, the infant's face with a little gauze veil. Claudine looks at the child, then at the mother, who is an ordinary working-class woman dressed all in black; she then looks at the door. We see her shadow slowly go back down the stairs, and below, on the bright street, she joins a crowd of people rushing about; they all disappear.

Meanwhile, the table is being set for the party.

One of the maids (disgusted): 'Those kids are making such a racket! I have a headache, what a celebration we had last night, didn't we!'

Angelic faces singing an old Christmas song around the piano. Two little boys in sailor suits, their mouths full of cake, are talking: 'They're still boring us to death with their music! Say, do you have the *Auto* magazine? Who won the Schneider Cup?'

In the small living room, Édouard and Marie-Laure are having an argument.

'You gullible fool, really, leave it to you to defend my holier-than-thou sister!'

'Why are you saying that?'

'Because . . .' and she whispers something in his ear.

At that moment, Claudine comes home. The children run across the room and hug her.

'Claudine! It's Claudine! Come and play with us.'

She gently pushes them away, goes into her room and locks the door; they start to follow her, but the Christmas pudding has been lit and appears. We see all their little expressions over their cups of hot chocolate, the nanny scolding them. Claudine is in her room, crushed against the window. She murmurs in a toneless, despairing voice:

'What am I going to do? What am I going to do?'

At that moment, we see her father adjusting his tie in front of the mirror, at his mistress's place. 'So you're sure you won't be able to come back tonight?' she asks, sounding hopeful.

'No, impossible.'

'Oh, good,' she sighs, relieved.

In the entrance hall to the bachelor pad where Claudine's mother meets her lover, we see a hand slipping a small wallet into a man's hand that quickly closes over it.

The image fades into a different hand, Claudine's; she is opening a small flask with the label: barbital.

The children dance around the tree.

Claudine carefully closes the doors and turns on the gas of the hot water tank above the bathtub, in the adjoining bathroom. Them she locks her door again. She walks over to the window, looks outside in despair as if she were hoping for something to come to help her, in vain.

'My God,' she whispers, 'forgive me; I'm an unfortunate wretch . . .'

She takes the barbital. (All we see is a full glass of water, then empty and the trembling hand holding it.) She lays down on her bed.

The children's voices are heard singing in the living room; they soon fade away under the sound of church bells, then return stronger, shrill. (This should give the impression of a nightmare Claudine is having while asleep.) When the singing stops, we clearly hear the sound of gas, like a hissing snake.

Édouard walks over to the children, who are now looking for some hidden object, accompanied by music, childish, obsessive music that is annoying.

He asks Christiane and Jeannot: 'Has your sister come back yet?'

The children barely reply. They are running around in all directions, shouting and talking all at once. The toys are given out; they pull them quite roughly from the branches of the tree and we see the tree shaking. A padded toy Santa Claus, badly attached, falls to the ground and all the little white shoes trample him, indifferent. The governesses blow out the candles. Jeannot, tears in his eyes, protests: 'Oh, what a shame, it was so beautiful!'

The nanny (dryly): 'You're nothing more than a little self-centred child. That's what Christmas trees are for.'

The children, shouting with joy, throw streamers, put on paper hats and blow into the cardboard trumpets. 'A farandole! A farandole!' One of the governesses sits down at the piano and plays vigorously. The children spin around quickly, more and more quickly; they get wild from their game. They run around the tree, then through the whole apartment, rushing through empty rooms and ending up in front of Claudine's door. It is locked and they begin banging on it: 'Let us in, let us in!'

Édouard, who has followed them, asks in surprise: 'What are you doing here?'

'Monsieur, Christiane and Jeannot's sister won't open the door. You see, it's locked.'

'Well, that's because she wants to be left alone.'

'Oh, no, of course not, she's playing a trick on us . . . Otherwise, she would have told us off by now,' replies a chubby-cheeked little boy wearing an Eton uniform.

Suddenly, Édouard is filled with anxiety and asks: 'Have you been calling her for a long time without her answering?'

'Oh, yes, a very long time!'

Édouard starts calling her, quietly at first, then much louder: 'Claudine! Claudine!'

No reply. The children, who have gradually become more and more worried, fall silent. Édouard kicks the door, bangs on it with his fists, but it remains firmly closed.

The hissing of gas. Claudine's head thrown back, her face white. The governess, in the empty living room, is being kissed by the butler but continues playing the piano, oblivious.

Édouard, determined, shouts: 'Be quiet, all of you! G . . . Damn it!'

While he is rattling the door, two of the kids have found a ladder and climbed up to the little skylight cut out of the roof, above the chimney, in Claudine's room. One of them calls out:

'Monsieur, Monsieur! Come quickly!'

Édouard, rushes up, sees Claudine fainted on her bed, goes back down and forces the door open with his shoulder. A long silence. Everyone is huddled in front of the door, the servants and the terrified children. Then, great chaos, children shouting:

'I'm scared! I'm scared! Is she dead?'

We see the living room and the candles on the tree that flicker and go out.

Claudine has opened her eyes. They are alone. He tries to laugh: 'Are you feeling better? You gave me quite a fright, you know, my dear.'

Claudine: 'Oh, why did you wake me up? I was in such a deep sleep.'

'Listen, I'm your friend, a true friend, Claudine . . . Tell me the truth . . . Is what Marie-Laure said true?'

Claudine smiles sadly: 'Ah, so Marie-Laure told you? Yes, it's true.'

Meanwhile, Christiane and Jeannot slip into the empty living room. They are holding a box of matches and light all the candles on the tree again, one by one. They are very excited.

'Wait 'til you see how pretty it will look . . . We didn't get to see it before with all the grown-ups pushing us around! Turn off the lights.'

But once the lights are off, all we see is the bare Christmas tree, bits of streamers and old wrapping paper on the floor.

'Oh!' the children say, sadly.

At that moment, a great commotion. Claudine's parents have been warned and rush into her room. Marie-Laure follows them.

'You miserable child! You have no pity, you don't care at all about your family,' etc.

Édouard: 'Monsieur, may I have the honour of asking for Claudine's hand in marriage?'

Her father (furious): 'Claudine's hand? I . . . yes . . . you can see I'm taken aback . . . I mean, deeply moved . . . (To Claudine, much more gently than before) So, no more foolishness, right? Ah, youth, fortunate youth . . . you get married, you kill yourself, just like that . . . Wait until you're my age, then you'll understand what it means to have real problems in life!'

Marie-Laure to Édouard, frowning, but making an effort in spite of her bad luck: 'Con . . . congratulations . . .'

Édouard (quietly): 'My dear, I prefer . . . someone who is blossoming rather than someone who is withering.'

Marie-Laure (annoyed): 'I don't understand.'

Claudine and Édouard are alone. 'Thank you, my dear friend,' she says softly. 'I will be ridiculously faithful to you, I swear it.'

We see their two faces. He looks at her, nods his head, brings her hand to his lips. She says quietly, over and over again, her eyes full of tears: 'Thank you for my child.'

Fade out.

That evening. Guests at the dinner table. Her father raises his glass: 'I have the pleasure of announcing the engagement of my daughter Claudine to Monsieur Saulnier.'

A discreet murmur of congratulations.

One lady to her mother: 'You must be very happy!'

'Oh, naturally, but it's so sad to lose one's children, and mine are still such babes . . . So when we send them out into the world all alone for the first time, we do worry so, don't we?'

Everyone leaves the table. Everything is discreet, proper. The servants walk by in silence, serving the coffee. On the sad Christmas tree, the candles have nearly burned out on its broken branches.

Jeannot and Christiane's room; they are in bed. We hear the nanny snoring. Little Jeannot is asleep, clutching his toys to his heart. Christiane, sitting on her bed, is crying softly; she wipes away her tears. Jeannot wakes up and whispers: 'Why are you crying?'

Christiane (pitifully): 'I don't know . . .'

Jeannot: 'Oh, but didn't you have a good time today? The Christmas tree, and now Claudine is going to get married . . . I'll be the ring bearer and you'll be the flower girl . . . didn't you have a good time?'

Christiane shakes her head.

'Why?'

Christiane buries her face in her pillow.

'Because . . . I don't know . . .'

Silence.

Faint melancholic music gradually fades away:

> *Childhood, Innocence, Dawn of the world . . .*
> *Dawn of love*
> *The most wonderful days . . .*

Dancing Dan's Christmas

Now one time it comes on Christmas, and in fact it is the evening before Christmas, and I am in Good Time Charley Bernstein's little speakeasy in West Forty-seventh Street, wishing Charley a Merry Christmas and having a few hot Tom and Jerrys with him.

This hot Tom and Jerry is an old-time drink that is once used by one and all in this country to celebrate Christmas with, and in fact it is once so popular that many people think Christmas is invented only to furnish an excuse for hot Tom and Jerry, although of course this is by no means true.

But anybody will tell you that there is nothing that brings out the true holiday spirit like hot Tom and Jerry, and I hear that since Tom and Jerry goes out of style in the United States, the holiday spirit is never quite the same.

Well, as Good Time Charley and I are expressing our holiday sentiments to each other over our hot Tom and Jerry, and I am trying to think up the poem about the night before Christmas and all through the house, which I know will interest Charley no little, all of a sudden there is a big knock at the front door, and when Charley opens the door, who comes in carrying a large package under one arm but a guy by the name of Dancing Dan.

This Dancing Dan is a good-looking young guy, who always seems well-dressed, and he is called by the name of Dancing Dan because he is a great hand for dancing around and about with dolls in night clubs, and other spots where there is any dancing. In fact, Dan never seems to be doing anything else, although I hear rumors that when he is not dancing he is carrying on in a most illegal manner at one thing and another. But of course you can always hear rumors in this town about anybody, and personally I am rather fond of Dancing Dan as he always seems to be getting a great belt out of life.

Anybody in town will tell you that Dancing Dan is a guy with no Barnaby whatever in him, and in fact he has about as much gizzard as anybody around, although I wish to say I always question his judgment in dancing so much with Miss Muriel O'Neill, who works in the Half Moon night club. And the reason I question his judgment in this respect is because everybody knows that Miss Muriel O'Neill is a doll who is very well thought of by Heine Schmitz, and Heine Schmitz is not such a guy as will take kindly to anybody dancing more than once and a half with a doll that he thinks well of.

Well, anyway, as Dancing Dan comes in, he weighs up the joint in one quick peek, and then he tosses the package he is carrying into a corner where it goes plunk, as if there is something very heavy in it, and then he steps up to the bar alongside of Charley and me and wishes to know what we are drinking.

Naturally we start boosting hot Tom and Jerry to Dancing Dan, and he says he will take a crack at it with us, and after one crack, Dancing Dan says he will have another crack, and Merry Christmas to us with it, and the first thing anybody knows it is a couple of hours later and we are still having cracks at the hot Tom and Jerry with Dancing Dan, and Dan says he never drinks anything so soothing in his life. In fact, Dancing Dan says he will recommend Tom and Jerry to everybody he knows, only he does not know anybody good enough for Tom and Jerry, except maybe Miss Muriel O'Neill, and she does not drink anything with drugstore rye in it.

Well, several times while we are drinking this Tom and Jerry, customers come to the door of Good Time Charley's little speakeasy and knock, but by now Charley is commencing to be afraid they will wish Tom and Jerry, too, and he does not feel we will have enough for ourselves, so he hangs out a sign which says 'Closed on Account of Christmas', and the only one he will let in is a guy by the name of Ooky, who is nothing but an old rum-dum, and who is going around all week dressed like Santa Claus and carrying a sign advertising Moe Lewinsky's clothing joint around in Sixth Avenue.

This Ooky is still wearing his Santa Claus outfit when Charley lets him in, and the reason Charley permits such a character as Ooky in his joint is because Ooky does the porter work for Charley when he is not Santa Claus for Moe Lewinsky, such as sweeping out, and washing the glasses, and one thing and another.

Well, it is about nine-thirty when Ooky comes in, and his puppies are aching, and he is all petered out generally from walking up and down and here and there with his sign, for any time a guy is Santa Claus for Moe Lewinsky he must earn his dough. In fact, Ooky is so fatigued, and his puppies hurt him so much that Dancing Dan and Good Time Charley and I all feel very sorry for him, and invite him to have a few mugs of hot Tom and Jerry with us, and wish him plenty of Merry Christmas.

But old Ooky is not accustomed to Tom and Jerry and after about the fifth mug he folds up in a chair, and goes right to sleep on us. He is wearing a pretty good Santa Claus make-up, what with a nice red suit trimmed with white cotton, and a wig, and false nose, and long white whiskers, and a big sack stuffed with excelsior on his back, and if I do not know Santa Claus is not apt to be such a guy as will snore loud enough to rattle the windows, I will think Ooky is Santa Claus sure enough.

Well, we forget Ooky and let him sleep, and go on with our hot Tom and Jerry, and in the meantime we try to think up a few songs appropriate to Christmas, and Dancing Dan finally renders 'My Dad's Dinner Pail' in a nice baritone and very loud, while I do first rate with 'Will You Love Me in December As You Do in May?'

About midnight Dancing Dan wishes to see how he looks as Santa Claus.

So Good Time Charley and I help Dancing Dan pull off Ooky's outfit and put it on Dan, and this is easy as Ooky only has this Santa Claus outfit on over his ordinary clothes, and he does not even wake up when we are undressing him of the Santa Claus uniform.

Well, I wish to say I see many a Santa Claus in my time, but I never see a better-looking Santa Claus than Dancing Dan, especially after he gets the wig and white whiskers fixed just right, and we put a sofa pillow that Good Time Charley happens to have around the joint for the cat to sleep on down his pants to give Dancing Dan a nice fat stomach such as Santa Claus is bound to have.

'Well,' Charley finally says, 'it is a great pity we do not know where there are some stockings hung up somewhere, because then,' he says, 'you can go around and stuff things in these stockings, as I always hear this is the main idea of a Santa Claus. But,' Charley says, 'I do not suppose anybody in this section has any stockings hung up, or if they have,' he says, 'the chances are they are so full of holes they will not hold anything. Anyway,' Charley says, 'even if there are any stockings hung up we do not have anything to stuff in them, although personally,' he says, 'I will gladly donate a few pints of Scotch.'

Well, I am pointing out that we have no reindeer and that a Santa Claus is bound to look like a terrible sap if he goes around without any reindeer, but Charley's remarks seem to give Dancing Dan an idea, for all of a sudden he speaks as follows:

'Why,' Dancing Dan says, 'I know where a stocking is hung up. It is hung up at Miss Muriel O'Neill's flat over here in West Forty-ninth Street. This stocking is hung up by nobody but a party by the name of Gammer O'Neill, who is Miss Muriel O'Neill's grandmamma,' Dancing Dan says. 'Gammer O'Neill is going on ninety-odd,' he says, 'and Miss Muriel O'Neill tells me she cannot hold out much longer, what with one thing and another, including being a little childish in spots.

'Now,' Dancing Dan says, 'I remember Miss Muriel O'Neill is telling me just the other night how Gammer O'Neill hangs up her stocking on Christmas Eve all her life, and,' he says, 'I judge from what Miss Muriel O'Neill says that the old doll always believes Santa Claus will come along some Christmas and fill the stocking full of beautiful gifts. But,' Dancing Dan says, 'Miss Muriel O'Neill tells me Santa Claus never does this, although Miss Muriel O'Neill personally always takes a few gifts home and pops them into the stocking to make Gammer O'Neill feel better.

'But, of course,' Dancing Dan says, 'these gifts are nothing much because Miss Muriel O'Neill is very poor, and proud, and also good, and will not take a dime off of anybody and I can lick the guy who says she will.

'Now,' Dancing Dan goes on, 'it seems that while Gammer O'Neill is very happy to get whatever she finds in her stocking on Christmas morning, she does not understand why Santa Claus is not more liberal, and,' he says, 'Miss Muriel O'Neill is saying to me that she only wishes she can give Gammer O'Neill one real big Christmas before the old doll puts her checks back in the rack.

'So,' Dancing Dan states, 'here is a job for us. Miss Muriel O'Neill and her grandmamma live all alone in this flat over in West Forty-ninth Street, and,' he says, 'at such an hour as this Miss Muriel O'Neill is bound to be working, and the chances are Gammer O'Neill is sound asleep, and we will just hop over there and Santa Claus will fill up her stocking with beautiful gifts.'

Well, I say, I do not see where we are going to get any beautiful gifts at this time of night, what with all the stores being closed, unless we dash into an all-night drugstore and buy a few bottles of perfume and a bum toilet set as guys always do when they forget about their ever-loving wives until after store hours on Christmas Eve, but Dancing Dan says never mind about this, but let us have a few more Tom and Jerrys first.

So we have a few more Tom and Jerrys, and then Dancing Dan picks up the package he heaves into the corner, and dumps most of the excelsior out of Ooky's Santa Claus sack, and puts the bundle in, and Good Time Charley turns out all the lights, but one, and leaves a bottle of Scotch on the table in front of Ooky for a Christmas gift, and away we go.

Personally, I regret very much leaving the hot Tom and Jerry, but then I am also very enthusiastic about going along to help Dancing Dan play Santa Claus, while Good Time Charley is practically overjoyed, as it is the first time in his life Charley is ever mixed up in so much holiday spirit.

As we go up Broadway, headed for Forty-ninth Street, Charley and I see many citizens we know and give them a large hello, and wish them Merry Christmas, and some of these citizens shake hands with Santa Claus, not knowing he is nobody but Dancing Dan, although later I understand there is some gossip among these citizens because they claim a Santa Claus with such a breath on him as our Santa Claus has is a little out of line.

And once we are somewhat embarrassed when a lot of little kids going home with their parents from a late Christmas party somewhere gather about Santa Claus with shouts of childish glee, and some of them wish to climb up Santa Claus' legs. Naturally, Santa Claus gets a little peevish, and calls them a few names, and one of the parents comes up and wishes to know what is the idea of Santa Claus using such language, and Santa Claus takes a punch at the parent, all of which is no doubt astonishing to the little kids who have an idea of Santa Claus as a very kindly old guy.

Well, finally we arrive in front of the place where Dancing Dan says Miss Muriel O'Neill and her grandmamma live, and it is nothing but a tenement house not far back of Madison Square Garden, and furthermore it is a walkup, and at this time there are no lights burning in the joint except a gas jet in the main hall, and by the light of this jet we look at the names on the letter boxes, such as you always find in the hall of these joints, and we see that Miss Muriel O'Neill and her grandmamma live on the fifth floor.

This is the top floor, and personally I do not like the idea of walking up five flights of stairs, and I am willing to let Dancing Dan and Good Time Charley go, but Dancing Dan insists we must all go, and finally I agree because Charley is commencing to argue that the right way for us to do is to get on the roof and let Santa Claus go down a chimney, and is making so much noise I am afraid he will wake somebody up.

So up the stairs we climb and finally we come to a door on the top floor that has a little card in a slot that says O'Neill, so we know we reach our destination. Dancing Dan first tries the knob, and right away the door opens, and we are in a little two- or three-room flat, with not much furniture in it, and what furniture there is, is very poor. One single gas jet is burning near a bed in a room just off the one the door opens into, and by this light we see a very old doll is sleeping on the bed, so we judge this is nobody but Gammer O'Neill.

On her face is a large smile, as if she is dreaming of something very pleasant. On a chair at the head of the bed is hung a long black stocking, and it seems to be such a stocking as is often patched and mended, so I can see that what Miss Muriel O'Neill tells Dancing Dan about her grandmamma hanging up her stocking is really true, although up to this time I have my doubts.

Finally Dancing Dan unslings the sack on his back, and takes out his package, and unties this package, and all of a sudden out pops a raft of big diamond bracelets, and diamond rings, and diamond brooches, and diamond necklaces, and I do not know what else in the way of diamonds, and Dancing Dan and I begin stuffing these diamonds into the stocking and Good Time Charley pitches in and helps us.

There are enough diamonds to fill the stocking to the muzzle, and it is no small stocking, at that, and I judge that Gammer O'Neill has a pretty fair set of bunting sticks when she is young. In fact, there are so many diamonds that we have enough left over to make a nice little pile on the chair after we fill the stocking plumb up, leaving a nice diamond-studded vanity case sticking out the top where we figure it will hit Gammer O'Neill's eye when she wakes up.

And it is not until I get out in the fresh air again that all of a sudden I remember seeing large headlines in the afternoon papers about a five-hundred-G's stickup in the afternoon of one of the biggest diamond merchants in Maiden Lane while he is sitting in his office, and I also recall once hearing rumors that Dancing Dan is one of the best lonehand git-'em-up guys in the world.

Naturally, I commence to wonder if I am in the proper company when I am with Dancing Dan, even if he is Santa Claus. So I leave him on the next corner arguing with Good Time Charley about whether they ought to go and find some more presents somewhere, and look for other stockings to stuff, and I hasten on home and go to bed.

The next day I find I have such a noggin that I do not care to stir around, and in fact I do not stir around much for a couple of weeks.

Then one night I drop around to Good Time Charley's little speakeasy, and ask Charley what is doing.

'Well,' Charley says, 'many things are doing, and personally,' he says, 'I'm greatly surprised I do not see you at Gammer O'Neill's wake. You know Gammer O'Neill leaves this wicked old world a couple of days after Christmas,' Good Time Charley says, 'and,' he says, 'Miss Muriel O'Neill states that Doc Moggs claims it is at least a day after she is entitled to go, but she is sustained,' Charley says, 'by great happiness in finding her stocking filled with beautiful gifts on Christmas morning.

'According to Miss Muriel O'Neill,' Charley says, 'Gammer O'Neill dies practically convinced that there is a Santa Claus, although of course,' he says, 'Miss Muriel O'Neill does not tell her the real owner of the gifts, an all-right guy by the name of Shapiro leaves the gifts with her after Miss Muriel O'Neill notifies him of the finding of same.

'It seems,' Charley says, 'this Shapiro is a tender-hearted guy, who is willing to help keep Gammer O'Neill with us a little longer when Doc Moggs says leaving the gifts with her will do it.

'So,' Charley says, 'everything is quite all right, as the coppers cannot figure anything except that maybe the rascal who takes the gifts from Shapiro gets conscience-stricken, and leaves them the first place he can, and Miss Muriel O'Neill receives a ten-G's reward for finding the gifts and returning them. And,' Charley says, 'I hear Dancing Dan is in San Francisco and is figuring on reforming and becoming a dancing teacher, so he can marry Miss Muriel O'Neill, and of course,' he says, 'we all hope and trust she never learn any details of Dancing Dan's career.'

Well, it is Christmas Eve a year later that I run into a guy by the name of Shotgun Sam, who is mobbed up with Heine Schmitz in Harlem, and who is a very, very obnoxious character indeed.

'Well, well, well,' Shotgun says, 'the last time I see you is another Christmas Eve like this, and you are coming out of Good Time Charley's joint, and,' he says, 'you certainly have your pots on.'

'Well, Shotgun,' I says, 'I am sorry you get such a wrong impression of me, but the truth is,' I say, 'on the occasion you speak of, I am suffering from a dizzy feeling in my head.'

'It is all right with me,' Shotgun says. 'I have a tip this guy Dancing Dan is in Good Time Charley's the night I see you, and Mockie Morgan, and Gunner Jack and me are casing the joint, because,' he says, 'Heine Schmitz is all sored up at Dan over some doll, although of course,' Shotgun says, 'it is all right now as Heine has another doll.

'Anyway,' he says, 'we never get to see Dancing Dan. We watch the joint from six-thirty in the evening until daylight Christmas morning, and nobody goes in all night but old Ooky the Santa Claus guy in his Santa Claus make-up, and,' Shotgun says, 'nobody comes out except you and Good Time Charley and Ooky.

'Well,' Shotgun says, 'it is a great break for Dancing Dan he never goes in or comes out of Good Time Charley's, at that, because,' he says, 'we are waiting for him on the second-floor front of the building across the way with some nice little sawed-offs, and are under orders from Heine not to miss.'

'Well, Shotgun,' I say, 'Merry Christmas.'

'Well, all right,' Shotgun says, 'Merry Christmas.'

DOROTHY L. SAYERS
The Necklace of Pearls

Sir Septimus Shale was accustomed to assert his authority once in the year and once only. He allowed his young and fashionable wife to fill his house with diagrammatic furniture made of steel; to collect advanced artists and anti-grammatical poets; to believe in cocktails and relativity and to dress as extravagantly as she pleased; but he did insist on an old-fashioned Christmas. He was a simple-hearted man, who really liked plum-pudding and cracker mottoes, and he could not get it out of his head that other people, 'at bottom', enjoyed these things also. At Christmas, therefore, he firmly retired to his country house in Essex, called in the servants to hang holly and mistletoe upon the cubist electric fittings; loaded the steel sideboard with delicacies from Fortnum & Mason; hung up stockings at the heads of the polished walnut bedsteads; and even, on this occasion only, had the electric radiators removed from the modernist grates and installed wood fires and a Yule log. He then gathered his family and friends about him, filled them with as much Dickensian good fare as he could persuade them to swallow, and, after their Christmas dinner, set them down to play 'Charades' and 'Clumps' and 'Animal, Vegetable and Mineral' in the drawing-room, concluding these diversions by 'Hide-and-Seek' in the dark all over the house. Because Sir Septimus was a very rich man, his guests fell in with this invariable programme, and if they were bored, they did not tell him so.

Another charming and traditional custom which he followed was that of presenting to his daughter Margharita a pearl on each successive birthday – this anniversary happening to coincide with Christmas Eve. The pearls now numbered twenty, and the collection was beginning to enjoy a certain celebrity, and had been photographed in the Society papers.

Though not sensationally large – each one being about the size of a marrow-fat pea – the pearls were of very great value. They were of exquisite colour and perfect shape and matched to a hair's-weight. On this particular Christmas Eve, the presentation of the twenty-first pearl had been the occasion of a very special ceremony. There was a dance and there were speeches. On the Christmas night following, the more restricted family party took place, with the turkey and the Victorian games. There were eleven guests, in addition to Sir Septimus and Lady Shale and their daughter, nearly all related or connected to them in some way: John Shale, a brother with his wife and their son and daughter Henry and Betty; Betty's fiancé, Oswald Truegood, a young man with parliamentary ambitions; George Comphrey, a cousin of Lady Shale's, aged about thirty and known as a man about town; Lavinia Prescott, asked on George's account; Joyce Trivett, asked on Henry Shale's account; Richard and Beryl Dennison, distant relations of Lady Shale, who lived a gay and expensive life in town on nobody precisely knew what resources; and Lord Peter Wimsey, asked, in a touching spirit of unreasonable hope, on Margharita's account. There were also, of course, William Norgate, secretary to Sir Septimus, and Miss Tomkins, secretary to Lady Shale, who had to be there because, without their calm efficiency, the Christmas arrangements could not have been carried through.

Dinner was over – a seemingly endless succession of soup, fish, turkey, roast beef, plum-pudding, mince-pies, crystallized fruit, nuts, and five kinds of wine, presided over by Sir Septimus, all smiles, by Lady Shale, all mocking deprecation, and by Margharita, pretty and bored, with the necklace of twenty-one pearls gleaming softly on her slender throat. Gorged and dyspeptic and longing only for the horizontal position, the company had been shepherded into the drawing-room and set to play 'Musical Chairs' (Miss Tomkins at the piano), 'Hunt the Slipper' (slipper provided by Miss Tomkins), and 'Dumb Crambo' (costumes by Miss Tomkins and Mr William Norgate). The back drawing-room (for Sir Septimus clung to these old-fashioned names) provided an admirable dressing-room, being screened by folding doors from the large drawing-room in which the audience sat on aluminium chairs, scrabbling uneasy toes on a floor of black glass under the tremendous illumination of electricity reflected from a brass ceiling.

It was William Norgate who, after taking the temperature of the meeting, suggested to Lady Shale that they should play at something less athletic. Lady Shale agreed and, as usual, suggested bridge. Sir Septimus, as usual, blew the suggestion aside.

'Bridge? Nonsense! Nonsense! Play bridge every day of your lives. This is Christmas time. Something we can all play together. How about "Animal, Vegetable and Mineral"?'

This intellectual pastime was a favourite with Sir Septimus; he was rather good at putting pregnant questions. After a brief discussion, it became evident that this game was an inevitable part of the programme. The party settled down to it, Sir Septimus undertaking to 'go out' first and set the thing going.

Presently they had guessed among other things Miss Tomkins's mother's photograph, a gramophone record of 'I Want to be Happy' (much scientific research into the exact composition of records, settled by William Norgate out of the *Encyclopaedia Britannica*), the smallest stickleback in the stream at the bottom of the garden, the new planet Pluto, the scarf worn by Mrs Dennison (very confusing, because it was not silk, which would be animal, or artificial silk, which would be vegetable, but made of spun glass – mineral, a very clever choice of subject), and had failed to guess the Prime Minister's wireless speech – which was voted not fair, since nobody could decide whether it was animal by nature or a kind of gas. It was decided that they should do one more word and then go on to 'Hide-and-Seek'. Oswald Truegood had retired into the back room and shut the door behind him while the party discussed the next subject of examination, when suddenly Sir Septimus broke in on the argument by calling to his daughter:

'Hullo, Margy! What have you done with your necklace?'

'I took it off, Dad, because I thought it might get broken in "Dumb Crambo". It's over here on this table. No, it isn't. Did you take it, Mother?'

'No, I didn't. If I'd seen it, I should have. You are a careless child.'

'I believe you've got it yourself, Dad. You're teasing.'

Sir Septimus denied the accusation with some energy. Everybody got up and began to hunt about. There were not many places in that bare and polished room where a necklace could be hidden. After ten minutes' fruitless investigation, Richard Dennison, who had been seated next to the table where the pearls had been placed, began to look rather uncomfortable.

'Awkward, you know,' he remarked to Wimsey.

At this moment, Oswald Truegood put his head through the folding-doors and asked whether they hadn't settled on something by now, because he was getting the fidgets.

This directed the attention of the searchers to the inner room. Margharita must have been mistaken. She had taken it in there, and it had got mixed up with the dressing-up clothes somehow. The room was ransacked. Everything was lifted up and shaken. The thing began to look serious. After half an hour of desperate energy it became apparent that the pearls were nowhere to be found.

'They must be somewhere in these two rooms, you know,' said Wimsey. 'The back drawing-room has no door and nobody could have gone out of the front drawing-room without being seen. Unless the windows –'

No. The windows were all guarded on the outside by heavy shutters which it needed two footmen to take down and replace. The pearls had not gone out that way. In fact, the mere suggestion that they had left the drawing-room at all was disagreeable. Because – because –

It was William Norgate, efficient as ever, who coldly and boldly faced the issue.

'I think, Sir Septimus, it would be a relief to the minds of everybody present if we could all be searched.'

Sir Septimus was horrified, but the guests, having found a leader, backed up Norgate. The door was locked, and the search was conducted – the ladies in the inner room and the men in the outer.

Nothing resulted from it except some very interesting information about the belongings habitually carried about by the average man and woman. It was natural that Lord Peter Wimsey should possess a pair of forceps, a pocket lens, and a small folding foot-rule – was he not a Sherlock Holmes in high life? But that Oswald Truegood should have two liver-pills in a screw of paper and Henry Shale a pocket edition of *The Odes of Horace* was unexpected. Why did John Shale distend the pockets of his dress-suit with a stump of red sealing-wax, an ugly little mascot, and a five-shilling piece? George Comphrey had a pair of folding scissors, and three wrapped lumps of sugar, of the sort served in restaurants and dining-cars – evidence of a not uncommon form of kleptomania; but that the tidy and exact Norgate should burden himself with a reel of white cotton, three separate lengths of string, and twelve safety-pins on a card seemed really remarkable till one remembered that he had superintended all the Christmas decorations. Richard Dennison, amid some confusion and laughter, was found to cherish a lady's garter, a powder-compact, and half a potato; the last-named, he said, was a prophylactic against rheumatism (to which he was subject), while the other objects belonged to his wife. On the ladies' side, the more striking exhibits were a little book on palmistry, three invisible hair-pins, and a baby's photograph (Miss Tomkins); a Chinese trick cigarette-case with a secret compartment (Beryl Dennison); a *very* private letter and an outfit for mending stocking-ladders (Lavinia Prescott); and a pair of eyebrow tweezers and a small packet of white powder, said to be for headaches (Betty Shale). An agitating moment followed the production from Joyce Trivett's handbag of a small string of pearls – but it was promptly remembered that these had come out of one of the crackers at dinnertime, and they were, in fact, synthetic. In short, the search was unproductive of anything beyond a general shamefacedness and the discomfort always produced by undressing and re-dressing in a hurry at the wrong time of the day.

It was then that somebody, very grudgingly and haltingly, mentioned the horrid word 'Police'. Sir Septimus, naturally, was appalled by the idea. It was disgusting. He would not allow it. The pearls must be somewhere. They must search the rooms again. Could not Lord Peter Wimsey, with his experience of – er – mysterious happenings, do something to assist them?

'Eh?' said his lordship. 'Oh, by Jove, yes – by all means, certainly. That is to say, provided nobody supposes – eh, what? I mean to say, you don't know that I'm not a suspicious character, do you, what?'

Lady Shale interposed with authority.

'We don't think *anybody* ought to be suspected,' she said, 'but, if we did, we'd know it couldn't be you. You know *far* too much about crimes to want to commit one.'

'All right,' said Wimsey. 'But after the way the place has been gone over –' He shrugged his shoulders.

'Yes, I'm afraid you won't be able to find any footprints,' said Margharita. 'But we may have overlooked something.'

Wimsey nodded.

'I'll try. Do you all mind sitting down on your chairs in the outer room and staying there. All except one of you – I'd better have a witness to anything I do or find. Sir Septimus – you'd be the best person, I think.'

He shepherded them to their places and began a slow circuit of the two rooms, exploring every surface, gazing up to the polished brazen ceiling, and crawling on hands and knees in the approved fashion across the black and shining desert of the floors. Sir Septimus followed, staring when Wimsey stared, bending with his hands upon his knees when Wimsey crawled, and puffing at intervals with astonishment and chagrin. Their progress rather resembled that of a man taking out a very inquisitive puppy for a very leisurely constitutional. Fortunately, Lady Shale's taste in furnishing made investigation easier; there were scarcely any nooks or corners where anything could be concealed.

They reached the inner drawing-room, and here the dressing-up clothes were again minutely examined, but without result. Finally, Wimsey lay down flat on his stomach to squint under a steel cabinet which was one of the very few pieces of furniture which possessed short legs. Something about it seemed to catch his attention. He rolled up his sleeve and plunged his arm into the cavity, kicked convulsively in the effort to reach farther than was humanly possible, pulled out from his pocket and extended his folding foot-rule, fished with it under the cabinet, and eventually succeeded in extracting what he sought.

It was a very minute object – in fact, a pin. Not an ordinary pin, but one resembling those used by entomologists to impale extremely small moths on the setting-board. It was about three-quarters of an inch in length, as fine as a very fine needle, with a sharp point and a particularly small head.

'Bless my soul!' said Sir Septimus. 'What's that?'

'Does anybody here happen to collect moths or beetles or anything?' asked Wimsey, squatting on his haunches and examining the pin.

'I'm pretty sure they don't,' replied Sir Septimus. 'I'll ask them.'

'Don't do that.' Wimsey bent his head and stared at the floor, from which his own face stared meditatively back at him.

'I see,' said Wimsey presently. 'That's how it was done. All right, Sir Septimus. I know where the pearls are, but I don't know who took them.

Perhaps it would be as well – for everybody's satisfaction – just to find out. In the meantime they are perfectly safe. Don't tell anyone that we've found this pin or that we've discovered anything. Send all these people to bed. Lock the drawing-room door and keep the key, and we'll get our man – or woman – by breakfast-time.'

'God bless my soul,' said Sir Septimus, very much puzzled.

Lord Peter Wimsey kept careful watch that night upon the drawing-room door. Nobody, however, came near it. Either the thief suspected a trap or he felt confident that any time would do to recover the pearls. Wimsey, however, did not feel that he was wasting his time. He was making a list of people who had been left alone in the back drawing-room during the playing of 'Animal, Vegetable and Mineral'. The list ran as follows:

Sir Septimus Shale
Lavinia Prescott
William Norgate
Joyce Trivett and Henry Shale (together, because they had claimed to
    be incapable of guessing anything unaided)
Mrs Dennison
Betty Shale
George Comphrey
Richard Dennison
Miss Tomkins
Oswald Truegood

He also made out a list of the persons to whom pearls might be useful or desirable. Unfortunately, this list agreed in almost all respects with the first (always excepting Sir Septimus) and so was not very helpful. The two secretaries had both come well recommended, but that was exactly what they would have done had they come with ulterior designs; the Dennisons were notorious livers from hand to mouth; Betty Shale carried mysterious white powders in her handbag, and was known to be in with a rather rapid set in town; Henry was a harmless dilettante, but Joyce Trivett could twist him round her little finger and was what Jane Austen liked to call 'expensive and dissipated'; Comphrey speculated; Oswald Truegood was rather

99

frequently present at Epsom and Newmarket – the search for motives was only too fatally easy.

When the second housemaid and the under-footman appeared in the passage with household implements, Wimsey abandoned his vigil, but he was down early to breakfast. Sir Septimus with his wife and daughter were down before him, and a certain air of tension made itself felt. Wimsey, standing on the hearth before the fire, made conversation about the weather and politics.

The party assembled gradually, but, as though by common consent, nothing was said about pearls until after breakfast, when Oswald True-good took the bull by the horns.

'Well now!' said he. 'How's the detective getting along? Got your man, Wimsey?'

'Not yet,' said Wimsey easily.

Sir Septimus, looking at Wimsey as though for his cue, cleared his throat and dashed into speech.

'All very tiresome,' he said, 'all very unpleasant. Hr'rm. Nothing for it but the police, I'm afraid. Just at Christmas, too. Hr'rm. Spoilt the party. Can't stand seeing all this stuff about the place.' He waved his hand towards the festoons of evergreens and coloured paper that adorned the walls. 'Take it all down, eh, what? No heart in it. Hr'rm. Burn the lot.'

'What a pity, when we worked so hard over it,' said Joyce.

'Oh, leave it, Uncle,' said Henry Shale. 'You're bothering too much about the pearls. They're sure to turn up.'

'Shall I ring for James?' suggested William Norgate.

'No,' interrupted Comphrey, 'let's do it ourselves. It'll give us something to do and take our minds off our troubles.'

'That's right,' said Sir Septimus. 'Start right away. Hate the sight of it.'

He savagely hauled a great branch of holly down from the mantelpiece and flung it, crackling, into the fire.

'That's the stuff,' said Richard Dennison. 'Make a good old blaze!' He leapt up from the table and snatched the mistletoe from the chandelier. 'Here goes! One more kiss for somebody before it's too late.'

'Isn't it unlucky to take it down before the New Year?' suggested Miss Tomkins.

'Unlucky be hanged. We'll have it all down. Off the stairs and out of the drawing-room too. Somebody go and collect it.'

'Isn't the drawing-room locked?' asked Oswald.

'No. Lord Peter says the pearls aren't there, wherever else they are, so it's unlocked. That's right, isn't it, Wimsey?'

'Quite right. The pearls were taken out of these rooms. I can't tell yet how, but I'm positive of it. In fact, I'll pledge my reputation that wherever they are, they're not up there.'

'Oh, well,' said Comphrey, 'in that case, have at it! Come along, Lavinia – you and Dennison do the drawing-room and I'll do the back room. We'll have a race.'

'But if the police are coming in,' said Dennison, 'oughtn't everything to be left just as it is?'

'Damn the police!' shouted Sir Septimus. 'They don't want evergreens.'

Oswald and Margharita were already pulling the holly and ivy from the staircase, amid peals of laughter. The party dispersed. Wimsey went quietly upstairs and into the drawing-room, where the work of demolition was taking place at a great rate, George having bet the other two ten shillings to a tanner that they would not finish their part of the job before he finished his.

'You mustn't help,' said Lavinia, laughing to Wimsey. 'It wouldn't be fair.'

Wimsey said nothing, but waited till the room was clear. Then he followed them down again to the hall, where the fire was sending up a great roaring and spluttering, suggestive of Guy Fawkes' night. He whispered to Sir Septimus, who went forward and touched George Comphrey on the shoulder.

'Lord Peter wants to say something to you, my boy,' he said.

Comphrey started and went with him a little reluctantly, as it seemed. He was not looking very well.

'Mr Comphrey,' said Wimsey, 'I fancy these are some of your property.' He held out the palm of his hand, in which rested twenty-two fine, small-headed pins.

'Ingenious,' said Wimsey, 'but something less ingenious would have served his turn better. It was very unlucky, Sir Septimus, that you should have mentioned the pearls when you did. Of course, he hoped that the loss wouldn't be discovered till we'd chucked guessing games and taken to "Hide-and-Seek". Then the pearls might have been anywhere in the house, we shouldn't have locked the drawing-room door, and he could have recovered them at his leisure. He had had this possibility in his mind when he came here, obviously, and that was why he brought the pins, and Miss Shale's taking off the necklace to play "Dumb Crambo" gave him his opportunity.

'He had spent Christmas here before, and knew perfectly well that "Animal, Vegetable and Mineral" would form part of the entertainment. He had only to gather up the necklace from the table when it came to his turn to retire, and he knew he could count on at least five minutes by himself while we were all arguing about the choice of a word. He had only to snip the pearls from the string with his pocket-scissors, burn the string in the grate, and fasten the pearls to the mistletoe with the fine pins. The mistletoe was hung on the chandelier, pretty high – it's a lofty room – but he could easily reach it by standing on the glass table, which wouldn't show footmarks, and it was almost certain that nobody would think of examining the mistletoe for extra berries. I shouldn't have thought of it myself if I hadn't found that pin which he had dropped. That gave me the idea that the pearls had been separated and the rest was easy. I took the pearls off the mistletoe last night – the clasp was there, too, pinned among the holly-leaves. Here they are. Comphrey must have got a nasty shock this morning. I knew he was our man when he suggested that the guests should tackle the decorations themselves and that he should do the back drawing-room – but I wish I had seen his face when he came to the mistletoe and found the pearls gone.'

'And you worked it all out when you found the pin?' said Sir Septimus.

'Yes; I knew then where the pearls had gone to.' 'But you never even looked at the mistletoe.' 'I saw it reflected in the black glass floor, and it struck me then how much the mistletoe berries looked like pearls.'

LANGSTON HUGHES

One Christmas Eve

Standing over the hot stove cooking supper, the colored maid, Arcie, was very tired. Between meals today, she had cleaned the whole house for the white family she worked for, getting ready for Christmas tomorrow. Now her back ached and her head felt faint from sheer fatigue. Well, she would be off in a little while, if only the Missus and her children would come on home to dinner. They were out shopping for more things for the tree which stood all ready, tinsel-hung and lovely in the living room, waiting for its candles to be lighted.

Arcie wished she could afford a tree for Joe. He'd never had one yet, and it's nice to have such things when you're little. Joe was five, going on six. Arcie, looking at the roast in the white folks' oven, wondered how much she could afford to spend tonight on toys for Joe. She only got seven dollars a week, and four of that went for her room and the landlady's daily looking after Joe while Arcie was at work.

'Lord, it's more'n a notion raisin' a child,' she thought.

She looked at the clock on the kitchen table. After seven. What made white folks so inconsiderate, she wondered. Why didn't they come on home here to supper? They knew she wanted to get off before all the stores closed. She wouldn't have time to buy Joe nothin' if they didn't hurry. And her landlady probably wanting to go out and shop, too, and not be bothered with little Joe.

'Doggone it!' Arcie said to herself. 'If I just had my money, I might leave the supper on the stove for 'em. I just got to get to the stores fo' they close.' But she hadn't been paid for the week yet. The Missus had promised to pay her Christmas Eve, a day or so ahead of time.

Arcie heard a door slam and talking and laughter in the front of the

103

house. She went in and saw the Missus and her kids shaking snow off their coats.

'Umm-m! It's swell for Christmas Eve,' one of the kids said to Arcie. 'It's snowin' like the deuce, and Mother came near driving through a stop light. Can't hardly see for the snow. It's swell!'

'Supper's ready,' Arcie said. She was thinking how her shoes weren't very good for walking in snow.

It seemed like the white folks took as long as they could to eat that evening. While Arcie was washing dishes, the Missus came out with her money.

'Arcie,' the Missus said, 'I'm so sorry, but would you mind if I just gave you five dollars tonight? The children have made me run short of change, buying presents and all.'

'I'd like to have seven,' Arcie said. 'I needs it.'

'Well, I just haven't got seven,' the Missus said. 'I didn't know you'd want all your money before the end of the week, anyhow. I just haven't got it to spare.'

Arcie took five. Coming out of the hot kitchen, she wrapped up as well as she could and hurried by the house where she roomed to get little Joe. At least he could look at the Christmas trees in the windows downtown.

The landlady, a big light yellow woman, was in a bad humor. She said to Arcie, 'I thought you was comin' home early and get this child. I guess you know I want to go out, too, once in a while.'

Arcie didn't say anything, for if she had, she knew the landlady would probably throw it up to her that she wasn't getting paid to look after a child both night and day.

'Come on, Joe,' Arcie said to her son, 'Let's us go in the street.'

'I hears they got a Santa Claus downtown,' Joe said, wriggling into his worn little coat. 'I want to see him.'

'Don't know 'bout that,' his mother said, 'But hurry up and get your rubbers on. Stores'll be closed directly.'

It was six or eight blocks downtown. They trudged along through the falling snow, both of them a little cold. But the snow was pretty!

The main street was hung with bright red and blue lights. In front of the City Hall there was a Christmas tree – but it didn't have no presents on it, only lights. In the store windows there were lots of toys – for sale.

Joe kept on saying, 'Mama, I want . . .'

But Mama kept walking ahead. It was nearly ten, when the stores were due to close, and Arcie wanted to get Joe some cheap gloves and something to keep him warm, as well as a toy or two. She thought she might come across a rummage sale where they had children's clothes. And in the ten-cent store, she could get some toys.

'O-oo! Lookee . . . ,' little Joe kept saying, and pointing at things in the windows. How warm and pretty the lights were, and the shops, and the electric signs through the snow.

It took Arcie more than a dollar to get Joe's mittens and things he needed. In the A&P Arcie bought a big box of hard candies for 49 cents. And then she guided Joe through the crowd on the street until they came to the dime store. Near the ten-cent store they passed a moving picture theater. Joe said he wanted to go in and see the movies.

Arcie said, 'Ump-un! No, child. This ain't Baltimore where they have shows for colored, too. In these here small towns, they don't let colored folks in. We can't go in there.'

'Oh,' said little Joe.

In the ten-cent store, there was an awful crowd. Arcie told Joe to stand outside and wait for her. Keeping hold of him in the crowded store would be a job. Besides she didn't want him to see what toys she was buying. They were to be a surprise from Santa Claus tomorrow.

Little Joe stood outside the ten-cent store in the light, and the snow, and people passing. Gee, Christmas was pretty. All tinsel and stars and cotton. And Santa Claus a-coming from somewhere, dropping things in stockings. And all the people in the streets were carrying things, and the kids looked happy.

But Joe soon got tired of just standing and thinking and waiting in front of the ten-cent store. There were so many things to look at in the other windows. He moved along up the block a little, and then a little more, walking and looking. In fact, he moved until he came to the picture show.

In the lobby of the moving picture show, behind the plate glass doors, it was all warm and glowing and awful pretty. Joe stood looking in, and as he looked his eyes began to make out, in there blazing beneath holly and colored streamers and the electric stars of the lobby, a marvelous

Christmas tree. A group of children and grown-ups, white, of course, were standing around a big man in red beside the tree. Or was it a man? Little Joe's eyes opened wide. No, it was not a man at all. It was Santa Claus!

Little Joe pushed open one of the glass doors and ran into the lobby of the white moving picture show. Little Joe went right through the crowd and up to where he could get a good look at Santa Claus. And Santa Claus was giving away gifts, little presents for children, little boxes of animal crackers and stick-candy canes. And behind him on the tree was a big sign (which little Joe didn't know how to read). It said, to those who understood, Merry Christmas from Santa Claus to our young patrons. Around the lobby, other signs said, When you come out of the show stop with your children and see our Santa Claus. And another announced, Gem Theater makes its customers happy – see our Santa.

And there was Santa Claus in a red suit and a white beard all sprinkled with tinsel snow. Around him were rattles and drums and rocking horses which he was not giving away. But the signs on them said (could little Joe have read) that they would be presented from the stage on Christmas Day to the holders of lucky numbers. Tonight, Santa Claus was only giving away candy, and stick-candy canes, and animal crackers to the kids.

Joe would have liked terribly to have a stick-candy cane. He came a little closer to Santa Claus. He was right in the front of the crowd. And then Santa Claus saw Joe.

Why is it that lots of white people always grin when they see a Negro child? Santa Claus grinned. Everybody else grinned, too, looking at little black Joe – who had no business in the lobby of a white theater. Then Santa Claus stooped down and slyly picked up one of his lucky number rattles, a great big loud tin-pan rattle like they use in cabarets. And he shook it fiercely right at Joe. That was funny. The white people laughed, kids and all. But little Joe didn't laugh. He was scared. To the shaking of the big rattle, he turned and fled out of the warm lobby of the theater, out into the street where the snow was and the people. Frightened by laughter, he had begun to cry. He went looking for his mama. In his heart he never thought Santa Claus shook great rattles at children like that – and then laughed.

In the crowd on the street he went the wrong way. He couldn't find the ten-cent store or his mother. There were too many people, all white people, moving like white shadows in the snow, a world of white people.

It seemed to Joe an awfully long time till he suddenly saw Arcie, dark and worried-looking, cut across the side-walk through the passing crowd and grab him. Although her arms were full of packages, she still managed with one free hand to shake him until his teeth rattled.

'Why didn't you stand there where I left you?' Arcie demanded loudly. 'Tired as I am, I got to run all over the streets in the night lookin' for you. I'm a great mind to wear you out.'

When little Joe got his breath back, on the way home, he told his mama he had been in the moving picture show.

'But Santa Claus didn't give me nothin',' Joe said tearfully. 'He made a big noise at me and I runned out.'

'Serves you right,' said Arcie, trudging through the snow. 'You had no business in there. I told you to stay where I left you.'

'But I seed Santa Claus in there,' little Joe said, 'so I went in.'

'Huh! That wasn't no Santa Claus,' Arcie explained. 'If it was, he wouldn't a-treated you like that. That's a theater for white folks – I told you once – and he's just a old white man.'

'Oh . . .' said little Joe.

MÁRIO DE ANDRADE

The Christmas Turkey

Translated by Gregory Rabassa

Our first family Christmas after the death of my father five months earlier had decisive consequences for family happiness. We hadn't always been happy in a family way, in that very abstract meaning of happiness: honorable people, no crimes, a home without internal strife or serious economic difficulties. But owing mainly to the gray nature of my father, a creature devoid of any lyricism, exemplary in his incapacity, well bedded down in mediocrity, we'd never been able to take full advantage of life, of the pleasures of material happiness, a good wine, a vacation at a resort, getting a refrigerator, things like that. My father had been one of those people who sought the good in a mistaken way, an almost full-blooded dramatic killjoy.

My father died, and we were all very sad, etc. As we were getting close to Christmas I still couldn't get that obstructive memory of the dead man out of my mind. He still seemed to have systematized the obligation of a mournful memory at every meal, in the most insignificant act of the family. Once, when I suggested to Mama the idea of going to see a movie, the result was tears. Where had I ever heard of such a thing as going to the movies during a period of deep mourning! Grief was already being cultivated for appearances and I, who'd only liked my father according to the rules, more out of filial instinct than any spontaneous love, saw myself getting to the point of hating the good dead man.

The reason for my having been born most certainly, yes, spontaneously, was the idea of performing one of my so-called crazy things. That had been, furthermore and from a very early age, my splendid victory over the family environment. From an early age, from the time of high school, when I managed to get failing grades every year; from the hidden kiss with a cousin at the age of ten, caught by Tia Velha, a detestable old aunt; and most of all since the time of the lessons I gave or received, I don't know which, with a servant girl of relatives: it got me imprisonment at home and within the vast array of relatives the conciliatory reputation of a 'nut'. 'He's crazy, poor thing!' they would say. My parents would speak with a certain condescending sadness; the rest of my relatives found an example for their children and probably had that pleasure of those who've convinced themselves of a certain superiority. There were no loonies among their children. Well, that was my salvation, that reputation. I did everything that life laid before me, and my being demanded that it be done with integrity. And they let me do it all because I was crazy, poor thing. The result of that was an existence without complexes, and I can't make one single complaint about it.

Christmas dinner had always been a custom in the family. A cheap dinner, as you've probably guessed: a dinner after the likes of my father, chestnuts, figs, raisins, after midnight mass. Stuffed with walnuts and almonds (the way we three children fought over the nutcrackers . . .), stuffed with chestnuts and monotony, we would embrace and go to bed. It was remembering it all that caused me to break out with one of my 'crazy things'.

'Well, I want to eat some turkey this Christmas.'

It was one of those shocks that are impossible to imagine. Immediately my saintly single aunt who lived with us gave notice that we couldn't invite anyone because of the mourning.

'But, who said anything about inviting anyone? That mania . . . When did we ever eat turkey in our lifetime? Turkey in this house is a party dish, all those devilish relatives come . . .'

'Don't talk like that, my son . . .'

'Well, I am talking like that, all right?'

And I unloaded my icy indifference concerning our infinite relatives who say they're the descendants of pioneers; what do I care? It was precisely the moment to develop my crazy, poor-thing theory; I couldn't let the opportunity slip by. I soaked myself in great tenderness for Mama and Aunty, my two mothers, three with my sister, the three mothers who always made my life a divine thing. It had always been like that: someone's birthday would come along and only then would they cook a turkey in that house. Turkey was a party dish: a whole stinking bunch of relatives, already prepared by tradition, would invade the house because of the turkey, the pastries and the sweets. My three mothers, three days before, no longer were aware of anything else in life except working, working in the preparation of sweetmeats and delicacies, exquisitely made. The relatives would devour everything and still carry off little packages for the ones who had been unable to come. My three mothers could barely get through, they were so exhausted. Only at its funeral the next day were Mama and Aunty then able to taste a slice of turkey leg, vague, dark, lost in the midst of the white rice. And Mama was the one who served, keeping everything for the old man and the children. No one really knew what turkey was like in our house; turkey meant party leftovers.

No, there'd be no guests; it was a turkey for us, five people. And it would be served with two kinds of manioc stuffing, the fatty kind with the giblets and the dry kind all golden with lots of butter. I only wanted to fill my gullet with the fatty stuffing, to which we had to add black plums, walnuts and a glass of sherry, as I'd learned at Rose's house; we went around together a lot. Naturally I omitted telling where I'd learned the recipe, but they all suspected. And they sat there afterward with that look of smoke, as if incense was being wafted around as if it were a temptation of the Devil to enjoy such a tasty recipe. And ice-cold beer, I guaranteed that, almost shouting. It's true that with my 'tastes', quite refined now away from home, I'd first thought of a good wine, a hundred percent French, but a tender feeling for Mama overcame the nut. Mama adored beer.

When I finished outlining my plans, I took good note of how very happy they were with a wild desire to follow along with the madness, but they all let themselves imagine that I alone was the only person who was wanting all that and it was an easy way to push them past me to . . . the guilt of their huge desires. They smiled, looking at one another, timid as distraught doves until my sister brought out the general feeling:

'He really is crazy!'

The turkey was bought, the turkey was cooked, etc. And after a poorly sung midnight mass we had our most delightful Christmas. It was funny: since I remembered that I was finally going to make Mama eat turkey, I couldn't do anything else those days except think about her, feel tenderness toward her, love my adorable little old lady. And my brother and sister were also caught up in the same fervent rhythm of love, all dominated by the new happiness that the turkey was giving the family. So that still covering up I very calmly watched Mama cutting the whole breast of the turkey. A moment later she paused, with strips from one side of the bird's breast, unable to resist those laws of frugality that had always held her prisoner in a meaningless near-poverty.

'No, ma'am, the whole piece! I could eat it all myself!'

It was a lie. Family love was burning so brightly in me that I was incapable of eating even a little bit in order for the other four to eat too much. And the others' tempo was the same. That turkey, eaten all by ourselves, was making each one rediscover what daily routine had completely smothered: love, the love of a mother, the love of children. God forgive me, but I'm thinking about Jesus . . . In that modest middle-class house a miracle worthy of a Christmas of God was taking place. The turkey's breast had been reduced completely to wide slices.

'I'll serve!'

'He really is crazy!' Because why should I serve since Mama always served in that house? In the midst of laughter the big full plates were passed to me and I began a heroic distribution while I told my brother to pour the beer. I immediately noticed an admirable piece of 'bark', skin full of fat, and I put it on the plate. Then some broad strips of white meat. Mama's voice, turning stern, cut through the anxious space in which everyone was aspiring for a particular part of the turkey:

'Don't forget your brother and sister, Juca!'

When would she realize, poor thing, that it was her plate, Mother's, that of my poor mistreated friend, who knew about Rose, about my crimes, to whom I only remembered telling things that made her suffer! The plate was sublime.

'Mama, this plate is for you! No! Don't pass it on, no!'

That was when she couldn't take any more of such commotion and began to cry. My aunt, too, perceiving that the next sublime plate would be hers, joined in the refrain of tears. And my sister, who could never see tears without opening her faucet, enlarged the area of weeping also. Then I began to say a lot of wild things so I wouldn't cry, too, I was nineteen . . . What kind of a family is this that looks at a turkey and cries? Things like that. They all made an effort to smile, but happiness had become impossible now. It was because the weeping, by association, had brought up the undesirable image of my dead father. My father, with his gray look, had come to ruin our Christmas once and for all. I was angry.

Well, we started eating in silence, mournfully, and the turkey was perfect. The soft meat, with such a delicate texture, was floating gently amidst the tastes of the stuffings and the ham, wounded from time to time, disturbed and redesired by the intervention of a black plum or the petulant annoyance of a walnut. But Papa, sitting there, gigantic, incomplete, a censure, a wound, an incapacity. And the turkey was so tasty with Mama's finally learning that turkey was a morsel worthy of the newborn Christ Child.

A dull battle began between the turkey and Papa's image. I thought that by praising the turkey I could help it in the fight and, naturally, I was on the turkey's side. But the dead have slippery and very hypocritical ways of winning: no sooner had I praised the turkey than Papa's image was victorious, insupportably obstructive.

'The only thing missing is your father . . .'

I wasn't eating. I couldn't enjoy that perfect turkey because I was so interested in that battle between the two dead creatures. I got to hate Papa. And I don't know what stroke of genius suddenly turned me political and hypocritical. At that moment, which today seems to me decisive to our family, I apparently took the side of my father. I pretended, sadly:

'That's right . . . But Papa, who loved us so much, who died from working so hard for us, Papa, up there in heaven, must be happy . . . (I hesitated, but I decided not to mention the turkey any more) happy to see all of us gathered here together as a family.'

And they all began, very calmly, to talk about Papa. His image grew smaller and smaller and became a bright little star in the sky. Now they were all eating the turkey sensually, because Papa had been very good, had always sacrificed himself for us, had been a saint who 'you, my children, will never be able to repay what you owe your father,' a saint. Papa had become a saint, a pleasant thing to contemplate, a steadfast little star in the sky. He wasn't harming anyone any more; he was only the object of sweet contemplation. The only dead one there was the turkey, dominating, completely victorious.

My mother, my aunt, all of us were overflowing with happiness. I was going to write 'gustatory happiness', but it wasn't just that. It was happiness with a capital *H*, a love for all, a forgetting of relationships that were a distraction of the great family love. And it was, I know it was, that first turkey ever eaten in the bosom of the family, the beginning of a new love, re-established, more complete, richer, and more inventive, more satisfied and aware of itself. A family happiness was born of that moment for us that – I'm not being an exclusionist – although there may be one as great, a more intense one than ours is impossible for me to imagine.

Mama ate so much turkey that I thought for a moment that it might do her harm. But then I thought: Oh, let her alone; even if it kills her, for once in her life at least she'll really have eaten turkey!

Such a lack of selfishness had been given to me by our infinite love . . . Afterwards there were light grapes and some cookies that in my country carry the name of *bem-casados*, the happily married. But not even that dangerous name was associated with the memory of my father, whom the turkey had already converted into a dignitary, something secure, a cult for contemplation.

We got up from the table. It was almost two o'clock, and all of us were merry, staggering from two bottles of beer. We all went off to sleep, to sleep or toss in bed, it didn't really matter which, because happy insomnia is good. The devilish part is that Rose, Catholic before she was Rose, had promised to wait for me with a bottle of champagne. In order to get out I lied, said that I was going to a male friend's party. I kissed Mama, winked at her as a way of letting her know where I was going and making her suffer a little. I kissed the two other women without winking. And now for Rose!

ELIZABETH BOWEN
Green Holly

Mr Rankstock entered the room with a dragging tread: nobody looked up or took any notice. With a muted groan, he dropped into an armchair – out of which he shot with a sharp yelp. He searched the seat of the chair, and extracted something. '*Your* holly, I think, Miss Bates,' he said, holding it out to her.

Miss Bates took a second or two to look up from her magazine. 'What?' she said. 'Oh, it must have fallen down from that picture. Put it back, please; we haven't got very much.'

'I regret,' interposed Mr Winterslow, 'that we have any: it makes scratchy noises against the walls.'

'It is seasonable,' said Miss Bates firmly.

'You didn't do this to us last Christmas.'

'Last Christmas,' she said, 'I had Christmas leave. This year there seems to be none with berries: the birds have eaten them. If there were not a draught, the leaves would not scratch the walls. I cannot control the forces of nature, can I?'

'How should I know?' said Mr Rankstock, lighting his pipe.

These three by now felt that, like Chevalier and his Old Dutch, they had been together for forty years: and to them it did seem a year too much. Actually, their confinement dated from 1940. They were Experts – in what, the Censor would not permit me to say. They were accounted for by their friends in London as 'being somewhere off in the country, nobody knows where, doing something frightfully hush-hush, nobody knows what'. That is, they were accounted for in this manner if there were still anybody who still cared to ask; but on the whole they had dropped out of human memory. Their reappearances in their former circles were infrequent, ghostly and unsuccessful: their friends could hardly disguise their pity, and for their own part they had not a word to say. They had come to prefer to spend leaves with their families, who at least showed a flattering pleasure in their importance.

This Christmas, it so worked out that there was no question of leave for Mr Rankstock, Mr Winterslow or Miss Bates: with four others (now playing or watching ping-pong in the next room) they composed in their high-grade way a skeleton staff. It may be wondered why, after years of proximity, they should continue to address one another so formally. They did not continue; they had begun again; in the matter of appellations, as in that of intimacy, they had by now, in fact by some time ago, completed the full circle. For some months, they could not recall in which year, Miss Bates had been engaged to Mr Winterslow; before that, she had been extremely friendly with Mr Rankstock. Mr Rankstock's deviation towards one Carla (now at her ping-pong in the next room) had been totally uninteresting to everybody; including, apparently, himself. If the war lasted, Carla might next year be called Miss Tongue; at present, Miss Bates was foremost in keeping her in her place by going on addressing her by her Christian name.

If this felt like their fortieth Christmas in each other's society, it was their first in these particular quarters. You would not have thought, as Mr Rankstock said, that one country house could be much worse than any other; but this had proved, and was still proving, untrue. The Army, for reasons it failed to justify, wanted the house they had been in since 1940; so they – lock, stock and barrel and files and all – had been bundled into another one, six miles away. Since the move, tentative exploration (for they were none of them walkers) had established that they were now surrounded by rather more mud but fewer trees. What they did know was, their already sufficient distance from the market town with its bars and movies had now been added to by six miles. On the other side of their new home, which was called Mopsam Grange, there appeared to be nothing; unless, as Miss Bates suggested, swineherds, keeping their swine. Mopsam village contained villagers, evacuees, a church, a public-house on whose never-open door was chalked 'No Beer, No Matches, No Teas Served', and a vicar. The vicar had sent up a nice note, saying he was not clear whether security regulations would allow him to call; and the doctor had been up once to lance one of Carla's boils.

Mopsam Grange was neither old or new. It replaced – unnecessarily, they all felt – a house on this site that had been burned down. It had a Gothic porch and gables, french windows, bow windows, a conservatory, a veranda, a hall which, puce-and-buff tiled and pitch-pine-panelled, rose to a gallery: in fact, every advantage. Jackdaws fidgeted in its many chimneys – for it had, till the war, stood empty: one had not to ask why. The hot-water system made what Carla called rude noises, and was capricious in its supplies to the (only) two mahogany-rimmed baths. The electric light ran from a plant in the yard; if the batteries were not kept charged the light turned brown.

The three now sat in the drawing-room, on whose walls, mirrors and fitments, long since removed, left traces. There were, however, some pictures: General Montgomery (who had just shed his holly) and some Landseer engravings that had been found in an attic. Three electric bulbs, naked, shed light manfully; and in the grate the coal fire was doing far from badly. Miss Bates rose and stood twiddling the bit of holly. 'Something,' she said, 'has got to be done about this.' Mr Winterslow and Mr Rankstock, the latter sucking in his pipe, sank lower, between their shoulder-blades, in their respective armchairs. Miss Bates, having drawn a breath, took a running jump at a table, which she propelled across the floor with a grating sound. *'Achtung!'* she shouted, at Mr Rankstock, who, with an oath, withdrew his chair from her route. Having got the table under General Montgomery, Miss Bates – with a display of long, slender leg, clad in ribbed scarlet sports stockings, that was of interest to no one – mounted it, then proceeded to tuck the holly back into position over the General's frame. Meanwhile, Mr Winterslow, choosing his moment, stealthily reached across her empty chair and possessed himself of her magazine.

What a hope! – Miss Bates was known to have eyes all the way down her spine. 'Damn you, Mr Winterslow,' she said, 'put that down! Mr Rankstock, interfere with Mr Winterslow: Mr Winterslow has taken my magazine!' She ran up and down the table like something in a cage; Mr Rankstock removed his pipe from his mouth, dropped his head back, gazed up and said: 'Gad, Miss Bates; you look fine . . .'

'It's a pretty *old* magazine,' murmured Mr Winterslow, flicking the pages over.

'Well, *you're* pretty old,' she said. 'I hope Carla gets you!'

'Oh, I can do better, thank you; I've got a ghost.'

This confidence, however, was cut off by Mr Rankstock's having burst into song. Holding his pipe at arm's length, rocking on his bottom in his armchair, he led them:

> '"Heigh-ho! sing Heigh-ho! unto the green holly:
> Most friendship is feigning, most loving mere folly –"'

'"*Mere folly, mere folly*,"' contributed Mr Winterslow, picking up, joining in. Both sang:

> '"*Then, heigh ho, the holly!*
> *This life is most jolly.*"'

'Now – *all*!' said Mr Rankstock, jerking his pipe at Miss Bates. So all three went through it once more, with degrees of passion: Miss Bates, when others desisted, being left singing 'Heigh-ho! sing heigh-ho! sing –' all by herself. Next door, the ping-pong came to an awe-struck stop. 'At any rate,' said Mr Rankstock, 'we all like Shakespeare.' Miss Bates, whose intelligence, like her singing, tonight seemed some way at the tail of the hunt, looked blank, began to get off the table, and said, 'But I thought that was a Christmas carol?'

Her companions shrugged and glanced at each other. Having taken her magazine away from Mr Winterslow, she was once more settling down to it when she seemed struck. 'What was that you said, about you had got a ghost?'

Mr Winterslow looked down his nose. 'At this early stage, I don't like to say very much. In fact, on the whole, forget it; if you don't mind –'

'Look,' Mr Rankstock said, 'if you've started seeing things –'

'I am only sorry,' his colleague said, 'that I've spoke.'

'Oh no, you're not,' said Miss Bates, 'and we'd better know. Just what *is* fishy about this Grange?'

'There is nothing "fishy",' said Mr Winterslow in a fastidious tone. It was hard, indeed, to tell from his manner whether he did or did not regret having made a start. He had reddened – but not, perhaps, wholly painfully – his eyes, now fixed on the fire, were at once bright and vacant; with unheeding, fumbling movements he got out a cigarette, lit it and dropped the match on the floor, to slowly burn one more hole in the fibre mat. Gripping the cigarette between tense lips, he first flung his arms out, as though casting off a cloak; then pressed both hands, clasped firmly, to the nerve-centre in the nape of his neck, as though to contain the sensation there. 'She was marvellous,' he brought out – 'what I could see of her.'

'Don't talk with your cigarette in your mouth,' Miss Bates said. '– Young?'

'Adorably, not so very. At the same time, quite – oh well, you know what I mean.'

'Uh-huh,' said Miss Bates. 'And wearing –?'

'I am certain she had a feather boa.'

'You mean,' Mr Rankstock said, 'that this brushed your face?'

'And when and where did this happen?' said Miss Bates with legal coldness.

Cross-examination, clearly, became more and more repugnant to Mr Winterslow in his present mood. He shut his eyes, sighed bitterly, heaved himself from his chair, said: 'Oh, well –' and stood indecisively looking towards the door. 'Don't let us keep you,' said Miss Bates. 'But one thing I don't see is: if you're being fed with beautiful thoughts, why you wanted to keep on taking my magazine?'

'I wanted to be distracted.'

'?'

'There *are* moments when I don't quite know where I am.'

'You surprise me,' said Mr Rankstock. – 'Good *God*, man, what is the matter?' For Mr Winterslow, like a man being swooped around by a bat, was revolving, staring from place to place high up round the walls of the gaunt, lit room. Miss Bates observed: 'Well, now we *have* started something.' Mr Rankstock, considerably kinder, said: 'That is only Miss Bates's holly, flittering in the wind.'

Mr Winterslow gulped. He walked to the inch of mirror propped on the mantelpiece and, as nonchalantly as possible, straightened his tie. Having done this, he said: 'But there isn't a wind tonight.'

The ghost hesitated in the familiar corridor. Her visibleness, even on Christmas Eve, was not under her own control; and now she had fallen in love again her dependence upon it began to dissolve in patches. This was a concentration of every feeling of the woman prepared to sail downstairs *en grande tenue*. Flamboyance and agitation were both present. But between these, because of her years of death, there cut an extreme anxiety: it was not merely a matter of, how was she? but of, *was* she – tonight – at all? Death had left her to be her own mirror; for into no other was she able to see.

For tonight, she had discarded the feather boa; it had been dropped into the limbo that was her wardrobe now. Her shoulders, she knew, were bare. Round their bareness shimmered a thousand evenings. Her own person haunted her – above her forehead, the crisped springy weight of her pompadour; round her feet the frou-frou of her skirts on a thick carpet; in her nostrils the scent from her corsage; up and down her forearm the glittery slipping of bracelets warmed by her own blood. It is the haunted who haunt.

There were lights in the house again. She had heard laughter, and there had been singing. From those few dim lights and untrue notes her senses, after their starvation, set going the whole old grand opera. She smiled, and moved down the corridor to the gallery, where she stood looking down into the hall. The tiles of the hall floor were as pretty as ever, as cold as ever, and bore, as always on Christmas Eve, the trickling pattern of dark blood. The figure of the man with the side of his head blown out lay as always, one foot just touching the lowest step of the stairs. It was too bad. She had been silly, but it could not be helped. They should not have shut her up in the country. How could she not make hay while the sun shone? The year round, no man except her husband, his uninteresting jealousy, his dull passion. Then, at Christmas, so many men that one did not know where to turn. The ghost, leaning further over the gallery, pouted down at the suicide. She said: 'You should have let me explain.' The man made no answer: he never had.

Behind a door somewhere downstairs, a racket was going on: the house sounded funny, there were no carpets. The morning-room door was flung open and four flushed people, headed by a young woman, charged out. They clattered across the man and the trickling pattern as though there were nothing there but the tiles. In the morning-room she saw one small white ball trembling to stillness upon the floor. As the people rushed the stairs and fought for place in the gallery the ghost drew back – a purest act of repugnance, for this was not necessary. The young woman, to one of whose temples was strapped a cotton-wool pad, held her place and disappeared round a corner exulting: '*My* bath, *my* bath!' 'Then may you freeze in it, Carla!' returned the scrawniest of the defeated ones. The words pierced the ghost, who trembled – they did not know!

Who were they? She did not ask. She did not care. She never had been inquisitive: information had bored her. Her schooled lips had framed one set of questions, her eyes a consuming other. Now the mills of death with their catching wheels had stripped her of semblance, cast her forth on an everlasting holiday from pretence. She was left with – nay, had become – her obsession. Thus is it to be a ghost. The ghost fixed her eyes on the other, the drawing-room door. He had gone in there. He would have to come out again.

The handle turned; the door opened; Winterslow came out. He shut the door behind him, with the sedulous slowness of an uncertain man. He had been humming, and now, squaring his shoulders, began to sing, '. . .*Mere folly, mere folly* –' as he crossed the hall towards the foot of the staircase, obstinately never raising his eyes. 'So it is you,' breathed the ghost, with unheard softness. She gathered about her, with a gesture not less proud for being tormentedly uncertain, the total of her visibility – was it possible diamonds should not glitter now, on her rising-and-falling breast – and swept from the gallery to the head of the stairs.

Winterslow shivered violently, and looked up. He licked his lips. He said: 'This cannot go on.'

The ghost's eyes, with tender impartiality and mockery, from above swept Winterslow's face. The hair receding, the furrowed forehead, the tired sag of the jowl, the strain-reddened eyelids, the blue-shaved chin – nothing was lost on her, nothing broke the spell. With untroubled wonder she saw his handwoven tie, his coat pockets shapeless as saddle-bags, the bulging knees of his flannel trousers. Wonder went up in rhapsody: so much chaff in the fire. She never had had illusions: *the* illusion was all. Lovers cannot be choosers. He'd do. He would have to do. – 'I know!' she agreed, with rapture, casting her hands together. 'We are mad – you and I. Oh, what is going to happen? I entreat you to leave this house tonight!'

Winterslow, in a dank, unresounding voice, said: 'And anyhow, what made you pick on me?'

'It's Kismet,' wailed the ghost zestfully. 'Why did you have to come here? Why you? I had been so peaceful, just like a little girl. People spoke of love, but I never knew what they meant. Oh, I could wish we had never met, you and I!'

Winterslow said: 'I have been here for three months; we have all of us been here, as a matter of fact. Why all this all of a sudden?'

She said: 'There's a Christmas Eve party, isn't there, going on? One Christmas Eve party, there was a terrible accident. Oh, comfort me! No one has understood. – Don't stand *there*; I can't bear it – not just *there*!'

Winterslow, whether he heard or not, cast a scared glance down at his feet, which were in slippers, then shifted a pace or two to the left. 'Let me up,' he said wildly. 'I tell you, I want my spectacles! I just want to get my spectacles. Let me by!'

'*Let* you up!' the ghost marvelled. 'But I am only waiting . . .'

She was more than waiting: she set up a sort of suction, an icy indrawing draught. Nor was this wholly psychic, for an isolated holly leaf of Miss Bates's, dropped at a turn of the staircase, twitched. And not, you could think, by chance did the electric light choose this moment for one of its brown fade-outs: gradually, the scene – the hall, the stairs and the gallery – faded under this fog-dark but glass-clear veil of hallucination. The feet of Winterslow, under remote control, began with knocking unsureness to mount the stairs. At their turn he staggered, steadied himself, and then stamped derisively upon the holly leaf. 'Bah,' he neighed – '*spectacles*!'

By the ghost now putting out everything, not a word could be dared. 'Where are you?'

Weakly, her dress rustled, three steps down: the rings on her hand knocked weakly over the panelling. 'Here, oh here,' she sobbed. 'Where I was before . . .'

'Hell,' said Miss Bates, who had opened the drawing-room door and was looking resentfully round the hall. 'This electric light.'

Mr Rankstock, from inside the drawing-room, said: 'Find the man.'

'The man has gone to the village. Mr Rankstock, if *you* were half a man –. Mr Winterslow, what are you doing, kneeling down on the stairs? Have you come over funny? Really, this is the end.'

At the other side of a baize door, one of the installations began ringing. 'Mr Rankstock,' Miss Bates yelled implacably, 'yours, this time.' Mr Rankstock, with an expression of hatred, whipped out a pencil and pad and shambled across the hall. Under cover of this Mr Winterslow pushed himself upright, brushed his knees and began to descend the stairs, to confront his colleague's narrow but not unkind look. Weeks of exile from any hairdresser had driven Miss Bates to the Alice-in-Wonderland style: her snood, tied at the top, was now thrust back, adding inches to her pale, polished brow. Nicotine stained the fingers she closed upon Mr Winterslow's elbow, propelling him back to the drawing-room. 'There is always drink,' she said. 'Come along.'

He said hopelessly: 'If you mean the bottle between the filing cabinets, I finished that when I had to work last night. – Look here, Miss Bates, why should she have picked on *me*?'

'It has been broken off, then?' said Miss Bates. 'I'm sorry for you, but I don't like your tone. I resent your attitude to my sex. For that matter, why did you pick on her? Romantic, nostalgic Blue-Danube-fixated – hein? There's Carla, an understanding girl, unselfish, getting over her boils; there are Avice and Lettice, due back on Boxing Day. There is me, as you have ceased to observe. But oh dear no; *we* do not trail feather boas –'

'– She only wore that in the afternoon.'

'Now let me tell you something,' said Miss Bates. 'When I opened the door, just now, to have a look at the lights, what do you think *I* first saw there in the hall?'

'Me,' replied Mr Winterslow, with returning assurance.

'O-*oh* no; oh indeed no,' said Miss Bates. 'You – why should I think twice of that, if you *were* striking attitudes on the stairs? You? – no, I saw your enchanting inverse. Extended, and it is true stone dead, I saw the man of my dreams. From his attitude, it was clear he had died for love. There were three pearl studs in his boiled shirt, and his white tie must have been tied in heaven. And the hand that had dropped the pistol had dropped a white rose; it lay beside him brown and crushed from having been often kissed. The ideality of those kisses, for the last of which I arrived too late –' here Miss Bates beat her fist against the bow of her snood – 'will haunt, and by haunting satisfy me. The destruction of his features, before I saw them, made their former perfection certain, where I am concerned. – And here I am, left, left, left, to watch dust gather on Mr Rankstock and you; to watch – yes, I who saw in a flash the ink-black perfection of *his* tailoring – mildew form on those clothes that you never change; to remember how both of you had in common that way of blowing your noses before you kissed me. He had been deceived – hence the shot, hence the fall. But who was *she*, your feathered friend, to deceive him? Who could have deceived him more superbly than I? – *I* could be fatal,' moaned Miss Bates, pacing the drawing-room. '*I* could be fatal – only give me a break!'

'Well, I'm sorry,' said Mr Winterslow, 'but really, what can I do, or poor Rankstock do? We are just ourselves.'

'You put the thing in a nutshell,' said Miss Bates. 'Perhaps I could bear it if you just got your hairs cut.'

'If it comes to that, Miss Bates, you might get yours set.'

Mr Rankstock's re-entry into the drawing-room – this time with brisker step, for a nice little lot of new trouble was brewing up – synchronized with the fall of the piece of holly, again, from the General's frame to the Rankstock chair. This time he saw it in time. '*Your* holly, I think, Miss Bates,' he said, holding it out to her.

'We must put it back,' said Miss Bates. 'We haven't got very much.'

'I cannot see,' said Mr Winterslow, 'why we should have any. I don't see the point of holly without berries.'

'The birds have eaten them,' said Miss Bates. 'I cannot control the forces of nature, can I?'

'*Then heigh-ho! sing heigh-ho! –*' Mr Rankstock led off.

'Yes,' she said, 'let us have that pretty carol again.'

FRANK O'CONNOR
Christmas Morning

We were living up Blarney Lane, in Cork, at the time, in one of the little whitewashed cottages at the top, on the edge of the open country. It was a tiny house – a kitchen with two little bedrooms off it – and the kitchen door opened to the street. There were only the four of us – my parents, my brother Sonny, and myself. I suppose, at the time I'm speaking of, Sonny was six or seven and I was two years older. I never really liked that kid. He was the mother's pet; a proper little Mummy's darling, always racing after her to tell her what mischief I was up to. I really believe it was to spite me that he was so smart at his books. In a queer sort of way, he seemed to know that that was what the mother valued most, and you might say he spelled his way into her favour. 'Mummy,' he'd say, 'will I call Larry in for his t-e-a?' Or 'Mummy, the k-e-t-e-l is boiling.' And, of course, if he made a mistake, the mother would correct him, and next time he'd have it right and get stuffed up with conceit. 'Mummy,' he'd say, 'aren't I a good speller?' We could all be good spellers if we went on like that. Mind you, it wasn't that I was stupid, or anything of the kind, but somehow I was restless and I could never fix my mind on the one thing for long. I'd do the lessons for the year before or the lessons for the next year – anything except the ones I should be doing. And in the evenings I loved to get out to the Dempseys, the kids who lived in the house opposite and were the leaders of all the blackguarding that went on in the road. Not that I was a rough child, either. It was just that I liked excitement, and I never could see what it was in schooling attracted the mother.

'I declare to goodness, Larry,' she said once, catching me with my cap in my hand, 'you ought to be ashamed of yourself, with your baby brother better than you at reading.'

'Ah, I'll do it when I come back,' I said.

'The dear knows what'll become of you,' she said. 'If you'd only mind your lessons, you might be something worth while – an engineer or a clerk.'

' 'Tis all right, Mummy,' Sonny said. '*I'll* be a clerk.'

'I'm going to be a soldier,' I said.

'God help us!' my mother said. 'I'm afraid that's all you'll ever be fit for.' Sometimes, I used to think she was just a shade simple. As if a fellow could be anything better than a soldier!

And then it began to draw on to Christmas, with the days getting shorter and, coming on to dusk, the crowds getting bigger in the streets, and I began to think of all the things I might get from Santa Claus. The Dempseys said there was no Santa Claus and that it was only what your mother and father gave you, but the Dempseys were a rough class of children and you wouldn't expect Santa Claus to come to them anyway. I was scouting round for whatever information I could pick up about it from the mother. I wasn't much good at writing, but it struck me that if a letter would do any good, I wouldn't mind having a shot at one.

'Ah, I don't know will he come at all this year,' my mother said with a distracted air. 'He has enough to do looking after good little boys that mind their lessons, without bothering about the others.'

'He only comes to good spellers, Mummy,' Sonny said. 'Isn't that right?'

'He comes to any little child that does his best,' my mother said firmly, 'whether they're good spellers or not.'

Well, from then on I tried to do my best. God knows, I tried. It was hardly my fault if my teacher, Flogger Dawley, gave us sums we couldn't do, within four days of the holidays, and I had to play hooky with Peter Dempsey. It wasn't for the pleasure of it. December is no month for playing hooky, and most of our time was spent sheltering from the rain in a store on the quays. The only mistake we made was imagining that we could keep it up until the holidays without being noticed. Of course, Flogger Dawley noticed and sent home to know what was keeping me. When I came home the third day, my mother gave me a look she had never given me before and said, 'Your dinner is there.' She was too full to talk. When I tried to explain to her, she only said, 'Ah, you have no word.' It wasn't the fact that I'd been playing hooky so much as all the lies I'd told her. For two days, she didn't open her mouth to me, and still I couldn't see what attraction schooling had for her or why she wouldn't let me grow up like anybody else.

That evening, Sonny stood at the front door with his hands in his trousers pockets, shouting to the other kids so that he could be heard all over the road, 'Larry isn't allowed to go out. He played hooky with Peter Dempsey. Me mother isn't talking to him.' And at night, when we were in our bed, he kept at me. 'Santa Claus isn't bringing you anything this year.'

'He is,' I said.

'No,' Sonny said.

'Why isn't he?'

'Because you played hooky with Dempsey,' Sonny said. 'I wouldn't play with them Dempsey fellows. They're no class. They had the bobbies up at the house.'

'And how would Santa Claus know that I played hooky with Dempsey?' I asked.

'He'd know,' Sonny said. 'Mummy would tell him.'

'And how could Mummy tell him and he up at the North Pole? Poor Ireland, she's rearing them still! 'Tis easy seen you're only a baby,' I said.

'I'm not a baby,' Sonny said, 'and I can spell better than you, and Santa Claus won't bring you anything.'

'You'll see whether he will or not,' said I, letting on to be quite confident about it. But in my own heart I wasn't confident at all. You could never tell what powers those superhuman chaps would have of knowing what you were up to. And I had a bad conscience about skipping school. I had never seen the mother like that before.

I decided there was really only one thing for me to do, and that was see Santa Claus and have a talk with him myself. Being a man, he'd probably understand that a fellow wouldn't want to spend his whole life over old books, as the mother wanted me to. I was a good-looking kid, and when I liked, I had a way with me. I had only to smile nicely at one old gent on the Mall to get a penny off him, and I felt sure if only I could get Santa Claus alone, I could explain it all to his satisfaction and maybe get round him to give me something really worth while, like a model railway. I started practising staying awake at night, counting five hundred and then a thousand and trying to hear first eleven and then midnight from the clock tower in Shandon. I felt sure Santa Claus would appear by midnight on Christmas Eve, seeing that he'd be coming from the north and would have the whole of the south side of town to do before morning. In some ways, I was quite an enterprising and farsighted kid. The only trouble was the things I was enterprising about.

I was so wrapped up in those plans of mine that I never noticed what a hard time my mother was having of it. Sonny and I used to go downtown with her, and while she was in the grocery shop, we stood outside the toyshop in the North Main Street, arguing about what we'd like for Christmas.

At noon the day before Christmas, my father came home to dinner and handed my mother some money. She stood looking at it doubtfully and her face went white.

'Well?' he said, getting angry. 'What's wrong with that?'

'What's wrong with it?' she asked. 'On Christmas Eve?'

'Why?' he said, sticking his hands in his trousers pockets and thrusting his head forward with an ugly scowl. 'Do you think I get more because 'tis Christmas Eve?'

'Lord God!' she said, and raised her hand to her cheek. 'Not a bit of cake in the house, nor a candle, nor anything!'

'All right!' he shouted. 'How much will buy the cake?'

'Ah, for pity's sake!' she cried. 'Will you give me the money and not argue with me in front of the children? Do you think I'm going to leave them with nothing on the one day of the year?'

'Bad luck to you and your children!' he said. 'Am I to be slaving from one year's end to another just for you to be throwing my money away on toys? There!' He threw two silver coins on the table. 'That's all you're going to get, so you can make the best of it,' he said, as he went out the door.

'I suppose the publicans will get the rest,' she called after him.

In the afternoon, she went downtown, but she didn't take us with her. She came back with several parcels, and in one of them was the big red Christmas candle. We waited for my father to come home to his tea, but he didn't, so we had our own and a slice of cake for each of us, and then my mother put Sonny on the kitchen chair with the holy-water stoup before the window by him, so that he could sprinkle the candle, and after that he lit it, and she said, 'The Light of Heaven to our Souls.' I could see she was upset because my father wasn't there. When Sonny and I hung up our stockings at either side of the bed in our room and got into bed, he was still out.

Then began the hardest couple of hours I ever put in. I don't think I was ever so sleepy, but I knew if I went to sleep, my chances were done, so I kept myself awake by making speeches to say to Santa when he came. The speeches were different, according to the sort of chap he turned out to be. When I had said them all, I nudged Sonny and tried to get him to wake up and keep me company, but he lay like the dead and neither moved nor opened his eyes. I knew by the light under the kitchen door that my mother hadn't gone to bed. Eleven struck from Shandon, and shortly afterward I heard the latch of the front door raised very softly, but it was only my father coming home.

'Hullo, little girl,' he said in an oily tone, and then he began to giggle. 'What is keeping you up so late?'

'Do you want your supper?' my mother asked in a low voice.

'Ah, no, I had a bit of pig's cheek in Daneen's on my way home,' he replied. 'My goodness, is it as late as that? If I knew that, I'd have strolled up to the North Chapel for Midnight Mass. I'd like to hear the "Adeste" again. That's a hymn I'm very fond of, a most touching hymn.' And he began to sing falsetto, as if he were a ladies' choir:

> 'Adeste, fideles,
> Solus domus dagos . . .'

My father was very fond of Latin hymns, particularly when he had a drop in, but he could never get the words right. He just made them up as he went along, and for some reason which I could never understand, that drove my mother into a fury. This night she said, 'Oh, you disgust me,' and closed the bedroom door behind her.

My father gave a low, pleased laugh. Then I heard him strike a match to light his pipe, and for a couple of minutes he puffed it noisily, and then the light under the door dimmed and went out. From the dark kitchen, I suddenly heard his falsetto voice quavering emotionally:

'Dixi medearum
Tutum tonum tantum,
Venite, adoremus . . .'

I knew that the chorus bit of it was the only thing he had right, but in a queer sort of way it lulled me to sleep, as if I were listening to choirs of angels singing.

I woke, coming on to dawn, with the feeling that something shocking had happened. The whole house was still, and our little room looking out on the foot and a half of back yard was pitch-dark. It was only when you looked at the tiny square of window that you could see that all the purple was gone out of the sky. I jumped out of bed and felt my stocking, and I knew at once that the worst had happened. Santa Claus had come while I was asleep, and had gone away with an altogether false impression of me, because all he had left me was a book like a reading book folded up, a pen and pencil, and a tuppenny bag of sweets. For a while, I was too stunned by the catastrophe to be able to think of anything else. Then I began to wonder what that foxy boy, Sonny, had got. I went to his side of the bed and examined his stocking.

For all his spelling and sucking up, Sonny hadn't done much better, because apart from a bag of sweets about the same size as my own, all Santa had left him was a gun, one that fired a cork, and you could get it in any toyshop for sixpence. All the same, it was a gun, and a gun was better than an old book, any day of the week. The Dempseys had a gang, and the gang fought the Strawberry Lane kids and never let them play ball on our road. That gun, it struck me, would be quite useful to me in a lot of ways, while it would be lost on Sonny, who wouldn't be let play with the gang, even if he wanted to.

Then I got the inspiration, as it seemed to me, direct from Heaven. Suppose I took the gun and gave Sonny the book. He was fond of spelling, and a studious child like him could learn a lot of spelling out of a big book like mine. Sonny hadn't seen Santa any more than I had, and what he didn't know wouldn't trouble him. I wasn't doing the least harm to anyone; in fact, I was doing him a genuine good turn, if only he knew it. So I put the book, pen and pencil into Sonny's stocking and the gun into my own, and then I got back into bed again and fell fast asleep. As I say, in those days I had quite a lot of initiative.

It was Sonny who waked me, shaking me like mad to tell me that Santa Claus had come and look what he'd brought me – a gun! I let on to be very surprised and rather disappointed, and I made him show me the book and told him it was much better than what Santa had brought me. As I knew, that child was prepared to believe anything, and within a few minutes he wanted to rush in to the mother to show her what he'd got. That was my bad moment. After the way she had carried on the previous time, I didn't like telling her the lie, though I had the satisfaction of knowing that the only person who could contradict me was at that particular moment somewhere by the North Pole. The thought gave me confidence, and Sonny and myself stormed in to the bedroom and wakened my father and mother, shouting at the top of our voices, 'Oh, look! Look what Santa Claus brought!'

My mother opened her eyes and smiled, and then, as she saw the gun in my hand, her face changed suddenly. It was just as it had been the day I had come home from playing hooky, when she said, 'You have no word.'

'Larry,' she said, 'where did you get that?'

'Santa Claus left it in my stocking, Mummy,' I said, and tried to look hurt.

'You stole it from that poor child's stocking while he was asleep,' my mother said. 'Larry, Larry, how could you be so mean?'

'Whisht, whisht, whisht!' said my father testily. ''Tis Christmas morning.'

'Ah!' she cried, turning to him. ''Tis easy it comes to you. Do you think I want my son to grow up a thief and a liar?'

'Ah, what thief, woman?' he said. He was as cross if you interrupted him in his rare moods of benevolence as in his commoner ones, of meanness, and this one was exacerbated by the feeling of guilt for the previous evening. 'Can't you let the child alone? Here, Larry,' he said, putting out his hand to the little table by the bed. 'Here's sixpence for you and another for Sonny. Don't lose it, now.'

I looked at my mother and saw the horror still in her eyes, and at that moment I understood everything. I burst into tears, threw the popgun on the floor by the bed, and rushed out by the front door. It was before a soul on the road was awake. I ran up the lane behind the house into the field, and threw myself on my face and hands in the wet grass as the sun was rising.

In some queer way, I understood all the things that had been hidden from me before. I knew there was no Santa Claus flying over the rooftops with his reindeer and his red coat – there was only my mother trying to scrape together a few pence from the housekeeping money that my father gave her. I knew that he was mean and common and a drunkard, and that she had been relying on me to study and rescue her from the misery which threatened to engulf her. And I knew that the horror in her eyes was the fear that, like him, I was turning out a liar, a thief, and a drunkard.

After that morning, I think my childhood was at an end.

DYLAN THOMAS
A Child's Christmas in Wales

One Christmas was so much like another, in those years around the sea-town corner now and out of all sound except the distant speaking of the voices I sometimes hear a moment before sleep, that I can never remember whether it snowed for six days and six nights when I was twelve or whether it snowed for twelve days and twelve nights when I was six.

All the Christmases roll down towards the two-tongued sea, like a cold and headlong moon bundling down the sky that was our street; and they stop at the rim of the ice-edged, fish-freezing waves, and I plunge my hands in the snow and bring out whatever I can find. In goes my hand into that wool-white bell-tongued ball of holidays resting at the rim of the carol-singing sea, and out come Mrs Prothero and the firemen.

It was on the afternoon of the day of Christmas Eve, and I was in Mrs Prothero's garden, waiting for cats, with her son Jim. It was snowing. It was always snowing at Christmas. December, in my memory, is white as Lapland, though there were no reindeers. But there were cats. Patient, cold and callous, our hands wrapped in socks, we waited to snowball the cats. Sleek and long as jaguars and horrible-whiskered, spitting and snarling, they would slink and sidle over the white back-garden walls, and the lynx-eyed hunters, Jim and I, fur-capped and moccasined trappers from Hudson Bay, off Mumbles Road, would hurl our deadly snowballs at the green of their eyes.

The wise cats never appeared. We were so still, Eskimo-footed arctic marksmen in the muffling silence of the eternal snows – eternal, ever since Wednesday – that we never heard Mrs Prothero's first cry from her igloo at the bottom of the garden. Or, if we heard it at all, it was, to us, like the far-off challenge of our enemy and prey, the neighbour's polar cat. But soon the voice grew louder. 'Fire!' cried Mrs Prothero, and she beat the dinner-gong.

And we ran down the garden, with the snowballs in our arms, towards the house; and smoke, indeed, was pouring out of the dining-room, and the gong was bombilating, and Mrs Prothero was announcing ruin like a town crier in Pompeii. This was better than all the cats in Wales standing on the wall in a row. We bounded into the house, laden with snowballs, and stopped at the open door of the smoke-filled room.

Something was burning all right; perhaps it was Mr Prothero, who always slept there after midday dinner with a newspaper over his face. But he was standing in the middle of the room, saying, 'A fine Christmas!' and smacking at the smoke with a slipper. 'Call the fire brigade,' cried Mrs Prothero as she beat the gong.

'They won't be there,' said Mr Prothero, 'it's Christmas.'

There was no fire to be seen, only clouds of smoke and Mr Prothero standing in the middle of them, waving his slipper as though he were conducting.

'Do something,' he said.

And we threw all our snowballs into the smoke – I think we missed Mr Prothero – and ran out of the house to the telephone box.

'Let's call the police as well,' Jim said.

'And the ambulance.'

'And Ernie Jenkins, he likes fires.'

But we only called the fire brigade, and soon the fire engine came and three tall men in helmets brought a hose into the house and Mr Prothero got out just in time before they turned it on. Nobody could have had a noisier Christmas Eve. And when the firemen turned off the hose and were standing in the wet, smoky room, Jim's aunt, Miss Prothero, came downstairs and peered in at them. Jim and I waited, very quietly, to hear what she would say to them. She said the right thing, always. She looked at the three tall firemen in their shining helmets, standing among the smoke and cinders and dissolving snowballs, and she said: 'Would you like anything to read?'

Years and years and years ago, when I was a boy, when there were wolves in Wales, and birds the colour of red-flannel petticoats whisked past the harp-shaped hills, when we sang and wallowed all night and day in caves that smelt like Sunday afternoons in damp front farmhouse parlours and we chased, with the jawbones of deacons, the English and the bears, before the motor-car, before the wheel, before the duchess-faced horse, when we rode the daft and happy hills bareback, it snowed and it snowed. But here a small boy says: 'It snowed last year, too. I made a snowman and my brother knocked it down and I knocked my brother down and then we had tea.'

'But that was not the same snow,' I say. 'Our snow was not only shaken from whitewash buckets down the sky, it came shawling out of the ground and swam and drifted out of the arms and hands and bodies of the trees; snow grew overnight on the roofs of the houses like a pure and grandfather moss, minutely white-ivied the walls and settled on the postman, opening the gate, like a dumb, numb thunderstorm of white, torn Christmas cards.'

'Were there postmen then, too?'

'With sprinkling eyes and wind-cherried noses, on spread, frozen feet they crunched up to the doors and mittened on them manfully. But all that the children could hear was a ringing of bells.'

'You mean that the postman went rat-a-tat-tat and the doors rang?'

'I mean that the bells that the children could hear were inside them.'

'I only hear thunder sometimes, never bells.'

'There were church bells, too.'

'Inside them?'

'No, no, no, in the bat-black, snow-white belfries, tugged by bishops and storks. And they rang their tidings over the bandaged town, over the frozen foam of the powder and ice-cream hills, over the crackling sea. It seemed that all the churches boomed for joy under my window; and the weathercocks crew for Christmas, on our fence.'

'Get back to the postmen.'

'They were just ordinary postmen, fond of walking and dogs and Christmas and the snow. They knocked on the doors with blue knuckles . . .'

'Ours has got a black knocker . . .'

'And then they stood on the white Welcome mat in the little, drifted porches and huffed and puffed, making ghosts with their breath, and jogged from foot to foot like small boys wanting to go out.'

'And then the Presents?'

'And then the Presents, after the Christmas box. And the cold post-man, with a rose on his button-nose, tingled down the tea-tray-slithered run of the chilly glinting hill. He went in his ice-bound boots like a man on fishmonger's slabs. He wagged his bag like a frozen camel's hump, dizzily turned the corner on one foot, and, by God, he was gone.'

'Get back to the Presents.'

'There were the Useful Presents: engulfing mufflers of the old coach days, and mittens made for giant sloths; zebra scarfs of a substance like silky gum that could be tug-o'-warred down to the galoshes; blinding tam-o'-shanters like patchwork tea-cosies and bunny-suited busbies and balaclavas for victims of head-shrinking tribes; from aunts who always wore wool next to the skin there were moustached and rasping vests that made you wonder why the aunts had any skin left at all; and once I had a little crocheted nose bag from an aunt now, alas, no longer whinnying with us. And pictureless books in which small boys, though warned with quotations not to, *would* skate on Farmer Giles' pond and did and drowned; and books that told me everything about the wasp, except why.'

'Go on to the Useless Presents.'

'Bags of moist and many-coloured jelly babies and a folded flag and a false nose and a tram-conductor's cap and a machine that punched tickets and rang a bell; never a catapult; once, by mistake that no one could explain, a little hatchet; and a celluloid duck that made, when you pressed it, a most unducklike sound, a mewing moo that an ambitious cat might make who wished to be a cow; and a painting book in which I could make the grass, the trees, the sea and the animals any colour I pleased, and still the dazzling sky-blue sheep are grazing in the red field under the rainbow-billed and pea-green birds.

'Hardboileds, toffee, fudge and allsorts, crunches, cracknels, humbugs, glaciers, marzipan, and butterwelsh for the Welsh. And troops of bright tin soldiers who, if they could not fight, could always run. And Snakes-and-Families and Happy Ladders. And Easy Hobbi-Games for Little Engineers, complete with instructions.

'Oh, easy for Leonardo! And a whistle to make the dogs bark to wake up the old man next door to make him beat on the wall with his stick to shake our picture off the wall.

'And a packet of cigarettes; you put one in your mouth and you stood at the corner of the street and you waited for hours, in vain, for an old lady to scold you for smoking a cigarette, and then with a smirk you ate it. And then it was breakfast under the balloons.'

'Were there Uncles like in our house?'

'There are always Uncles at Christmas.

'The same Uncles. And on Christmas mornings, with dog-disturbing whistle and sugar fags, I would scour the swatched town for the news of the little world, and find always a dead bird by the white Post Office or by the deserted swings; perhaps a robin, all but one of his fires out. Men and women wading or scooping back from chapel, with taproom noses and wind-bussed cheeks, all albinos, huddled their stiff black jarring feathers against the irreligious snow.

'Mistletoe hung from the gas brackets in all the front parlours; there was sherry and walnuts and bottled beer and crackers by the dessert-spoons; and cats in their fur-abouts watched the fires; and the high-heaped fire spat, all ready for the chestnuts and the mulling pokers.

'Some few large men sat in the front parlours, without their collars, Uncles almost certainly, trying their new cigars, holding them out judiciously at arms' length, returning them to their mouths, coughing, then holding them out again as though waiting for the explosion; and some few small Aunts, not wanted in the kitchen, nor anywhere else for that matter, sat on the very edges of their chairs, poised and brittle, afraid to break, like faded cups and saucers.'

Not many those mornings trod the piling streets: an old man always, fawn-bowlered, yellow-gloved and, at this time of year, with spats of snow, would take his constitutional to the white bowling green and back, as he would take it wet or fine on Christmas Day or Doomsday; sometimes two hale young men, with big pipes blazing, no overcoats and wind-blown scarfs, would trudge, unspeaking, down to the forlorn sea, to work up an appetite, to blow away the fumes, who knows, to walk into the waves until nothing of them was left but the two curling smoke clouds of their inextinguishable briars. Then I would be slap-dashing home, the gravy smell of the dinners of others, the bird smell, the brandy, the pudding and mince, coiling up to my nostrils, when out of a snow-clogged side lane would come a boy the spit of myself, with a pink-tipped cigarette and the violet past of a black eye, cocky as a bullfinch, leering all to himself.

I hated him on sight and sound, and would be about to put my dog whistle to my lips and blow him off the face of Christmas when suddenly he, with a violet wink, put *his* whistle to *his* lips and blew so stridently, so high, so exquisitely loud, that gobbling faces, their cheeks bulged with goose, would press against their tinselled windows, the whole length of the white echoing street. For dinner we had turkey and blazing pudding, and after dinner the Uncles sat in front of the fire, loosened all buttons, put their large moist hands over their watch chains, groaned a little and slept. Mothers, aunts and sisters scuttled to and fro, bearing tureens. Auntie Bessie, who had already been frightened, twice, by a clock-work mouse, whimpered at the sideboard and had some elderberry wine. The dog was sick. Auntie Dosie had to have three aspirins, but Auntie Hannah, who liked port, stood in the middle of the snowbound back yard, singing like a big-bosomed thrush. I would blow up balloons to see how big they would blow up to; and, when they burst, which they all did, the Uncles jumped and rumbled. In the rich and heavy afternoon, the Uncles breathing like dolphins and the snow descending, I would sit among festoons and Chinese lanterns and nibble dates and try to make a model man-o'-war, following the Instructions for Little Engineers, and produce what might be mistaken for a sea-going tramcar.

Or I would go out, my bright new boots squeaking, into the white world, on to the seaward hill, to call on Jim and Dan and Jack and to pad through the still streets, leaving huge deep footprints on the hidden pavements.

'I bet people will think there's been hippos.'

'What would you do if you saw a hippo coming down our street?'

'I'd go like this, bang! I'd throw him over the railings and roll him down the hill and then I'd tickle him under the ear and he'd wag his tail.'

'What would you do if you saw *two* hippos?'

Iron-flanked and bellowing he-hippos clanked and battered through the scudding snow towards us as we passed Mr Daniel's house.

'Let's post Mr Daniel a snowball through his letter-box.'

'Let's write things in the snow.'

'Let's write, "Mr Daniel looks like a spaniel" all over his lawn.'

Or we walked on the white shore.

'Can the fishes see it's snowing?'

The silent one-clouded heavens drifted on to the sea. Now we were snow-blind travellers lost on the north hills, and vast dewlapped dogs, with flasks round their necks, ambled and shambled up to us, baying 'Excelsior'. We returned home through the poor streets where only a few children fumbled with bare red fingers in the wheel-rutted snow and cat-called after us, their voices fading away, as we trudged uphill, into the cries of the dock birds and the hooting of ships out in the whirling bay. And then, at tea the recovered Uncles would be jolly; and the ice cake loomed in the centre of the table like a marble grave. Auntie Hannah laced her tea with rum, because it was only once a year.

Bring out the tall tales now that we told by the fire as the gaslight bubbled like a diver. Ghosts whooed like owls in the long nights when I dared not look over my shoulder; animals lurked in the cubbyhole under the stairs where the gas meter ticked. And I remember that we went singing carols once, when there wasn't the shaving of a moon to light the flying streets. At the end of a long road was a drive that led to a large house, and we stumbled up the darkness of the drive that night, each one of us afraid, each one holding a stone in his hand in case, and all of us too brave to say a word. The wind through the trees made noises as of old and unpleasant and maybe webfooted men wheezing in caves. We reached the black bulk of the house.

'What shall we give them? "Hark the Herald"?'

'No,' Jack said, '"Good King Wenceslas". I'll count three.'

One, two, three, and we began to sing, our voices high and seemingly distant in the snow-felted darkness round the house that was occupied by nobody we knew. We stood close together, near the dark door.

Good King Wenceslas looked out
On the Feast of Stephen . . .

And then a small, dry voice, like the voice of someone who has not spoken for a long time, joined our singing: a small, dry, eggshell voice from the other side of the door: a small dry voice through the keyhole. And when we stopped running we were outside *our* house; the front room was lovely; balloons floated under the hot-water-bottle-gulping gas; every-thing was good again and shone over the town.

'Perhaps it was a ghost,' Jim said.

'Perhaps it was trolls,' Dan said, who was always reading.

'Let's go in and see if there's any jelly left,' Jack said. And we did that.

Always on Christmas night there was music. An uncle played the fiddle, a cousin sang 'Cherry Ripe', and another uncle sang 'Drake's Drum'. It was very warm in the little house.

Auntie Hannah, who had got on to the parsnip wine, sang a song about Bleeding Hearts and Death, and then another in which she said her heart was like a Bird's Nest; and then everybody laughed again; and then I went to bed. Looking through my bedroom window, out into the moonlight and the unending smoke-coloured snow, I could see the lights in the windows of all the other houses on our hill and hear the music rising from them up the long, steadily falling night. I turned the gas down, I got into bed. I said some words to the close and holy darkness, and then I slept.

GEORGES SIMENON

The Little Restaurant near Place des Ternes

A Christmas Story for Grown-Ups

Translated by David Coward

The clock in its black case, which regular customers had always known to stand in the same place, over the rack where the serviettes were kept, showed four minutes to nine. The advertising calendar behind the head of the woman sitting at the till, Madame Bouchet, showed that it was the twenty-fourth day of December.

Outside, a fine rain was falling. Inside, it was warm. A pot-bellied stove, like the ones there used to be in railway stations, sat in the very centre of the room. Its black chimney pipe rose through empty space before disappearing into a wall.

Madame Bouchet's lips moved as she counted the banknotes. The bar's owner stood patiently by, watching her, while in his hand he was already holding the grey linen bag into which he put the contents of the till every evening.

Albert, the waiter, glanced up at the clock, drifted over to them and with a wink motioned towards a bottle which stood apart from the others on the counter. The landlord in turn looked at the time, gave a shrug and nodded his assent.

'Just because they're the last ones here, there's no reason, why we shouldn't give them a drink like the others,' he muttered under his breath as he walked off with the tray.

He had a habit of talking to himself while he was working.

The landlord's car stood waiting by the kerb outside. He lived some distance away, at Joinville, where he had had a villa built for him. His wife had previously worked the tills in cafés. He had been a waiter. He still had painful feet from those days, as all waiters in bars and restaurants do, and wore special shoes. The back of his car was filled with attractively wrapped parcels which he was taking home for the Christmas Eve festivities.

Madame Bouchet would get the bus to Rue Coulaincourt, where she would be spending Christmas with her daughter, whose husband worked as a clerk at the town hall.

Albert had two young kids, and their toys had been hidden for several days on top of the tall linen cupboard.

He began with the man, putting a small glass on the table, which he then filled with Armagnac.

'It's on the house,' he said.

He made his way past several empty tables to the corner where Jeanne – Long Tall Jeanne – had just lit a cigarette, carefully positioned himself between her and the till and muttered:

'Drink up quick so I can pour you another! Compliments of the landlord!'

Finally, he got to the last table in the row. A young woman was taking her lipstick out of her handbag as she looked at herself in a small hand mirror.

'With the compliments of the house . . .'

She looked up at him in surprise.

'It's the custom here at Christmas.'

'Thank you.'

He would gladly have poured her a second glass too, but he did not know her well enough. Besides she was sitting too near the till.

All done! He tipped the landlord another wink by way of asking him if it was at last time for him to go outside and pull down the shutters. It was already stretching hospitality to have stayed open this late just for three customers. At this point in the evening in most of the restaurants in Paris, staff would be scurrying around setting out tables for the late-night Christmas Eve supper trade. But this was a small restaurant which offered a regular clientele modestly priced menus, a quiet place to eat just off Place des Ternes in the least frequented part of the Faubourg Saint-Honoré.

Few people had eaten there that evening. More or less everyone had family or friends to go to. The last ones left were these two women and a man, and the waiter was not bold enough to show them the door. But the fact that they went on sitting at their tables, from which the cloths had been removed, surely meant that they had no one waiting for them.

He lowered the left-hand shutter, then the right, came back in, wavered over lowering the shutter over the door, which would force the reluctant customers to crouch down to get out. But it was now nine o'clock. The takings had been counted. Madame Bouchet had put on her black hat, her coat and her tippet of marten fur and was looking for her gloves. The landlord, his feet turned outwards, advanced a few steps. Long Tall Jeanne was still smoking her cigarette, and the young woman had clumsily caked her mouth with lipstick. The restaurant was about to close. It was time. It was past the time. The landlord was about to say, as politely as he could, the time-honoured words:

'Ladies and gentlemen . . .'

But before he could pronounce one syllable, there was a single, crisp sound, and the only male customer, his eyes suddenly wide open as if he'd been taken completely by surprise, swayed before toppling sideways on the bench seat that ran along the wall.

He had walked in casually, without saying a word, without warning anybody that just as they were about to close he would put a bullet in his head.

'It would be best if you waited here for a few moments,' the landlord told the two women. 'There's a policeman on duty on the corner of the street. Albert has gone to get him.'

Long Tall Jeanne had stood up to get a look at the dead man and, pausing by the stove, she lit another cigarette. The young woman in her corner sucked her handkerchief and, although it was hot there, was shaking all over.

The policeman came in. His cape glistened with rain and gave off a barrack-room smell.

'Do you know him?'

'He's been eating here every day for years. He's Russian.'

'Are you sure he's dead? If he is, we'd better wait for the inspector. I've phoned through to him.'

They did not have long to wait. The police station was close by, in Rue de l'Étoile. The inspector wore an overcoat which was either badly cut or had shrunk in the rain, and a hat that had faded to no particular colour. He did not seem in a good mood.

'The first of tonight's crop!' he muttered as he bent over. 'He's early. Usually it comes on them around midnight, when everybody else is having most fun.'

He straightened up, holding a wallet in his hand. He opened it and from it took a thick, green identity card.

'Alexis Borine, fifty-six years old, born in Vilna.'

He recited the words in an undertone, as a priest says mass and the way Albert talked to himself.

'Hôtel de Bordeaux, Rue Brey . . . Engineer . . . Was he an engineer?' he asked the landlord.

'He might have been, a long time ago, but ever since he's been coming here he's been working as an extra in films. I recognized him several times up on the screen.'

'Any witnesses?' asked the inspector as he turned round.

'There's me, my cashier, the waiter and the two ladies there. If you'd like to take their names first . . .'

The inspector found himself face to face with Jeanne, who really was tall, half a head taller than him.

'Fancy seeing you here. Papers.'

She handed him her card. He wrote down:

'Jeanne Chartrain. Age: twenty-eight. Profession, none . . . Oh come on! No profession? . . .'

'It's what they put me down as at the town hall.'

'Have you got the other card?'

She nodded.

'Up to date, is it?'

'Still as charmless as ever, I see,' she said with a smile.

'What about you?'

The question was directed at the badly made-up young woman, who stammered:

'I haven't got my identity card on me. My name is Martine Cornu. I am nineteen and I was born at Yport . . .'

The tall woman gave a start and looked at her more closely. Yport was very near where she came from, not more than five kilometres away. And there were lots of people in the area by the name of Cornu. The people who ran Yport's largest café, overlooking the beach, were called Cornu.

'Address?' growled Inspector Lognon, who was known locally as 'Inspector Hard-Done-By'.

'I live in an apartment building in Rue Brey. Number 17.'

'You will probably be called for questioning at the station one of these days. And now you can go.'

He was waiting for the municipal ambulance. Madame Bouchet asked:

'Can I go too?'

'If you want.'

Then, as she left, he called Long Tall Jeanne back as she was making her way to the door.

'You didn't happen to know him?'

'I turned a trick with him ages ago, maybe six months . . . At least six months, because it was at the start of summer . . . He was the sort of client who goes with girls to talk more than for any other reason, who asks you questions and thinks you're a sad case . . . Since then he's never said hello, though whenever he comes in here he always gives me a little nod.'

The young woman left. Jeanne followed her out, keeping very close behind her. She was wearing a cheap fur coat which was far too short for her. She had always worn clothes which were too short. Everyone told her so, but she persisted without knowing why, and the effect was to make her look even taller.

'Home' for her was fifty metres further along on the right, in the total darkness of Square du Roule, where there were only artists' studios and single-storey maisonettes. She had a small first-floor apartment with a private staircase and a door opening directly on to the street to which she had the key.

She had promised herself she would go straight home that evening. She never stayed out on Christmas Eve. She had hardly any make-up on and was wearing very ordinary clothes. So much so that she had been shocked in the restaurant to see the young woman piling on the lipstick.

She took a few steps into the cul de sac perched on her high heels, which she could hear clacking on the cobbles. Then she realized that her spirits had drooped because of the Russian: she felt she needed to walk in light and fill her ears with noise. So she turned and headed towards Place des Ternes, where the broad, brilliantly illuminated swathe that runs down from the Arc de Triomphe comes to an end. The cinemas, the theatres, the restaurants were all lit up. In the windows, printed pennants advertised the prices and menus of Christmas Eve suppers and on every door could be read the word 'Full'.

The streets were almost unrecognizable, for there was hardly anyone about.

The young woman was now walking ten metres ahead of her, looking like someone who is not sure which way to go. She kept stopping in front of a shop window or at a street corner, uncertain whether to cross, standing and staring at the photographs hanging on the walls of the warm foyer of a cinema.

'Anybody would think she's the one touting for custom!'

When he saw the Russian, Lognon had muttered:

'The first of tonight's crop . . . He's early.'

Maybe he'd done it there rather than in the street, because it would have been an even more miserable end outside, or alone in his furnished room. In the restaurant, it had been quiet and peaceful, almost a family atmosphere. There a man could feel he was surrounded by familiar faces. It was warm. He'd even been offered a drink on the house!

She gave a shrug. She had nothing else to do. She too halted outside shop windows and looked at the photos while the luminous neon signs turned her red and green and violet, and all the time she was aware of the young woman who was still walking just ahead of her.

Who knows, perhaps she had come across her when she was a little girl. There were ten years between them. When she'd worked for the Fisheries at Fécamp – she was already as tall but very skinny – many a Sunday she had gone out with boys to dances at Yport. Sometimes she had gone dancing at the Café Cornu, and the owner's children were always running around the place.

'Don't trip over the tadpoles,' she would tell her partners.

She called the kids tadpoles. Her own brothers and sisters were tadpoles too. She'd had six or seven of them back then, but there wouldn't be as many left there now.

It was strange to think that this girl was probably one of the tadpoles from the Café Cornu!

Above the shops all along the avenue were apartments, and nearly all of their windows were lit up. She gazed up at them, raising her head to the refreshing drizzle, sometimes catching a glimpse of shadows moving behind the curtains, and she wondered:

'What are they doing?'

Most likely they would be reading the newspaper or decorating the Christmas tree as they waited for midnight. In some cases, the lady of the house would soon be receiving guests and was now worrying about whether the dinner would turn out right.

Thousands of children were sleeping, or pretending to be asleep. And almost all the people who had flocked to the cinemas and theatres had booked tables in restaurants for their Christmas Eve supper or reserved their seats in church for midnight mass.

For you had to book your seat in churches too. Otherwise perhaps the girl might have gone there?

All the people she passed either were in groups, already in high spirits, or were couples clinging to each other more tightly, it seemed, than on ordinary days.

Lone pedestrians were also in more of a hurry than on normal days. They gave the impression that they were on their way somewhere, that they had people waiting for them.

Was that why the Russian had put a bullet in his head? And also why Inspector Hard-Done-By had said that there would be more to follow?

It was the day that did it, of course it was! The girl in front of her had halted on the corner of Rue Brey. The third tenement along was a hotel, and there were others too, discreet establishments where rooms could be taken for short periods. Actually it was there that Jeanne had gone with her first ever customer. The Russian had been living until today in the hotel next door, very probably on the very top floor, because only the poorest rooms were let by the month or the week.

What was the Cornu girl looking at? Fat Émilie? Now there was a tart without either shame or religion. She was there, even though it was

Christmas, and she couldn't even bother to walk a few steps up and down so that she wouldn't look quite so obvious.

She stayed put in the doorway, with the words 'Furnished Rooms' emblazoned just above her purple hat. But there she was, old, well past forty, enormously fat now, and her feet, which over time had become as sensitive as those of the owner of the restaurant, were almost terminally tired of ferrying all that flab around.

'Evening, Jeanne!' she sang out across the street.

Jeanne did not answer. Why was she following the girl? For no particular reason. Probably because she didn't have anything else to do and was afraid of going home.

But the Cornu girl did not know where she was going either. She had turned into Rue Brey automatically and was mincing along unhurriedly, tightly buttoned up in her blue two-piece suit, which was far too thin for the time of year.

She was a pretty girl. A touch chubby. With a diverting little rear end which she wiggled as she walked. In the restaurant, seen from the side, the way her full, high breasts had pushed out the front of her jacket had been very noticeable.

'If any man comes on to you tonight, dearie,' thought Jeanne, 'it'll be your own stupid fault!'

Especially that evening, because respectable men, the ones with family, friends or just social acquaintances, weren't out wandering the streets.

But the little fool did not know that. Did she even know what Fat Émilie was doing standing outside the entrance of the hotel? From time to time, as she walked past a bar, she would stand on tiptoe and look inside.

Ah! She was going into one. Albert had done her no favours by giving her that drink. At the beginning, it had been the same with Jeanne too. Unfortunately for her, if she'd had one drink, she'd have to have another. And when she'd had three, she no longer knew what she was doing. It wasn't like that any more, not by a long chalk! Nowadays she could certainly put it away before she'd had enough!

The bar was called Chez Fred. It had a long, mahogany counter and the kind of high stools on which women cannot perch without showing a lot of leg. It was virtually empty. Just one man at the back, a musician or maybe a dancer, already in a dinner jacket, who would shortly be going to work in some night-spot nearby. He was eating a sandwich and drinking beer.

Martine Cornu hoisted herself on to a stool by the door, against the wall. Jeanne went in and sat down a little further along.

'Armagnac,' she ordered, since that was what she had begun drinking.

The girl looked at the rows of bottles which, lit from above, formed a rainbow of subtle colours.

'A Benedictine . . .' she said.

The barman turned the knob of a radio, and sickly-sweet music filled the bar.

Why didn't Jeanne just walk up to her and ask her straight out if she really was a Cornu from Yport? There were Cornus in Fécamp too, cousins, but they were butchers in Rue du Havre.

The musician – or dancer – at the back of the bar had already noticed Martine and was languidly giving her the eye.

'Got any cigarettes?' the girl asked the barman.

She wasn't used to smoking, as was patently obvious from the way she opened the packet and blinked as she released the smoke.

It was ten o'clock. Another two hours and it would be midnight. Everyone would kiss and hug. In every house, the radio would blare out verses of 'O Holy Night', and everybody would join in.

Really, it was all very silly. Jeanne, who never had problems speaking to anybody, felt quite incapable of approaching this girl who hailed from her part of the world and whom she had probably met when she was just a child.

But it wouldn't have been unpleasant. She'd have said:

'Seeing as how you're all alone and looking sorry for yourself, why don't we spend a quiet Christmas Eve together?'

She knew exactly how to mind her manners. She wouldn't talk to her about men or about being on the game. There must be a whole lot of people they both knew at Fécamp and Yport whom they could talk about. And why shouldn't she take her home with her?

Her place was very neat, very tidy. She had lived for long enough in rented rooms to know what it meant to have a place of her own. She could take the girl there without feeling any sense of shame, because she never brought men home with her. Other girls did. For Long Tall Jeanne, it was a matter of principle. And few apartments were as trim and spotless as hers. She even kept felt undersoles behind the front door which she used like skates on rainy days so as not to dirty the wooden floor, which she kept highly polished, like an ice-rink.

They would buy a couple of bottles, something good but not too strong. There were *charcutiers* still open which sold different kinds of pâté, lobster, scallops and assorted tasty and attractively presented dishes which they could not afford to eat every day of the week.

She watched her out of the corner of her eye. Perhaps eventually she would have spoken to her if the door hadn't opened at that moment and two men hadn't come in, the kind Jeanne disliked, the sort of men who, when they enter a room, always look around as if they owned the place.

'Evening, Fred!' said the shorter of the two, who was also fatter.

They had already taken stock of the bar. An uninterested glance at the musician sitting at the back, and a closer look at Jeanne who, now that she was sitting down, did not seem as tall as she did standing up – which, incidentally, was why she often worked out of bars.

Of course, they knew at a glance exactly what she was. On the other hand they stared insistently at Martine then sat very close to her.

'Do you mind?'

She shrank back against the wall, still holding her cigarette as clumsily as before.

'What are you having, Willy?'

'The usual.'

'The usual, Fred.'

They were the type of men who often have foreign accents and are heard talking about horse-racing or discussing cars. They were also the sort who knew how to choose the right moment to give a woman the glad eye, walk her into a corner of the room and whisper sweet nothings into her ear. And wherever they happen to be they always need to make a phone call.

The barman started mixing them a complicated drink while they watched him closely.

'Hasn't the baron been in?'

'He said he wanted one of you to call him. He's gone to see Francis.'

The taller of the pair went into the phone booth. The other moved closer to Martine.

'That stuff's no good for the stomach,' he said, clicking the catch of a gold cigarette case.

She looked at him in surprise. Jeanne wanted to call out to her:

'Don't answer!'

Because the moment she started talking to him it would be difficult to shake him off.

'What's no good for the stomach?'

She was behaving like the dumb cluck that she was. She even forced herself to smile, probably because she had been taught to smile when talking to people, or maybe because she really believed it made her look like something off the cover of a magazine.

'That stuff you're drinking.'

'But it's Benedictine!'

She really was from Fécamp, way out in the sticks! She honestly thought that saying the name was the last word on the subject.

'Of course it is! There's nothing like it for upsetting the insides! Fred!'

'Yes, sir.'

'Bring us another here, for the lady, and make it snappy.'

'Coming up.'

'But . . .' she tried to protest.

'Just a drink between friends, no need to be scared! It's Christmas Eve, isn't it, yes or no?'

The tall one straightened his tie in the mirror as he stepped out of the phone booth. He cottoned on quickly.

'Do you live around here?'

'Not far.'

'Barman!' call Jeanne, 'give me one of the same.'

'Armagnac?'

'No. One of whatever it was you just poured.'

'A sidecar?'

'Go on, then.'

She felt furious, for no good reason, and wanted to say:

'Listen, darling, it won't be long now before you pass out . . . These guys play dirty . . . If you wanted a drink, couldn't you have chosen a more suitable bar? Or gone home and got drunk there?'

Of course she herself hadn't gone home either, even though she was used to living alone. But does anybody want to go home on Christmas Eve knowing there is no one waiting there and with the prospect of lying in bed listening to the sound of music and happy voices coming through the wall?

Soon the doors of cinemas and theatres would open and out would spill impatient crowds who would rush away to the tens of thousands of tables they had reserved in the most modern restaurants in the most far-flung parts of town. Christmas Eve junketings to suit all pockets!

Except – and this was the point – you couldn't reserve a table for one. Not least because it wouldn't be fair on folk who go out to have a good time with friends, not fair at all for you to sit by yourself in a corner and watch the goings-on. What would that make you? A wet blanket! You would see them form into huddles and whisper to each other, wondering if they should ask you to join them because they felt sorry for you.

Nor could you go out and roam around the streets, because if you did, every cop on the beat would eye you suspiciously, curious to see if you intended to use some dark corner to do what the Russian had done, or if, despite the cold, one of them was going to have to jump into the Seine and fish you out.

'What do you think of it?'

'It's not very strong.'

If her parents really ran a bistro, she should have known about such things. But it was what women always say. It's as if they're always expecting to be given liquid fire in a glass. But when it turns out to be not as strong as they'd thought, they stop being so suspicious.

'Work in a shop, do you?'

'No . . .'

'Typist? . . .'

'Yes.'

'Been in Paris long?'

He had teeth like a film star's and a moustache made of two commas.

'Do you like dancing?'

'Sometimes.'

Oh, they were laying it on very thick! How pleasant the thought of exchanging idle chat like this in such company! Maybe the girl believed they really were men of the world? The gold case held out to her and the Egyptian cigarettes too probably dazzled her eyes, as did the large diamond ring worn by the man closest to her.

'Fill us up again, Fred.'

'Not for me, thanks. Anyway, it's time I . . .'

'Time you? . . .'

'I'm sorry?'

'It's time you . . . did what? You can't be going home to bed at half past ten on Christmas Eve! . . .'

It was weird! Sitting on the sidelines and watching a scene like this being acted out always makes it look so utterly stupid. But to be involved, to play a part in it . . .

'What a birdbrain!' Jeanne muttered as she smoked one cigarette after another without taking her eyes off the trio.

Naturally, Martine did not dare to admit that, yes, she was, actually, intending to go home to bed.

'Have you got a date?'

'Don't be so nosy.'

'Got a boyfriend?'

'What's it to you?'

'Well, I'd be more than happy to keep him waiting for a bit.'

'Why?'

Long Tall Jeanne could have recited the whole script for them. She knew it by heart. She had also caught the look aimed at the barman which meant:

'Keep it coming!'

But in her present condition, the erstwhile tadpole from Yport could have been plied with the stiffest of cocktails and she would have found them not strong at all. Likewise her lipstick: didn't she have enough on already? Yet she still felt the need for more, to open her handbag and show she used Houbigant lipstick, but also to demonstrate her pout, because all women believe they are irresistible when they push out their lips to receive that impudent little implement.

'Think you're gorgeous? If you could only see yourself in a mirror, you'd soon realize which of the two of us looks most like a tart!'

But not quite, because the difference is not just a matter of a little more or less warpaint. The proof of this was provided by the two men who, as they came in, had needed only a quick look to pigeonhole Jeanne.

'Ever been to the Monico?'

'No. What is it?'

'Hear that, Albert? She's never been to the Monico!'

'Don't make me laugh!'

'But you do like dancing? Now look, sweetheart . . .'

Jeanne was expecting the word, but later rather than sooner. The man wasn't wasting any time. His leg was already pressed tight against one of the girl's in such a way that she could not draw it back, for she was too close to the wall.

'It's one of the most amazing night-spots in Paris. Regulars only. Bob Alisson and his jazz band. Never heard of Bob Alisson either?'

'I don't go out much.'

The two men exchanged winks. Obvious where this was leading. A few minutes from now, the small fat one would remember that he had an urgent appointment so that he could leave the field clear for his friend.

'Not so fast, you creeps!' Jeanne murmured, her mind made up.

She herself had also downed three drinks one after the other, not counting the free ones she'd had courtesy of the landlord of the restaurant. She was not drunk, she never was, not completely, but she was beginning to attach great importance to certain notions.

For example, the idea that this silly kid came from the same place as she did, that she was a tadpole. Then she thought of fat Émilie standing in the doorway of the hotel. It was in that very hotel, though not on a Christmas Eve, that she had gone upstairs with a man for the first time.

'Could you give me a light?'

She had slid off her stool and, with a cigarette dangling between her lips, now joined the smaller of the two men.

He was also aware what this meant and was not best pleased. He gave her a critical once-over. Standing upright, he must have been a good head shorter than her, and the way she carried herself was mannish.

'Like to buy a girl a drink?'

'If you insist . . . Fred!'

'Coming up.'

While this was going on, the kid eyed her with a feeling close to indignation, as if an attempt was being made to steal something that belonged to her.

'Hey, you three don't look like you're having much fun!'

And, laying one hand on the shoulder of the man next to her, Jeanne started belting out the words of the song the radio was playing softly in the background.

'Of all the bird-brained . . .' she kept saying to herself every ten minutes. 'How can anyone be so . . . ?'

But, oddest of all, the birdbrain in question continued looking at her with an expression of the utmost contempt.

But one of Willy's arms had now entirely disappeared behind Martine's back, and the hand wearing the diamond ring lay heavily on the front of her blouse.

She now lay slumped – literally – on the red plush seat against the wall of the Monico, and there was now no need to put her glass in her hand because more often than not she herself kept clamouring for it and gulped down the champagne greedily.

Each time she drained her glass, she burst into a fit of convulsive laughter and then clung even more tightly to the man she was with.

It was not yet midnight. Most of the tables were unoccupied. Sometimes the two of them had the dance floor to themselves. Willy kept his nose buried in the short hair at the back of his partner's head and ran his lips over the pimply skin of the nape of her neck.

'You in a bad mood or something?' Jeanne asked the other man.

'Why?'

'Because you didn't win first prize. Think I'm too tall?'

'A bit . . .'

'It doesn't show lying down.'

It was a crack she had made thousands of times. It was almost a chat-up line and just as vapid as the sweet nothings the two others were whispering to each other – but at least she wasn't soft-soaping him because she was enjoying it.

'Do you reckon Christmas Eve is fun?'

'Not especially.'

'Do you think anyone really enjoys it?'

'I suppose some people must . . .'

'Earlier on, in the restaurant where I had dinner, this man shot himself in a corner, without making a fuss, looking like he was sorry for disturbing us and making a mess on the floor.'

'Haven't you got anything more cheerful to say?'

'All right, order another bottle. I'm thirsty.'

It was the only option remaining. Get the tadpole blind drunk, because she was stubbornly refusing to realize what was happening. Make her sick to her stomach, so sick that she puked, then all she'd be fit for was to be packed off home and put to bed.

'Cheers, sweetie, and likewise to all the Cornus of Yport town and district!'

'You're from there?'

'From Fécamp. There was a time when I used to go dancing in Yport every Sunday.'

'Cut it out!' snapped Willy. 'We've not come here to listen to your life stories . . .'

When they'd been in the bar in Rue Brey, it had seemed on the cards that one more glass would have finished the tadpole off. But instead the opposite had happened.

Perhaps being out in the fresh air for a few minutes had been enough to revive her? Maybe it was the champagne? The more she drank the wider awake she became. But she was no longer the same young girl she had been in the restaurant. Willy was now slotting cigarettes ready-lit between her lips, and she was drinking out of his glass. It was sickening to see. And that hand of his never stopped pawing her blouse and skirt!

Not much longer now until everyone would be hugging and kissing and that repulsive man would clamp his lips on the mouth of the girl, who would be stupid enough to faint away in his arms.

'That's what we're all like at her age! They should ban Christmas altogether . . .'

And all the other public holidays too! . . . But now it was Long Tall Jeanne who wasn't thinking straight.

'What say we go on to some other place?'

Maybe this time the fresh air would have the opposite effect, and

Martine would finally pass out. And if she did, most likely the two-bit gigolo wouldn't try to take her home and go up to her room!

'We're fine here . . .'

Meanwhile, Martine, still glaring suspiciously at Jeanne, talked about her in a whisper to her beau. She was probably saying:

'Why is she interfering? Who is she? She looks like a . . .'

Suddenly the sound of jazz stopped. For a few seconds, there was silence. People rose to their feet.

The band struck up 'O Holy Night'.

Oh yes, it was here too! And Martine found herself squeezed tightly to Willy's chest, their bodies melded into one from feet to foreheads and their mouths scandalously stuck together.

'Hey, you disgusting pair! . . .'

Long Tall Jeanne bore down on them, shrill and loud-mouthed, arms and legs moving jerkily like a puppet with its strings crossed.

'Aren't you going to give anyone else a look in?'

And then raising her voice:

'Shift yourself, girl, and make a bit of room for me!'

When they didn't move, she grabbed Martine by the shoulder and yanked her back.

'You still haven't got it, have you, you stupid cow! Maybe you think your precious Willy here has got eyes only for you? But what if I got jealous?'

People at other tables were listening and watching.

'I haven't said anything up to now. I didn't interfere, because I'm a decent sort of girl. But that punter is mine . . .'

Startled, the girl said: 'What's she saying?'

Willy tried to push her away but failed.

'What am I saying? What am I saying? I'm saying you're a rotten little tart and that you stole him off of me! I'm saying you're not going to get away with it and that I'm going to smash your pretty face in. I'm saying . . . Take that for starters! . . . And that! . . . And this! . . .'

She went at it with a will, punching, scratching, grabbing handfuls of hair, while onlookers tried in vain to separate them.

Long Tall Jeanne was as strong as a man.

'You've been treating me like dirt! You were asking for it! . . .'

Martine did her best to fight her off, scratching back, even sinking her small teeth into the hand of her opponent, who had her by one ear.

'Calm down, ladies! . . . Gentlemen, please! . . .'

But Jeanne kept screeching at the top of her voice and managed to knock the table over. Glasses and bottles shattered. Women customers fled from the battle zone screaming while Jeanne finally succeeded in tripping the girl and putting her on the floor.

'Ah! You've been asking for trouble and you've come to the right place for it! . . .'

They were now both on the floor, grappling with each other, spattered with flecks of blood from cuts caused by the broken glass.

The band was playing 'O Holy Night' as loudly as possible to cover the noise. Some of the customers went on singing. Eventually the door opened. Two officers from the cycle-mounted police patrol marched in and headed for the fighting women.

Unceremoniously they nudged them with the toes of their boots.

'Come on you two! On your feet!'

'It was that bitch who . . .'

'Shut up! You can explain down at the station . . .'

As chance would have it, the two men, Willy and his pal, seemed to have vanished.

'Come along with us.'

'But . . .' Martine protested.

'Keep your mouth shut! Save it for later!'

Long Tall Jeanne turned to look for her hat, which she had lost in the scuffle. Outside on the pavement, she called to the doorman:

'Jean, keep my hat safe for me. I'll come and get it tomorrow. It's almost new!'

'If you don't keep quiet . . .' said one of the policemen jangling his handcuffs.

'Aw, put a sock in it, dumbo. We'll be as good as gold!'

Martine's legs gave way. It was only now, all of a sudden, that she started to feel sick. They had to stop in a dark recess to let her empty her stomach against a wall on which was written in white letters: 'No Urinating'.

She was crying, a mixture of sobs and hiccups.

'I don't know what's got into her. We were having such a nice time . . .'

'Come off it!'

'I'd like a glass of water.'

'You'll get one at the station.'

It wasn't far to the police station in Rue de l'Étoile. It turned out that Lognon, the hard-done-by inspector, was still on duty. A pair of glasses was perched on his nose. He was busy, probably writing up his report about the death of the Russian. He recognized Jeanne, then the girl. He looked at each of them in turn, not understanding.

'You two knew each other?'

'Looks like it, sunshine.'

'You're drunk!' he barked at Jeanne. 'What about the friend? . . .'

One of the policemen explained:

'They were both rolling on the floor of the Monico, tearing each other's hair out . . .'

'Inspector . . .' Martine started to protest.

'That's enough! Lock 'em up till the van comes on its round.'

The men were on one side, not many, mostly old down-and-outs, and the women on the other, at the far end, separated from them by a wire grille.

There were benches along the walls. A pint-size flower-seller was crying.

'What are you here for?'

'They found cocaine in my posies. It wasn't nothing to do with me . . .'

'You don't say!'

'Who's she?'

'A tadpole.'

'A what?'

'A tadpole. Don't try to work it out. Careful! She's going to throw up again. That'll make it smell like roses in here if the paddy-wagon's late!'

By three in the morning, there were a good hundred of them in the lockup at police HQ on Quai de l'Horloge, men still on one side and women on the other.

In thousands of houses, people were still probably dancing around Christmas trees. Digestive systems were certain to be struggling with turkey, foie gras and black pudding. The restaurants and bars would not close until it started to get light.

'Have you got the message at last, you silly cow?'

Martine was curled up on a bench as highly polished by use as any church pew. She was still feeling sick. Her features were drawn, her eyes unfocused, and her lips pursed.

'I don't know what I ever did to you.'

'You didn't do anything, girl.'

'You're a common . . .'

'Shush! Don't say that word in this place! Because there are several dozen of them here who might skin you alive.'

'I hate you!'

'You could be right. Even so, maybe you wouldn't be feeling so clever at this moment if you were in some hotel room in Rue Brey!'

The girl was clearly trying to make a big effort to understand.

'Don't bother trying to work it out! Just believe me when I say you're better off here even if it isn't comfortable and don't smell so good. Come eight o'clock, the inspector will give you a short lecture that you thoroughly deserve and then you can get the Métro back to Place des Ternes. Me? They'll give me the usual medical and take my card off me so I can't work for a week.'

'I don't understand.'

'Oh forget it! Did you really think that spending the night with that creep – and on Christmas Eve too – would have been nice? Did you? And how proud of your precious Willy you'd have been tomorrow morning! Do you really think people didn't feel disgusted when they saw you hanging round the neck of that cheap crook? But now at least your future is still in your hands. And you have the Russian to thank for it, you know!'

'Why?'

'I dunno exactly. Just a thought. First because it was on his account that I didn't go straight home. Then again maybe it was him who made me want to be Father Christmas for once in my life. Now move up and make room for me . . .'

Then she added, already more than drowsy:

'Just imagine if, once in their lives, everybody behaved like Father Christmas . . .'

Her voice grew softer the deeper she drifted into sleep.

'Just imagine it, right? . . . Just once . . . And when you think of how many people there are on this earth . . .'

Then finally, still muttering, with her head on Martine's thigh for a pillow:

'Can't you stop your legs jumping all the time . . .'

RAY BRADBURY

The Gift

Tomorrow would be Christmas, and even while the three of them rode to the rocket port the mother and father were worried. It was the boy's first flight into space, his very first time in a rocket, and they wanted everything to be perfect. So when, at the customs table, they were forced to leave behind his gift which exceeded the weight limit by no more than a few ounces and the little tree with the lovely white candles, they felt themselves deprived of the season and their love.

The boy was waiting for them in the Terminal room. Walking towards him, after their unsuccessful clash with the Interplanetary officials, the mother and father whispered to each other.

'What shall we do?'

'Nothing, nothing. What *can* we do?'

'Silly rules!'

'And he so wanted the tree!'

The siren gave a great howl and people pressed forward into the Mars Rocket. The mother and father walked at the very last, their small pale son between them, silent.

'I'll think of something,' said the father.

'What? . . .' asked the boy.

And the rocket took off and they were flung headlong into dark space.

The rocket moved and left fire behind and left Earth behind on which the date was December 24th, 2052, heading out into a place where there was no time at all, no month, no year, no hour. They slept away the rest of the first 'day'. Near midnight, by their Earth-time New York watches, the boy awoke and said, 'I want to go look out the porthole.'

There was only one port, a 'window' of immensely thick glass of some size, up on the next deck.

'Not quite yet,' said the father. 'I'll take you up later.'

'I want to see where we are and where we're going.'

'I want you to wait for a reason,' said the father.

He had been lying awake, turning this way and that, thinking of the abandoned gift, the problem of the season, the lost tree and the white candles. And at last, sitting up, no more than five minutes ago, he believed he had found a plan. He need only carry it out and this journey would be fine and joyous indeed.

'Son,' he said, 'in exactly one half-hour it will be Christmas.'

'Oh,' said the mother, dismayed that he had mentioned it. Somehow she had rather hoped that the boy would forget.

The boy's face grew feverish and his lips trembled. 'I know, I know. Will I get a present, will I? Will I have a tree? You promised –'

'Yes, yes, all that, and more,' said the father.

The mother started. 'But –'

'I mean it,' said the father. 'I really mean it. All and more, much more. Excuse me, now. I'll be back.'

He left them for about twenty minutes. When he came back he was smiling. 'Almost time.'

'Can I hold your watch?' asked the boy, and the watch was handed over and he held it ticking in his fingers as the rest of the hour drifted by in fire and silence and unfelt motion.

'It's Christmas *now*! Christmas! Where's my present?'

'Here we go,' said the father and took his boy by the shoulder and led him from the room, down the hall, up a rampway, his wife following.

'I don't understand,' she kept saying.

'You will. Here we are,' said the father.

They had stopped at the closed door of a large cabin. The father tapped three times and then twice in a code. The door opened and the light in the cabin went out and there was a whisper of voices.

'Go on in, son,' said the father.

'It's dark.'

'I'll hold your hand. Come on, Mama.'

They stepped into the room and the door shut, and the room was very dark indeed. And before them loomed a great glass eye, the porthole, a window four feet high and six feet wide, from which they could look out into space.

The boy gasped.

Behind him, the father and the mother gasped with him, and then in the dark room some people began to sing.

'Merry Christmas, son,' said the father.

And the voices in the room sang the old, the familiar carols, and the boy moved forward slowly until his face was pressed against the cool glass of the port. And he stood there for a long long time, just looking and looking out into space and the deep night at the burning and the burning of ten billion billion white and lovely candles . . .

SHIRLEY JACKSON

A Visit to the Bank

Our local bank is an informal and neighborly spot, lavish with its hard-covered checkbooks, always ready to look up the value of the Swiss franc, eager to advise on investments or make wills. Its atmosphere is substantially less hushed and reverent than, say, a good movie theater, with a loudspeaker system which plays soft music for depositors, an air-cooling device which clears the air of the acrid scent of ten-dollar bills, richly upholstered benches for nervous mortgagees; it is a bank dedicated to every friendly pursuit except the swift transference of money. I have had occasion, over the past few years, to deal frequently with the bank's Mr Andrews, a man of chilling questions and a very cynical view of me, over some minor monies which have passed reluctantly from Mr Andrews' hands into our bank account, and rapidly from there into the hands of various milkmen, doctors, department stores, and sundry poker cronies of my husband's. Mr Andrews likes to believe that he is giving me this money as a favor. 'We are always glad to lend funds,' he is apt to say, with a dim smile, 'after all, that's what a bank is *for*, isn't it?' Since Mr Andrews so obviously believes that that is the main thing that a bank is *not* for, my answer to this is usually a gay laugh and a quick question about how ninety days is six months, isn't it? Mr Andrews is also fond of saying things like, 'Well, *we* have our obligations to meet, too, you realize,' and 'If we were to accommodate *every*one who asks us . . .'

Mr Andrews never says 'money', just like that, the way the rest of us do so often; he refers to it reverently as 'Credit' or 'Funds' or 'Equity'. I have fallen into the habit of taking one or more of my children with me when I drop in to speak to Mr Andrews about equity or funds or credit, in the unexpressed hope that their soft pathetic eyes might touch Mr

Andrews' heart, although I know by now that their soft pathetic little eyes might as easily open the door to the vault; the only time, I think, that I have ever seen Mr Andrews really taken aback was when Laurie, when he had just commenced coin-collecting, asked if he might look over the bank's small change for V nickels.

At any rate, shortly before Christmas, then – and Christmas is of course always a time of great monetary discomfort around our house – I came timidly to Mr Andrews' bank, at the back of my mind the thought that the children's presents had at least been bought and duly hidden, although not paid for, and holding by one hand my daughter Jannie, in a blue snow suit, and holding by the other hand my daughter Sally, in a red snow suit. The girls had their hair brushed and their boots on the right feet, and if I could raise the cash from Mr Andrews they were each going to have an ice cream cone. We came into the bank, where the loudspeaker system was playing 'Joy to the World', and found that the center paddock, where they usually foreclose mortgages, had been given over to a tall and gracious Christmas tree; because of the holiday season, they were foreclosing their mortgages in a sort of little recess behind the tellers. I sat the girls down on a velvet-covered bench directly in front of the Christmas tree, and told them to stay right where they were and Mommy would be back in a minute and then we would all go and get our ice cream cones. They sat down obediently, and I made my way over to Mr Andrews' secretary.

'Good morning,' I said to her.

'Good morning,' she said. 'Merry Christmas.'

'Oh,' I said. 'Merry Christmas.'

She nodded brightly and turned back to the papers on her desk. I twined my fingers around the ornamental iron work of the railing, and said, 'I wonder if I might perhaps be able to see Mr Andrews?'

'Mr Andrews? And what did you want to see him about?'

'Well,' I said, coming a little closer, 'it was to have been about our loan.'

'Your loan?' she said, in that peculiarly penetrating tone all bank employees use when there is a question of money going the unnatural, or reverse-English direction. 'You wanted to pay back your loan?'

'I hoped,' I said, 'that perhaps I could speak to Mr Andrews.'

'Isn't that sweet?' she said unexpectedly.

After a minute I realized that she was staring past me to where my girls were sitting, and I turned and saw without belief that Santa Claus, complete with sack of toys, had come out from behind the Christmas tree and was leaning over the railing and beckoning my daughters to him.

'I didn't know the bank had a Santa Claus,' I said.

'Every year,' she said. 'At Christmas, you know.'

Jannie and Sally slid off the bench and trotted over to Santa Claus; I could hear Sally's delighted, 'Hello, Santa Claus!' and see Jannie's half-embarrassed smile; people all over the bank were turning to look and to beam and to smile at one another and murmur appreciatively. Because I have known Jannie and Sally for rather a long time, I untwined my fingers from the ironwork and made across the bank for their bench, reaching them just as Santa Claus opened the little gate in the railing and ushered them inside. He sat down under the warm lights of the Christmas tree and took Jannie onto one knee and Sally onto the other.

'Well, well, well,' he said, and laughed hugely. 'And have you been a *good* girl?' he asked Jannie.

Jannie nodded, her mouth open, and Sally said, 'I've been *very* good.'

'And do you brush your teeth?'

'Twice,' said Sally, and Jannie said, '*I* brush *my* teeth every morning and every night and every morning.'

'Well, well, well,' Santa Claus said, nodding his head appreciatively. 'So you've been good little girls, have you?'

'I've been very *very* good,' Sally said insistently.

Santa Claus thought. 'And have you washed your faces?' was what he finally achieved.

'I wash *my* face,' said Sally, and Jannie, inspired, said, 'I wash my face and my hands and my arms and my ears and my neck and –'

'Well, that's just *fine*,' Santa Claus said, and again he laughed merrily, caroming Jannie and Sally off his round little belly. 'Fine, fine,' he said, 'and now,' he said to Jannie, 'what is old Santa going to bring you for Christmas?'

'A doll?' Jannie said tentatively, 'are you going to bring me a doll?'

'I most certainly *am* going to bring you a doll,' said Santa Claus. 'I'm going to bring you the prettiest doll you ever *saw*, because you've been such a *good* girl.'

'And a wagon?' Jannie said, 'and doll dishes and a little stove?'

'That's *just* what I'm going to bring you,' Santa Claus said. 'I'm going to bring good little girls *every*thing they ask for.'

The fatuous smile I had been wearing on my face began to slip a little; there was a handsome doll dressed in blue waiting for Jannie in the guest room closet, and a handsome doll dressed in pink waiting for Sally; I began trying to signal surreptitiously to Santa Claus.

'And me,' Sally said, 'and me, and *me*, I want a bicycle.'

I shook my head most violently at Santa Claus, smiling nervously. 'That's right,' Santa Claus said, 'for good little girls, I bring bicycles.'

'You're *really* going to bring me a bicycle?' Sally asked incredulously, '*and* a doll *and* a wagon?'

'I most certainly am,' Santa Claus told her.

Sally gazed raptly at Jannie. 'He's going to bring my bicycle after all,' she said.

'*I* want a bicycle too,' Jannie said.

'Allllllll right,' said Santa Claus. 'But have you been a *good* girl?' he asked Jannie anxiously.

'I've been so good,' Jannie told him with ardor, 'you just don't *know*, I've been so good.'

'I've been good,' Sally said. 'I want blocks, too. And a doll carriage for my doll, and a bicycle.'

'And our brother wants a microscope,' Jannie told Santa Claus, 'and he's been a very good boy. And a little table and chairs, I want.'

'Santa Claus,' I said, '*excuse* me, Santa Claus . . .'

'Aren't they darling?' a woman said behind me.

'And candy, and oranges, and nuts,' Santa Claus was going on blissfully, 'and all sorts of good things in your stockings, and candy canes –'

'I forgot, I want a party dress.'

'But you must be *good* little girls, and do just what your mommy and daddy tell you to, and never *never* forget to brush your teeth.'

I went with haste back to Mr Andrews' secretary. 'I've *got* to see Mr Andrews,' I told her, 'I've got to see him *fast*.'

'You'll have to wait,' she said, looking fondly over to where my daughters were receiving a final pat on the head from Santa Claus.

The loudspeaker system was playing 'O Come, All Ye Faithful', I was thinking wildly: bicycle, microscope, bicycle, table and chairs, doll dishes, and my daughters came running across the floor to me. 'Look,' Sally was shrieking, 'look at what Santa Claus gave to us.'

'Santa Claus was here,' Jannie confirmed, 'he came right into the bank where we were and he gave us each a present, look, a little bag of chocolate money.'

'Oh, fine, fine, fine,' I said madly.

'And I *am* going to have my bicycle, Santa said he was *too* bringing it.'

'– and me a bicycle too, and doll carriages and dishes and –'

'– and in our stockings.'

'Mr Andrews will see you now,' said the secretary.

I sat my daughters down again and made my entrance into Mr Andrews' office. His nose still retained a trace of jovial redness, but the jolly old elf's eye was the familiar agate, and the faint echo of jingle bells around him sounded more like the clinking of half dollars.

'Well,' said Santa Claus, selecting my loan slip from the stack on his desk, 'and what brings *you* here again so soon?'

BIENVENIDO SANTOS

The Prisoners

In Hays, Kansas, I saw some German prisoners. It was a late evening on a melancholy winter day. They marched in the snow through the deserted campus, four abreast, with a quick, eager motion in their strides that was somehow dignified. They were young, all of them, their faces flushed, and some were smiling as they walked, as though they were not prisoners, but happy workers in a happy land.

It was to have been my last day on the campus. My itinerary allowed me a Christmas vacation which I could spend anywhere I wished to, so I began planning as soon as I arrived in Kansas. From Emporia I went on to Hays, and from there it was up to me. 'You could move to your next city and await the opening of classes there,' read Dr Hager's instructions, 'or you could return to Washington, if you wish . . . It's up to you.' The note included the usual season's greetings which did not cheer me up at all, but through no fault of the good doctor.

It was quite depressing, travelling through snow-covered places. The cold streets of the little cities looked unhappy as though bearing more than their winter share of snow. And people were always hurrying to get to a room where there was a lighted stove. All the way, long before Thanksgiving, from Shippensburg in Pennsylvania, the snow had been falling all over the land. In Oneonta in New York, the frost came early. Shortly before I left the town, the trees on the hills had lost their gold.

After Hays, the next stop on my schedule was Evanston. So I decided to go to Chicago. I had been there before during my first year in America. I had run away from the deserted campus in Urbana, thinking it would be much better spending Christmas in Chicago, but it turned out differently. Now I remembered the winds, the soot, and the indifferent strangers, their impersonal faces. But, too, I remembered the huge manger where the Child Jesus lay surrounded by Mary and Joseph, and the beasts and the adoring kings. Especially at night, this familiar scene, right at the foot of the bridge on the riverside, glowed with life as though the Birth were just now, a few moments back and the cause for great rejoicing was fresh, was real.

I had made arrangements to leave for Chicago. I was coming from the railway depot when I saw those prisoners. The station agent spoke of a great snowstorm that had developed somewhere along the way, and it might be that there would be no transportation available for the next few days.

'Please give me your telephone number and I'll keep in touch with you,' he said.

I told him I was staying at the college campus. Hays was not a big city and at that time of the year, with all the college boys and girls away, it was a pretty lonesome place. The snow was still falling. Earlier in the day, during the noon hour, it looked like twilight and felt like twilight; dusk and ashes and a shadowy vagueness were over all things.

The building superintendent who gave me back the key to my room was sorry to hear that I could not go, but I told him it was all right, I expected to hear from the station agent any time.

'I'm lucky,' I said, 'I've the entire campus to myself.'

'That's right,' he laughed, 'but you're not quite alone. There are some German prisoners of war assigned to the compound temporarily. I guess you've seen them.'

'Oh, yes, I have,' I said, thinking of the tall, blond men marching in the snow.

Then I was alone in my room.

As I removed my coat, I noticed that the room had been made up, readied for the next guest of the school. Strange, but nothing in it looked familiar, nothing in it I remembered as though I had just come. Of course, there had been many other rooms like this in all my wanderings, simply furnished, warm, and comfortable. Always there was a clean smell; and mostly the walls were bare, but cool and easy on the eyes. Now I turned off the light and looked through the glass window. Outside, the snow was falling, thickest, it seemed, under the lamplights. In the distance was the highway. Headlights glared occasionally and passed on. That was the only difference, the view from the window. It was a highway now, winding somewhere through a wide expanse of level whiteness. Sometimes it was a river as in Natchatoches or a church as in Cape Girardeau.

That night, it was Christmas Eve. I could not sleep at once. The room felt too warm and the radiator made a lot of noise that was like the scampering of rats in the attic. At first I thought I had caught a fever, my ears burned and I had difficulty breathing. So I tiptoed to the window and raised the shutter a little. A whiff of the night air filled the room at once and I felt better under the thick blankets.

Then the night was filled with sounds, distant and near: the crunch of tyres on the snow, somewhere the honking of a horn, but far away; a door banging as though a house had fallen, then silence again, the noiseless fall of snow upon the earth. I remembered home; perhaps I dreamed. Now the night was filled with music, soft, muted strains of a familiar Christmas song . . . silent night, holy night . . .

My brother and I had come from Manila. It was Christmas Eve. By mistake we got off the wrong station. We had not been home for so long, we had forgotten it was to have been the next station yet, a flagstop, not the main town station. But we were so excited to be home at last, we had not remembered. So we walked a long way, in the dark, through sandy pathways, under the bamboo trees. We told our way by the sound of the river. We kept going towards it. We knew that our house was somewhere in that darkness on the river bank.

It was a beautiful night. Stars filled the sky. Choose the brightest, Greg said, and that would be the star that led the wise men to the Child in the manger. We are the wise men now, I said, although we aren't so wise, we have forgotten the way home. But the old Santiago river would lead us. Dogs barked and we shouted at them. When we passed by a nipa shack where a light shone through the nipa walls, we would call, in God's name, may we pass? And a voice or voices would answer, pass on, please, and God watch over you . . . Merry Christmas!

When we came to more houses, we could almost see our way from the lights by the windows. The air was sweet with the odour of native cakes and candies. We felt tired and hungry, but we walked on. And we kept walking till we saw the river under the stars and the familiar house on the sands. Father and Mother were there and the little ones. As we unpacked the presents we had bought for them, Father said, you didn't have to spend all your money.

Mother was having quite a time with the sticky stuff she was cooking, so I came to her and took the ladle from her hand; but instead of helping her, I put it aside and flung my arms around her thin body and squeezed her hard, crying as I did so; I had missed her so much, the smell of betel nut in her breath and the fragrance of lime in her hair. Let me go, let me go, she screamed, you're breaking my bones. As I relaxed my hold, she put her arms around my neck. She was crying also. You have stayed away too long, my son, she said. Greg was looking out of the window, towards the river. Father had turned away. Suddenly from somewhere in the night, above the noise of the river, floated the Christmas song, silent night . . . holy night . . .

Maybe I had fallen asleep after all and had dreamed all this. In my devastated country only the river perhaps had not changed.

It was daylight when I opened my eyes. I was shivering. Hurriedly, I reached for the shutter and pulled it down. The snow had stopped falling, yet there was no sun.

Merry Christmas, I said, looking at the ceiling, thinking of warm, old arms around my neck, sniffing the air for the smell of betel nut and the odour of lime. Don't be silly, I chided myself, as I always did when I was feeling quite lonesome and was missing home too much. Then I started on the usual thoughts that were supposed to make me less miserable during such moments.

About my being not too really badly off. Think of the places you have seen, the many good people you have met. You are to be envied. You are treated well wherever you go. People have been kind to you. They give you standing ovations. They hold parties in your honour. Sweet young American girls ask for your autograph as though you were a celebrity. And they write you letters. They say nice, lovely things . . . Think of other men, less fortunate, who walk alone. Think of the prisoners of war. An Ohio private in the jungles of New Guinea had written to his wife in America: 'It will be a different Christmas this year. The altar will be a fallen tree in this stinking jungle. All around there will be the stink of sweat, unwashed clothes and the fainter, sweeter smell of death. But as I kneel to pray I know you will be alongside me, praying too, and that will make it a Happy Christmas, darling.'

Suddenly I felt a great need to go to church. I should not have forgotten in the first place. It was Christmas Day. There should be a church somewhere. It was not yet too late.

Downtown, a few well-dressed people walked the streets. Some were coming from church, others were just walking, hand in hand, or alone. The things I really wanted to say, on my knees, were not too easily said. For a time I just knelt there, listening to organ music, not saying anything in particular, just thinking how it was, back home, beside the Santiago river.

At the depot, the station agent recognized me at once. 'I'm sorry for you, fellow,' he said, 'having to spend Christmas away from home like this, but I'll ring you up as soon as I have some definite news for you.'

I thanked him and walked out and the sun was shining. The streets were dirty and slushy now. I wondered whether the restaurants were open on Christmas Day. In Chicago, during that first year, I had to walk many blocks, and found one open in the dingier section of the city where the shiftless roamed in rags. Fortunately, it was not that difficult in Hays. There was a food shop open on a side street. A coloured picture of Santa Claus dispensing cigarettes was nailed on the wall above the counter.

In the afternoon, after wandering around in the sun I was back at the campus. As I was about to open the door to the main entrance, I saw the man hacking away with a shovel at the ice-covered fountain. He was one of the prisoners I had seen the day before. He wore gloves and a thick uniform. I stopped to watch him. The exertion kept him warm, I supposed. When he looked my way, I said, 'Merry Christmas,' hoping he would understand. He bowed slightly, and smiled, mumbling words. Then he resumed his work.

Soon a young man in the uniform of a US soldier came along and saluted me politely. When I greeted him, he grinned back, 'Same to you, sir.'

Then both of us watched the prisoner. The guard knew who I was and why I was still on the campus. The building superintendent had told him. Then he said that the German prisoners were keeping quarters temporarily at the boys' dormitory, the squat brick building on the west side of the hall where I was staying.

'This fellow here,' he said, 'is not supposed to work today. But ever since he saw the ice-covered fountain and learned that there were fishes there, he has been wanting to get them out. His companions don't pay any attention to him. They're feeling good and warm in their quarters, playing chess, and writing or listening to the radio.'

'Do they speak English?' I asked.

'Hardly. Just what they pick up when we talk to them and what they learn in class. Some are diligent. They learn. They try to read the papers. Others just look at the pictures.'

The prisoner had cracked the ice open. He smiled at us.

'Success, eh?' the guard said.

The prisoner rolled his sleeves up close to the armpit, and kneeling on the ground, dipped his hand into the water. He winced as the ice-cold water bit into his flesh. But after a while, perhaps it was not too cold any more. He kept his arm in the water for some time, searching the bottom for fish.

'No, no!' the prisoner said, straining to reach farther down.

'He's stubborn,' the guard said, walking away.

Then the prisoner rose to his feet. In his hand he held a tiny golden fish.

'See?' he said, smiling as though he was about to perform a trick.

'But it's stiff. It's dead,' I said.

'No, no!' the man protested, 'Will live, will live.'

He made a sign for me to follow, and together we walked to the prisoners' quarters. As the door closed behind us, the warmth of the room sent a pleasant tingle through my body. I did not realize I had stayed quite long out in the cold.

Some of the men were sipping coffee. Their bunks were clean and very neatly made. When they saw what my companion had in his hand, they turned their attention away from me. And they spoke loudly at the same time, with a lot of grimaces and gestures. My companion shook them all away, angrily it seemed, and walked towards one of the bunks and got out a glass tumbler like the ones students use in the laboratory. With this he ran out, back to the fountain.

The guard invited me to a cup of coffee and we sat among the men. They looked at me and smiled and talked among themselves in their language.

'Look,' said the guard to them, 'this gentleman comes from the Philippines.'

The prisoners took up the word, mouthing it with difficulty. 'Philippines . . . Philippines,' and it sounded strange as they pronounced the word. Some of them seemed to say that they knew the place, others didn't seem to know. They talked and they laughed. A group of them had started to open a book that lay on a table where there were magazines and a radio. A man was sitting at a corner of the long table, writing something. The noise didn't seem to bother him.

'They're all right,' I said, putting down my cup.

'You bet they are,' said the guard, 'they got to be.'

Then the group, which was interested in the book, gave out a shout, 'Philippines . . . here . . . here.' And they came to me with a map of the Orient. They were pointing at the archipelago. I glanced at it and nodded. The island looked so small.

'Very far . . . very far,' one of the prisoners was saying.

'You like the snow?' I asked the men, wanting to talk about something else. They didn't understand me at once, but when they did they said a lot in German. Then one of them spoke. 'Snow, huh? Plenty snow in Germany.'

'In the Philippines,' I said, 'we have no snow.'

The same fellow translated this to the others and they began another discussion among themselves.

Then this man who seemed to know more English than the rest, asked, 'Why not go home to Philippines. Must be nice, huh? No snow.'

'I can't go home,' I said, 'the war, you know.'

The meaning of these words was relayed to the others and suddenly there was boisterous laughter among them. They were saying a lot of things that certainly amused them, but this word they kept repeating as they looked at me, '*Gefangener . . . Gefangener,*' the word spreading in the room like a refrain. Even the man writing at the table turned to look at me.

'What's all this about?' I asked the guard.

Their interpreter answered quickly, 'They say, you're prisoner, too.'

'Well,' I began, trying to smile, but just then the prisoner came in, holding in both hands the glass tumbler half-filled with water, where many fishes floated, all dead stiff.

The other prisoners gathered around him, looking at the fish, saying things, and this man shook them all away.

'He insists,' said the guard, 'that the fish will live.'

The man had placed the tumbler on the long table and sat on the bench and stared at the fish. I came over, sitting beside him, and watched the fish for some sign of life. It looked like a vigil. Someone had turned on the radio and soft church music filled the room.

'Maybe you're right,' I said to the man beside me.

'Yes, yes,' he said without looking away from the tumbler. And softly, in a half-whisper, he kept muttering to himself, '*Wird leben. Wird leben. Hoffnung. Es besteht hoffnung.*' Then he looked at me briefly and his eyes didn't look so young, and again he turned to the fish, murmuring, 'Will live . . . will live. There is hope.'

I have learned the words since then, trying hard especially in desperate moments to believe in them. As it turned out, I never got to know whether the prisoner was right.

The station agent had been on the phone right after I had seen him, but it was not until evening that he was able to talk to me. When I left the prisoners' quarters to take the phone call, I didn't know that I was not going to see them again.

The station agent said that the Chief was coming through on its way to the East Coast. There was barely time to get packed again, although I could have returned to the prisoner's quarters and said goodbye and found out perhaps whether the fish in the tumbler had showed any signs of life, but I was too excited.

I paused under the lighted doorway as the cab-driver started putting my luggage inside the car. I looked towards the prisoners' quarters, but their lights were out. They had turned in early, but some of them must be awake, looking out through the windows. Perhaps they could see me. I waved towards them. It could be that they waved back.

MURIEL SPARK

The Leaf-Sweeper

Behind the town hall there is a wooded parkland which, towards the end of November, begins to draw a thin blue cloud right into itself; and as a rule the park floats in this haze until mid-February. I pass every day, and see Johnnie Geddes in the heart of this mist, sweeping up the leaves. Now and again he stops, and jerking his long head erect, looks indignantly at the pile of leaves, as if it ought not to be there; then he sweeps on. This business of leaf-sweeping he learnt during the years he spent in the asylum; it was the job they always gave him to do; and when he was discharged the town council gave him the leaves to sweep. But the indignant movement of the head comes naturally to him, for this has been one of his habits since he was the most promising and buoyant and vociferous graduate of his year. He looks much older than he is, for it is not quite twenty years ago that Johnnie founded the Society for the Abolition of Christmas.

Johnnie was living with his aunt then. I was at school, and in the Christmas holidays Miss Geddes gave me her nephew's pamphlet, *How to Grow Rich at Christmas*. It sounded very likely, but it turned out that you grow rich at Christmas by doing away with Christmas, and so pondered Johnnie's pamphlet no further.

But it was only his first attempt. He had, within the next three years, founded his society of Abolitionists. His new book, *Abolish Christmas or We Die*, was in great demand at the public library, and my turn for it came at last. Johnnie was really convincing, this time, and most people were completely won over until after they had closed the book. I got an old copy for sixpence the other day, and despite the lapse of time it still proves conclusively that Christmas is a national crime. Johnnie demonstrates that every human-unit in the kingdom faces inevitable starvation within a period inversely proportional to that in which one in every six industrial-productivity units, if you see what he means, stops producing toys to fill the stockings of the educational-intake units. He cites appalling statistics to show that 1.024 per cent of the time squandered each Christmas in reckless shopping and thoughtless churchgoing brings the nation closer to its doom by five years. A few readers protested, but Johnnie was able to demolish their muddled arguments, and meanwhile the Society for the Abolition of Christmas increased. But Johnnie was troubled. Not only did Christmas rage throughout the kingdom as usual that year, but he had private information that many of the Society's members had broken the Oath of Abstention.

He decided, then, to strike at the very roots of Christmas. Johnnie gave up his job on the Drainage Supply Board; he gave up all his prospects, and, financed by a few supporters, retreated for two years to study the roots of Christmas. Then, all jubilant, Johnnie produced his next and last book, in which he established, either that Christmas was an invention of the Early Fathers to propitiate the pagans, or it was invented by the pagans to placate the Early Fathers, I forget which. Against the advice of his friends, Johnnie entitled it *Christmas and Christianity*. It sold eighteen copies. Johnnie never really recovered from this; and it happened, about that time, that the girl he was engaged to, an ardent Abolitionist, sent him a pullover she had knitted, for Christmas; he sent it back, enclosing a copy of the Society's rules, and she sent back the ring. But in any case, during Johnnie's absence, the Society had been undermined by a moderate faction. These moderates finally became more moderate, and the whole thing broke up.

Soon after this, I left the district, and it was some years before I saw Johnnie again. One Sunday afternoon in summer, I was idling among the crowds who were gathered to hear the speakers at Hyde Park. One little crowd surrounded a man who bore a banner marked 'Crusade against Christmas'; his voice was frightening; it carried an unusually long way. This was Johnnie. A man in the crowd told me Johnnie was there every Sunday, very violent about Christmas, and that he would soon be taken up for insulting language. As I saw in the papers, he was soon taken up for insulting language. And a few months later I heard that poor Johnnie was in a mental home, because he had Christmas on the brain and couldn't stop shouting about it.

After that I forgot all about him until three years ago, in December, I went to live near the town where Johnnie had spent his youth. On the afternoon of Christmas Eve I was walking with a friend, noticing what had changed in my absence, and what hadn't. We passed a long, large house, once famous for its armoury, and I saw that the iron gates were wide open.

'They used to be kept shut,' I said.

'That's an asylum now,' said my friend; 'they let the mild cases work in the grounds, and leave the gates open to give them a feeling of freedom.

'But,' said my friend, 'they lock everything inside. Door after door. The lift as well; they keep it locked.'

While my friend was chattering, I stood in the gateway and looked in. Just beyond the gate was a great bare elm tree. There I saw a man in brown corduroys, sweeping up the leaves. Poor soul, he was shouting about Christmas.

'That's Johnnie Geddes,' I said. 'Has he been here all these years?'

'Yes,' said my friend as we walked on. 'I believe he gets worse at this time of year.'

'Does his aunt see him?'

'Yes. And she sees nobody else.'

We were, in fact, approaching the house where Miss Geddes lived. I suggested we call on her. I had known her well.

'No fear,' said my friend.

I decided to go in, all the same, and my friend walked on to the town.

Miss Geddes had changed, more than the landscape. She had been a solemn, calm woman, and now she moved about quickly, and gave short agitated smiles. She took me to her sitting-room, and as she opened the door she called to someone inside:

'Johnnie, see who's come to see us!'

A man, dressed in a dark suit, was standing on a chair, fixing holly behind a picture. He jumped down.

'Happy Christmas,' he said. 'A Happy and a Merry Christmas indeed. I do hope,' he said, 'you're going to stay for tea, as we've got a delightful

Christmas cake, and at this season of goodwill I would be cheered indeed if you could see how charmingly it's decorated; it has "Happy Christmas" in red icing, and then there's a robin and –'

'Johnnie,' said Miss Geddes, 'you're forgetting the carols.'

'The carols,' he said. He lifted a gramophone record from a pile and put it on. It was 'The Holly and the Ivy'.

'It's "The Holly and the Ivy",' said Miss Geddes. 'Can't we have something else? We had that all morning.'

'It is sublime,' he said, beaming from his chair, and holding up his hand for silence.

While Miss Geddes went to fetch the tea, and he sat absorbed in his carol, I watched him. He was so like Johnnie, that if I hadn't seen poor Johnnie a few moments before, sweeping up the asylum leaves, I would have thought he really was Johnnie. Miss Geddes returned with the tray, and while he rose to put on another record, he said something that startled me.

'I saw you in the crowd that Sunday when I was speaking at Hyde Park.'

'What a memory you have!' said Miss Geddes.

'It must be ten years ago,' he said.

'My nephew has altered his opinion of Christmas,' she explained. 'He always comes home for Christmas now, and don't we have a jolly time, Johnnie?'

'Rather!' he said. 'Oh, let me cut the cake.'

He was very excited about the cake. With a flourish he dug a large knife into the side. The knife slipped, and I saw it run deep into his finger. Miss Geddes did not move. He wrenched his cut finger away, and went on slicing the cake.

'Isn't it bleeding?' I said.

He held up his hand. I could see the deep cut, but there was no blood.

Deliberately, and perhaps desperately, I turned to Miss Geddes.

'That house up the road,' I said, 'I see it's a mental home now. I passed it this afternoon.'

'Johnnie,' said Miss Geddes, as one who knows the game is up, 'go and fetch the mince pies.'

He went, whistling a carol.

'You passed the asylum,' said Miss Geddes wearily.

'Yes,' I said.

'And you saw Johnnie sweeping up the leaves.'

'Yes.'

We could still hear the whistling of the carol.

'Who is *he*?' I said.

'That's Johnnie's ghost,' she said. 'He comes home every Christmas. But,' she said, 'I don't like him. I can't bear him any longer, and I'm going away tomorrow. I don't want Johnnie's ghost, I want Johnnie in flesh and blood.'

I shuddered, thinking of the cut finger that could not bleed. And I left, before Johnnie's ghost returned with the mince pies.

Next day, as I had arranged to join a family who lived in the town, I started walking over about noon. Because of the light mist, I didn't see at first who it was approaching. It was a man, waving his arm to me. It turned out to be Johnnie's ghost.

'Happy Christmas. What do you think,' said Johnnie's ghost, 'my aunt has gone to London. Fancy, on Christmas Day, and I thought she was at church, and here I am without anyone to spend a jolly Christmas with, and, of course, I forgive her, as it's the season of goodwill, but I'm glad to see you, because now I can come with you, wherever it is you're going, and we can all have a Happy . . .'

'Go away,' I said, and walked on.

It sounds hard. But perhaps you don't know how repulsive and loath-some is the ghost of a living man. The ghosts of the dead may be all right, but the ghost of mad Johnnie gave me the creeps.

'Clear off,' I said.

He continued walking beside me. 'As it's the time of goodwill, I make allowances for your tone,' he said. 'But I'm coming.'

We had reached the asylum gates, and there, in the grounds, I saw Johnnie sweeping the leaves. I suppose it was his way of going on strike, working on Christmas Day. He was making a noise about Christmas.

On a sudden impulse I said to Johnnie's ghost, 'You want company?'

'Certainly,' he replied. 'It's the season of . . .'

'Then you shall have it,' I said.

I stood in the gateway. 'Oh, Johnnie,' I called.

He looked up.

'I've brought your ghost to see you, Johnnie.'

'Well, well,' said Johnnie, advancing to meet his ghost. 'Just imagine it!'

'Happy Christmas,' said Johnnie's ghost.

'Oh, really?' said Johnnie.

I left them to it. And when I looked back, wondering if they would come to blows, I saw that Johnnie's ghost was sweeping the leaves as well. They seemed to be arguing at the same time. But it was still misty, and really, I can't say whether, when I looked a second time, there were two men or one man sweeping the leaves.

Johnnie began to improve in the New Year. At least, he stopped shouting about Christmas, and then he never mentioned it at all; in a few months, when he had almost stopped saying anything, they discharged him.

The town council gave him the leaves of the park to sweep. He seldom speaks, and recognizes nobody. I see him every day at the late end of the year, working within the mist. Sometimes, if there is a sudden gust, he jerks his head up to watch a few leaves falling behind him, as if amazed that they are undeniably there, although, by rights, the falling of leaves should be stopped.

TRUMAN CAPOTE

A Christmas Memory

Imagine a morning in late November. A coming of winter morning more than twenty years ago. Consider the kitchen of a spreading old house in a country town. A great black stove is its main feature; but there is also a big round table and a fireplace with two rocking chairs placed in front of it. Just today the fireplace commenced its seasonal roar.

A woman with shorn white hair is standing at the kitchen window. She is wearing tennis shoes and a shapeless gray sweater over a summery calico dress. She is small and sprightly, like a bantam hen; but, due to a long youthful illness, her shoulders are pitifully hunched. Her face is remarkable – not unlike Lincoln's, craggy like that, and tinted by sun and wind; but it is delicate too, finely boned, and her eyes are sherry-colored and timid. 'Oh my,' she exclaims, her breath smoking the windowpane, 'it's fruitcake weather!'

The person to whom she is speaking is myself. I am seven; she is sixty-something. We are cousins, very distant ones, and we have lived together – well, as long as I can remember. Other people inhabit the house, relatives; and though they have power over us, and frequently make us cry, we are not, on the whole, too much aware of them. We are each other's best friend. She calls me Buddy, in memory of a boy who was formerly her best friend. The other Buddy died in the 1880s, when she was still a child. She is still a child.

'I knew it before I got out of bed,' she says, turning away from the window with a purposeful excitement in her eyes. 'The courthouse bell sounded so cold and clear. And there were no birds singing; they've gone to warmer country, yes indeed. Oh, Buddy, stop stuffing biscuit and fetch our buggy. Help me find my hat. We've thirty cakes to bake.'

It's always the same: a morning arrives in November, and my friend, as though officially inaugurating the Christmas time of year that exhilarates her imagination and fuels the blaze of her heart, announces: 'It's fruitcake weather! Fetch our buggy. Help me find my hat.'

The hat is found, a straw cartwheel corsaged with velvet roses out-of-doors has faded: it once belonged to a more fashionable relative. Together, we guide our buggy, a dilapidated baby carriage, out to the garden and into a grove of pecan trees. The buggy is mine; that is, it was bought for me when I was born. It is made of wicker, rather unraveled, and the wheels wobble like a drunkard's legs. But it is a faithful object; springtimes, we take it to the woods and fill it with flowers, herbs, wild fern for our porch pots; in the summer, we pile it with picnic paraphernalia and sugar-cane fishing poles and roll it down to the edge of a creek; it has its winter uses, too: as a truck for hauling firewood from the yard to the kitchen, as a warm bed for Queenie, our tough little orange and white rat terrier who has survived distemper and two rattlesnake bites. Queenie is trotting beside it now.

Three hours later we are back in the kitchen hulling a heaping buggyload of windfall pecans. Our backs hurt from gathering them: how hard they were to find (the main crop having been shaken off the trees and sold by the orchard's owners, who are not us) among the concealing leaves, the frosted, deceiving grass. Caarackle! A cheery crunch, scraps of miniature thunder sound as the shells collapse and the golden mound of sweet oily ivory meat mounts in the milk-glass bowl. Queenie begs to taste, and now and again my friend sneaks her a mite, though insisting we deprive ourselves. 'We mustn't, Buddy. If we start, we won't stop. And there's scarcely enough as there is. For thirty cakes.' The kitchen is growing dark. Dusk turns the window into a mirror: our reflections mingle with the rising moon as we work by the fireside in the firelight. At last, when the moon is quite high, we toss the final hull into the fire and, with joined sighs, watch it catch flame. The buggy is empty, the bowl is brimful.

We eat our supper (cold biscuits, bacon, blackberry jam) and discuss tomorrow. Tomorrow the kind of work I like best begins: buying. Cherries and citron, ginger and vanilla and canned Hawaiian pineapple, rinds and raisins and walnuts and whiskey and oh, so much flour, butter, so many eggs, spices, flavorings: why, we'll need a pony to pull the buggy home.

But before these purchases can be made, there is the question of money. Neither of us has any. Except for skinflint sums persons in the house occasionally provide (a dime is considered very big money); or what we earn ourselves from various activities: holding rummage sales, selling buckets of handpicked blackberries, jars of homemade jam and apple jelly and peach preserves, rounding up flowers for funerals and weddings. Once we won seventy-ninth prize, five dollars, in a national football contest. Not that we know a fool thing about football. It's just that we enter any contest we hear about: at the moment our hopes are centered on the fifty-thousand-dollar Grand Prize being offered to name a new brand of coffee (we suggested 'A.M.'; and, after some hesitation, for my friend thought it perhaps sacrilegious, the slogan 'A.M.! Amen!'). To tell the truth, our only *really* profitable enterprise was the Fun and Freak Museum we conducted in a back-yard woodshed two summers ago. The Fun was a stereopticon with slide views of Washington and New York lent us by a relative who had been to those places (she was furious when she discovered why we'd borrowed it); the Freak was a three-legged biddy chicken hatched by one of our own hens. Everybody hereabouts wanted to see that biddy: we charged grownups a nickel, kids two cents. And took in a good twenty dollars before the museum shut down due to the decease of the main attraction.

But one way and another we do each year accumulate Christmas savings, a Fruitcake Fund. These moneys we keep hidden in an ancient bead purse under a loose board under the floor under a chamber pot under my friend's bed. The purse is seldom removed from this safe location except to make a deposit, or, as happens every Saturday, a withdrawal; for on Saturdays I am allowed ten cents to go to the picture show. My friend has never been to a picture show, nor does she intend to: 'I'd rather hear you tell the story, Buddy. That way I can imagine it more. Besides, a person my age shouldn't squander their eyes. When the Lord comes, let me see him clear.' In addition to never having seen a movie, she has never: eaten in a restaurant, traveled more than five miles from home, received or sent a telegram, read anything except funny papers and the Bible, worn cosmetics, cursed, wished someone harm, told a lie on purpose, let a hungry dog go hungry. Here are a few things she has done, does do: killed with a hoe the biggest rattlesnake ever seen in this country (sixteen rattles), dip snuff (secretly), tame humming-birds (just try it) till they balance on her finger, tell ghost stories (we both believe in ghosts) so tingling they chill you in July, talk to herself, take walks in the rain, grow the prettiest japonicas in town, know the recipe for every sort of old-time Indian cure, including a magical wart-remover.

Now, with supper finished, we retire to the room in a faraway part of the house where my friend sleeps in a scrap-quilt-covered iron bed painted rose pink, her favorite color. Silently, wallowing in the pleasures of conspiracy, we take the bead purse from its secret place and spill its contents on the scrap quilt. Dollar bills, tightly rolled and green as May buds. Somber fifty-cent pieces, heavy enough to weight a dead man's eyes. Lovely dimes, the liveliest coin, the one that really jingles. Nickels and quarters, worn smooth as creek pebbles. But mostly a hateful heap of bitter-odored pennies. Last summer others in the house contracted to pay us a penny for every twenty-five flies we killed. Oh, the carnage of August: the flies that flew to heaven! Yet it was not work in which we took pride. And, as we sit counting pennies, it is as though we were back tabulating dead flies. Neither of us has a head for figures; we count slowly, lose track, start again. According to her calculations we have $12.73. According to mine, exactly $13. 'I do hope you're wrong, Buddy. We can't mess around with thirteen. The cakes will fall. Or put somebody in the cemetery. Why, I wouldn't dream of getting out of bed on the thirteenth.' This is true: she always spends thirteenths in bed. So, to be on the safe side, we subtract a penny and toss it out the window.

Of the ingredients that go into our fruitcakes, whiskey is the most expensive, as well as the hardest to obtain: State laws forbid its sale. But everybody knows you can buy a bottle from Mr Haha Jones. And the next day, having completed our more prosaic shopping, we set out for Mr Haha's business address, a 'sinful' (to quote public opinion) fish-fry and dancing café down by the river. We've been there before, and on the same errand; but in previous years our dealings have been with Haha's wife, an iodine-dark Indian woman with brazzy peroxided hair and a dead-tired disposition. Actually, we've never laid eyes on her husband, though we've heard that he's an Indian too. A giant with razor scars across his cheeks. They call him Haha because he's so gloomy, a man who never laughs. As we approach his café (a large log cabin festooned inside and out with chains of garish-gay naked lightbulbs and standing by the river's muddy edge under the shade of river trees where moss drifts through the branches like gray mist) our steps slow down. Even Queenie stops prancing and sticks close by. People have been murdered in Haha's café. Cut to pieces. Hit on the head. There's a case coming up in court next month. Naturally these goings-on happen at night when the colored lights cast crazy patterns and the victrola wails. In the daytime Haha's is shabby and deserted. I knock at the door, Queenie barks, my friend calls: 'Mrs Haha, ma'am? Anyone to home?'

Footsteps. The door opens. Our hearts overturn. It's Mr Haha Jones himself! And he *is* a giant; he *does* have scars; he *doesn't* smile. No, he glowers at us through Satan-tilted eyes and demands to know: 'What you want with Haha?'

For a moment we are too paralyzed to tell. Presently my friend half-finds her voice, a whispery voice at best: 'If you please, Mr Haha, we'd like a quart of your finest whiskey.'

His eyes tilt more. Would you believe it? Haha is smiling! Laughing, too. 'Which one of you is a drinkin' man?'

'It's for making fruitcakes, Mr Haha. Cooking.'

This sobers him. He frowns. 'That's no way to waste good whiskey.' Nevertheless, he retreats into the shadowed café and seconds later appears carrying a bottle of daisy yellow unlabeled liquor. He demonstrates its sparkle in the sunlight and says: 'Two dollars.'

We pay him with nickels and dimes and pennies. Suddenly, jangling the coins in his hand like a fistful of dice, his face softens. 'Tell you what,' he proposes, pouring the money back into our bead purse, 'just send me one of them fruitcakes instead.'

'Well,' my friend remarks on our way home, 'there's a lovely man. We'll put an extra cup of raisins in *his* cake.'

The black stove, stoked with coal and firewood, glows like a lighted pumpkin. Eggbeaters whirl, spoons spin round in bowls of butter and sugar, vanilla sweetens the air, ginger spices it; melting, nose-tingling odors saturate the kitchen, suffuse the house, drift out to the world on puffs of chimney smoke. In four days our work is done. Thirty-one cakes, dampened with whiskey, bask on window sills and shelves.

Who are they for?

Friends. Not necessarily neighbor friends: indeed, the larger share are intended for persons we've met maybe once, perhaps not at all. People who've struck our fancy. Like President Roosevelt. Like the Reverend and Mrs J. C. Lucey, Baptist missionaries to Borneo who lectured here last winter. Or the little knife grinder who comes through town twice a year. Or Abner Packer, the driver of the six o'clock bus from Mobile, who exchanges waves with us every day as he passes in a dust-cloud whoosh. Or the young Wistons, a California couple whose car one afternoon broke down outside the house and who spent a pleasant hour chatting with us on the porch (young Mr Wiston snapped our picture, the only one we've ever had taken). Is it because my friend is shy with everyone *except* strangers that these strangers, and merest acquaintances, seem to us our truest friends? I think yes. Also, the scrapbooks we keep of thank-you's on White House stationery, time-to-time communications from California and Borneo, the knife grinder's penny post cards, make us feel connected to eventful worlds beyond the kitchen with its view of a sky that stops.

Now a nude December fig branch grates against the window. The kitchen is empty, the cakes are gone; yesterday we carted the last of them to the post office, where the cost of stamps turned our purse inside out. We're broke. That rather depresses me, but my friend insists on celebrating with two inches of whiskey left in Haha's bottle. Queenie has a spoonful in a bowl of coffee (she likes her coffee chicory-flavored and strong). The rest we divide between a pair of jelly glasses. We're both quite awed at the prospect of drinking straight whiskey; the taste of it brings screwed-up expressions and sour shudders. But by and by we begin to sing, the two of us singing different songs simultaneously. I don't know the words to mine, just: *Come on along, come on along, to the dark-town strutters' ball.* But I can dance: that's what I mean to be, a tap dancer in the movies. My dancing shadow rollicks on the walls; our voices rock the chinaware; we giggle: as if unseen hands were tickling us. Queenie rolls on her back, her paws plow the air, something like a grin stretches her black lips. Inside myself I feel warm and sparky as those crumbling logs, carefree as the wind in the chimney. My friend waltzes round the stove, the hem of her poor calico skirt pinched between her fingers as though it were a party dress: *Show me the way to go home*, she sings, her tennis shoes squeaking on the floor. *Show me the way to go home.*

Enter: two relatives. Very angry. Potent with eyes that scold, tongues that scald. Listen to what they have to say, the words tumbling together into a wrathful tune: 'A child of seven! whiskey on his breath! are you out of your mind? feeding a child of seven! must be loony! road to ruination! remember Cousin Kate? Uncle Charlie? Uncle Charlie's brother-in-law? shame! scandal! humiliation! kneel, pray, beg the Lord!'

Queenie sneaks under the stove. My friend gazes at her shoes, her chin quivers, she lifts her skirt and blows her nose and runs to her room. Long after the town has gone to sleep and the house is silent except for the chimings of clocks and the sputter of fading fires, she is weeping into a pillow already as wet as a widow's handkerchief.

'Don't cry,' I say, sitting at the bottom of her bed and shivering despite my flannel nightgown that smells of last winter's cough syrup, 'don't cry,' I beg, teasing her toes, tickling her feet, 'you're too old for that.'

'It's because,' she hiccups, 'I *am* too old. Old and funny.'

'Not funny. Fun. More fun than anybody. Listen. If you don't stop crying you'll be so tired tomorrow we can't go cut a tree.'

She straightens up. Queenie jumps on the bed (where Queenie is not allowed) to lick her cheeks. 'I know where we'll find pretty trees, Buddy. And holly, too. With berries big as your eyes. It's way off in the woods. Farther than we've ever been. Papa used to bring us Christmas trees from there: carry them on his shoulder. That's fifty years ago. Well, now: I can't wait for morning.'

Morning. Frozen rime lusters the grass; the sun, round as an orange and orange as hot-weather moons, balances on the horizon, burnishes the silvered winter woods. A wild turkey calls. A renegade hog grunts in the undergrowth. Soon, by the edge of knee-deep, rapid-running water, we have to abandon the buggy. Queenie wades the stream first, paddles across barking complaints at the swiftness of the current, the pneumonia-making coldness of it. We follow, holding our shoes and equipment (a hatchet, a burlap sack) above our heads. A mile more: of chastising thorns, burs and briers that catch at our clothes; of rusty pine needles brilliant with gaudy fungus and molted feathers. Here, there, a flash, a flutter, an ecstasy of shrillings remind us that not all the birds have flown south. Always, the path unwinds through lemony sun pools and pitch vine tunnels. Another creek to cross: a disturbed armada of speckled trout froths the water round us, and frogs the size of plates practice belly flops; beaver workmen are building a dam. On the farther shore, Queenie shakes herself and trembles. My friend shivers, too: not with cold but enthusiasm. One of her hat's ragged roses sheds a petal as she lifts her head and inhales the pine-heavy air. 'We're almost there; can you smell it, Buddy?' she says, as though we were approaching an ocean.

And, indeed, it is a kind of ocean. Scented acres of holiday trees, prickly-leafed holly. Red berries shiny as Chinese bells: black crows swoop upon them screaming. Having stuffed our burlap sacks with enough greenery and crimson to garland a dozen windows, we set about choosing a tree. 'It should be,' muses my friend, 'twice as tall as a boy. So a boy can't steal the star.' The one we pick is twice as tall as me. A brave handsome brute that survives thirty hatchet strokes before it keels with a creaking rending cry. Lugging it like a kill, we commence the long trek out. Every few yards we abandon the struggle, sit down and pant. But we have the strength of triumphant huntsmen; that and the tree's virile, icy perfume revive us, goad us on. Many compliments accompany our sunset return along the red clay road to town; but my friend is sly and noncommittal when passers-by praise the treasure perched on our buggy: what a fine tree and where did it come from? 'Yonderways,' she murmurs vaguely. Once a car stops and the rich mill owner's lazy wife leans out and whines: 'Giveya two-bits cash for that ol tree.' Ordinarily my friend is afraid of saying no; but on this occasion she promptly shakes her head: 'We wouldn't take a dollar.' The mill owner's wife persists. 'A dollar, my foot! Fifty cents. That's my last offer. Goodness, woman, you can get another one.' In answer, my friend gently reflects: 'I doubt it. There's never two of anything.'

Home: Queenie slumps by the fire and sleeps till tomorrow, snoring loud as a human.

A trunk in the attic contains: a shoebox of ermine tails (off the opera cape of a curious lady who once rented a room in the house), coils of frazzled tinsel gone gold with age, one silver star, a brief rope of dilapidated, undoubtedly dangerous candy-like light bulbs. Excellent decorations, as far as they go, which isn't far enough: my friend wants our tree to blaze 'like a Baptist window', droop with weighty snows of ornament. But we can't afford the made-in-Japan splendors at the five-and-dime. So we do what we've always done: sit for days at the kitchen table with scissors and crayons and stacks of colored paper. I make sketches and my friend cuts them out: lots of cats, fish too (because they're easy to draw), some apples, some watermelons, a few winged angels devised from saved-up sheets of Hershey-bar tin foil. We use safety pins to attach these creations to the tree; as a final touch, we sprinkle the branches with shredded cotton (picked in August for this purpose). My friend, surveying the effect, clasps her hands together. 'Now honest, Buddy. Doesn't it look good enough to eat?' Queenie tries to eat an angel.

After weaving and ribboning holly wreaths for all the front windows, our next project is the fashioning of family gifts. Tie-dye scarves for the ladies, for the men a home-brewed lemon and licorice and aspirin syrup to be taken 'at the first Symptoms of a Cold and after Hunting'. But when it comes time for making each other's gift, my friend and I separate to work secretly. I would like to buy her a pearl-handled knife, a radio, a whole pound of chocolate-covered cherries (we tasted some once, and she always swears: 'I could live on them, Buddy, Lord yes I could – and that's not taking His name in vain'). Instead, I am building her a kite. She would like to give me a bicycle (she's said so on several million occasions: 'If only I could, Buddy. It's bad enough in life to do without something *you* want; but confound it, what gets my goat is not being able to give somebody something you want *them* to have. Only one of these days I will, Buddy. Locate you a bike. Don't ask how. Steal it, maybe'). Instead, I'm fairly certain that she is building me a kite – the same as last year, and the year before: the year before that we exchanged slingshots. All of which is fine by me. For we are champion kite-fliers who study the wind like sailors; my friend, more accomplished than I, can get a kite aloft when there isn't enough breeze to carry clouds.

Christmas Eve afternoon we scrape together a nickel and go to the butcher's to buy Queenie's traditional gift, a good gnawable beef bone. The bone, wrapped in funny paper, is placed high in the tree near the silver star. Queenie knows it's there. She squats at the foot of the tree staring up in a trance of greed: when bedtime arrives she refuses to budge. Her excitement is equaled by my own. I kick the covers and turn my pillow as though it were a scorching summer's night. Somewhere a rooster crows: falsely, for the sun is still on the other side of the world.

'Buddy, are you awake?' It is my friend, calling from her room, which is next to mine; and an instant later she is sitting on my bed holding a candle. 'Well, I can't sleep a hoot,' she declares. 'My mind's jumping like a jack rabbit. Buddy, do you think Mrs Roosevelt will serve our cake at dinner?' We huddle in the bed, and she squeezes my hand I-love-you. 'Seems like your hand used to be so much smaller. I guess I hate to see you grow up. When you're grown up, will we still be friends?' I say always. 'But I feel so bad, Buddy. I wanted so bad to give you a bike. I tried to sell my cameo Papa gave me. Buddy' – she hesitates, as though embarrassed – 'I made you another kite.' Then I confess that I made her one, too; and we laugh. The candle burns too short to hold. Out it goes, exposing the starlight, the stars spinning at the window like a visible caroling that slowly, slowly daybreak silences. Possibly we doze; but the beginnings of dawn splash us like cold water: we're up, wide-eyed and wandering while we wait for others to waken. Quite deliberately my friend drops a kettle on the kitchen floor. I tap-dance in front of closed doors. One by one the household emerges, looking as though they'd like to kill us both; but it's Christmas, so they can't. First, a gorgeous breakfast: just everything you can imagine – from flapjacks and fried squirrel to hominy grits and honey-in-the-comb. Which puts everyone in a good humor except my friend and I. Frankly, we're so impatient to get at the presents we can't eat a mouthful.

Well, I'm disappointed. Who wouldn't be? With socks, a Sunday school shirt, some handkerchiefs, a hand-me-down sweater and a year's subscription to a religious magazine for children. *The Little Shepherd*. It makes me boil. It really does.

My friend has a better haul. A sack of Satsumas, that's her best present. She is proudest, however, of a white wool shawl knitted by her married sister. But she *says* her favorite gift is the kite I built her. And it *is* very beautiful; though not as beautiful as the one she made me, which is blue and scattered with gold and green Good Conduct stars; moreover, my name is painted on it, 'Buddy'.

'Buddy, the wind is blowing.'

The wind is blowing, and nothing will do till we've run to a pasture below the house where Queenie has scooted to bury her bone (and where, a winter hence, Queenie will be buried, too). There, plunging through the healthy waist-high grass, we unreel our kites, feel them twitching at the string like sky fish as they swim into the wind. Satisfied, sun-warmed, we sprawl in the grass and peel Satsumas and watch our kites cavort. Soon I forget the socks and hand-me-down sweater. I'm as happy as if we'd already won the fifty-thousand-dollar Grand Prize in that coffee-naming contest.

'My, how foolish I am!' my friend cries, suddenly alert, like a woman remembering too late she has biscuits in the oven. 'You know what I've always thought?' she asks in a tone of discovery, and not smiling at me but a point beyond. 'I've always thought a body would have to be sick and dying before they saw the Lord. And I imagined that when He came it would be like looking at the Baptist window: pretty as colored glass with the sun pouring through, such a shine you don't know it's getting dark. And it's been a comfort: to think of that shine taking away all the spooky feeling. But I'll wager it never happens. I'll wager at the very end a body realizes the Lord has already shown Himself. That things as they are' – her hand circles in a gesture that gathers clouds and kites and grass and Queenie pawing earth over her bone – 'just what they've always seen, was seeing Him. As for me, I could leave the world with today in my eyes.'

This is our last Christmas together.

Life separates us. Those who Know Best decide that I belong in a military school. And so follows a miserable succession of bugle-blowing prisons, grim reveille-ridden summer camps. I have a new home too. But it doesn't count. Home is where my friend is, and there I never go.

And there she remains, puttering around the kitchen. Alone with Queenie. Then alone. ('Buddy dear,' she writes in her wild hard-to-read script, 'yesterday Jim Macy's horse kicked Queenie bad. Be thankful she didn't feel much. I wrapped her in a Fine Linen sheet and rode her in the buggy down to Simpson's pasture where she can be with all her Bones . . .') For a few Novembers she continues to bake her fruitcakes single-handed; not as many, but some: and, of course, she always sends me 'the best of the batch'. Also, in every letter she encloses a dime wadded in toilet paper: 'See a picture show and write me the story.' But gradually in her letters she tends to confuse me with her other friend, the Buddy who died in the 1880s; more and more thirteenths are not the only days she stays in bed:

a morning arrives in November, a leafless birdless coming of winter morning, when she cannot rouse herself to exclaim: 'Oh my, it's fruitcake weather!'

And when that happens, I know it. A message saying so merely confirms a piece of news some secret vein had already received, severing from me an irreplaceable part of myself, letting it loose like a kite on a broken string. That is why, walking across a school campus on this particular December morning, I keep searching the sky. As if I expected to see, rather like hearts, a lost pair of kites hurrying toward heaven.

WOLFDIETRICH SCHNURRE

The Loan

Translated by Lyn Marven

Father generally went to a lot of trouble at Christmas. It was admittedly particularly difficult at that time to get over the fact that we were unemployed. Other festivals you either celebrated or you didn't; but Christmas was something you lived for, and when it finally came you held on to it; and as for the shop windows, they often couldn't bring themselves to part from their chocolate Father Christmases even in January.

It was the dwarves and the Kasperles that did it for me particularly. If Father was there, I would look away; but that was more conspicuous than staring at them; and so gradually I started to look at the shops again.

Father was not insensitive to the shop window displays either, he just hid it better. Christmas, he said, was a festival of joy; the important thing now was not to be sad, even if one didn't have any money.

'Most people,' Father said, 'are just happy on the first and second days of Christmas, maybe again later at New Year. But that's not enough; you have to start the being happy at least a month before. At New Year,' Father said, 'you can feel free to be sad again; for it is never nice when a year simply goes, just like that. But now, before Christmas, being sad is inappropriate.'

Father himself always made a big effort not to be sad around this time of year; but for some reason he found it harder than I did; probably because he no longer had a father who could say to him what he always said to me. And things would definitely also have been much easier if Father had still had his job. He would even have worked as an assistant lab technician now; but they didn't need any assistant lab technicians at the moment. The director had said that he could certainly stay in the museum, but for work he would have to wait until better times.

'And when will that be, do you think?' Father had asked.

'I don't want to upset you,' the director had said.

Frieda had had better luck; she had been taken on as a kitchen help in a large pub on Alexanderplatz and had also got lodgings there straight away. It was quite pleasant for us not to be with her constantly; now we only saw each other at lunchtime and in the evening she was much nicer.

But on the whole we didn't live badly. For Frieda kept us well supplied with food and if it was too cold at home, we went over to the museum; and when we had looked at all the exhibits, we would lean against the heating underneath the dinosaur skeleton, look out the window or start up a conversation with the museum attendant about breeding rabbits.

So actually it was entirely fitting that the year be brought to an end in peace and tranquillity. That was, if Father hadn't worried so much about a Christmas tree. It came up quite suddenly.

We had collected Frieda from the pub and walked her home and lain down in bed, when Father slammed shut his book, *Brehm's Life of Animals*, which he still used to read in the evening, and called over to me, 'Are you asleep yet?'

'No,' I said, because it was too cold to sleep.

'It's just occurred to me,' Father said, 'we need a Christmas tree, don't we?' He paused for a second and waited for my answer.

'Do you think so?' I said.

'Yes,' Father said, 'and a proper, pretty one at that; not one of those wee ones that falls over as soon as you hang so much as a walnut on it.'

At the word walnut I sat up. Maybe we could also get some gingerbread biscuits to hang on it as well?

Father cleared his throat. 'God –,' he said, 'why not; we'll talk to Frieda.'

'Maybe Frieda knows someone who would give us a tree too,' I said.

Father doubted it. In any case: the kind of tree he had in mind no one would give away, it would be a treasure, a treat.

Would it be worth one mark, I wanted to know.

'One mark?!' Father snorted through his nose scornfully, 'Two at least!'

'And where is this tree?'

'See,' Father said, 'that's just what I'm wondering.'

'But we can't actually buy it though,' I said. 'Two marks: where could you possibly get that money?'

Father lifted the paraffin lamp and looked around the room. I knew he was wondering whether there was anything else he could take to the pawn shop; but everything had already gone, even the gramophone; I had cried so much when the fellow behind the grille had shuffled away with it.

Father put the lamp back down and cleared his throat. 'Go to sleep now; I'll have a think about the situation.'

The next few days we simply hung around the Christmas tree stalls. Tree after tree grew legs and walked off; but we still didn't have one.

'Could we not –?' I asked on the fifth day, once we were leaning against the heating in the museum underneath the dinosaur skeleton again.

'Could we what?' Father asked sharply.

'I mean, should we not just try to get a normal tree?'

'Are you mad?!' Father was indignant. 'Maybe one of those cabbage stalks that you don't know afterwards if it's supposed to be a sweeping brush or a toothbrush? Out of the question.'

But it was no good; Christmas was getting closer and closer. At first the forests of Christmas trees in the streets were still well stocked; but gradually they developed clearings, and one afternoon we watched as the fattest Christmas tree seller on Alexanderplatz, Strapping-Jimmy, sold his last little tree, a real matchstick of a tree, for three marks fifty, spat on the money, jumped on his bike and cycled off.

Now we did begin to feel sad. Not very sad; but at any rate it was enough for Frieda to furrow her brows even more than she usually did and ask us what was up.

We had got used to keeping our troubles to ourselves, but not this time; and Father told her.

Frieda listened carefully. 'That's it?'

We nodded.

'You're funny,' Frieda said. 'Why don't you just go to the Grunewald forest and steal one?'

I have seen father outraged many times, but never as outraged as he was this evening.

He went pale as chalk. 'Are you serious?' he asked hoarsely.

Frieda was very surprised. 'Of course,' she said, 'that's what everyone does.'

'Everyone!' Father echoed, 'everyone!' He stood up stiffly and took my hand. 'You'll permit me,' he said, 'to take the boy home first before I give you the answer that deserves.'

He never gave her the answer. Frieda was sensible; she played along with Father's prudery and the next day she apologized.

But it didn't make any difference; we still didn't have a tree, never mind the stately tree Father had in mind.

But then – it was 23 December and we had just taken up our usual position under the dinosaur skeleton – inspiration struck Father.

'Do you have a spade?' he asked the museum attendant, who had nodded off next to us on his folding chair.

'What?!' he yelled with a start, 'Do I have a what?!'

'A spade, man,' Father said impatiently, 'do you have a spade?'

Yes, he had one.

I looked up at Father uncertainly. However he looked reasonably normal; only his gaze seemed a touch more unsteady than usual.

'Good,' he said then, 'we'll come back to your place tonight and you can lend it to us.'

It was later that night before I discovered what he had planned.

'Come on,' Father said and shook me, 'get up.'

Still drowsy I crawled over the bars of the bed. 'What on earth is going on?'

'Now listen,' Father said and stood in front of me, 'stealing a tree, that's bad; but borrowing one, that's okay.'

'Borrowing?' I asked, blinking.

'Yes,' Father said. 'We're going to go to Friedrichshain park and dig up a blue spruce. We'll put it in the bath in some water at home, celebrate Christmas with it tomorrow and then afterwards we'll plant it back in the same place. Well?' He gave me a piercing stare.

'A fantastic idea,' I said.

Humming and whistling we set off; Father with the spade on his back, me with a sack under my arm. Every now and then Father would stop whistling and we sang in two-part harmony, 'Deck the Halls' and 'The First Noël the Angel Did Say'. As always with such carols, Father had tears in his eyes and I too was in a very solemn mood.

Then Friedrichshain park appeared before us and we fell silent.

The blue spruce that Father had his eye on stood in the middle of a round flowerbed of roses covered in straw. It was a good metre and a half tall and a model of regular growth.

As the earth was only frozen just under the surface it didn't take long at all before Father had exposed the roots. Then we carefully tipped the tree over, put it roots first into the sack, Father hung his jacket over the end sticking out, we shovelled the earth back into the hole, spread straw over the top, Father loaded the tree onto his shoulder and we went home. Here we filled the big tin bath with water and put the tree in.

When I woke the next morning Father and Frieda were already busy decorating the tree. It had been fastened to the ceiling with string and Frieda had cut a selection of stars out of tinfoil which she was hanging on its branches; they looked very pretty. I also saw some gingerbread men hanging there. I didn't want to spoil their fun; so I pretended I was still asleep. While I did, I thought about how I could repay them for their kindness. Eventually it occurred to me: Father had borrowed a Christmas tree, why shouldn't I also manage to get a loan of our pawned gramophone for the holidays? I acted like I had just woken up, admired the tree in seemly fashion, and then I got dressed and went out.

The pawnbroker was a horrible person, even the first time we were there and Father had given him his coat. I would have happily given him something else too; but now it was necessary to be friendly to him.

I also made a great effort. I told him a story of two grandmothers and 'especially at Christmas' and 'enjoying the old days one more time' and so on, and suddenly the pawnbroker struck out and clouted me one and said quite calmly, 'I don't care how much you fib otherwise; but at Christmas you tell the truth, got it?' Then he shuffled into the next room and brought out the gramophone. 'But woe betide you if you break anything! And only for three days! And only because it's you.'

I made a bow, so low that I nearly bumped my head against my knee-cap; then I took the turntable under one arm, the horn under the other and ran back home.

First I hid both bits in the wash-kitchen. I did have to let Frieda in on the secret, for she had the records; but Frieda kept mum.

Frieda's boss, the landlord of the pub, had invited us for lunch. There was impeccable noodle soup followed by mashed potato and giblets. We ate until we were unrecognizable; afterwards in order to save coal we went to the museum and the dinosaur skeleton for a while; and in the afternoon Frieda came and collected us.

At home we lit a fire. Then Frieda brought out a huge bowl full of the leftovers of the giblets, three bottles of red wine and a square metre of Bienenstich, Father put his volume of *Brehm's Life of Animals* on the table for me, and the moment he wasn't looking I ran down to the wash-kitchen and brought up the gramophone and told Father to face the other way.

He did as he was told; Frieda spread out the records and put the lights on, and I fixed the horn and wound the gramophone.

'Can I turn around yet?' Father asked; when Frieda had switched the light off he could stand it no longer.

'Wait a second,' I said, 'this damn horn – I can't get it to stay put!' Frieda coughed.

'What horn do you mean?' Father asked.

But then it started. It was 'O Come Little Children'; it crackled a bit and the record obviously had a scratch, but that didn't matter. Frieda and I sang along and then Father turned around. First he swallowed and rubbed his nose, but then he cleared his throat and sang along too. When the record was finished we shook hands and I told Father how I'd managed to get the gramophone.

He was thrilled. 'Well!' he kept on saying to Frieda and nodded at me as he did so, 'well!'

It turned into a very lovely Christmas evening. First we sang and played all the records through; then we played them again without singing; then Frieda sang along with all of the records on her own; then she sang with Father again, and then we ate and finished the wine and after that we made some music; then we walked Frieda home and we went to bed too.

The next morning the tree stayed standing in all its finery. I was allowed to lie in bed and Father played gramophone music all night and whistled the harmony.

Then, the following night, we took the tree out of the bath, put it in the sack, still decorated with tinfoil stars, and took it back to Friedrichshain park. Here we planted it back in the round rose bed. Then we

stamped the earth firm and went home. In the morning I took the gramophone away too.

We visited the tree frequently; the roots grew back again. The tinfoil
stars hung in its branches for quite a while, some even until Spring.

I went to see the tree again a few months ago. It's now a good two
storeys high and has the circumference of a medium-sized factory chimney.
It seems strange to think that we once invited it into our one-room flat.

SOPHIA DE MELLO BREYNER ANDRESEN

Christmas Eve

Translated by Margaret Jull Costa

The friend

Once upon a time, there was a yellow house with a garden all around it. In the garden grew lime trees, birches, a very ancient cedar, a cherry tree and two plane trees. Joana used to play beneath the cedar tree. She would make little houses out of moss and grass and twigs and lean them against the wide, dark trunk. Then she would imagine the dwarves who – always assuming they existed – might live in those houses. And she planned to make a bigger, more complicated house for the king of the dwarves.

Joana had no brothers or sisters and so she played alone. Now and then, her two cousins or some other children would come to play with her, and sometimes she was invited to parties, but the children whose houses she went to or who came to her house weren't really friends. They were visitors. They made fun of her moss houses and found her garden terribly boring.

And Joana was very sad because she didn't know how to play with other children. She only knew how to be alone.

One October morning, though, she found a friend.

Joana was sitting perched on the garden wall, and a boy came walking down the road. His clothes were very old and patched, and his eyes shone like two stars. He was walking slowly along the edge of the pavement, smiling up at the autumn leaves. Joana's heart gave a leap.

'Ah,' she thought. 'He looks like a friend, yes, he's exactly how a friend should look.'

And from her perch on the wall, she said:

'Good morning!'

The boy turned, smiled and said:

'Good morning!'

The two remained silent for a moment, then Joana asked:

'What's your name?'

'Manuel,' said the boy.

'My name's Joana.'

And another light, airy silence passed between them.

In a neighbouring garden a bell rang.

Then the boy said.

'Your garden's really beautiful.'

'Yes, it is, why don't you come in and see for yourself?'

And Joana climbed down from the wall and went and opened the gate.

And together they strolled through the garden. The boy looked at everything. Joana showed him the pond and the goldfish. She showed him the orchard, the orange trees and the vegetable patch. And she called to the dogs so that she could introduce them to him as well. And she showed him the wood stack where a cat was sleeping. And she showed him all the trees and the lawns and the flowers.

'Oh, it's lovely, really lovely,' said the boy gravely.

'And this,' said Joana, 'is the cedar tree. This is where I play.'

And they sat down in the round shade of the cedar.

The morning light encircled the garden. Everything was full of peace and coolness. Occasionally, a yellow seed pod would fall from the lime tree, spinning as it fell.

Joana went to look for pebbles, twigs and moss and, together, she and the boy began building the house for the king of the dwarves.

They played like this for a long time, until a factory siren sounded in the distance.

'Midday,' said the boy. 'I have to go.'

'Where do you live?'

'On the other side of the pine forest.'

'Is that where your house is?'

'Yes, but it's not really a house.'

'What is it then?'

'My father is in heaven, which is why we're so poor. My mother works all day, but we still don't have enough to be able to afford a house.'

'But where do you sleep at night?'

'The owner of the forest has a hut where he keeps a cow and a donkey. Out of charity, he lets me sleep there too.'

'And where do you play?'

'Oh, I play everywhere. We used to live in the centre of the city, and then I'd play on the pavement and in the gutter. I'd play with empty cans and old newspapers, with bits of rag and pebbles. Now I play in the pine forest and on the road. I play with the grass and the weeds and the animals and the flowers. You can play anywhere.'

'I'm not allowed to leave this garden, so why don't you come back tomorrow and play with me again?'

From then on, every morning, the boy would come walking down the street, and Joana would perch on the wall waiting for him.

She would open the gate, and they would both go and sit in the round shade of the cedar tree. And that was how Joana found a friend.

He was a particularly marvellous friend too. The flowers would turn to look at him when he passed, the light shone more brightly around him, and when Joana brought breadcrumbs from the kitchen, the birds would come and eat them from his hand.

The party

After many days and many weeks, Christmas came around.

And on Christmas Eve, Joana put on her blue velvet dress and her black patent-leather shoes, and then, at half past seven, with her hair carefully brushed and combed, she left her room and went downstairs.

There she heard voices coming from the big living room: the grown-ups talking. And because Joana knew they had closed the door so as to keep her out, she went into the dining room to see if the glasses were already on the table.

The glasses spent their lives shut up in a big dark wooden cabinet in the corridor. The cabinet was kept locked with a large key, and its two doors were never fully opened. Inside were all kinds of shadows and lights. It was like a cave full of marvels and secrets. Many things were kept locked up inside, things that weren't needed for everyday life, glittering, rather magical things: china cups, bottles, little boxes, goblets and birds made of glass. There was even a dish containing three wax apples and a silver bell in the shape of a little girl. There was also a big Easter egg made of red porcelain and decorated with golden flowers.

Joana had never seen right to the back of the cabinet. She wasn't allowed to open the doors herself, and she only occasionally managed to persuade the maid to let her peer inside.

On party days, the glasses would emerge from that dark shadowy interior. They were clear, transparent, glinting, and they tinkled when carried on a tray. For Joana that tinkling sound was the music of parties.

Joana walked round the table. The glasses were already there, so cold and luminous that they looked more as if they had come from some mountain spring than from the dark depths of a cabinet.

The candles were lit and their flickering light pierced the glass. The table was full of other extraordinary, marvellous things too: glass baubles, golden pinecones and a plant with prickly leaves and red berries.

It was a party. It was Christmas.

Then Joana went out into the garden, because she knew that the stars are different on Christmas Eve.

She opened the door and went down the steps from the verandah. It was very cold, but even the cold seemed to glow. The lime trees, the birches and the cherry trees had all lost their leaves. Their bare branches stood silhouetted in the air like black lace. Only the branches of the cedar tree were still covered in needles.

And very high up, above the trees, was the vast, dark dome of the sky. And in that darkness, the stars sparkled more brightly than anything else. Down below, it was party time, which is why there were so many shining things: candles, glass baubles and crystal glasses. But there was an even bigger party in the sky, with millions and millions of stars.

For a while, Joana stood looking up, not thinking about anything. She was simply gazing in wonderment at the vast joy of the night in the dark, luminous sky, with not a cloud or a shadow to be seen.

Then she went back into the house and closed the door.

'Will it be very long until supper?' she asked a maid she met in the corridor.

'It'll be a little while yet,' said the maid.

Then Joana went into the kitchen to see Gertrude the cook, who was a remarkable person, because she could touch hot things and not get burned and pick up the sharpest of knives without cutting herself, and she was in charge of everything and knew everything. Joana thought her the most important person she knew.

Gertrude had opened the oven to inspect the two Christmas turkeys. She was turning them and basting them with the cooking juices. The taut skin of the turkey breasts was already golden.

'May I ask you something, Gertrude?' said Joana.

Gertrude raised her head and her face looked as golden and roasted as the turkeys.

'What's that?' she asked.

'What presents do you think I'm going to get?'

'I don't know,' said Gertrude. 'I've no idea.'

Joana, however, had such confidence in Gertrude's knowledge of the world that she continued to ask questions.

'And do you think my friend will get many presents?'

'Which friend is that?'

'Manuel.'

'No, Manuel won't get any presents.'

'None at all?'

'No,' said Gertrude, shaking her head.

'But why?'

'Because he's poor, and poor people don't get presents.'

'But that's wrong, Gertrude.'

'Well, that's the way it is,' said Gertrude, closing the oven door.

Joana stood motionless in the middle of the kitchen. She accepted Gertrude's 'that's the way it is' because she knew that Gertrude understood how the world worked. Every morning, she would hear her haggling with the butcher, the fisherwoman and the woman selling fruit, and no one ever got the better of her.

She had been a cook for thirty years. And for thirty years she had been getting up at seven in the morning and working until eleven at night. And she knew everything that went on in the neighbourhood and everything that went on in other people's houses. And she knew all the gossip too. She knew all the recipes, she knew how to make all the cakes and knew all the different sorts of meat and fish and fruit and vegetables. She was never wrong. She knew everything there was to know about the world, and the things and the people in it.

However, what Gertrude had said grated on her as if it were a lie. Joana said nothing, though, and stood in the kitchen, thinking.

Suddenly, the door opened, and a maid appeared, saying:

'Your cousins have arrived.'

And Joana went to greet her cousins. A few minutes later, the grown-ups appeared too, and everyone went and sat round the table.

The Christmas Eve party had begun.

There was a smell of cinnamon and pinewood in the air. And everything on the table shone: the candles, the knives, the crystal glasses, the glass baubles, the golden pine cones. And the guests laughed and exchanged 'Happy Christmases'. The glasses tinkled with the sound of happiness and parties. And Joana thought:

'Gertrude must be wrong. Christmas is a party for everyone. Tomorrow, Manuel will come and tell me all about his Christmas. He's sure to get presents too.'

And consoled by this thought, Joana felt almost as happy as she had before.

Christmas Eve supper was the same as it was every year. First came the chicken soup, then the baked cod, then the roast turkey, then the crème caramel, then the eggy bread, and, finally, the pineapples. At the end, everyone stood up, the doors were flung wide, and they all went into the living room.

The lights were turned off, leaving only the candles on the tree.

Joana was nine years old, and although she had already seen the Christmas tree nine times, each time always felt as if it were the first.

The tree gave off a wonderful glow that touched everything with its light. It was as if a star had come down to Earth. It was Christmas. And that's why the tree was decorated with lights and its branches hung with exotic fruit, a reminder of the joy that had spread throughout the world on that other night many, many years ago.

And in the Christmas crib, the clay figures, the Child, the Virgin, St Joseph, the cow and the donkey, seemed to be continuing a quiet conversation that had never been interrupted – a conversation you could see but not hear.

Joana looked and looked and looked.

Sometimes her thoughts turned to her friend Manuel, then one of her cousins came and tugged at her sleeve and said:

'Joana, here are your presents.'

Joana opened the parcels and boxes one by one: a doll, a ball, books full of colourful drawings, a paintbox. Around her, everyone was laughing and chatting, showing each other the presents they'd received and all talking at the same time.

And Joana was thinking:

'Perhaps Manuel was given a toy car.'

And so the Christmas party went on.

The grown-ups sat on the chairs and sofas to talk, and the children sat on the floor to play.

Until someone said:

'It's half past eleven and almost time for midnight mass. And high time the children went to bed.'

Then people began to leave.

Joana's father and mother also left.

'Goodnight, my dear. Happy Christmas,' they said.

And the door shut.

A moment later, the maids left too.

The house became very silent. They had all gone to midnight mass, apart from old Gertrude, who was in the kitchen tidying up.

And so Joana went down to the kitchen. This would be a good time to talk to Gertrude.

'Happy Christmas, Gertrude,' said Joana.

'Happy Christmas,' said Gertrude.

Joana fell silent then, before asking:

'Gertrude, is it true what you said before supper?'

'What did I say?'

'You said Manuel wouldn't get any Christmas presents because poor people don't get presents.'

'Of course it's true. I don't tell lies. He wouldn't have had presents or a Christmas tree or a stuffed turkey or any eggy bread. Poor people are poor and all they have is their poverty.'

'So what would his Christmas have been like?'

'Just like every other day.'

'And what is every other day like?'

'A bowl of soup and a bit of bread.'

'Is that true, Gertrude?'

'Of course it's true. But you'd better go to bed now, because it's nearly midnight.'

'Goodnight,' said Joana, and left the kitchen.

She went up the stairs to her bedroom. Her presents lay on her bed. She looked at them one by one. And she was thinking:

'A doll, a ball, a paintbox and books. Those are exactly the presents I wanted. I was given everything I wanted, but no one gave Manuel anything.'

And sitting on the edge of the bed with her presents, Joana started imagining what coldness and darkness and poverty would be like. She started imagining what Christmas Eve would be like in that house that wasn't really a house, but a hut, a stable.

'It must be so cold!' she thought.

'It must be so dark!' she thought.

'It must be so sad!' she thought.

And she began imagining the dark, freezing cold stable where Manuel would be sleeping on the straw, warmed only by the breath of a cow and a donkey.

'Tomorrow, I'm going to give him my presents,' she said.

Then she sighed and thought:

'No, tomorrow it won't be the same. Christmas Eve is when you should get your presents, and it's Christmas Eve now.'

She went over to the window, opened the shutters and peered out at the street. No one was passing. Manuel would be sleeping. He would only come to see her the next morning. In the distance, she could see a large, dark shadow: the pine forest.

Then, coming from the church tower, loud and clear, she heard the twelve strokes of midnight.

'Now,' thought Joana. 'I have to go now. I have to go there now, tonight, so that he'll have some presents on Christmas Eve.'

She went over to her wardrobe, took out a coat and put it on. Then she picked up the ball, the paintbox and the books. She considered taking him the doll as well, but thought better of it. After all, he was a boy and wouldn't be interested in dolls.

Joana tiptoed down the stairs, and every stair creaked, but Gertrude was making so much clatter in the kitchen putting things away that she heard nothing.

A door in the dining room gave directly onto the garden. Joana opened it and went out, leaving it on the latch.

Then she crossed the garden. Alex and Chiribita both barked.

'It's me,' Joana said.

And when they heard her voice, the two dogs stopped barking.

Then she opened the garden gate and went out.

The star

When she found herself alone in the street, she was tempted to turn back. The trees seemed gigantic, and their bare branches filled the sky with shapes like fantastical birds. And the street seemed to be alive, even though it was completely deserted. At that hour, no one was passing. Everyone was at midnight mass. Safe inside their gardens, the houses had all their doors and windows closed. There wasn't a soul to be seen, only things, but Joana had the feeling that the things were looking at her and listening to her as if they were people.

'I'm afraid,' she thought, but resolved to keep walking straight ahead and not look at anything.

When she reached the end of the road, she turned down an alleyway between two walls. At the end of that alleyway, she saw flat, empty fields. There, without walls or trees or houses, she could see the night more clearly, the lofty, brilliant dome of the night sky. The silence was so loud it seemed to be singing. Far off in the distance, she could see the dark mass of the pine trees.

'Will I ever get there?' thought Joana, but kept walking.

Her feet sank into the icy grass. Out in the open, a sharp snowy wind cut her face like a knife.

'I'm cold,' thought Joana, but kept walking.

As she came closer, the pine forest grew and grew until it was vast.

Joana stopped for a moment in the middle of the fields.

'I wonder where the hut is?' she thought.

And she looked all around her for a path to follow.

But there was no path to her right, no path to her left and no path straight ahead.

'How am I going to find the way?' she thought.

Then she looked up, and saw a star moving very slowly across the sky.

'That star looks like a friend,' she thought.

And she began to follow the star.

Until, that is, she entered the forest. Then, in an instant, the shadows closed about her, huge shadows, green and purple and black and blue, were dancing around her, waving their arms. And the breeze blowing through the needles of the pine trees seemed to be murmuring incomprehensible words. Finding herself surrounded by voices and shadows, Joana felt afraid and wanted to run away, but, looking up, she saw that, high in the sky, beyond all the shadows, the star continued to move. And so she followed the star.

She was already deep in the forest when she seemed to hear footsteps.

'Could it be a wolf?' she thought.

She stopped to listen. The sound of footsteps came closer, until she saw, emerging from the trees, a very tall figure coming towards her.

'Could it be a thief?' she thought.

But the figure stopped right in front of her, and she saw that the 'figure' was, in fact, a king. He had a gold crown on his head and around his shoulders a long blue cloak embroidered with diamonds.

'Good evening,' said Joana.

'Good evening,' said the king. 'What's your name?'

'Joana,' she said.

'And my name is Melchior,' said the king.

Then he asked:

'Where are you going all alone and at this late hour?'

'I'm following that star,' she said.

'So am I,' said the king, 'I'm following that star too.'

And together they continued through the forest.

Again Joana heard footsteps. And another figure emerged out of the shadows of the night.

This figure wore a crown studded with diamonds and, around his shoulders, a red mantle sewn with emeralds and sapphires.

'Good evening,' she said. 'My name's Joana and I'm following the star.'

'I'm following the star too,' said the king, 'and my name is Gaspar.'

And they continued together through the forest.

Again Joana heard the sound of footsteps, and a third figure emerged out of the blue shadows and the dark pine trees.

He was wearing a white turban and around his shoulders a long green mantle embroidered with pearls. His face was black.

'Good evening,' she said. 'My name is Joana, and we're all following the star.'

'I'm following the star too,' said the king, 'and my name is Balthasar.'

And together the four of them continued through the night forest.

Dry twigs snapped beneath their feet, the breeze murmured in the branches, and the great embroidered cloaks of the three kings from the Orient glittered among the green, purple and blue shadows.

When they were almost at the edge of the forest, they saw a light in the distance, and above that light the star stopped.

And they continued to walk until they reached the place where the star had stopped, and there Joana saw a hut with no door, but she saw no darkness or shadows or sadness, for the hut was filled with light, with the glow from the angels.

And then Joana saw her friend Manuel. He was lying on the straw between the cow and the donkey and was fast asleep, a smile on his face.

Around him, kneeling on the air, were the angels. His body seemed weightless and made of a light that cast no shadows.

The angels kneeling on the air had their hands clasped in prayer. This then was Manuel's Christmas, lit by the light of the angels.

'Oh,' said Joana, 'it's just like the Nativity scene!'

'Yes,' said King Balthasar, 'it's exactly like the Nativity.'

Then Joana knelt down and placed her presents on the ground.

GRACE PALEY

The Loudest Voice

There is a certain place where dumbwaiters boom, doors slam, dishes crash; every window is a mother's mouth bidding the street shut up, go skate somewhere else, come home. My voice is the loudest.

There, my own mother is still as full of breathing as me and the grocer stands up to speak to her. 'Mrs Abramowitz,' he says, 'people should not be afraid of their children.'

'Ah, Mr Bialik,' my mother replies, 'if you say to her or her father "Ssh," they say, "In the grave it will be quiet."'

'From Coney Island to the cemetery,' says my papa. 'It's the same subway; it's the same fare.'

I am right next to the pickle barrel. My pinky is making tiny whirlpools in the brine. I stop a moment to announce: 'Campbell's Tomato Soup. Campbell's Vegetable Beef Soup. Campbell's S-c-otch Broth . . .'

'Be quiet,' the grocer says, 'the labels are coming off.'

'Please, Shirley, be a little quiet,' my mother begs me.

In that place the whole street groans: Be quiet! Be quiet! but steals from the happy chorus of my inside self not a tittle or a jot.

There, too, but just around the corner, is a red brick building that has been old for many years. Every morning the children stand before it in double lines which must be straight. They are not insulted. They are waiting anyway.

I am usually among them. I am, in fact, the first, since I begin with 'A'.

One cold morning the monitor tapped me on the shoulder. 'Go to Room 409, Shirley Abramowitz,' he said. I did as I was told. I went in a hurry up a down staircase to Room 409, which contained sixth-graders.

213

I had to wait at the desk without wiggling until Mr Hilton, their teacher, had time to speak.

After five minutes he said, 'Shirley?'

'What?' I whispered.

He said, 'My! My! Shirley Abramowitz! They told me you had a particularly loud, clear voice and read with lots of expression. Could that be true?'

'Oh yes,' I whispered.

'In that case, don't be silly; I might very well be your teacher someday. Speak up, speak up.'

'Yes,' I shouted.

'More like it,' he said. 'Now, Shirley, can you put a ribbon in your hair or a bobby pin? It's too messy.'

'Yes!' I bawled.

'Now, now, calm down.' He turned to the class. 'Children, not a sound. Open at page 39. Read till 52. When you finish, start again.' He looked me over once more. 'Now, Shirley, you know, I suppose, that Christmas is coming. We are preparing a beautiful play. Most of the parts have been given out. But I still need a child with a strong voice, lots of stamina. Do you know what stamina is? You do? Smart kid. You know, I heard you read "The Lord is my shepherd" in Assembly yesterday. I was very impressed. Wonderful delivery. Mrs Jordan, your teacher, speaks highly of you. Now listen to me, Shirley Abramowitz, if you want to take the part and be in the play, repeat after me, "I swear to work harder than I ever did before."'

I looked to heaven and said at once, 'Oh, I swear.' I kissed my pinky and looked at God.

'That is an actor's life, my dear,' he explained. 'Like a soldier's, never tardy or disobedient to his general, the director. Everything,' he said, 'absolutely everything will depend on you.'

That afternoon, all over the building, children scraped and scrubbed the turkeys and the sheaves of corn off the schoolroom windows. Goodbye Thanksgiving. The next morning a monitor brought red paper and green paper from the office. We made new shapes and hung them on the walls and glued them to the doors.

The teachers became happier and happier. Their heads were ringing like the bells of childhood. My best friend, Evie, was prone to evil, but she did not get a single demerit for whispering. We learned 'Holy Night' without an error. 'How wonderful!' said Miss Glacé, the student teacher. 'To think that some of you don't even speak the language!' We learned 'Deck the Halls' and 'Hark! The Herald Angels' . . . They weren't ashamed and we weren't embarrassed.

Oh, but when my mother heard about it all, she said to my father: 'Misha, you don't know what's going on there. Cramer is the head of the Tickets Committee.'

'Who?' asked my father. 'Cramer? Oh yes, an active woman.'

'Active? Active has to have a reason. Listen,' she said sadly, 'I'm surprised to see my neighbors making tra-la-la for Christmas.'

My father couldn't think of what to say to that. Then he decided: 'You're in America! Clara, you wanted to come here. In Palestine the Arabs would be eating you alive. Europe you had pogroms. Argentina is full of Indians. Here you got Christmas . . . Some joke, ha?'

'Very funny, Misha. What is becoming of you? If we came to a new country a long time ago to run away from tyrants, and instead we fall into a creeping pogrom, that our children learn a lot of lies, so what's the joke? Ach, Misha, your idealism is going away.'

'So is your sense of humor.'

'That I never had, but idealism you had a lot of.'

'I'm the same Misha Abramovitch, I didn't change an iota. Ask anyone.'

'Only ask me,' says my mama, may she rest in peace. 'I got the answer.'

Meanwhile the neighbors had to think of what to say too.

Marty's father said: 'You know, he has a very important part, my boy.'

'Mine also,' said Mr Sauerfeld.

'Not my boy!' said Mrs Klieg. 'I said to him no. The answer is no. When I say no! I mean no!'

The rabbi's wife said, 'It's disgusting!' But no one listened to her. Under the narrow sky of God's great wisdom she wore a strawberry-blond wig.

Every day was noisy and full of experience. I was Right-hand Man. Mr Hilton said: 'How could I get along without you, Shirley?'

He said: 'Your mother and father ought to get down on their knees every night and thank God for giving them a child like you.'

He also said: 'You're absolutely a pleasure to work with, my dear, dear child.'

Sometimes he said: 'For godsakes, what did I do with the script? Shirley! Shirley! Find it.'

Then I answered quietly: 'Here it is, Mr Hilton.'

Once in a while, when he was very tired, he would cry out: 'Shirley, I'm just tired of screaming at those kids. Will you tell Ira Pushkov not to come in till Lester points to that star the second time?'

Then I roared: 'Ira Pushkov, what's the matter with you? Dope! Mr Hilton told you five times already, don't come in till Lester points to that star the second time.'

'Ach, Clara,' my father asked, 'what does she do there till six o'clock she can't even put the plates on the table?'

'Christmas,' said my mother coldly.

'Ho! Ho!' my father said. 'Christmas. What's the harm? After all, history teaches everyone. We learn from reading this is a holiday from pagan times also, candles, lights, even Hanukkah. So we learn it's not altogether Christian. So if they think it's a private holiday, they're only ignorant, not patriotic. What belongs to history belongs to all men. You want to go back to the Middle Ages? Is it better to shave your head with a second-hand razor? Does it hurt Shirley to learn to speak up? It does not. So maybe someday she won't live between the kitchen and the shop. She's not a fool.'

I thank you, Papa, for your kindness. It is true about me to this day. I am foolish but I am not a fool.

That night my father kissed me and said with great interest in my career, 'Shirley, tomorrow's your big day. Congrats.'

'Save it,' my mother said. Then she shut all the windows in order to prevent tonsillitis.

In the morning it snowed. On the street corner a tree had been decorated for us by a kind city administration. In order to miss its chilly shadow our neighbors walked three blocks east to buy a loaf of bread. The butcher pulled down black window shades to keep the colored lights from shining on his chickens. Oh, not me. On the way to school, with both my hands I tossed it a kiss of tolerance. Poor thing, it was a stranger in Egypt.

I walked straight into the auditorium past the staring children. 'Go ahead, Shirley!' said the monitors. Four boys, big for their age, had already started work as propmen and stagehands.

Mr Hilton was very nervous. He was not even happy. Whatever he started to say ended in a sideward look of sadness. He sat slumped in the middle of the first row and asked me to help Miss Glacé. I did this, although she thought my voice too resonant and said, 'Show-off!'

Parents began to arrive long before we were ready. They wanted to make a good impression. From among the yards of drapes I peeked out at the audience. I saw my embarrassed mother.

Ira, Lester and Meyer were pasted to their beards by Miss Glacé. She almost forgot to thread the star on its wire, but I reminded her. I coughed a few times to clear my throat. Miss Glacé looked around and saw that everyone was in costume and on line waiting to play his part. She whispered, 'All right . . .' Then:

Jackie Sauerfeld, the prettiest boy in first grade, parted the curtains with his skinny elbow and in a high voice sang out:

> *Parents dear*
> *We are here*
> *To make a Christmas play in time.*
> *It we give*
> *In narrative*
> *And illustrate with pantomime.*

He disappeared.

My voice burst immediately from the wings to the great shock of Ira Lester and Meyer, who were waiting for it but were surprised all the same.

'I remember, I remember, the house where I was born . . .'

Miss Glacé yanked the curtain open and there it was, the house – an old hayloft, where Celia Kornbluh lay in the straw with Cindy Lou, her favorite doll. Ira, Lester and Meyer moved slowly from the wings toward her, sometimes pointing to a moving star and sometimes ahead to Cindy Lou.

It was a long story and it was a sad story. I carefully pronounced all the words about my lonesome childhood, while little Eddie Braunstein wandered upstage and down with his shepherd's stick, looking for sheep. I brought up lonesomeness again, and not being understood at all except by some women everybody hated. Eddie was too small for that and Marty Groff took his place, wearing his father's prayer shawl. I announced twelve friends, and half the boys in the fourth grade gathered round Marty, who stood on an orange crate while my voice harangued. Sorrowful and loud, I declaimed about love and God and Man, but because of the terrible deceit of Abie Stock we came suddenly to a famous moment. Marty, whose remembering tongue I was, waited at the foot of the cross. He stared desperately at the audience. I groaned, 'My God, my God, why hast thou forsaken me?' The soldiers who were sheiks grabbed poor Marty to pin him up to die, but he wrenched free, turned again to the audience, and spread his arms aloft to show despair and the end. I murmured at the top of my voice, 'The rest is silence, but as everyone in this room, in this city – in this world – now knows, I shall have life eternal.'

That night Mrs Kornbluh visited our kitchen for a glass of tea.

'How's the virgin?' asked my father with a look of concern.

'For a man with a daughter, you got a fresh mouth, Abramovitch.'

'Here,' said my father kindly, 'have some lemon, it'll sweeten your disposition.'

They debated a little in Yiddish, then fell in a puddle of Russian and Polish. What I understood next was my father, who said, 'Still and all, it was certainly a beautiful affair, you have to admit, introducing us to the beliefs of a different culture.'

'Well, yes,' said Mrs Kornbluh. 'The only thing . . . you know Charlie Turner – that cute boy in Celia's class – a couple others? They got very small parts or no part at all. In very bad taste, it seemed to me. After all, it's their religion.'

'Ach,' explained my mother, 'what could Mr Hilton do? They got very small voices; after all, why should they holler? The English language they know from the beginning by heart. They're blond like angels. You think it's so important they should get in the play? Christmas . . . the whole piece of goods . . . they own it.'

I listened and listened until I couldn't listen any more. Too sleepy, I climbed out of bed and kneeled. I made a little church of my hands and said, 'Hear, O Israel . . .' Then I called out in Yiddish, 'Please, good night, good night. Ssh.' My father said, 'Ssh yourself,' and slammed the kitchen door.

I was happy. I fell asleep at once. I had prayed for everybody: my talking family, cousins far away, passers-by, and all the lonesome Christians. I expected to be heard. My voice was certainly the loudest.

LAURIE LEE

A Cold Christmas Walk in the Country

The women in the kitchen are wrapped in their ritual vapours, having swapped dreamy beds for the clanging hellfires of ovens, spitting bird-roasts, bastings, boiling suds of greens, baked piecrusts and mysterious stuffings. Distracted but agile they shove me against the wall as I grope to look for my boots. Women preparing a meal, like women at their make-up, inhabit a similar chaos that is not to be tampered with.

'Think I'll take a small walk. Up the road,' I say. 'Past the wood. Down the Pond. I think.'

Spoons flashing in bowls, they raise their heads vaguely as though they'd heard an odd sound in the plumbing. Their eyes look through me but do not see me. I belong to an army of men-in-the-way. I get some raw mince on my fingers, lick it off, wish I hadn't, muffle myself up, and go . . .

Outside there is no surprise in the coldness of the morning. It lies on the valley like a frozen goose. The world is white and keen as a map of the Poles and as still as the paper it's printed on. Icicles hang from the gutters like glass silk stockings and drip hot drops in my hand as I breathe on them.

Taking the air in my teeth I feel the old excitement, the raw echoes of an ancestral world, crammed with bull-headed mammoths and tusk-toothed tigers, of flint spears and boasting in caves. Today is the winter as it always was, and when it wasn't it was not remembered. Forgotten, now, are the small freaks of weather, the offbeat heatwaves and wet-warm Decembers that have cropped up now and then in the past. Winter was always like this since the beginning of winters, since the first man learned to sneeze.

Pushing the cold before me like a sheet of tin, I set off up the Christmas road. I have a new thorn stick with a silver band round it and new gloves with an itchy price tag. Before the New Year I shall no doubt lose the lot. But it doesn't matter, they were made for this day.

It is a morning for heroes and exhilarating exile, a time to shock the blood back to life, while I go stamping frost-footed along pathways of iron, over grass that is sharp as wire, past cottages hollowed out like Hallowe'en turnips all seething with lights and steam.

'Same to you, Miss Kirk!' An old lady totters by, bent double like a tyre round a dartboard. Ancient spirit of the season, she is distributing tea to the peasants, which she has done for the last fifty years. She doesn't have to worry where all the peasants have got to; we all admit to being her peasants today.

I climb up the valley, breathing hard the sharp air which prickles the nostrils and turns to vapour. To be walking today is to be followed every-where by private auras of pearly cloud. The wandering cows are exhaling too – pale balloons of unheard conversation. The ploughed fields below me have crusts like bread pudding, delicately sugared with twinkling frost. The distant pastures are slivered, crumpled and bare. Even the light they reflect seems frozen.

Where was this valley last summer? It was not here then. Winter and summer are different places. This beech wood, for instance, so empty now, no more than a fissure of cracks in the sky – where is the huge lazy heaving of those June-thick leaves, reeking of sap and the damp roots of orchids, rustling with foxes and screaming with jays and crammed to the clouds with pigeons? The wood, for the moment, is but the scaffold of summer. It stands stripped to the bruising cold. A dark bird or two sit along the bare branches. None of them move. They might be caged.

Approaching the pond at last I notice a sweet smell of ice – or perhaps it is the only memory of it. We could certainly smell ice when we were boys; even in bed, before getting up. One sniff of the air at the moment of waking and one knew whether the pond was frozen, knew the quality of the ice, whether it was rough or smooth, and even (I swear) its thickness.

This morning it is a plate of dark-green glass, wind-polished and engraved with reeds. An astonished swan walks slowly around it, testing the ice for a hole to sit in, then unable to find one it rises up on its webs and flogs the air with its puzzled wings.

Like the wood, the pond is under a spell, silent as a loaded gun, its explosions of moorhens, coots and lilies held in check for a suspended moment. I look through the ice and see tiny bubbles of air bright as lights in a Christmas tree. I see lily leaves, too, frozen solid in bunches. I wonder what the fish are doing . . .

'Come on Eff!' croaks a voice. 'It's froze! Didn't I tell ya?' Two kids have arrived. Tommy Bint and his sister, wrapped in scarves and hot for the ice. They jump up and down and caramels shower from their pockets like nuts from a hazel tree.

'Ain't you goin' on, mister?' Course I'm going on. I test the ice as delicately as the swan. It buckles and groans like an old attic floor but we've soon got a good slide going. All is as it was – the hollow ring of our boots, the panting run and the swooning glide, the brief oiled passage across the face of winter, the magic anarchy of pleasure for nothing.

After an hour we stop, our faces pink as crab apples, a feeling of wings still about our heels. 'Got to get home to dinner. Yummy-yum,' says Tom. 'Baked spuds and a gurt great goose.' 'And fritters,' says his sister. 'And plum puddin' and custard and nobble minces and brizzle nuts and . . . and . . .' 'You'll be sick.' 'I'll be sick.' She goes joyously through the motions. Then they trot off like two rubber balls.

I climb back to the village sliding on frozen puddles. They are like holes of sky in the road. A sudden blackbird alarmed skids out of a bush chipping chains of sharp cries behind him. A true note of winter, like an axe on a tree, a barking dog or a daylight owl – each pure and solitary in the pause of silence from which the past and the future hang.

It has now turned noon and the day slides slowly from the roofs of the sloping village. It freezes harder than ivory; one can almost see it in the air, as though the light was being stretched on nails. A clear cold radiance hangs over the landscape and a crow crosses it on creaking wings. The rich earth, with all its seeds and humming fields and courtships, is now closed and bound in white vellum. Only one colour remains, today's single promise, pricked in red over the ashen world – seen in a flitting robin, some rosehips on a bush, the sun hanging low by the wood, and through the flushed cottage windows the berries of the holly and the russet faces of the feasting children.

It is good to have been walking on such a day, feeling the stove of one's body alive, to be walking in winter on the ground of one's birth, and good to be walking home. The table's laid when I get there. The women are taking off their aprons. It is also good to arrive in time.

ITALO CALVINO

Santa's Children

Translated by William Weaver

No period of the year is more gentle and good, for the world of industry and commerce, than Christmas and the weeks preceding it. From the streets rises the tremulous sound of the mountaineers' bagpipes; and the big companies, till yesterday coldly concerned with calculating gross product and dividends, open their hearts to human affections and to smiles. The sole thought of Boards of Directors now is to give joy to their fellow man, sending gifts accompanied by messages of goodwill both to other companies and to private individuals; every firm feels obliged to buy a great stock of products from a second firm to serve as presents to third firms; and those firms, for their part, buy from yet another firm further stocks of presents for the others; the office windows remain aglow till late, specially those of the shipping department, where the personnel work overtime wrapping packages and boxes; beyond the misted panes, on the sidewalks covered by a crust of ice, the pipers advance. Having descended from the dark mysterious mountains, they stand at the downtown intersections, a bit dazzled by the excessive lights, by the excessively rich shop windows; and heads bowed, they blow into their instruments; at that sound, among the businessmen the heavy conflicts of interest are placated and give way to a new rivalry: to see who can present the most conspicuous and original gift in the most attractive way.

At Sbav and Co. that year the Public Relations Office suggested that the Christmas presents for the most important persons should be delivered at home by a man dressed as Santa Claus.

The idea won the unanimous approval of the top executives. A complete Santa Claus outfit was bought: white beard, red cap and tunic edged in white fur, big boots. They had the various delivery men try it on to see whom it fitted best, but one man was too short and the beard touched the ground; another was too stout and couldn't get into the tunic; another was too young; yet another was too old and it wasn't worth wasting make-up on him.

While the head of the Personnel Office was sending for other possible Santas from the various departments, the assembled executives sought to develop the idea: the Human Relations Office wanted the employees' Christmas packages also to be distributed by Santa Claus, at a collective ceremony; the Sales Office wanted Santa to make a round of the shops as well; the Advertising Office was worried about the prominence of the firm's name, suggesting that perhaps they should tie four balloons to a string with the letters S.B.A.V.

All were caught up in the lively and cordial atmosphere spreading through the festive, productive city; nothing is more beautiful than the sensation of material goods flowing on all sides and, with it, the goodwill each feels toward the others; for this, this above all, as the skirling sound of the pipes reminds us, is what really counts.

In the shipping department, goods – material and spiritual – passed through Marcovaldo's hands, since it represented merchandise to load and unload. And it was not only through loading and unloading that he shared in the general festivity but also by thinking that at the end of that labyrinth of hundreds of thousands of packages there waited a package belonging to him alone, prepared by the Human Relations Office – and even more, by figuring how much was due him at the end of the month, counting the Christmas bonus and his overtime hours. With that money, he too would be able to rush to the shops and buy, buy, buy, to give presents, presents, presents, as his most sincere feelings and the general interests of industry and commerce decreed.

The head of the Personnel Office came into the shipping department with a fake beard in his hand. 'Hey, you!' he said to Marcovaldo. 'See how this beard looks on you. Perfect! You're Santa then. Come upstairs. Get moving. You'll be given a special bonus if you make fifty home deliveries per day.'

Got up as Santa Claus, Marcovaldo rode through the city on the saddle of the motorbike-truck laden with packages wrapped in varicoloured paper, tied with pretty ribbons, and decorated with twigs of mistletoe and holly.

The white cotton beard tickled him a little, but it protected his throat from the cold air.

His first trip was to his own home, because he couldn't resist the temptation of giving his children a surprise. At first, he thought, they won't recognize me. Then I bet they'll laugh!

The children were playing on the stairs. They barely looked up. 'Hi, Papà.'

Marcovaldo was let down. 'Hmph . . . Don't you see how I'm dressed?'

'How are you supposed to be dressed?' Pietruccio said. 'Like Santa Claus, right?'

'And you recognized me first thing?'

'Easy! We recognized Signor Sigismondo, too; and he was disguised better than you!'

'And the janitor's brother-in-law!'

'And the father of the twins across the street!'

'And the uncle of Ernestina – the girl with the braids!'

'All dressed like Santa Claus?' Marcovaldo asked, and the disappointment in his voice wasn't due only to the failure of the family surprise but also because he felt that the company's prestige had somehow been impaired.

'Of course. Just like you,' the children answered. 'Like Santa Claus. With a fake beard, as usual.' And turning their backs on him, the children became absorbed again in their games.

It so happened that the Public Relations Offices of many firms had had the same idea at the same time; and they had recruited a great number of people, jobless for the most part, pensioners, street vendors, and had dressed them in the red tunic with the cotton-wool beard. The children, the first few times, had been amused, recognizing acquaintances under that disguise, neighbourhood figures, but after a while they were jaded and paid no further attention.

The game they were involved in seemed to absorb them entirely. They had gathered on a landing and were seated in a circle. 'May I ask what you're plotting?' Marcovaldo inquired.

'Leave us alone, Papà; we have to fix our presents.'

'Presents for whom?'

'For a poor child. We have to find a poor child and give him presents.'

'Who said so?'

'It's in our school reader.'

Marcovaldo was about to say: 'You're poor children yourselves!' But during this past week he had become so convinced that he was an inhabitant of the Land of Plenty, where all purchased and enjoyed themselves and exchanged presents, that it seemed bad manners to mention poverty; and he preferred to declare: 'Poor children don't exist any more!'

Michelino stood up and asked: 'Is that why you don't bring us presents, Papà?' Marcovaldo felt a pang at his heart. 'I have to earn some overtime now,' he said hastily, 'and then I'll bring you some.'

'How do you earn it?'

'Delivering presents,' Marcovaldo said.

'To us?'

'No, to other people.'

'Why not to us? It'd be quicker.'

Marcovaldo tried to explain. 'Because I'm not the Human Relations Santa Claus, after all; I'm the Public Relations Santa Claus. You understand?'

'No.'

'Never mind.' But since he wanted somehow to apologize for coming home empty-handed, he thought he might take Michelino with him on his round of deliveries. 'If you're good, you can come and watch your Papà taking presents to people,' he said, straddling the seat of the little delivery wagon.

'Let's go. Maybe I'll find a poor child,' Michelino said and jumped on, clinging to his father's shoulders.

In the streets of the city Marcovaldo encountered only other red-and-white Santas, absolutely identical with him, who were driving panel trucks or delivery carts or opening the doors of shops for customers laden with packages or helping carry their purchases to the car. And all these Santas seemed concentrated, busy, as if they were responsible for the operation of the enormous machine of the Holiday Season.

And exactly like them, Marcovaldo ran from one address to another, following his list, dismounted from his seat, sorted the packages in the wagon, selected one, presented it to the person opening the door, pronouncing the words: 'Sbav and Company wish a Merry Christmas and a Happy New Year,' and pocketed the tip.

This tip could be substantial and Marcovaldo might have been considered content, but something was missing. Every time, before ringing at a door, followed by Michelino, he anticipated the wonder of the person who, on opening the door, would see Santa Claus himself standing there before him; he expected some fuss, curiosity, gratitude. And every time he was received like the postman, who brings the newspaper day after day.

He rang at the door of a luxurious house. A governess answered the door. 'Oh, another package. Who's this one from?'

'Sbav and Company wish a . . .'

'Well, bring it in,' and she led Santa Claus down a corridor filled with tapestries, carpets and majolica vases. Michelino, all eyes, followed his father.

The governess opened a glass door. They entered a room with a high ceiling, so high that a great fir tree could fit beneath it. It was a Christmas tree lighted by glass bubbles of every colour, and from its branches hung presents and sweets of every description. From the ceiling hung heavy crystal chandeliers, and the highest branches of the fir caught some of the glistening drops. Over a large table were arrayed glass, silver, boxes of candied fruit and cases of bottles. The toys, scattered over a great rug, were as numerous as in a toyshop, mostly complicated electronic devices and model spaceships. On that rug, in an empty corner, there was a little boy about nine years old, lying prone, with a bored, sullen look. He was leafing through an illustrated volume, as if everything around him were no concern of his.

'Gianfranco, look. Gianfranco,' the governess said. 'You see? Santa Claus has come back with another present.'

'Three hundred twelve,' the child sighed, without looking up from his book. 'Put it over there.'

'It's the three hundred and twelfth present that's arrived,' the governess said. 'Gianfranco is so clever. He keeps count; he doesn't miss one. Counting is his great passion.'

On tiptoe Marcovaldo and Michelino left the house.

'Papà, is that little boy a poor child?' Michelino asked.

Marcovaldo was busy rearranging the contents of the truck and didn't answer immediately. But after a moment, he hastened to protest: 'Poor? What are you talking about? You know who his father is? He's the president of the Society for the Implementation of Christmas Consumption/Commendatore –'

He broke off, because he didn't see Michelino anywhere. 'Michelino! Michelino! Where are you?' He had vanished.

I bet he saw another Santa Claus go by, took him for me, and has gone off after him . . . Marcovaldo continued his rounds, but he was a bit concerned and couldn't wait to get home again.

At home, he found Michelino with his brothers, good as gold.

'Say, where did you go?'

'I came home to collect our presents . . . the presents for that poor child . . .'

'What? Who?'

'The one that was so sad . . . the one in the villa, with the Christmas tree . . .'

'Him? What kind of a present could you give him?'

'Oh, we fixed them up very nice . . . three presents, all wrapped in silver paper.'

The younger boys spoke up: 'We all went together to take them to him! You should have seen how happy he was!'

'I'll bet!' Marcovaldo said. 'That was just what he needed to make him happy: your presents!'

'Yes, ours! . . . He ran over right away to tear off the paper and see what they were . . .'

'And what were they?'

'The first was a hammer: that big round hammer, the wooden kind . . .'

'What did he do then?'

'He was jumping with joy! He grabbed it and began to use it!'

'How?'

'He broke all the toys! And all the glassware! Then he took the second present . . .'

'What was that?'

'A slingshot. You should have seen him. He was so happy! He hit all the glass balls on the Christmas tree. Then he started on the chandeliers . . .'

'That's enough. I don't want to hear any more! And the . . . third present?'

'We didn't have anything left to give, so we took some silver paper and wrapped up a box of kitchen matches. That was the present that made him happiest of all. He said: They never let me touch matches! He began to strike them, and . . .'

'And?'

'. . . and he set fire to everything!'

Marcovaldo was tearing his hair. 'I'm ruined!'

The next day, turning up at work, he felt the storm brewing. He dressed again as Santa Claus, in great haste, loaded the presents to be delivered onto the truck, already amazed that no one had said anything to him, and then he saw, coming toward him, the three section chiefs: the one from Public Relations, the one from Advertising, and the one from Sales.

'Stop!' they said to him. 'Unload everything. At once!'

This is it, Marcovaldo said to himself, and could already picture himself fired.

'Hurry up! We have to change all the packages!' the three section chiefs said. 'The Society for the Implementation of Christmas Consumption has launched a campaign to push the Destructive Gift!'

'On the spur of the moment like this,' one of the men remarked. 'They might have thought of it sooner . . .'

'It was a sudden inspiration the President had,' another chief explained. 'It seems his little boy was given some ultramodern gift articles, Japanese, I believe, and for the first time the child was obviously enjoying himself . . .'

'The important thing,' the third added, 'is that the Destructive Gift serves to destroy articles of every sort: just what's needed to speed up the pace of consumption and give the market a boost . . . All in minimum time and within a child's capacities . . . The President of the Society sees a whole new horizon opening out. He's in seventh heaven, he's so enthusiastic . . .'

'But this child . . .' Marcovaldo asked, in a faint voice: 'did he really destroy much stuff?'

'It's hard to make an estimate, even a hazy one, because the house was burned down . . .'

Marcovaldo went back to the street, illuminated as if it were night, crowded with mamas and children and uncles and grannies and packages and balloons and rocking horses and Christmas trees and Santa Clauses and chickens and turkeys and fruit cakes and bottles and bagpipers and chimney sweeps and chestnut vendors shaking pans of chestnuts over round, glowing black stoves.

And the city seemed smaller, collected in a luminous vessel, buried in the dark heart of a forest among the age-old trunks of the chestnut trees and an endless cloak of snow. Somewhere in the darkness the howl of the wolf was heard; the hares had a hole buried in the snow, in the warm red earth under a layer of chestnut burrs.

A jack-hare came out, white, onto the snow; he twitched his ears, ran beneath the moon, but he was white and couldn't be seen, as if he weren't there. Only his little paws left a light print on the snow, like little clover leaves. Nor could the wolf be seen, for he was black and stayed in the black darkness of the forest. Only if he opened his mouth, his teeth were visible, white and sharp.

There was a line where the forest, all black, ended and the snow began, all white. The hare ran on this side, and the wolf on that.

The wolf saw the hare's prints on the snow and followed them, always keeping in the black, so as not to be seen. At the point where the prints ended there should be the hare, and the wolf came out of the black, opened wide his red maw and his sharp teeth, and bit the wind.

The hare was a bit farther on, invisible; he scratched one ear with his paw and escaped, hopping away.

Is he here? There? Is he a bit farther on?

Only the expanse of snow could be seen, white as this page.

TOVE JANSSON

Christmas

Translated by Kingsley Hart

The smaller you are, the bigger Christmas is. Underneath the Christmas Tree, Christmas is vast. It is a green jungle with red apples and sad, peaceful angels twirling around on cotton thread keeping watch over the entrance to the primaeval forest. In the glass balls the primaeval forest is never-ending; Christmas is a time when you feel absolutely safe, thanks to the Christmas tree.

There outside is the studio which is very big and very cold. The only warm place is close to the stove, with the fire and the shadows on the floor and the pillar-like legs of the statues.

The studio is full of sculpture, large white women who have always been there. They are everywhere, the movements of their arms are vague and shy and they look straight past one because they are uninterested, and sad in quite a different way from my angels. Some of them have clay rags on their heads and the largest one has a clothesline round her tummy. The rags are wet and when one goes past they brush one's face like cold white birds in the dark. It's always dark in the evening.

The studio window must never be cleaned because it gives a very beautiful light, it has a hundred little panes, some of them darker than others, and the lanterns outside swing to and fro and draw a window of their own on the wall. There are stout shelves, one under the other, and on each shelf white ladies stand, but they are quite tiny. They face one another and turn away from one another but their movements are just as hesitant and shy as those of the big women. All of them get dusted just before Christmas. But only Mummy is allowed to touch them and the grenades from the 1918 war aren't dusted at all.

Daddy's women are sacred. He doesn't care about them after they are cast in plaster, but for everybody else they are sacred.

Apart from the women, the window and the stove, everything else is in shadow. Against the wall there is a sinister heap of things that mustn't be examined; armatures, boxes with clay and plaster, moulds, wood, rags and modelling stands, and behind them all creeps the mysterious thing with eyes as black as night.

But the middle of the room is empty. All there is is a single modelling stand with a woman in wet rags, and she is the most sacred thing of all. The stand has three legs and they throw stiff shadows across the blank patch of concrete floor and up towards the ceiling which is so far away that no one can get up there, at least not before the Christmas tree arrives. We have the finest and tallest tree in the town and it's probably worth a fortune because it has to reach right up to the ceiling and be of the bristly kind. All other sculptors have small and scruffy Christmas trees, not to mention certain painters who hardly have what you could call trees at all. People who live in ordinary flats have their tree on a table with a *cloth* on it, poor things! They buy their tree as an afterthought.

On the morning agreed upon beforehand we, that is Daddy and I, get up at six o'clock because Christmas trees must be bought in the dark. We walk from Skatudden to the other end of town because the big harbour there is just the right setting for buying a Christmas tree. We generally spend hours choosing, looking at every branch very suspiciously, because they can be stuck in. It's always cold. Once Daddy got the top of a tree in his eye. The early morning darkness is full of freezing bundles hunting for trees and the snow is scattered with fir twigs. There is a menacing enchantment about the harbour and the market place.

Then the studio is transformed into a primaeval forest where one can make oneself unget-at-able deep in under the Christmas tree. Under the tree one must feel full of love. There are also other places where one can feel full of grief or hate, between the hall doors where the letters drop through the letter-box, for example. The hall door has small red and green glass panes, it is narrow and solemn, and the hall is full of clothes, skis and packing cases, but it is between the two doors that there is just enough room to stand and hate. If one hates in a big space one dies immediately.

But if the space is narrow the hate turns inwards again and goes round and round one's body and never reaches God.

But it's quite different with Christmas trees, particularly when the glass balls have been hung up. They are store-places for love and that's why it's so terribly dangerous to drop them.

As soon as the Christmas tree was in the studio everything took on a fresh significance, and was charged with a holiness that had nothing to do with Art. Christmas began in earnest.

Mummy and I went to the icy rocks behind the Russian Church and scratched around for some moss. We built the Land of the Nativity with the desert and Bethlehem in clay, with new streets and houses each time, we filled the whole of the studio window, we made lakes with pieces of mirror and placed the shepherds and gave them new lambs and new legs because the old ones had broken up in the moss and we placed the sand carefully so that the clay could be used later. Then we took out the manger with the thatched roof which they had got in Paris in nineteen hundred and ten. Daddy was very moved and had to have a snorter.

Mary was always right in the front, but Joseph had to be at the back with the cattle because he had been damaged by water and, besides, in perspective he was smaller.

Last of all came the Baby Jesus, who was made of wax and had real curly hair which they had made in Paris before I was born. When he was in place we had to be quite quiet for a long while.

Once Poppolino got out and devoured the Baby Jesus. He climbed up Daddy's Statue of Liberty, sat on the hilt of the sword, and ate up Jesus.

There was nothing we could do, and we didn't dare to look at each other. Mummy made a new Baby Jesus of clay and painted it. We thought that it turned out too red and too fat round the middle, but no one said anything.

Christmas always rustled. It rustled every time, mysteriously, with silver paper and gold paper and tissue paper and a rich abundance of shiny paper decorating and hiding everything and giving a feeling of reckless extravagance.

There were stars and rosettes everywhere, even on the vegetable dishes and on the expensive shop-bought sausages which we used to have before we began to have real ham.

One could wake up at night to the reassuring sound of Mummy wrapping up presents. One night she painted the tiles of the stove with little blue landscapes and bunches of flowers on every tile all the way to the top.

She made gingerbread biscuits shaped like goats with the pastry-cutter and gave the Lucy-pussies, small flat pastry scrolls, curly legs and a raisin in the middle of the tummy. When they came here from Sweden the pussies had only four legs but every year they got more and more until they had a wild and curly ornamentation all over.

Mummy weighed sweets and nuts on a letter-balance so that everyone would get exactly the same amount. During the year everything is measured roughly, but at Christmas everything has to be absolutely fair. That's why it's such a strenuous time.

In Sweden people stuff their own sausages and make candles and carry small baskets to the poor for several months and all mothers sew presents at night. On Christmas Eve they all become Lucias, with a great wreath with lots of candles in it on their heads.

The first time Daddy saw a Lucia he was very scared, but when he realised it was only Mummy he began to laugh. Then he wanted her to be a Lucia every Christmas Eve because it was such fun.

I lay on my bunk and heard Lucia starting to climb the steps, and it wasn't easy for her. The whole thing was as beautiful as being in heaven and she had modelled a pig in marzipan as they do in Sweden. Then she sang a little and climbed up the steps to Daddy's bunk. Mummy only sings once a year because her vocal cords are crossed.

There were hundreds of candles on the balustrade round our bunks waiting to be lit just before the Story of the Nativity. Then they flutter in all directions round the studio like so many pearl necklaces, maybe there are thousands of them. These candles are very interesting when they burn down because the cardboard dividing-wall could easily catch fire.

Later in the morning Daddy used to get very worked up because he took Christmas very seriously and could hardly stand all the preparations. He was quite exhausted. He put every single candle straight and warned us about the danger of fire. He rushed out and bought mistletoe, a tiny twig of it, because it had to hang from the ceiling and is more expensive than orchids. He kept on asking whether we were quite sure that everything was in order and suddenly thought that the composition of the Land of the Nativity was all wrong. Then he had a snorter to calm himself. Mummy wrote poetry and picked sealing-wax off wrapping-paper and gold ribbon from the previous Christmas.

Twilight came and Daddy went to the churchyard with nuts for the squirrels and to look at the graves. He has never been particularly concerned about the relations lying there and they didn't particularly like him either because they were distant relatives and rather bourgeois. But when Daddy got back home again he was sad and twice as worked up because the churchyard had been so wonderfully beautiful with all the candles burning there. Anyway, the squirrels had buried masses of nuts along with the relatives although it was forbidden to do so, and that was a consoling thought at least.

After dinner there was a long pause to allow Christmas a breathing-space. We lay on our bunks in the dark listening to Mummy rustling down by the stove and in the street outside all was quiet.

Then the long lines of candles were lit and Daddy leaped down from his bunk to make sure that the ones on the Christmas tree were all upright and that the candle behind Joseph wasn't setting fire to the thatched roof.

And then we had the Story of the Nativity. The most solemn part was when Mary pondered these things in her heart and it was almost as beautiful when they departed into their own country another way. The rest of it wasn't so special.

We recovered from this and Daddy had a snorter. And now I was triumphantly certain that Christmas belonged to me.

I crept into the green primaeval forest and pulled out parcels. Now the feeling of love under the branches of the tree was almost unbearable, a compact feeling of holiness made up of Marys and angels and mothers and Lucias and statues, all of them blessing me and forgiving everything during the year that was past, including that business of hating in the hall, forgiving everything on earth as long as they could be sure that everybody loved one another.

And just then the largest glass ball fell on the concrete floor and it smashed into the world's tiniest and nastiest splinters.

The silence afterwards was unbelievable. At the neck of the ball there was a little ring with two metal prongs. And Mummy said: actually, that ball has always been the wrong colour.

And so night came and all the candles had burnt down and all the fires had been put out and all the ribbons and paper had been folded up for next Christmas. I took my presents to bed with me.

Every now and then Daddy's slippers shuffled down there in the studio and he ate a little pickled herring and had a snorter and tried to get some music out of the wireless he had built himself. The feeling of peace everywhere was complete.

Once something happened to the wireless and it played a whole tune before the interference came back. In its own way interference is something of a miracle, mystifying isolated signals from somewhere out in space.

Daddy sat in the darkened studio for a long time eating pickled herring and trying to get proper tunes on the wireless. When it didn't work at all he climbed up on to his bunk again and rustled his newspapers. Mummy's candles had gone out much earlier, and there was a general smell of Christmas tree and burning and benediction all over.

Nothing is as peaceful as when Christmas is over, when one has been forgiven for everything and one can be normal again.

After a while we packed the holy things away in the hall cupboard and the branches of the Christmas tree burnt in the stove with small violent explosions. But the trunk wasn't burnt until the following Christmas. All the year it stood next to the box of plaster, reminding us of Christmas and the absolute safety in everything.

CYPRIAN EKWENSI
Just Because of Xmas

She had heard it said: 'Nobody goes so far as the man who does not know where he is going.' Perhaps that was why she spent so much time at her dressing-table. Ma Bimbo had no idea where she was going. She knew only that she was leaving the house.

By the time she stood at the bus stop, she was a picture in blue. The colour flattered her dark chocolate skin, while the trace of silver in her head-tie added just that touch of glamour that distinguished her from the other beauties that roamed the city streets at this festive season. She had tied the cloth around her waist in the manner of husband stealers: in front, it came down like the point of an arrow to her toes; but at the back, it scarcely concealed her knees. The result was that young men's eyes followed greedily the lines of her smooth legs. Ma Bimbo did not mind. She had nothing to feel self-conscious about: on her feet were blue suede shoes with red soles that looked baked in the sun; and with gold glittering around her throat, on her ears and fingers and wrists, she was confident that she would conquer all Lagos.

She stood leaning against the post, smiling. But beneath that smile was a heart groaning under the stress of want, poverty, and the prospect of a bleak Christmas. The buses would not stop. They merely slowed down at the stop, the conductors poked out their heads and shouted: 'No more room,' and with a snort, they rolled on. They were over-loaded. People had money to spend; they were not like herself, widowed, with two children to look after and a nagging 'Antie' to obstruct, rather than help her. She had often thought of marrying again, but it was too early yet to forget her husband.

The crowd around the bus stop grew. They surged impatiently, stamping their feet and muttering. Some of the braver ones stood in the shade, their anxious eyes scanning the hot black road that stretched away towards Yaba. Buses came roaring in . . . the occupants yelled and waved handkerchiefs . . . the conductors yelled, 'No more room' . . . and the disgruntled waiting crowd swore and exploded.

Many of the women grouped around the stop looked up and down the street, crossed it, and started walking away resolutely. Ma Bimbo knew they were going to Lagos on their bare feet. Five miles was not much of a distance to walk in the hot sun, especially as there was so much to see on the way, but she was bent on adventure. It was the festive season. People did reckless things just because of Christmas.

Only that morning, she had tried to sell the very dress she was now wearing. They had refused to buy it because this was the Christmas season and many things were going at half-price. There was no sense in buying expensive second-hand clothes, however good.

Later, she had gone to call on Ma Shola and Sisi Tola, to find out how they were preparing for Christmas. They lived along Kwasie Street, near the private hospital. She saw that the shutters were down and knew they must be in the backyard. She had gone in, but had checked herself along the corridor. Sisi Tola was talking:

'Come and take your child,' she said, 'she's messing up my clothes . . .'

'I'm coming!' That was Ma Shola. She knew the voice. 'Is that how you'll treat your own?'

Sisi Tola laughed. '*Epe!* People are thinking of Christmas, and you are washing clothes.'

'Why not?'

'Ma Shola! What d'you think of this my dress? I want to sell it!'

'What!'

'I'm tired of it. I must buy something new for Christmas.'

'You're brave. So you're one of those people who'll do anything – just because of Christmas?'

'Nothing shameful in that!'

'Please, get me more water . . . thank you. Pour it on my hands . . . now, I'll take the child . . . Not me! If I don't get enough to eat, or drink, or put on my body, I'll not disgrace myself. After all, Christmas is how you feel, not what you put on. Christmas is of the mind.'

Christmas is of the mind. Ma Bimbo stood still in the corridor. She wiped the sweat off her face. The powder smeared the handkerchief red. She turned round quietly, and tiptoed out of the household.

On the street, she moved fast. She kept glancing back until she had rounded the corner beyond the telegraph pole. Then she sighed. No one had seen her. When she got home, she thought over Ma Shola's words – Chirstmas is of the mind – there was plenty of truth in that. Ma Shola was a woman who loved nice clothes and nice clothes became her. She was not saying those words out of spite; she meant them.

But for Ma Bimbo, Christmas time was not the time to restrain oneself. It was the time for reckless decisions, always based upon goodwill towards others. It was a time to dress well and join the groups of colourful women who followed drums about the streets and raised dust in their wake. It was a time for senselessness and good-humoured stupidity.

Her children had to have new clothes; they had to send rockets streaking into the night air; they had to yell like the others and watch the *Eguns*, the masquerades. What was Christmas without all these? If they missed that now, it would be until next year: another twelve months!

Her bus came at last and in she went. There was just room for one and she took it, perching herself on the tip of the bench so that those who came and went along the narrow corridor used her suede shoes as a foot-mat. A noisy woman carrying a large basket was wedged in by the window. Part of her load formed a hurdle along the narrow passage between the rows of seats, and she was weeping.

'Oh, my scarf! Oh, my scarf!'

'Where did you leave it?' moaned the other women.

'Oh, my scarf! Oh! What shall I do?'

At the other end, the conductor had already started to collect the fares. Ma Bimbo's heart leapt to her throat. She had not a penny on her. It was not that she had left the money in the house, but she just didn't have it. The conductor came nearer and nearer. She heard him counting the money behind her. He collected fares from passengers on both sides of her, and by-passed her. Must be some mistake, she thought. She turned round, and there, behind her was a large man smiling at her.

She understood. He had paid her fare. At Tinubu she got down to thank her benefactor, but there were many buses and he had disappeared before she could weave her way to the back. She stood undecided for a moment. Glancing up, she saw that the time was 9.00 a.m. She walked along Broad Street for a while, avoiding the taxi-park. But the drivers whistled appreciatively, though rudely, and swung their cars before her.

'Taxi, Ma! Take mah own; clean, see? Yes, here, Ma! Taxi? Where to?'

She laughed inwardly. These people did not know whom they had been offering a ride. She had spent all her money on the burial, first of her husband, and shortly after, of her mother-in-law. And how much money had she ever had before she became a widow? She had never before thought of money; her husband had always been the provider. This was the first Christmas she had ever worried about.

She walked down towards the Marina. The huge shops, looking like exaggerated modern liners, towered to the very clouds. Shoppers jostled along the street, four to five deep, so that the traffic was pushed nearer the Lagoon.

She went into the first shop. A crowd had gathered at the entrance, and she knew that a sensation of some sort was going on. Some of the men were opening parcels. A few cried out in glee, but most of them flung their parcels away and bemoaned the loss of their money. Their dip had not been 'lucky'. Ma Bimbo wanted to try her 'luck', but she had not got two shillings. She stood there longingly for a few moments. Then she went into the shop. Everything was being given away for practically nothing: shoes, underwear, toys . . . just the right toys for the children.

She came down the steps slowly. Outside, she stood watching the cars parked under the coconut palms. One or two women she knew greeted her.

'What have you bought?' they asked, but she merely smiled, and said she had not yet seen what she came for.

She was just about to move when a Chevrolet parked itself under the coconuts. A big man in a white shirt outside trousers, his fleshy face beaming with Christmas joy, strode over and eyed her appraisingly. There was something in his look which annoyed her. He seemed to be too confident of his personal charm and his eyes went beyond the surface into her very soul. She did not like to be made to feel so naked.

'Hello, what have you bought?' And she recognized him as her benefactor of the bus.

'Nothing,' she said. 'Thank you for this morning . . . I looked for you at Tinubu, but . . .'

'Oh! Forget that! But why so serious? Come along, let us make up the quarrel. I do not like to quarrel with women. *I have been expecting you back all this time.* Won't you come home?'

She looked more closely at him. She was sure now: the man was crazy. His eyes were red and watery, and he must have been drinking far too much.

'Come along, what d'you want to buy?'

'I have not come to buy anything,' she said with spirit. 'I came to meet my husband, but he is busy with the boss . . .'

'Your husband? But I am your husband.'

Ma Bimbo could not help laughing. But the man somehow got her across the street and into his car before she could decide on his sanity. They were whirling through the pressing Christmas mob, and suddenly they stopped in front of a house which looked slightly smaller than the shop they had just come from.

'*Ekabo-O!*' came the welcoming greeting of the women. '*Ekabo-O!*'

They rushed out to embrace her, but one of them – the bulky one in the lead – stopped. 'She looks like your first wife, chief!'

'She does not look like her: she is!'

'But that cannot be, chief! The dead do not come back!'

'They come back: she is my wife!'

He took her into his innermost room and ordered the women to make things ready, because he had a big visitor. Ma Bimbo was speechless. Surely this was a dream, and it was a crazy dream. She heard them getting things ready: the clatter of plates, the click of glasses, the shuffle of feet . . . then a young slim girl with big eyes and a protruding lower lip slipped in, carrying a tray heaped with all kinds of glasses. She was in blue too, and as she set it down on a stool, she whispered, 'Welcome, Ma,' and left.

'That's my number two wife,' the chief explained, 'the one I married after you ran away.'

Ma Bimbo looked away. The room was in the wildest disorder. Mirrors seemed to reflect her image from every wall, and what was left after the bed had occupied half of it was full of half-open trunks and jumbled clothes.

'You will drink this wine,' the chief said, and she accepted it.

She sipped it slowly, and the taste pleased her. His excitement was beginning to affect her and she found herself returning smile for smile and compliment for compliment: the Christmas feeling was on her. But somewhere in her she heard a note of warning. The door was half open, and the words that came floating in now and again were not encouraging. 'Lost his senses? . . . Is it just Christmas or is he mad?'

'Go now,' said the chief, 'go and get your things. I need you back. Or shall I send the car? It is not fair for you to leave me like this.'

'I want to go shopping,' Ma Bimbo wailed in her smallest voice.

'Then wait!' roared the chief. 'I'll go with you.'

Ma Bimbo could not understand how he remained sane enough to take her through all the shops and buy her all she wanted; all that Alaba and Koyinde and Antie wanted. She was intoxicated when the chief's driver stopped outside her residence and unloaded the parcels that were now hers. She gave the driver a few bottles and parcels and he became quite communicative.

'Ah been drive them man for ten year,' he said. 'Ah never see am act like dis before!'

He went on to reveal how the chief had married young, and his wife had died. He had married others, and had even become a polygamist, but every time he saw a woman who reminded him – however faintly – of his beloved Alake, he always lost his head. In Ma Bimbo's case, the driver went on, the resemblance was too great. She looked like a twin sister. Did Ma Bimbo not see how startled the chief's wives were when she stepped out of the car?

'It is true,' said Ma Bimbo. She was touched. 'Poor man! With so much money, and so many people around him, he's still not happy . . .'

'Some time, he will come marry you,' the driver said.

'Nonsense!' said Ma Bimbo, but she was uneasy.

'Ekabo! 'Kabo!' said Koyinde and Alaba.

The two children, arms outstretched before them, came to welcome their mother. Ma Bimbo embraced them, laughing at their weak efforts to lift parcels they could not carry. Her Christmas had become everything she had desired.

LUCIA BERLIN

Noël. Texas. 1956

'Tiny's on the roof! Tiny's on the roof!'

That's all they can talk about down there. So what, I'm on the roof. What they don't know is I may just never get off.

I didn't mean to be so dramatic. Would have simply gone to my room and slammed the door, but my mother was in my room. So I slammed out the kitchen door. And there was a ladder, to the roof.

I flung myself down, still in a tizzy, and took some sips from my flask of Jack Daniel's. Well, I declare, I thought, it's right nice up here. Sheltered, but with a view of the pastures and the Rio Grande and Mount Cristo Rey. Real pleasant. Especially now that Esther has me all set up with an extension cord. A radio, electric blanket, crossword puzzles. She empties my chamber pot and brings me food and bourbon. For sure I'll be up here until after Christmas.

Christmas.

Tyler knows how I hate and despise Christmas. He and Rex Kipp run plumb amok every year . . . donating to charities, toys to crippled children, food to old folks. I heard them plotting to drop toys and food on Juarez shantytown Christmas Eve. Any excuse to show off, spend money, and act like a couple of royal assholes.

This year Tyler said I was in for a big surprise. A surprise for *me*? I'm embarrassed to admit this. You know I actually imagined that he was taking me to Bermuda or Hawaii. Never in my wildest dreams did I figure on a family reunion.

He finally admitted he was really doing it for Bella Lynn. Bella Lynn is our spoiled rotten daughter who's back home now that her husband,

Cletis, left her. 'She's so blue,' Tyler says. 'She needs a sense of roots.' Roots? I'd rather see Gila monsters in my hatbox.

First off he invites my mother. Up and takes her out of the Bluebonnet nursing home. Where they keep her tied up, where she belongs. Then he asks his one-eyed alcoholic brother, John, and his alcoholic sister, Mary. Now, I drink. Jack Daniel's is my *friend*. But I still have my sense of humor, not mean like her. Besides she has incestuous feelings for Tyler, always has. Plus he asks her boring boring husband, who didn't come, praise the Lord. Their daughter Lou is here, with a baby. Her husband left her too. She's about as empty-headed as my Bella Lynn. Oh well, in no time they'll both be running off with some new illiterate misfits.

Tyler went and invited eighty people to a party Christmas Eve. That's tomorrow. This is when our new maid Lupe went and stole our ivory-handled carving knives. She hid them in her girdle, bent over for some fool reason crossing the bridge to Juarez. Stabbed herself, almost bled to death and it all ended up Tyler's fault. He had to pay for the ambulance and the hospital and a huge old fine because she was a wetback. And of course they found out about the wetback gardeners and the wash woman. So now there's no help at all. Just poor Esther and some part-time strangers. Thieves.

But the worst worst top of everything is he invited my relatives from Longview and Sweetwater. Terrible people. They are all very thin or grotesquely fat, and all they do is eat. They all look as if they have seen hard times. Drought. Tornadoes. Point is these are people I don't even know, don't ever want to know. People I married him for so I'd never have to see again.

Not that I need any more reasons to stay up here, but there is another one. Once in a while, clear as a bell, I can hear every single word Tyler and Rex are saying down in the shop.

I'm ashamed to admit this, but, what the hell, it's the truth. I'm jealous of Rex Kipp. Now I know Tyler's been sleeping with that tacky little secretary of his, Kate. Well, I.C.C.L. Which means I couldn't care less. Keeps him from huffin and puffin top of me.

But Rex. Now Rex is year in, year out. We spent half of our honeymoon at Cloudcroft, other half on Rex's ranch. Those two fish and hunt and gamble together and fly all around Lord knows where in Rex's plane.

What galls me the most is how they talk together, out in the shop, for hours and hours. I mean to say this has nagged me to death. What in Sam Hill are those old farts talking about out there?

Well, now I know.

Rex: You know, Ty, this is a damn good whiskey.

Tyler: Yep. *Damn* good.

Rex: Goes down like mother's milk.

Tyler: Smooth as silk.

(They've only been swilling that rotgut for forty-some years.)

Rex: Look at them old clouds . . . billowing and tumbling.

Tyler: Yep.

Rex: I expect that's my favorite kind of cloud. Cumulus. Full of rain for my cattle and just as pretty as can be.

Tyler: Not me. Not my favorite.

Rex: How come?

Tyler: Too much commotion.

Rex: That's what's fine, Ty, the commotion. It's majestic as all git out.

Tyler: God *damn*, this is a nice mellow hooch.

Rex: That is just one hell of a beautiful sky.

(Long silence.)

Tyler: My kind of sky is a cirrus sky.

Rex: What? Them wispy no-count little clouds?

Tyler: Yep. Now up in Ruidoso, that sky is blue. With those light cirrus clouds skipping along so light and easy.

Rex: I know that very sky you're talking about. Day I shot me two buck antelope.

(That's it. The entire conversation. Here's one more:)

Rex: But do Mexkin kids like the same toys white kids do?

Tyler: Course they do.

Rex: Seems to me they play with things like sardine cans for boats.

Tyler: That's the whole point of our Juarez operation. Real toys. But, what kind? How bout guns?

Rex: Give Mexkins guns? No way.

Tyler: They're all crazy about cars. And the women about babies.

Rex: That's it! Cars and dolls!

Tyler: Tinker-toys and erector sets!

Rex: Balls. Real baseballs and footballs!

Tyler: We've got everything figured out just fine, Rex.

Rex: Perfect.

(I mean, what existential dilemma these dickheads got figured out beats all hell out of me.)

Tyler: How you going to find it, flying in the dark?

Rex: I can find anyplace. Anyhow, we'll have the star.

Tyler: What star?

Rex: The star of Bethlehem!

I watched the whole party from up here. Boy was I a relaxed hostess, lying under the starry sky, my little radio playing 'Away in a Manger' and 'White Christmas'.

Esther was up at four, cooking and cleaning. Have to admit Bella and Lou helped her out. The florist arrived and the caterers with more food and booze, bartenders in tuxedos. A truck came to deliver a giant bubble machine Tyler had set up inside the front door. I can't think about my carpet. Loudspeakers started blaring Roy Rogers and Dale Evans singing 'Jingle Bells' and 'I Saw Momma Kissing Santa Claus'. Then cars and more cars kept on coming with even more people I never want to see again in my life. Esther, bless her heart, brought me up a tray of food and pitcher of eggnog, a fresh bottle of old Jack. She was all dressed up in black, with a white lace apron, her white hair coiled in braids around her head. She looked like a queen. She's the only person I like in this whole wide world or maybe it's that she's the only one who likes me.

'What's my slut of a sister-in-law up to?' I asked her.

'Playing cards. Some men started up a poker game in the library and she asks real sweet, "Ooh, can I play?"'

'That'll teach them.'

'That's the very thing I says to myself minute she started to shuffle. Zip zip zip.'

'And my mama?'

'She's running around telling folks Jesus is our blessit redeemer.'

I didn't have to ask her about Bella Lynn, who was on the back porch swing with old Jed Ralston. His wife, mongoose Martha, we call her, probably too loaded down with diamonds to walk, find out what he's up to. Then Lou comes out with Orel, Willa's boy, an overgrown mutant who plays tight end for the Texas Aggies. The four of them start strolling around the garden, giggling and squealing, ice cubes rattling. Strolling? Those girls were half-lit, their skirts so tight and their spike heels so high they could barely walk. I yelled down at them,

'Tar-paper floozies! White trash!'

'What's that?' Jed asks.

'It's just Mama. Up on the roof.'

'Tiny's on the roof?'

So I lay me back down, went back to looking up at the stars. Turned my Christmas music high to drown out the party. I sang, too, to myself. It came upon a midnight clear. Fog came from my mouth and I sounded like a child, singing. I just lay there and sang and sang.

It was around ten when Tyler and Rex and the two girls came sneaking out, whispering and stumbling in the dark. They loaded our Lincoln with two big sacks, drove in two cars down the back pasture to the field by the ditch where Rex lands the Piper Cub. The four of them tied the bags onto the outside of the plane and then Tyler and Rex climbed in. Bella Lynn and Lou turned on the car's headlights to light Rex up a runway. Although seems like it was such a clear night he could have seen by stars.

The plane was so loaded down it barely got off the ground. When it finally did it took a god-awful time to get any altitude. Just missed the wires and then the cottonwoods at the river. The wings dipped a few times, and he wasn't showing off. At last he was headed for Juarez and the tiny red taillight disappeared. I breathed and said thank God and drank.

I lay back down, shaking. I couldn't bear it if Tyler were to crash. Just then the radio played 'Silent Night', which always gets me. I cried, just plain bawled my eyes out. It's not true, what I said about him and Kate. I mind it a lot.

The girls were waiting in the dark by the tamarisk bushes. Fifteen, twenty minutes, seemed like hours. I didn't see the plane, but they must have, because they turned the car lights on and it landed.

I couldn't hear a word because of the racket from the party and they had the shop door and windows shut, but I could see the four of them in front of the fireplace. It looked so sweet just like *A Christmas Carol* with them toasting champagne, their faces all glowing and happy.

That's about when the news came on my radio. 'A short while ago a mystery Santa dropped toys and much needed food onto Juarez shantytown. But marring this Christmas surprise is the tragic news that an elderly shepherd has been killed, allegedly struck by a falling can of ham. More details at midnight.'

'Tyler! Tyler!' I hollered.

Rex opened the shop door and came out.

'What is it? Who's there?'

'It's me. Tiny.'

'Tiny? Tiny's still on the roof!'

'Get Tyler, dick-face.'

Tyler came out and I told him about the bulletin, said how Rex better hightail it on out to Silver City.

They drove back down to light him out. By the time they got back the house was quiet, except for Esther, cleaning up. The girls went inside. Tyler came over, underneath where I was. I held my breath, listening to him whisper Tiny? Tiny? for a while and then I leaned over the ledge.

'What do you want?'

'Come down off that roof now, Tiny. Please.'

ANGELA CARTER

The Ghost Ships

A Christmas Story

> Therefore that whosoever shall be found observing any such day as Christmas or the like, either by forbearing of labor, feasting, or any other way upon any such account aforesaid, every person so offending shall pay for every offense five shillings as a fine to the country.
>
> *Statute enacted by the General Court of*
> *Massachusetts, May 1659, repealed 1681*

'Twas the night before Christmas. Silent night, holy night. The snow lay deep and crisp and even. Etc. etc. etc.; let these familiar words conjure up the traditional anticipatory magic of Christmas Eve, and then – forget it.

Forget it. Even if the white moon above Boston Bay ensures that all is calm, all is bright, there will be no Christmas *as such* in the village on the shore that now lies locked in a precarious winter dream.

(Dream, that uncensorable state. They would forbid it if they could.)

At that time, for we are talking about a long time ago, about three and a quarter hundred years ago, the newcomers had no more than scribbled their signatures on the blank page of the continent that was, as it lay under the snow, no whiter nor more pure than their intentions.

They plan to write more largely; they plan to inscribe thereon the name of God.

And that was why, because of their awesome piety, tomorrow, on Christmas Day, they will wake, pray and go about their business as if it were any other day.

For them, all days are holy but none are holidays.

New England is the new leaf they have just turned over; Old England is the dirty linen their brethren at home have just – did they not recently

250

win the English Civil War? – washed in public. Back home, for the sake of spiritual integrity, their brothers and sisters have broken the graven images in the churches, banned the playhouses where men dress up as women, chopped down the village Maypoles because they welcome in the spring in altogether too orgiastic a fashion.

Nothing particularly radical about that, given the Puritans' basic premises. Anyone can see at a glance that a Maypole, proudly erect upon the village green as the sap is rising, is a godless instrument. The very thought of Cotton Mather, with blossom in his hair, dancing round the Maypole makes the imagination reel. No. The greatest genius of the Puritans lay in their ability to sniff out a pagan survival in, say, the custom of decorating a house with holly for the festive season; they were the stuff of which social anthropologists would be made!

And their distaste for the icon of the lovely lady with her bonny babe – Mariolatry, graven images! – is less subtle than their disgust at the very idea of the festive season itself. It was the *festivity* of it that irked them.

Nevertheless, it assuredly is a gross and heathenish practice, to welcome the birth of Our Saviour with feasting, drunkenness, and lewd displays of mumming and masquerading.

We want none of that filth in this new place.

No, thank you.

As midnight approached, the cattle in the byres lumbered down upon their knees in homage, according to the well-established custom of over sixteen hundred English winters when they had mimicked the kneeling cattle in the Bethlehem stable; then, remembering where they were in the nick of time, they hastily refrained from idolatry and hauled themselves upright.

Boston Bay, calm as milk, black as ink, smooth as silk. And, suddenly, at just the hour when the night spins on its spindle and starts to unravel its own darkness, at what one could call, elsewhere, the witching hour –

> I saw three ships come sailing in,
> Christmas Day, Christmas Day,

I saw three ships come sailing in
On Christmas Day in the morning.

Three ships, silent as ghost ships; ghost ships of Christmas past.

And what was in those ships all three?

Not, as in the old song, 'the Virgin Mary and her baby'; that would have done such grievous damage to the history of the New World that you might not be reading this in the English language even. No; the imagination must obey the rules of actuality. (Some of them, anyway.)

Therefore I imagine that the first ship was green and leafy all over, built of mossy Yule logs bound together with ivy. It was loaded to the gunwales with roses and pomegranates, the flower of Mary and the fruit that represents her womb, and the mast was a towering cherry tree which, now and then, leaned down to scatter ripe fruit on the water in memory of the carol that nobody in New England now sang. The Cherry Tree Carol, that tells how, when Mary asked Joseph to pick her some cherries, he was jealous and spiteful and told her to ask the father of her unborn child to help her pick them – and, at that, the cherry tree bowed down so low the cherries dangled in her lap, almost.

Clinging to the mast of this magic cherry tree was an abundance of equally inadmissible mistletoe, sacred since the dawn of time, when the Druids used to harvest it with silver sickles before going on to perform solstitial rites of memorable beastliness at megalithic sites all over Europe.

Yet more mistletoe dangled from the genial bundle of evergreens, the kissing bough, that invitation to the free exchange of precious bodily fluids.

And what is that bunch of holly, hung with red apples and knots of red ribbon? Why, it is a wassail bob.

This is what you did with your wassail bob. You carried it to the orchard with you when you took out a jar of hard cider to give the apple trees their Christmas drink. All over Somerset, all over Dorset, everywhere in the apple-scented cider country of Old England, time out of mind, they souse the apple trees at Christmas, get them good and drunk, soak them.

You pour the cider over the tree trunks, let it run down to the roots. You fire off guns, you cheer, you shout. You serenade the future apple crop and next year's burgeoning, you 'wassail' them, you toast their fecundity in last year's juices.

But not in *this* village. If a sharp smell of fruit and greenery wafted from the leafy ship to the shore, refreshing their dreams, all the same, the immigration officials at the front of the brain, the port of entry for memory, sensed contraband in the incoming cargo and snapped: 'Permission to land refused!'

There was a furious silent explosion of green leaves, red berries, white berries, of wet, red seeds from bursting pomegranates, of spattering cherries and scattering flowers; and cast to the winds and scattered was the sappy, juicy, voluptuous flesh of all the wood demons, tree spirits and fertility goddesses who had ever, once upon a time, contrived to hitch a ride on Christmas.

Then the ship and all it had contained were gone.

But the second ship now began to belch forth such a savoury aroma from a vent amidships that the most abstemious dreamer wrinkled his nose with pleasure. This ship rode low in the water, for it was built in the unmistakable shape of a pie dish and, as it neared shore, it could be seen that the deck itself was made of piecrust just out of the oven, glistening with butter, gilded with egg yolk.

Not a ship at all, in fact, but a Christmas pie!

But now the piecrust heaved itself up to let tumbling out into the water a smoking cargo of barons of beef gleaming with gravy, swans upon spits and roast geese dripping hot fat. And the figurehead of this jolly vessel was a boar's head, wreathed in bay, garlanded in rosemary, a roasted apple in its mouth and sprigs of rosemary tucked behind its ears. Above, hovered a pot of mustard, with wings.

Those were hungry days in the new-found land. The floating pie came wallowing far closer in than the green ship had done, close enough for the inhabitants of the houses on the foreshore to salivate in their sleep.

But then, with one accord, they recalled that burnt offerings and pagan sacrifice of pig, bird and cattle could never be condoned. In unison, they rolled over on to their other sides and turned their stern backs.

The ship span round once, then twice. Then, the mustard pot swooping after, it dove down to the bottom of the sea, leaving behind a bobbing mass of sweetmeats that dissipated itself gradually, like sea wrack, leaving behind only a single cannonball of the plum-packed Christmas pudding of Old England that the sea's omnivorous belly found too much, too indigestible, and rejected it, so that the pudding refused to sink.

The sleepers, freed from the ghost not only of gluttony but also of dyspepsia, sighed with relief.

Now there was only one ship left.

The silence of the dream lent this apparition an especial eeriness.

This last ship was packed to the gunwales with pagan survivals of the most concrete kind, the ones in – roughly – human shape. The masts and spars were hung with streamers, paperchains and balloons, but the gaudy decorations were almost hidden by the motley crew of queer types aboard, who would have been perfectly visible from the shore in every detail of their many-coloured fancy dress had anyone been awake to see them.

Reeling to and fro on the deck, tumbling and dancing, were all the mummers and masquers and Christmas dancers that Cotton Mather hated so, every one of them large as life and twice as unnatural. The rouged men dressed as women, with pillowing bosoms; the clog dancers, making a soundless rat-a-tat-tat on the boards with their wooden shoes; the sword dancers whacking their wooden blades and silently jingling the little bells on their ankles. All these riotous revellers used to welcome in the festive season back home; it was they who put the 'merry' into Merry England!

And now, horrors! they sailed nearer and nearer the sanctified shore, as if intent on forcing the saints to celebrate Christmas whether they wanted to or no.

The saint the Church disowned, Saint George, was there, in paper armour painted silver, with his old foe, the Turkish knight, a chequered tablecloth tied round his head for a turban, fencing with clubs as they used to every Christmas in the Old Country, going from house to house with the mumming play that was rooted far more deeply in antiquity than the birth it claimed to celebrate.

This is the plot of the mumming play: Saint George and the Turkish knight fight until Saint George knocks the Turkish knight down. In comes the Doctor, with his black bag, and brings him back to life again – a shocking mockery of death and resurrection. (Or else a ritual of revivification, depending on one's degree of faith, and also, of course, depending on one's degree of faith in what.)

The master of these floating revels was the Lord of Misrule himself, the clown prince of Old Christmas, to which he came from fathoms deep in time. His face was blackened with charcoal. A calf's tail was stitched on to the rump of his baggy pants, which constantly fell down, to be hitched up again after a glimpse of his hairy buttocks. His top hat sported paper roses. He carried an inflated bladder with which he merrily battered the dancing heads around him. He was a true antique, as old as the festival that existed at midwinter before Christmas was ever thought of. Older.

His descendants live, all year round, in the circus. He is mirth, anarchy and terror. Father Christmas is his bastard son, whom he has disowned for not being obscene enough.

The Lord of Misrule was there when the Romans celebrated the Winter Solstice, the hinge on which the year turns. The Romans called it Saturnalia and let the slaves rule the roost for the duration, when all was topsy-turvy and almost everything that occurred would have been illegal in the Commonwealth of Massachusetts at the time of the ghost ships, if not today.

Yet from the phantom festival on the bedizened deck came the old, old message: during the twelve days of Christmas, nothing is forbidden, everything is forgiven.

A merry Christmas is Cotton Mather's worst nightmare.

If a little merriment imparts itself to the dreams of the villagers, they do not experience it as pleasure. They have exorcised the vegetables, and the slaughtered beasts; they will not tolerate, here, the riot of unreason that used to mark, over there, the inverted season of the year when nights are longer than days and the rivers do not run and you think that when the sun sinks over the rim of the sea it might never come back again.

The village raised a silent cry: Avaunt thee! Get thee hence!

The riotous ship span round once, twice – a third time. And then sank, taking its Dionysiac crew with it.

But, just as he was about to be engulfed, the Lord of Misrule caught hold of the Christmas pudding that still floated on the water. This Christmas pudding, sprigged with holly, stuffed with currants, raisins, almonds, figs, compressed all the Christmas contraband into one fearful sphere.

The Lord of Misrule drew back his arm and bowled the pudding towards the shore.

Then he, too, went down. The Atlantic gulped him. The moon set, the snow came down again and it was a night like any other winter night.

Except, next morning, before dawn, when all rose to pray in the shivering dark, the little children, thrusting their feet reluctantly into their cold shoes, found a juicy resistance to the progress of their great toes and, investigating further, discovered to their amazed and secret glee, each child a raisin the size of your thumb, wrinkled with its own sweetness, plump as if it had been soaked in brandy, that came from who knows where but might easily have dropped out of the sky during the flight overhead of a disintegrating Christmas pudding.

About the Authors and Stories

HANS CHRISTIAN ANDERSEN (1805–1875) was born on the island of Funen, in Denmark, the son of a cobbler and a washerwoman. As a teenager, he made his debut on the stage of the Royal Theatre of Copenhagen playing a troll. His matchless fairy tales – 'The Little Mermaid', 'Thumbelina', 'The Emperor's New Clothes', 'The Ugly Duckling', 'The Snow Queen' and 'The Red Shoes' – were inspired by folk tales his grandmother told him as a boy. 'The Fir Tree' was first published in 1844, and Andersen read it aloud at a Christmas party the following year to an audience that included one of the Brothers Grimm.

Inspired by the work of the Brothers Grimm in Germany, old school friends PETER CHRISTEN ASBJØRNSEN (1812–1885) and JØRGEN MOE (1813–1882) decided as young men to collect and publish Norway's own folk tales. Asbjørnsen (a zoologist) and Moe (a poet and later a bishop) spent their holidays wandering the mountains in search of good material. The result was *Norwegian Folktales* (*Norske Folkeeventyr*) which first appeared as a slim pamphlet in 1841 and was expanded over the years to encompass some sixty tales. Many of the stories, like 'The Cat on the Dovrefjell', feature ugly trolls who live in caves and mountains (the Dovrefjell is a range in central Norway) and terrorize local humans.

FYODOR DOSTOYEVSKY (1821–1881) was born in Moscow, a doctor's son. His first published novel, *Poor Folk*, appeared in 1845 and he wrote 'A Christmas Party and a Wedding' in 1848. His burgeoning literary career was interrupted the following year when he was arrested and sentenced to death for belonging to a group that discussed banned books. He was reprieved at the last minute but sent to prison in Siberia for four years. Dostoyevsky recovered from this terrible experience to write some of the greatest works of Russian literature, including *Crime and Punishment*, *The Idiot* and *The Brothers Karamazov*.

PAUL ARÈNE (1843–1896) was born in Provence, France, the son of a clockmaker. After studying in Marseille and working as a teacher, he turned to journalism at the age of 23 and became part of the Parisian literary scene. He fought in the Franco-Prussian war in 1870 and was awarded the Legion of Honour for his efforts. Arène was best known for his writing on Provençal life and landscape, but Christmas was another favourite theme. 'Saint Anthony and his Pig' ('La vraie tentation du grand Saint Antoine') is taken from his festive collection of 1880, *Contes de Noël*.

ANTON CHEKHOV (1860–1904), the grandson of a former serf and son of a grocer, was born in Taganrog, a port in Southern Russia. His childhood was overshadowed by his frightening father, but he was close to his mother. While he was at university, his father was defrauded and went bankrupt, leaving the family in dire financial straits; Chekhov supported them almost single-handedly by selling stories and sketches to magazines. Although a doctor by profession, he soon became famous for his brilliant stories and plays. 'Boys' was published in 1887 in a St Petersburg newspaper, and was counted by Leo Tolstoy (later Chekhov's neighbour) as one of his favourite stories by the younger writer.

JOAQUIM MARIA MACHADO DE ASSIS (1839–1908) is widely regarded as Brazil's greatest writer. His father, the son of freed slaves, was a wall painter and his mother was a washerwoman, and Machado de Assis grew up poor in the outskirts of Rio de Janeiro. Despite receiving only a basic education, he became a journalist, then a novelist and story writer, then Knight of the Imperial Order of the Rose and founder of the Brazilian Academy of Letters. His most famous novels include *Dom Casmurro* and *Posthumous Memoirs of Brás Cubas*. 'Midnight Mass' ('A Missa do Galo'), which first appeared in 1899, is one of the most beloved stories of Brazilian literature.

SAKI (1870–1916) was the pen name of Hector Hugh Munro, whose irreverent stories mischievously satirized Edwardian society. The son of the Inspector General for the Indian Imperial Police, he was born in Burma (now Myanmar) but raised in Devon by two drearily puritanical aunts. Like George Orwell thirty years later, Saki joined the Burmese police force as a young man, before moving to London to dedicate himself to writing. He chose the pen name Saki after the 'cypress-slender Minister of Wine' in the *Rubáiyát of Omar Khayyám* and his short stories about the debonair young Reginald began appearing from 1901. 'Reginald's Christmas Revel' was published in the 1904 collection *Reginald*. Gay at a time when sexual activity between men was illegal, Saki was forced to keep his romantic life a secret. Deeply patriotic, he signed up on the outbreak of the First World War despite being over the age of enlistment and rose to the rank of lance-sergeant. He was killed by a sniper during the Battle of the Ancre. His last words were 'Put that bloody cigarette out!'.

SELMA LAGERLÖF (1858–1940) was born into a wealthy military family in Western Sweden. Like Hans Christian Andersen in Denmark, she was deeply inspired by the Swedish fairy tales and legends her grandmother told her as a child. She began her debut novel, *Gösta Berling's Saga*, while working as a teacher; it was later turned into a silent film starring Greta Garbo in her first major role. Lagerlöf's most famous and best-loved book, *The Wonderful Adventures of Nils Holgersson*, is about a naughty boy who is turned into a tiny imp and flies with a flock of wild geese over Sweden. 'The Legend of the Christmas Rose' ('Legenden om julrosorna') was published in 1908. In addition to her writing, Lagerlöf was a major figure in the Swedish movement for women's suffrage. She was the first woman to win the Nobel Prize in Literature, in 1909, and also saved the life of a future Nobel Prize winner, by securing the passage of the German-Jewish writer Nelly Sachs on the last flight from Nazi Germany to Sweden in 1940.

O. HENRY (1862–1910) had a short but colourful life. Born William Porter in Greensboro, North Carolina, he became licensed as a pharmacist at the age of nineteen and moved to Austin, Texas, where he met and eloped with his future wife. His career as a journalist and writer began to really take off following a move to Houston, but in 1896 he was arrested for embezzling funds while working as a bookkeeper for a bank. In a moment of madness, he absconded while changing trains on his way to the courthouse before his trial. He fled to Honduras where he befriended a notorious train robber and laid low in a hotel for six months, but returned to face trial after learning that his wife was dying of tuberculosis. He was sentenced and served three years in jail before being freed and reunited with his young daughter.

While in prison, he adopted the pen name O. Henry, and after his release he found great fame and popularity as a short story writer. 'A Chaparral Christmas Gift' first appeared in the 1910 collection *Whirligigs*.

IRÈNE NÉMIROVSKY (1903–42) was born in Kiev, then part of the Russian Empire, into a wealthy Jewish family. After her family fled the Russian Revolution for Paris when Némirovsky was a teenager, she studied at the Sorbonne and began to write. She married a banker and had two daughters, and enjoyed immediate success with her first two books, both of which were made into films. Happiness was short-lived, however. Despite converting to Roman Catholicism in 1939, the Némirovskys were denied French citizenship and forced to stop working because of their Jewish heritage. As the Nazis approached Paris, the family fled to the village of Issy-l'Evêque in the east of France, where Némirovsky was arrested in July 1942. She was taken to Auschwitz and died a month later, of typhus. In the 1990s, her daughter discovered her unfinished masterpiece *Suite Française* in a notebook; it was published in 2004 and became an international bestseller. 'Noël' was first published in 1932.

DAMON RUNYON (1880–1946) is best known for his short stories featuring a motley assortment of high-living, fast-talking gamblers, drinkers and hustlers in New York City – as in 'Dancing Dan's Christmas', which was published in *Collier's* magazine in December 1932. He was born into a family of newspapermen in Kansas, and became a journalist himself after enlisting to fight in the Spanish-American War in his late teens. In 1910 he moved to New York City where he specialized in sports writing, especially baseball and boxing. The musical *Guy and Dolls*, which premiered in 1950, was based on two of his stories, and he is also credited with coining the term 'Hooray Henry', in his story 'Tight Shoes'.

DOROTHY L. SAYERS (1893–1957) grew up in a tiny village in Cambridgeshire, England. She won a scholarship to study at Somerville College, Oxford, but despite finishing with first-class honours in 1915, she had to leave without a degree because the university didn't award them to women at the time. She later worked in advertising, coming up with famous campaigns for Colman's Mustard and Guinness beer. Her personal life was chequered by romantic disappointments, however. One boyfriend, a Russian émigré poet, married another detective writer; a second only admitted to being married when she told him she was pregnant with their child. She later wed a Scottish journalist but was never able to live with her son, who was raised by relatives. The poet Dante was her last great passion, and she considered her translation of the *Divine Comedy* for the new Penguin Classics series to be her best work. Her most enduring character, the debonair, aristocratic amateur sleuth Lord Peter Wimsey was introduced in the novel *Whose Body?* in 1923. 'The Necklace of Pearls' was first published in 1933.

LANGSTON HUGHES (1901–67) was born in Joplin, Missouri. His grandfather had been a prominent member of the anti-slavery movement; his grandmother, who helped raise him, had been the first woman to attend Oberlin College and instilled in him a sense of the importance of fighting for racial justice. Hughes attended Columbia University but dropped out because of the racism he experienced there. He got a job as a crewman on a ship and sailed to Paris and England, where he settled for some time in the 1920s. After returning to the USA, he spent most of the rest of his life in Harlem, becoming a leading figure in the Harlem Renaissance movement. Famous especially as a poet, he also wrote stories, plays, works of non-fiction and the novel *Not Without Laughter*. 'One Christmas Eve' was first published in the journal *Opportunity* in December 1933.

MÁRIO DE ANDRADE (1893–1945) was a polymath and one of the founders of Brazilian modernism. He was born in São Paulo, where he lived almost his whole life. A musical child prodigy, he originally intended to become a pianist, but became affected by trembling in his hands following the sudden death of his teenage brother. Instead, he turned to poetry and photography, and began to extensively document Brazilian culture and folklore, while also working as a music professor. His great novel, *Macunaíma*, was published in 1928; the semi-autobiographical 'The Christmas Turkey' ('Peru de Natal') appeared in 1942.

ELIZABETH BOWEN (1899–1973) was born in Dublin and moved to England as child. She attended art school and mixed with the Bloomsbury Group. Her marriage to a BBC employee was happy but sexless, and she had several affairs with both men and women. In 1930, she inherited her family's home, Bowen's Court, in County Cork, and was visited there by an extraordinary array of literary visitors over the years, including Virginia Woolf, Eudora Welty, Carson McCullers and Iris Murdoch. During the Second World War, she worked for the British Ministry of Information, reporting mostly on Irish affairs. Best known for novels such as *The Last September*, *The Death of the Heart* and *The Heat of the Day*, she was also a celebrated writer of ghost stories. 'Green Holly' was first published in the Christmas edition of *The Listener* in 1944.

FRANK O'CONNOR (1903–66) was the pseudonym of Michael O'Donovan. Born in Cork, Ireland, his childhood was blighted by his father's alcoholism and ill-treatment of his adored mother. Largely self-educated, he began to prepare a collected edition of his works at the age of twelve and later worked as a librarian, translator and journalist. In 1918 he joined the Irish Republican Army and served in combat during the Irish War of Independence. While interned by the Free State Government he took the opportunity to learn several languages. In later life, he became acclaimed especially for his short stories. Many of these first appeared in the *New Yorker*, including 'Christmas Morning', which was published in the December 1946 issue.

DYLAN THOMAS (1914–53), who was born in Swansea, Wales, was still a teenager when he wrote many of his most famous poems. At twenty he made his way to London, where he met Caitlin Macnamara, a dancer who had run away from home. They married, moved to the Welsh village of Laugharne and had three children together, but their relationship was tempestuous and marred by financial difficulties, infidelity and heavy drinking. During the Second World War Thomas scripted films for the British Ministry of Information, and he became a familiar voice reading his poetry on BBC Radio. 'A Child's Christmas in Wales' first appeared in *Harper's Bazaar* in 1950 and Thomas later read it aloud for a recording during a tour of America in 1952. He died the following year, while on another tour of America, following a catastrophically heavy drinking session. *Under Milk Wood*, Thomas's evocative 'play for voices', was broadcast after his death with an all-Welsh cast starring Richard Burton.

GEORGES SIMENON (1903–89) was the creator of the iconic pipe-smoking detective Maigret, scourge of the Parisian criminal underworld. Simenon was born in Liège, Belgium and took a job at the age of fifteen on the local newspaper, which introduced him to the city's insalubrious corners and gave him material for his future writing. He published his first book in 1921 and moved to Paris the following year, later living in Canada, the USA, France and Switzerland. Maigret first appeared in print in 1930 and would become the protagonist of 75 novels and 28 short stories, including 'The Little Restaurant near Place des Ternes' in *Un Noël de Maigret* in 1951.

RAY BRADBURY (1920–2012) is most famous for the 1953 dystopian novel *Fahrenheit 451*, about a sinister future society in which books are outlawed. He grew up in Illinois and Los Angeles, and spent much of his time in the local library as he couldn't afford college. Rejected from the military during the Second World War due to poor eyesight, he was able to devote himself to writing and became a full-time writer by the age of 24. He was married for 56 years and had four daughters. A prolific writer into his eighties, he wrote nearly 600 short stories in addition to many novels and screenplays. 'The Gift' was first published in *Esquire* in December 1952; the version here is from the collection *R is for Rocket* (1962).

SHIRLEY JACKSON (1916–65) was born in San Francisco, USA and met her husband, the future critic Stanley Edgar Hyman, while at university. The couple moved to a rambling house in Vermont, which she sometimes claimed to be haunted, and had four children together. The idea for her explosive short story 'The Lottery' came to Jackson while out running errands with her infant daughter; published in 1948 in the *New Yorker*, it initially prompted a furious response from readers but has since become one of the most iconic American stories of all time. As well as her dark, brilliant stories and novels such as *The Haunting of Hill House* and *We Have Always Lived in the Castle*, Jackson wrote witty semi-fictionalized magazine pieces about family life. These were gathered in the 1952 book *Life Among the Savages*, from which 'A Visit to the Bank' is taken.

BIENVENIDO SANTOS (1911–1996) was born in Manila, Philippines. In 1941, he was awarded a government scholarship to study in the United States, and spent time at the universities of Illinois, Columbia and Harvard. But two months into his trip, and two weeks before Christmas, the Philippines were invaded by Japan, and Santos found himself an exile in America, cut off from his homeland, and his wife and daughters. This experience was central to his first published book, *You Lovely People* (1955), from which the story 'The Prisoners' has been taken. Santos did return home after the war, but moved back to the United States in the sixties to teach creative writing.

MURIEL SPARK (1918–2006) was born in Edinburgh, Scotland. She worked as a secretary before moving to Southern Rhodesia (now Zimbabwe), where she married and had a son. After the breakup of her marriage, she returned to England and worked in intelligence during the Second World War. Despite not publishing her first novel until she was nearly forty, she wrote over thirty acclaimed books in the course of her long life, including the novels *The Ballad of Peckham Rye*, *The Driver's Seat* and *The Prime of Miss Jean Brodie*, and many works of poetry, biography and criticism. She settled in Tuscany in the 1970s, where she lived for the rest of her life. 'The Leaf-Sweeper' was published in the Christmas 1956 issue of the *London Mystery Magazine*.

TRUMAN CAPOTE (1924–1984) is best known for the sparkling novella *Breakfast at Tiffany's* and the chilling true crime book *In Cold Blood*. He was born in New Orleans and raised by relatives in Monroeville, Alabama following the divorce of his parents. He left school when he was fifteen and subsequently worked for the *New Yorker* which provided his first – and last – regular job. 'A Christmas Memory', published in *Mademoiselle* magazine in December 1956, was based on Capote's own childhood and his memories of the real-life Sook, a distant relative of his mother's named Nanny Rumbley Faulk.

WOLFDIETRICH SCHNURRE (1920–1989) was born in Frank-furt, the son of a librarian and ornithologist father who moved the family to Berlin in 1928. Schnurre served as a soldier in the Second World War before fleeing to Westphalia in 1945. He returned to Berlin after the war, living first in the east, then in the western part of the city, and made his living as a theatre and film critic. 'The Loan' is from his largely autobio-graphical book *When Father's Beard was Still Red* (*Als Vaters Bart noch rot war*), which was first published in 1958.

SOPHIA DE MELLO BREYNER ANDRESEN (1919–2004) was one of Portugal's most beloved twentieth-century writers, commonly referred to as 'Sophia'. Born in Porto to an aristocratic family, she was given a strict Catholic upbringing and remained a passionate believer to the end. In addition to her writing life, she was married with five children, served as an MP and was openly critical of the Portuguese dictator Sala-zar. She was acclaimed especially for her poetry and children's stories, and she translated both Dante and Shakespeare into Portuguese. 'Christ-mas Eve' ('A Noite de Natal') was first published in 1959.

GRACE PALEY (1922–2007) was the daughter of Jewish Ukrainian immigrants and grew up in the Bronx, New York. She studied with W. H. Auden at the progressive New School for Social Research in New York and at the age of nineteen married a cinematographer with whom she had two children. As well as being a poet, short story writer and teacher, she was a passionate social activist who campaigned for peace and women's rights. In 1978, she was arrested as one of 'The White House Eleven' for unfurling an anti-nuclear banner on the White House lawn. 'The Loudest Voice' was published in her first collection, *The Little Dis-turbances of Man*, in 1959.

LAURIE LEE (1914–97) grew up in the village of Slad, Gloucestershire. He would later immortalize the village and surrounding countryside in his classic memoir *Cider With Rosie*, in which he recalled how he and other local boys used to walk miles in the snow to go 'carol-barking' at Christmas time. At the age of nineteen Lee walked to London and then travelled to Spain, where he was trapped by the outbreak of the Civil

War – experiences he recounted in *As I Walked Out One Midsummer Morning* and *A Moment of War*. 'A Cold Christmas Walk in the Country' has been taken from *Village Christmas*, which was published in 2015 after Lee's daughter Jessy stumbled upon lost essays in the British Library that her father had written years earlier.

ITALO CALVINO (1923–85) was born in Cuba and grew up in San Remo, Italy. When the Germans occupied northern Italy during the Second World War, he managed to evade the Fascist draft and joined the partisans, an experience that inspired his first novel *The Path to the Spiders' Nests*. Best known for his experimental masterpieces *Invisible Cities* and *If on a Winter's Night a Traveller*, Calvino was also an essayist, journalist and story writer. 'Santa's Children' ('I figli di Babbo Natale') is from *Marcovaldo* (1963), a collection of stories that unfold across the four seasons in an unnamed industrial city in northern Italy.

TOVE JANSSON (1914–2001) was brought up in an artistic, Swedish-speaking family in Helsinki, Finland. Her father was a sculptor, her mother an illustrator, and Jansson herself would go on to study art in Stockholm and Paris. From the 1930s to 50s she worked as an illustrator for a satirical magazine, garnering notoriety for her drawings lampooning Hitler and Stalin at a time when Finland was cooperating with Nazi Germany. In 1945 she introduced her most famous creation, a family of trolls named the Moomins, with *The Moomins and the Great Flood*. Jansson turned to literature for adults with the semi-autobiographical *Sculptor's Daughter* (*Bildhuggarens dotter*, 1968), from which 'Christmas' is taken.

CYPRIAN EKWENSI (1921–2007) was born in Minna, Nigeria, the son of a famed storyteller and elephant hunter. In early life, he worked as a forestry officer in Nigeria and as a pharmacist in Romford, England. On returning home, he wrote his first novel, *People of the City* (1954), which was one of the first Nigerian novels to be published internationally. *Jagua Nana*, his most famous book, appeared in 1961 and won an international literary prize, though it was banned in schools and attacked by the church. In later life Ekwensi worked in broadcasting, politics and as a pharmacist, while writing over forty books and scripts. 'Just Because of Xmas' is from his story collection *Restless City and Christmas Gold* (1975).

LUCIA BERLIN (1936–1994) was born in Alaska and spent her childhood moving between mining camps in the USA and Chile because of her father's job. She married and divorced three times and had four sons, while working as a teacher, hospital clerk and cleaner, among other jobs. She struggled with alcohol and severe health problems, but became a popular writing professor at the University of Colorado and her short stories enjoyed the acclaim of a small band of devoted followers. Eleven years after her death, she became a sudden literary sensation with the publication of the collection *A Manual for Cleaning Women*, an international bestseller. 'Noel. Texas. 1956' is from the 2018 follow-up collection *Evening in Paradise*, though written many years earlier.

ANGELA CARTER (1940–1992) was born in Eastbourne, England, the daughter of a journalist and a Selfridge's cashier. After an unsuccessful early stint working on a local newspaper, she married a chemist and embarked on an English degree at Bristol University, where she became captivated by the romances and legends of medieval literature. She used prize money awarded for her third novel to leave her husband and move to Japan, where she worked as a bar hostess. *The Bloody Chamber*, her brilliant feminist reimagining of traditional fairy tales, appeared in 1979. 'The Ghost Ships' was published posthumously, in *American Ghosts and Old World Wonders*, in 1993.

Acknowledgements

Hans Christian Andersen, 'The Fir Tree', from *Fairy Tales* (Penguin Classics, 2004). Translation copyright © Tiina Nunnally, 2004. Used by permission of Viking Books, an imprint of Penguin Publishing Group, a division of Penguin Random House LLC.

Peter Christen Asbjørnsen and Jørgen Moe, 'The Cat on the Dovrefjell'. Revised translation copyright © D. L. Ashliman, 2000.

Fyodor Dostoyevsky, 'A Christmas Party and a Wedding', from *The Gambler and Other Stories* (Penguin Classics, 2010). Translation copyright © Ronald Meyer, 2010.

Paul Arène, 'St Anthony and his Pig', from *A Very French Christmas* (New Vessel Press, 2016). Translation copyright © J. M. Lancaster and New Vessel Press, 2016.

Joaquim Maria Machado de Assis, 'Midnight Mass', from *The Collected Stories* (Liveright, 2018). Translation copyright © Margaret Jull Costa and Robin Patterson, 2018. Used by permission of Liveright Publishing Corporation.

Irène Némirovsky, 'Noël', from *A Very French Christmas* (New Vessel Press, 2016). Translation © Sandra Smith and New Vessel Press, 2016.

Damon Runyon, 'Dancing Dan's Christmas', from *Guys and Dolls and Other Writings* (Penguin Classics, 2008). Copyright 1932 by P. F. Collier and Son, Inc.; copyright renewed © 1959 by Damon Runyon, Jr., and Mary Runyon McCann. Used by permission of Viking Books, an imprint of Penguin Publishing Group, a division of Penguin Random House LLC.

Dorothy L. Sayers, 'The Necklace of Pearls', from *Lord Peter Wimsey: The Complete Stories* (Hodder & Stoughton; HarperCollins USA, 2018). Reprinted by permission of David Higham Ltd and HarperCollins Ltd, USA.

Langston Hughes, 'One Christmas Eve', from *The Ways of White Folks* (Vintage Classics, 1990). Copyright © 1934 by Penguin Random House LLC, copyright renewed 1962 by Langston Hughes. Used by permission of Alfred A. Knopf, an imprint of the Knopf Doubleday Publishing Group, a division of Penguin Random House LLC.

Mario de Andrade, 'The Christmas Turkey', from *The Oxford Book of Latin American Short Stories* (Oxford University Press, 1997). Translation © Gregory Rabassa, 1997. Used by permission of Oxford University Press through PLSclear.

Elizabeth Bowen, 'Green Holly', from *Collected Stories* (Vintage Classics, 1999). Copyright © Elizabeth Bowen 1944. Reproduced with permission of Curtis Brown Group Ltd, London on behalf of the Estate of Elizabeth Bowen.

Frank O'Connor, 'Christmas Morning' from *Collected Stories* (Vintage, 1982). Copyright © Estate of Frank O'Connor, 1981. Reprinted by permission of Peters Fraser & Dunlop on behalf of the Estate of Frank O'Connor.

Dylan Thomas, 'A Child's Christmas in Wales' (Orion, 1993; New Directions, 2017). Copyright © the Trustees for the copyrights of Dylan Thomas, 1950 and © New Directions Publishing Corp, 1954. Reprinted by permission of Orion Publishing Group Limited, and New Directions Publishing, Corp.

Georges Simenon, 'The Little Restaurant near Place Les Ternes (A Christmas Story for Grown-Ups)', from *A Maigret Christmas and Other Stories* (Penguin Classics, 2017). Copyright © Georges Simenon Limited, 1951. Translation © David Coward, 2017.

Ray Bradbury, 'The Gift', from *R is for Rocket* (Pan Books, 1972). Copyright © Ray Bradbury, 1962. Reprinted by permission of Abner Stein.

Shirley Jackson, 'A Visit to the Bank', from *Life Among the Savages* (Penguin Classics, 2019). Copyright © Shirley Jackson, 1948-53. Copyright renewed © Laurence Hyman, Joanne Schnurer, Barry Hyman and Sarah Webster, 1975-81.

Bienvenido Santos, 'The Prisoners', from *Philippine Short Stories 1941–1955: Part II* (University of the Philippines Press, 2009). Reprinted by permission of the University of the Philippines Press.

Muriel Spark, 'The Leaf Sweeper' from *The Complete Short Stories* (Canongate, 2018). Copyright © Muriel Spark, 1953–1997. Reproduced by permission of David Higham Associates and New Directions Publishing, Corp.

Truman Capote, 'A Christmas Memory', from *The Complete Stories*

(Penguin Classics, 2005). Copyright © Truman Capote Literary Trust, 2004. Reprinted by permission of Vintage Books, an imprint of Penguin Publishing Group, a division of Penguin Random House LLC.

Wolfdietrich Schnurre, 'The Loan', from *Berlin Tales* (Oxford University Press, 2009). Copyright © Piper Verlag, Berlin, 1996. Translation © Lyn Marven 2009. Reprinted by permission of Piper Verlag and Oxford University Press through PLSclear.

Sophia de Mello Breyner Andresen, 'Christmas Eve', from *The Girl from the Sea and Other Stories* (Dedalus, 2019). Copyright © Heirs of Sophia de Mello Breyner Andresen. Translation © Margaret Jull Costa, 2019.

Grace Paley, 'The Loudest Voice', from *The Collected Stories* (Virago, 2018). Reproduced by permission of Union Literary.

Laurie Lee, 'A Cold Christmas Walk', from *Village Christmas* (Penguin Classics, 2015). Copyright © The Partners of the Literary Estate of Laurie Lee, 2015. Reprinted by permission of Curtis Brown Group Ltd, London, on behalf of The Partners of the Literary Estate of Laurie Lee.

Italo Calvino, 'Santa's Children'. From *Marcovaldo* (Vintage Classics, 2001). Copyright © Giulio Eianudi editore, 1963. Translation © Martin Secker and Warburg Ltd, 1983. Reprinted by permission of The Random House Group Limited.

Tove Jansson, 'Christmas' from *Sculptor's Daughter* (Sort Of Books, 2015). Copyright © Tove Jansson 1968, Moomin Characters™. Translation copyright © Schildts Förlags Ab, Finland, 1969. Reprinted by permission of Rights & Brands Helsinki and Sort Of Books.

Cyprien Ekwensi, 'Just Because of Xmas', from *Restless City and Christmas Gold* (Heinemann, 1975). Copyright © Cyprian Ekwensi, 1975. Publisher's note: a line is missing in the original edition, so the words 'Later, she had gone to call on Ma Shola and . . . ' on p. 239 have been added conjecturally.

Lucia Berlin, 'Noel, Texas, 1956' from *Evenings in Paradise* (Farrar, Straux and Giroux; Picador, 2018). Copyright © the Literary Estate of Lucia Berlin LP, 2018. Reprinted by permission of the Licensor through PLSclear.

Angela Carter, 'The Ghost Ships' from *American Ghosts and Old World Wonders* (Vintage, 2012). Copyright © The Estate of Angela Carter, 1993. Reprinted by permission of the Estate c/o Rogers, Coleridge and White.

ISBN 978-0-241-45565-4